Praise for

THE DEVIL INSIDE

Nominated for the 2007 *Romantic Times*
Reviewers' Choice Awards for Best Urban Fantasy
Finalist for LR Café's Best of 2007 Awards
for Best Book All Around

"Kick-ass exorcist Morgan Kingsley is sure to win Black a
legion of fans."   —KELLEY ARMSTRONG

"A sassy heroine who's not afraid to do what it takes to
get the job done or to save a loved one's life. Add to that a
sexy hero, great secondary characters and a story line
that keeps you reading, and this one is definitely a
keeper."   —KERI ARTHUR

"[Black's] got a winning heroine, a well-crafted contem-
porary world where demonic possession is just a part of
life, and a nice balance of mystery, action and sex, making this light but engaging novel an urban fantasy series
kickoff full of promise."   —*Publishers Weekly*

"Talk about your odd couples! The delicious irony of trap-
ping a sexy demon and a cranky exorcist in the same
body gives rising star Black lots of room for conflict and
action. It's inventive in the extreme! 4½ stars. Top pick!"
                                            —*Romantic Times*

"The plot is nonstop from the first page and the romance
sprinkled throughout....A wonderful new addition to
the genre, *The Devil Inside* is an intriguing story and
Morgan Kingsley an engaging heroine. I can't wait to see
what the next book, *The Devil You Know,* has to offer."
                                      —Romance Reviews Today

ALSO BY JENNA BLACK

THE MORGAN KINGSLEY SERIES

The Devil Inside

The Devil You Know

The Devil's Due

Speak of the Devil

&

Watchers in the Night

Secrets in the Shadow

Shadows on the Soul

Hungers of the Heart

THE DEVIL'S
PLAYGROUND

JENNA BLACK

■ A DELL BOOK | NEW YORK

A Dell Books Mass Market Original

Copyright © 2010 by Jenna Black

Published in the United States by Dell Books, an imprint of
The Random House Publishing Group, a division
of Random House, Inc., New York.

DELL is a registered trademark of Random House, Inc.,
and the colophon is a registered trademark of Random House, Inc.

978-0-440-24494-3

Cover illustration: Don Sipley

Printed in the United States of America

www.bantamdell.com

9 8 7 6 5 4 3 2 1

Title-page photo courtesy of Agnieszka Michalska

To the Heart of Carolina Romance Writers,
for all their support and encouragement

acknowledgments

Thanks as always to my fantastic editor, Anne Groell, and to my fabulous agent, Miriam Kriss. Thanks to my critique partner, Kelly Gay, for being a sounding board and helping me develop this story. Special thanks go to Rinda Elliott for helping me find my way out of the corner I wrote myself into near the end. And finally, thanks to the Deadline Dames (yes, Rinda, this means I'm technically thanking you twice), who are always there for me through the peaks and valleys of this crazy, wonderful business of writing.

THE DEVIL'S
PLAYGROUND

N O ONE WOULD HAVE CALLED MY LIFE NORMAL EVEN before I became the human host of Lugh, the demon king, who was embroiled in a mostly covert war for the throne. So the fact that I was beginning to think of my life as "normal" now could have been a cause for alarm. But hey, it had been more than two months since anyone had tried to kill me, torture me, or frame me for murder. These days, that was about as normal as it got.

The truth is, my life had settled into something that resembled a routine, and I was beginning to get pretty comfortable with it. Since I was no longer under suspension by the U.S. Exorcism Board, I spent time at my office almost every day. I performed an exorcism maybe once or twice a month, and there was enough paperwork and general office management to keep me busy for a couple hours a day. Not exactly a nine-to-five, but routine enough to lull me into something like complacency. Before I'd become Lugh's host, I'd routinely done one or two exorcisms a week, but that required me to travel all around the country—something I couldn't afford to do anymore. Lugh and all the members of his royal council on the Mortal Plain agreed—possibly a first—that it would be "unwise" for me to venture too far from home when a crisis could pop up at the drop of a hat.

After the disastrous exorcism of Jordan Maguire Jr., which had almost cost me my career and my freedom, I'd been on a lucky streak, with more hosts than usual coming out of the exorcisms with their minds intact. My lucky streak had just ended, however. I'd had an early morning exorcism—a teenaged boy with a face only a mother could love. When I'd cast out the demon who'd possessed him, he'd been catatonic. There was no way of knowing if he would ever snap out of it. I could still hear the mother's heartbroken sobs when the authorities gave her the news.

Naturally, I was a bit depressed afterward. I went to my office and tried to bury myself in paperwork, but I wasn't exactly being productive. So when someone knocked on my office door, I was glad for the interruption. Until said interruption opened the door at my invitation.

I hadn't seen Shae, owner of The Seven Deadlies—a demon sex club that made my stomach curdle just thinking about it—in over two months, and that was just fine by me. I'd have been happy never to see her again in my entire life. She was a mercenary and a predator. She was also an illegal demon—one who'd taken an unwilling human host—and a snitch for Special Forces, the Philly police department's demon-crime unit. I'd have loved nothing more than to exorcize her ass, but her status as a police snitch protected her.

I'm not what you'd call a conservative dresser—I love low-rise jeans and low-cut tops—but I could never compete with Shae for sheer flamboyance. If her tight white pants dipped any lower, she'd need a bikini wax to wear them, and her sheer red lace top made no attempt to hide the black bra she wore beneath. On most people, that outfit would have looked silly at best, and slutty at worst. On Shae, it reminded me of the plumage on a tropical bird, showy and exotic.

My first impulse was to tell her to get the hell out of my office, but I was getting better at this whole impulse-control thing. There was no way Shae was here on a social call, and I probably needed to hear what she had to say, whether I wanted to or not. I flashed her my best imitation of a welcoming smile.

"Well, this ought to be interesting," I said. "Have a seat." I gestured toward one of the chairs in front of my desk, then frowned theatrically. "If you're capable of sitting down in those pants, that is. I wouldn't want you mooning passersby." Never mind that Shae and I were alone in my office with the door closed.

Shae's smile always reminded me of a shark. Or the Big Bad Wolf. I don't think her teeth are really any sharper than a normal person's, but they always looked it. Plus, they were movie-star white against her Heart of Africa skin. She made a big production out of sitting gingerly on the edge of the chair and craning her neck for any signs of visible butt cheek.

I rolled my eyes and refrained from comment. "So, what brings you to my neck of the woods?"

Shae's smile turned sly and calculating. "I have some information you might be interested in hearing."

"Okay, lay it on me." But I knew it wouldn't be that simple. Shae did *nothing* out of the goodness of her heart. If she was offering information, then it would be for a price.

"What's it worth to you?" she asked, right on cue.

I laughed. "How should I know? You haven't told me what 'it' is yet."

She pursed her lips, and a hint of annoyance flared in her eyes. "I'm doing you a favor by coming to you. I can just as easily walk right back out that door."

If she thought I'd find that option unappealing, she was very much mistaken. "You don't get to call it a favor when you're offering it for a price."

"Fine." She stood up and made to leave. I let her get as far as the door before I caved.

"All right, I'll quit being a smart-ass," I said. "Come and sit down."

She didn't leave, but she didn't come sit down, either. Instead, she just stared at me, her head cocked to one side. It was hard not to squirm under that intense regard. I'm not at my best when I'm uncomfortable, so I did what I usually do at such times—I lashed out.

"I wonder what Raphael would do if I told him you were trying to sell me information," I mused, and was gratified to see a momentary break in Shae's composure.

Raphael, Lugh's youngest brother and member of the royal council, had a reputation for cruelty that was, as far as I could tell, unparalleled. The fact that I knew he deserved it didn't make our alliance an easy one. But he was one hell of a bogeyman to threaten Shae with. She was the only person outside the royal council who knew who was hosting Raphael on the Mortal Plain, and she was scared enough of him to keep the secret.

Unfortunately, Shae regained her legendary composure almost before I had a chance to see the flash of terror in her eyes. Her spine straightened, and she bared her teeth in something that bore little resemblance to a smile.

"I know more about the demons of this city—both legal and illegal—than anyone. I can be a valuable asset. But if you sic Raphael on me, I swear to you I will never volunteer another scrap of information again, no matter how important it might be."

I pondered that for a moment, but she continued before I came to any conclusions.

"Raphael can't intimidate information out of me if he doesn't know I have it. I'm much more useful to you in the long run as a willing business partner."

Her logic was impeccable, though I didn't like it. Sure, Raphael could probably "coax" her into spitting out whatever it was she had now, but I knew her threat wasn't an empty one. I might not much want her as a friend, but I wanted her as an enemy even less.

"Okay, fine. I'll leave Raphael out of this. But until you give me some hint what it is you have, I can't even begin to figure out what it's worth to me."

The last time I'd had to negotiate with Shae, we'd determined beyond a shadow of a doubt that I didn't have the kind of money I'd need to pay for her...services. Hell, I barely had any money at all! My insurance company had *finally* come through with the money they owed me after my house burned down, but since I wasn't exactly raking in the bucks with my one to two exorcisms a month, I knew I'd have to make that money last. Though I yearned for my quaint little cottage in the suburbs, I couldn't afford to rebuild it and was still living in a cookie-cutter apartment in Center City.

"What if I told you my information pertained to Dougal's ambition to take the demon throne?"

I really hated the fact that Shae knew I had any involvement in Lugh's struggle with Dougal, but since information was her currency of choice when cash wasn't available, and since I'd been forced to negotiate with her before, she knew far more than I was comfortable with. I suspect that the moment those words left her lips, my face froze in some kind of ridiculously transparent expression of interest mingled with alarm. I'm finally starting to accept the reality that I will never have what you'd call a poker face.

"Okay, you've got my full attention," I told Shae, since she could see that already.

"Glad to hear it. Now let's talk payment."

I'm a sucky negotiator, and I wasn't in the mood to spar with Shae. "Why don't you just tell me what you want?"

Shae blinked, like the idea that I might not want to spend half an hour playing cat and mouse came as a complete surprise to her. Maybe those tight pants were giving her the wedgie from hell, or maybe my bluntness genuinely made her uncomfortable, but I swear Shae actually squirmed.

Then she rallied her mental troops and tossed out what she had to know would be an impossibly outrageous demand. "I want to know exactly what your involvement is with Lugh and his...family troubles."

I snorted. "Not going to happen. Nice doing business with you. Bye-bye." I crossed my arms over my chest and waited for her next offer.

Shae clucked her tongue. "Perhaps you don't understand how this game is played. I make an offer, then you make a counteroffer, and we go back and forth until we find a mutually agreeable middle ground."

"Do I look like someone who plays by the rules?" I asked with an arched eyebrow. Sitting there in my office wearing jeans and a crop-top, with a total of seven earrings in my ears and a tattoo on my lower back that would be on prominent display if I stood up, I looked about as far removed from your typical, businesslike exorcist as it was possible to look. Not that there's any kind of official dress code for exorcists; it's just that most of them tend to dress somberly, in respect for the gravity of their jobs. Don't get me wrong: I take my job as seriously as anyone. I just don't feel that I have to dress like a business-school clone to show it.

Apparently refusal to negotiate was a pretty good negotiation tactic, at least for me. Shae was tapping one bloodred fingernail against the arm of her chair, the gesture no doubt an unconscious one, as she regarded me through narrowed eyes.

"You hang out with Adam, one of Lugh's chief lieutenants, and with Raphael, one of his brothers. And yet you're a human exorcist." I think despite her usual mercenary sangfroid, Shae was actually dying of curiosity, above and beyond whatever advantage she could take out of figuring out my relationship with Lugh. "Your involvement makes no sense. Explain to me exactly what your role is, and I'll tell you what I know."

Since my role was as host to the demon king, and since Dougal would burn me at the stake—thus killing his brother so the throne could pass to him—if he found out, this wasn't information I could divulge. I shook my head.

"I could have sworn I'd already said no to that," I said with a false smile. "I hear the third time's the charm."

Shae stopped tapping her nail, and I think that signaled an end to her uncertainty. "I have information that is important to anyone who supports Lugh and some of his more radical plans for change. I don't plan to share that information with you unless you tell me what your involvement is with Lugh. That's my price. Take it or leave it."

So much for the give-and-take of negotiations. I gritted my teeth as I leaned back in my chair and wondered what to do. On the one hand, the bait Shae was dangling in front of my nose was pretty tempting. On the other hand, the price she was demanding was pretty steep. *Too* steep. Shae already knew that Tommy Brewster was Raphael's host, which, considering Raphael had betrayed Dougal and was on his hit list, was a terrible risk. Raphael was confident his fearsome reputation would keep Shae from telling anyone who was hosting him, but I couldn't see taking the same risk with Lugh.

Any ideas, Lugh?

Once upon a time, I'd only been able to communicate with Lugh through dreams, but the barriers between my mind and his were considerably thinner now than they had once been, and I could converse with him silently while I was awake.

You can tell her the truth without telling her the whole *truth,* he suggested. *It's common knowledge amongst Dougal's henchmen that you were once my host, but it'll be news to Shae.*

That was true. For a while, Raphael had been something of a double agent, pretending to support Dougal in his attempted coup while remaining loyal to Lugh. During that time, he'd fed Dougal the story that I had been coerced into summoning Lugh, but that Lugh had taken a new host in an attempt to escape the assassins Dougal had sent after him.

I'm a really shitty liar, but I hoped Shae would attribute any awkwardness in my delivery to my discomfort over revealing delicate information. Bracing myself as if for battle, I sat up straight and looked Shae in the eye.

"I was Lugh's host when he first came to the Mortal Plain."

Shae's eyes dilated with an almost sexual excitement at that news. "Well, well," she said, licking her lips, "that explains a lot. Fascinating."

I refrained from informing her that Dougal already knew this. The more forbidden she thought the knowledge was, the more it would buy me.

"Okay, I answered your question. Now it's your turn. What is this mysterious information that's so important to Lugh's cause?"

I was pretty sure Shae was giving serious consideration to trying to pry more out of me, so I put on my most implacable expression, just to let her know it wouldn't work. The corner of her mouth twitched, and I didn't know if it was a hint of a smile or a grimace of disappointment.

"I would be more inclined to talk if I knew for certain that my information would make its way to Lugh's ears."

Curiosity stopped the instant refusal that had sprung to my lips. "Why do you care if Lugh hears it?"

"Because if he finds his way back to the throne, he will make possession of an unwilling host a crime in the Demon Realm, which it currently is not."

Interesting that Shae would volunteer that bit of information. The demons didn't exactly run around advertising that their law had no problem with them taking whatever host they wanted, even if it was a capital crime to take an unwilling host under *human* law. I'd learned a hell of a lot about demons since I'd become Lugh's host, and most of it was shit they kept secret for a very good reason.

"If he makes possessing unwilling hosts illegal," Shae continued, "I want to make sure I am granted immunity. Though I have walked the Mortal Plain more than eighty years now, I would someday like to go home, and I don't want to return to a prison sentence. If Lugh knows I've supported him ..." She shrugged.

I'd seen before that Shae had no compunction about playing both sides, so it came as no great surprise to know that her offer of information served more than one purpose.

"I can't guarantee that Lugh will hear about your co-operation immediately," I said, hoping the lie didn't show on my face, "but I can promise I'll do my best to get a message to him, which probably won't be that hard if he does end up on the throne again. Now I've already given you the information you asked for. Time for you to start talking."

There was still a calculating gleam in her eye, but thankfully she didn't press for any more. "I've had a notable increase in demon membership in my club over the last several weeks," she said. "I've been in business for going on fifteen years now, and I've never seen a membership spike like this before."

Not immediately knowing what to make of this news, I decided to inject a little of my usual snark. "I thought you had a months-long waiting list for membership." It went without saying that the waiting list only applied to humans.

Shae gave me a dirty look but didn't rise to my bait. "Most of these demons are clearly illegals, and when they first show up at the club, they look pretty rough. Lots of track marks, too skinny, weatherbeaten. They clean up pretty fast once the demon has been in residence for a while, but still ... It isn't hard to imagine that their hosts are the kind of people who can drop off the face of the earth without anyone noticing or caring."

"They aren't exactly dropping off the face of the earth," I muttered, but I knew what she meant. These were people who didn't have friends and family who would raise a stink over their loved one being illegally possessed.

"Why are you telling *me*?" I asked. "Isn't this more up Adam's alley than mine?"

Shae just looked at me, her eyes cold and hard. I guess I already knew the answer to that question. She might be forced to work with Adam in her role of police snitch, but she sure as hell didn't *like* it. Or him.

"Forget I asked," I said. "Do you know how these demons are getting to the Mortal Plain?"

Once a demon was on the Mortal Plain, it could transfer from host to host via skin-to-skin contact. However, it couldn't come here from the Demon Realm in the first place without an invitation from a willing host.

"Don't know," Shae said. "I don't seem to be missing any regulars, though, so it isn't a case of legal demons moving to new hosts. These demons are definitely new arrivals."

The implications made me shudder. Although a host had to voluntarily invite a demon onto the Mortal Plain, there were any number of ways someone could be forced to "volunteer." I was a prime example, having been drugged and manipulated by Raphael so that I would invite Lugh to the Mortal Plain and into my body, even though being possessed was—at the time—my worst nightmare. Luckily, because of my, er, special genetic makeup, I retain control of my body, except on rare occasions where Lugh takes over—usually by mutual agreement, and once in a while by brute force. But whoever these hapless "volunteers" were, they were worse than dead, their minds fully intact, trapped inside bodies they could not control.

"I don't know how these demons are gaining access to the Mortal Plain," Shae said, "but I don't think it's a coincidence that there would be this sudden influx while Dougal is keeping Lugh's seat warm."

I didn't, either. Because Lugh was still king even though he was AWOL, Dougal was only the regent, and his powers were limited. But since Lugh hadn't officially outlawed the possession of unwilling hosts yet, and since there were always way more demons wanting to come to the Mortal Plain than there were willing hosts, it wasn't much of a stretch to imagine that Dougal had arranged to make more hosts available.

"I need to know exactly how they're getting here," I muttered, more to myself than to Shae.

"I'd love to tell you," Shae said. "For a price." I opened my mouth to say something indignant, but she cut me off. "I'd love to, but I can't. I've been told in no uncertain terms that I am not to ask any questions about these new members."

"By whom?" I asked sharply.

Shae shook her head and didn't answer.

"You're not the type to let someone come into your place and tell you what to do," I said. Yeah, Raphael had been able to intimidate her into keeping quiet about his identity, but I doubted there was anyone else who would inspire the kind of terror that Raphael did.

"I'm not," she said, and there was a faint gleam of malice in her eyes.

And suddenly I understood. I felt like slapping myself on the forehead. "That's why you came here to tell me about this. Not because you really wanted to trade information, but because you're pissed off at whoever gave you the gag order and you want to sic Lugh's supporters on him."

A slight grin curved her lips, though the gleam remained in her eye and turned the grin into something decidedly unwholesome. "I've told you nothing that I was forbidden to say, so technically I have broken no agreements. What you decide to do with the information I've given you is your concern, not mine."

She rose from the chair, the motion strangely sinuous. "As always, it's been a pleasure doing business with you," she said, then turned toward the door without awaiting a response. Which was just as well, because I hadn't the faintest idea what to say.

two

HADN'T BEEN GETTING A WHOLE LOT DONE BEFORE Shae's visit, and I suspected I would get even less done afterward, so I closed up my office and headed home, lost in thought. It was a nasty, miserably hot and humid day, and I was soaked with sweat as soon as I stepped outside.

My apartment is conveniently located only three blocks from my office, but unfortunately, I'd chosen the height of lunch hour for my short sojourn home, so the streets were flooded with grumpy, overheated business-people. Horns blared as similarly grumpy, overheated drivers complained about every minuscule delay. To add to the lovely atmosphere, a road crew was doing some kind of work that involved hot tar *and* jackhammers. The sound of the jackhammers made my teeth rattle, and there's nothing that stinks quite so much as hot tar on a hot day. How I missed my quaint little house in the suburbs!

The air conditioner in my apartment building's lobby was set to stun, and it felt like the sweat on my skin turned to ice on contact with the frigid air. I shivered, though it wasn't necessarily an unpleasant sensation after the heat. Mike, the doorman, gave me his usual pleasant smile and greeting, but I caught his quick, no doubt involuntary glance at my chest. Guess my flimsy lace bra had been a bad choice for today. Even really nice guys can be tempted by the sight of a well-endowed woman entering a cold building. If he'd stared, I might have complained, but I could forgive that little peek. I crossed my arms over my chest while I was waiting for the elevator. The majority of the population in my building was retirees, and I got enough "What's wrong with young people these days?" looks without showing off my perky nipples.

By the time I made it up to my apartment, my clothes were wet and clammy against my skin, and I couldn't wait to get out of them. I beelined for my bedroom, stripping as I went, looking forward to a soothing hot shower.

My building is old and cranky, and it takes approximately forever and a day for the water to heat up. I didn't have the patience to wait for it, so I plunged into the "refreshing" spray and gritted my teeth against the chill.

I shivered for what felt like about five minutes before the water finally warmed up. I closed my eyes and let the water stream over my face, washing away any traces of sweat.

There's nothing like being in the shower to make a woman feel vulnerable. You're nude, you're usually in some kind of enclosed space that cuts off your line of sight—my shower door was that crappy, pseudofrosted plastic that blocked out much of the light—and the sound of water hitting tile masks any sounds from outside the bathroom. So when I opened my eyes and saw a man-shaped shadow silhouetted against the door, I jumped about a mile into the air and yelped like a dog whose foot has been stepped on.

Adrenaline flooded my system, and I quickly catalogued my collection of soaps, shampoos, and conditioners in search of a makeshift weapon. My rational brain kicked in right about the time Brian said, "It's just me."

I let out a groan of mingled relief and embarrassment. My knees were practically knocking, so I leaned my back against the cool tile and pressed a hand to my chest, ordering my heart to resume beating at a normal speed. Brian and I spent enough time at each other's apartments that we had agreed to trade keys. Obviously, I hadn't gotten used to the idea of someone else having access to my apartment yet.

Brian slid the shower door open just a crack, peeking in cautiously. "Am I risking bodily injury if I open this door a little wider?"

I huffed out a deep breath and pushed away from the wall, not sure if I wanted to punch him or kiss him. "You just scared about ten years off my life! You've seen *Psycho*. You should know better than to sneak up on a woman in the shower."

The door cracked open a little more, and Brian gave me a mock pout as he started working the knot in his tie loose. "How can I make it up to you?" The knot came loose, and the tie slithered to the floor. He untucked his shirt and began slowly unbuttoning it.

A new kind of heat flooded my veins, but I'm never one to give in easily. "What are you doing here, anyway? Aren't you supposed to be at work?"

Brian's a lawyer, and a relatively young one, which means he spends way too much time at work in my opinion. "Paying my dues," he calls it, but I have other less charitable ways to describe it.

"I've had to work the last three weekends in a row," he said as he shed his shirt. "My boss decided to give me some time off for good behavior."

I had to resist the urge to reach out and help him with his belt to hurry him along. He's disgustingly patient and loves to tease me until I beg. I hate begging.

"I hope it's not good behavior you have in mind at the moment," I said, though the tent in his pants was stunning evidence of exactly what his plans entailed.

"Trust me," he said with a waggle of his brows, "good behavior is the furthest thing from my mind." And he dropped his pants to prove it.

My nipples hardened, and desire licked at my belly. Barely able to keep my hands to myself, I slid the door open wide enough to let Brian in. The shower always felt kind of small even when I was in it all by myself, but somehow I didn't mind the crowded feeling when Brian was in there with me. I wrapped my arms around his neck and pulled his head down to mine for a kiss.

We both moaned faintly as our lips touched. He pulled me tightly to him, his hands skimming down my back until they cupped my ass. When he did, I heard the faintest of moans in my head—a moan that only I could hear. I froze, my eyes popping open, and my arousal disappearing with record speed.

Brian pulled away. "What's wrong?"

Sorry, Lugh whispered in my mind.

My cheeks glowed with heat that had nothing to do with the temperature. Lugh had told me before how much he enjoyed it when I had sex with Brian, but I had forcibly blocked that thought from my mind, and Lugh had never before made a sound. I wanted to pretend that Brian and I were the only two people in that shower, but Lugh had just reminded me that we weren't. Although he'd apologized, I wasn't sure it had been an accident. He had his own ideas on how I should structure my love life, and he wasn't above imposing those ideas on me when he had the chance.

I felt the tension mounting in Brian's body as I struggled with myself. I'd never been very good about opening up to him, and admitting that Lugh lusted after him would be…embarrassing at best. Once upon a time, Brian had been patient with me and my need for a certain amount of privacy, but that wasn't the case anymore. He drew away a little further, and I realized he was seriously considering getting out of the shower. I grabbed for him, and he got the message, though he was giving me his lawyer face, which was never a good thing.

I didn't like feeling pressured, and I didn't want to have to explain myself. Every instinct of a long history of contrariness urged me to let him go. But even that contrary part of me agreed he had a right to know what was going on.

I shifted uncomfortably and couldn't meet Brian's eyes. "This is going to be kind of awkward to explain," I said. It would have been nice if he'd rushed in with reassurances that I didn't have to, but of course he didn't. I swallowed hard and forced myself to look up at him.

"You know how I told you that Lugh was kinda putting the moves on me a while back?" I'd never quite explained just how hard Lugh had pushed—and how much success he had had—but I had told Brian the truth. Under duress, naturally.

Brian nodded, and his jaw jutted out just slightly. Jealousy flared in his eyes. "I thought Lugh and I had an understanding about that," he grated.

It wasn't quite the understanding that Brian imagined. Lugh understood that Brian was not willing to share, but that was about as far as it went. However, there was no need to bring that up right this moment.

"Yeah, well, the thing is he, uh, kinda likes *you*, too. If you know what I mean." Crap. I sounded like a Monty Python sketch. But really, can there be anything more awkward than telling your boyfriend the male demon by whom you are possessed lusts after him?

"Oh." Twin spots of color rose in his cheeks, and it was his turn to avoid eye contact.

"Thanks a lot, Lugh," I muttered under my breath.

This had to come out in the open sometime, he responded, typically unrepentant.

Brian scratched the back of his head, his face frozen in a perplexed frown. I couldn't blame him for not knowing how to handle this. I certainly had no clue. At least he wasn't a complete homophobe. I'm sure there are plenty of men who would have run screaming by this point.

Figuring our sexy, romantic shower together wasn't going to happen, I reached over and turned the water off. Brian looked like he was going to protest, then thought better of it. The erection he'd sported when he'd joined me was long gone.

Boy, you sure know how to spoil the mood, I told Lugh sourly, but he had no response this time.

"Demons don't have the same gender hang-ups that humans do," I said in an effort to fill the awkward silence. "To Lugh, it's perfectly natural to be attracted to both of us."

"Uh-huh," Brian said as he slid the shower door open and grabbed for a towel. He handed me one without looking at me, then wrapped his own around his waist and stepped out.

Damn it, damn it, damn it!

I blotted off the worst of the water as Brian gathered up his clothes and disappeared into the bedroom. Too bad Lugh resided inside my body and there was no way to give him a smack upside the head without giving myself one as well. I took a deep breath and followed Brian into the bedroom.

He'd already managed to get his pants back on. I must have looked pretty stricken, because he paused with one arm in his shirt when he saw my face. With a sigh, he let the shirt fall back to the ground and crossed the distance between us, pulling me into a hug.

"I'm sorry, Morgan," he said into my hair. "I can't help being a bit weirded out right now. But it doesn't mean that I don't love you."

I knew that, but it still hurt to feel him withdraw from me as he was doing now. I held on tight and tried to think of something clever to say, something that would deflect the tension. Nothing leapt to mind.

Despite my clingy monkey hold, Brian managed to escape my arms, but he didn't resume dressing, so I tried not to despair. He sat on the edge of the bed, his brow still furrowed with thought. I wanted to kiss that furrow away, but suspected he wouldn't appreciate an overture right now.

He didn't even look up as I dropped the towel and slipped into a comfy, beat-up bathrobe. I gathered the robe tightly around me and climbed onto the bed, sitting with my back against the headboard, giving Brian his space.

"So whenever we make love, he's, uh...*there*?" Brian asked.

I blinked in surprise. "Brian, he's *always* there."

He waved that away. "I know he's always in residence, as it were. I just thought..." He shook his head. "I don't know what I thought. Maybe that he politely shut his eyes when we were in bed."

I refrained from pointing out that *my* eyes were Lugh's eyes. "I don't think he could even if he wanted to."

Brian nodded mutely, and I had a feeling he was going through some of our more...exotic encounters in his mind. I know *I* was.

"Lugh and I are a package deal," I said, though why I felt the need to restate the obvious I don't know. I guess I just don't do that well with awkward silences.

"Yeah." He rubbed his chin, lost in thoughts he chose not to share with me.

Hurt stabbed through me, though there was really no reason for it. It wasn't *me* Brian was withdrawing from. But for the first time, I started thinking about what my future would be like with my demon passenger. Maybe I should have thought about it before, but since I'd first found out I was possessed, my future had looked so uncertain—as in I was unlikely to *have* a future—that I hadn't put much thought into it.

I still didn't know what would happen between Brian and me, even if I managed to get rid of Lugh somehow. We'd put some jumbo-sized Band-Aids on our relationship, and so far they seemed to be holding strong. But how long would that last? Sure, I was being more open and honest with Brian now than I had been in the past, trusting him when trust had always eluded me before. But my life had taught me a fundamental truth: People don't change, even if your perceptions of them do. So where did that leave me?

Wallowing in self-pity, apparently.

I shook it off as best I could, forcing a semicheerful smile. "Guess I'm not getting laid this afternoon, huh?"

Brian gave a little huff of what might have been

laughter. "Guess not. But I still have high hopes for later tonight." He reached over and took my hand, squeezing it firmly. "Just give me a little time to get used to the idea, okay?"

I wasn't sure which idea it was he needed to get used to: Lugh's desire, or just the fact that Lugh was our silent partner when we had sex, the ultimate voyeur. Maybe it didn't matter.

I nodded my acceptance, then leaned in for a kiss—the action instinctive rather than planned. Brian hesitated for a fraction of a second before he pressed his lips to mine, giving me a firm but closed-mouth kiss.

Brian is way too perceptive not to notice that his halfhearted kiss stung me, but he pretended not to.

"How about dinner tonight?" he asked. He glanced at his watch. "I'll pick you up around seven, okay?"

"Sure," I said as my heart sank a little lower. Something told me a single afternoon wasn't going to be enough time for Brian to sort things through, and our dinner tonight was going to be an awkward and uncomfortable affair. But I just didn't have it in me to turn him down.

three

WHEN I'M STRESSED OUT, I CLEAN. THESE LAST TWO months of relative peace had kept my stress level manageable, which meant my apartment was a pigsty. Worrying about what was going to happen with Brian was enough to galvanize me into action, so I got to work practically as soon as the door closed behind him.

I quickly lost myself in the familiar rhythm, my thoughts focused on nothing except the task at hand. Some people meditate; I scrub toilets. What can I say?

At around five, Brian called and told me his boss had suddenly ordered him back to work, so he'd have to take a rain check on dinner. My throat tightened with worry, though I tried not to show it. I gracefully accepted his apology and his offer of a rain check, then hung up the phone before I started to hyperventilate.

It was true that in Brian's line of work, it wouldn't be that unusual for his boss to call him out of the blue at any hour of the day or night. Certainly it had happened before. But with this afternoon's discussion looming large in my mind, I couldn't help wondering if this had been a convenient excuse, rather than a genuine need to work.

Just give him a little time, Lugh said, and I snarled softly.

"Easy for you to say when you're the one who screwed me over in the first place!"

Of course, he didn't answer. I resisted the urge to throw the phone across the room. There was no point in arguing with Lugh—his ability to rummage around in my head gives him an unfair advantage. But I was sick of cleaning house, and I didn't think it would absorb my thoughts so effectively anymore. What I needed right now, I decided, was human contact. And what better human was there than someone who could understand *exactly* what Brian and I were going through?

Dominic Castello is the former host of the demon Saul, Raphael's son. But what made him singularly perfect as a confidant under the circumstances was that his boyfriend, Adam, was still possessed, making their relationship into a really weird ménage à trois very similar to my own situation.

Among his other sterling qualities, Dominic is also a fantastic cook, and he'd finally taken the plunge and bought a restaurant. Actually, I'm pretty sure it was Adam who'd bought the restaurant, because Dominic didn't have that kind of money, but Dominic was the official owner. The grand opening wasn't for another week yet, but I knew Dom was in the process of training his staff right now, so I decided to take a gamble in hopes of combining a free meal with good company.

Dominic's restaurant was within walking distance,

but when I stepped outside, I almost wished I'd called a cab. The air was like a wet, stifling blanket, and I was drenched with sweat by the time I got to the restaurant.

A smile stretched my lips when I saw the newly installed sign over the front door. Apparently, the restaurant was going to be called "Dominic's." Simple, and to the point. And probably Adam's idea, because Dom was way too modest to want to name the place after himself. A handwritten sign in the doorway said, "Opening soon," but I could see shadows of movement behind the closed curtains.

I rapped on the door a couple of times, and eventually one of those shadows moved in my direction. The door opened, and a rail-thin Italian woman with discreetly graying hair gave me the once-over before saying, "We're not open yet. The grand opening is in one week."

She started closing the door before I had a chance to say anything, and I was momentarily flummoxed by her rudeness. If this was the kind of staff Dom was hiring, I had to wonder what he was thinking.

Luckily, Dominic emerged from the kitchen at that moment and saw me.

"Morgan!" he said, sounding delighted as he waved to me from across the room.

The bitch at the door pursed her lips in obvious disapproval, but she halted her effort to slam the door in my face. I wondered what her problem was, then reminded myself that many people her age found my outlandish appearance somewhat disconcerting. Aside

from the multiple piercings in my ears and my conspic-
uously sexy wardrobe, I'm also a five-foot-nine redhead,
so I tend to make an impression everywhere I go. She
fingered a truly hideous crucifix that was tucked away
under the collar of her white blouse, and for a moment
I feared she was going to shove it in my face like I was a
vampire.

Dominic said something to her in Italian, and she
replied with something I suspected was less than com-
plimentary. I don't speak a word of Italian, but the sour
expression on her face was a pretty good clue. She
sniffed disdainfully, then spun on her heel and headed
toward the kitchen without another word.

I gaped at Dom, who gave me a wry smile and a
shrug.

"Sorry," he said. "She's my stepmother, and when
she wanted to help out with the restaurant I didn't have
the heart to say no. But she's, uh, rather conservative."
The smile turned into a hint of a grimace.

I knew next to nothing about Dom's family, except
that they were all Italian and Catholic, but I could certainly read between the lines well enough to guess they
weren't happy about his choices in life. They probably
adhered to the theory that demons were the Spawn of
Satan, and I bet they'd disapproved heartily of his decision to host one. I bet they weren't too happy about him
being gay, either, and they would probably expire of
horror if they knew any of the details of his relationship
with Adam, which involved S&M.

"Has she met Adam yet?" I asked, though I figured
the answer was no or she'd either have run screaming

or be buried in some secret grave. Adam isn't one to suffer fools, and when he wants to be intimidating…Let's just say no sane person would mess with him.

Dom shrugged. "So far, I've been able to keep them apart. She knows I live with Adam, but I think she's convinced herself that we're just roommates. I've told her the truth, but she's developed a case of selective hearing."

Better and better. Sometimes I seriously wondered if love was worth all the trouble it caused.

Dom ushered me into the restaurant, closing and locking the door behind us. I hadn't seen the place since he'd first bought it, and I gave a soft whistle of appreciation for the changes. It had been an Italian restaurant even before Dom had bought it, but the previous owners had had delusions of grandeur and had gone out of their way to make the place look like Snob Central, with everything cold and super formal.

Dom had transformed it into a warm, intimate space, retaining all the class while doing away with the formality. Tables for two lined the windows, while tables for four and six dotted the center of the room. There was even a long table that looked like it would seat about twelve tucked into a corner in the back.

"It's gorgeous," I told Dom, and smiled as he beamed in obvious pride. He is one of the nicest people I've ever met, and I was really hoping the restaurant would take off for him.

"Are you here just to sightsee?" he asked, "or would you mind being a test subject for my staff?"

I grinned. "Well, it would be a real hardship for me, but I guess I can spare a little time to help you out. That's what friends are for, right?"

"Then let me show you to your table."

He pulled a chair back from one of the tables by the window. Only Dominic can get away with holding a chair out for me and not get his head bitten off. I'm not big on the whole chivalry thing.

"Shouldn't your hostess be taking care of this part of the job?" I couldn't help teasing.

Dom darted a quick, surreptitious glance at the kitchen, then bent to whisper in my ear. "To tell you the truth, I suspect she won't last until opening day. I can't keep her and Adam apart much longer, and they're destined to get along about as well as your average snake and mongoose."

I grinned. "Sounds like you've got a really passive-aggressive plan to get rid of her."

He gave me a "Who, me?" face while his eyes twinkled with humor. "I'll send a server out with a menu. They just came back from the printer today."

He started to head toward the kitchen, excited to show me the menu, but I grabbed his sleeve to stop him.

"Just to warn you," I said, "I did come here with ulterior motives."

"Other than wanting a free meal?"

I grinned. "Let's say *in addition* to wanting a free meal."

"Okay."

"Can I chat with you for a while when you have a few spare minutes?"

He heaved a dramatic sigh. "What's going on between you and Brian *now*?" he asked.

I think I blushed, though I supposed I should be used to being transparent by now. "Actually, it's between me, *Lugh*, and Brian."

His eyes widened. "Oh." He picked up the napkin from my plate and shook it out, laying it over my lap as though I wasn't capable of doing so myself. "Better order an appetizer and dessert. This might be a long conversation."

I made vague grumbling noises at him, which he ignored completely. I've never been one to share my troubles with anyone, having pretended to be an island for as long as I can remember. But Dom is different. I've talked to him about things I'd never dreamed I could talk about. And though the idea still made me uncomfortable, I knew it was good for me.

"I'll set things in motion in the kitchen," he told me, "and then I'll be right back."

"Thanks," I said, fighting my usual urge to flee from conversation.

A couple of minutes later, a waiter who obviously had an unhealthy love of hair gel emerged from the kitchen carrying a menu. I politely listened to his spiel while he told me which items on the menu were actually available tonight. Next Wednesday night they were going to have a special dinner service just for friends and family so that everyone got to practice before the grand opening, but tonight they only had a few basics available.

I couldn't remember ever eating something Dom

had cooked that was less than delicious, so I made some snap decisions and sent the waiter on his way.

I'd never considered Dom a control freak—and I'm an expert on the subject—but he remained ensconced in the kitchen until the waiter arrived with the bowl of minestrone I'd ordered. Dom took the seat across from me as the waiter laid a second bowl of soup in front of him. Dom cast a wistful glance at the kitchen door as the waiter retreated, and I had to smother a laugh.

"It's just me, Dom," I said as I inhaled the fragrant steam that wafted from my soup. "I promise I won't be writing any scathing reviews."

He laughed, and some of the tension eased from his shoulders. "I know, I know. I'm just getting a head start on being nervous for the grand opening."

I tasted the soup and sighed in contentment. "Trust me, you have nothing to be nervous about."

"Do you have any idea how many Italian restaurants there are in this city? Or how many restaurants of any kind fail in their first year? Adam's sunk a lot of money into this place, and—" He cut himself off with a look of annoyance. "But never mind all that. You came here to talk about what's going on with you and Brian. And Lugh."

I was tempted to spend more time reassuring Dom about how great his restaurant would be, but I doubted it would do any good. Despite the confidence I had in him, I couldn't blame him for being nervous. Only a successful grand opening could hope to calm his jitters.

The bowl of piping hot soup in front of me made

it easier for me to tell Dominic all about this afternoon's ... complications with Brian and Lugh. No, I didn't give him a play-by-play recounting, but I did tell him that Lugh "liked" Brian, and that he had made that known today.

By the time I'd finished talking, my entrée—a seafood risotto that looked so rich it was probably illegal in some states—arrived. I hadn't finished the soup yet, and Dom scolded the waiter for serving the entrée too early. It was a gentle scolding, though, and I figured Dom was probably a really great boss.

I waited until the waiter was back in the kitchen before I resumed talking. This was *not* the kind of conversation I wanted strangers overhearing.

"So," I asked in a conspiratorial whisper, "how do you deal with it? Knowing that there are two different people in Adam's body? Do you just ... I don't know, pretend that the human Adam isn't there?"

In a usual demonic possession, the demon has total control of its host's body, but the host's personality is still alive and kicking inside. Which meant that even though Adam's human host couldn't interact with the outside world, he was always there, just like Lugh was always there in me.

Dom looked thoughtful. "I think our situation is pretty different from yours. Adam ... that is, Adam's host ... and I knew each other before we both volunteered to host, so I've known both the demon and the human. I think it's easier for me to remember that they're two separate people that way. And having been a

host myself, I've always known how intimate the relationship is. Brian's never really known Lugh, so while he
might understand in theory that you and Lugh are different people, it might be hard for him to really absorb.
At least not if Lugh isn't shoving it in his face."

I cocked my head at him. "Don't think I didn't notice
that you didn't answer the question." It wasn't like Dom
to be evasive. He was a hell of a lot more open and honest than I was.

His mouth tugged down in a hint of a frown. "I guess
it's because I don't like the answer," he said softly. "I
suppose I *do* sometimes kind of forget about the human
half of Adam. I know the two of them talk a lot and that
they get along very well, but the human Adam never…
talks to me, like Lugh talks to the rest of us."

Except for the rare occasions when Lugh ended up in
control, all other communication between him and his
council came through me. I guess that made me something like Lugh's mouthpiece, at least some of the time.

"If you were friends before you became hosts, why
doesn't Adam's host talk to you?"

Dom thought about that for a moment before answering. "When I was hosting Saul, I never felt the need
to communicate with anyone else. He was the only person I could interact with directly, and I guess it seemed
like too much trouble to reach out to other people. Especially when Saul could give me everything I needed." He
shrugged. "It's easier than you think to just kind of…
let yourself fade into the background."

I snorted softly. Easy for Dom, maybe. There was no
way in hell it'd be easy for *me*. "So you think Adam's

host just kind of sits behind the scenes twiddling his thumbs and has no feelings one way or another about your relationship with Adam?"

Dom looked distinctly uncomfortable. "No, of course not. But it doesn't do anyone any good to dwell on that."

My temper is prickly at the best of times, and a low simmer started in my veins. "You think it's best for Adam's *host* if you and Adam don't dwell on the fact that he's there?"

My voice had risen only a little, but Dom's stepmother peeked out from the kitchen anyway. I think she was hoping to have a front-row seat for my eviction from the restaurant, but even though Dom's back was to the kitchen, he seemed to know she was there. He glared over his shoulder at her, reinforcing his message with words that I'm sure meant "Mind your own business" in Italian.

The little distraction gave me a moment to rein in my temper. "Sorry," I said to Dom when he turned to face me again. "You know me—I get bitchy when I'm uncomfortable."

Anger still flushed his cheeks, but he managed to smile. "And when you're scared. And when you're sick. And when—"

"I get the point," I said, but I couldn't help laughing a bit. It didn't last long, though. "I guess the upshot of all this is that you and Adam haven't really worked everything out into some neat agreement that I can try to emulate with Brian."

"I wouldn't say that. I think we *are* all comfortable with how things have worked out."

"Yeah, and that's why you started squirming when I brought it up."

"No relationship is perfect. So yeah, sometimes I think it's awkward that Adam's host is there and it's easier for me pretend he isn't. But that's just part of the territory when your lover is a demon. I'm not going to give Adam up just because he's not alone in that body."

I leaned back in my chair, unreasonably frustrated that Dom couldn't solve my romantic difficulties with a few well-chosen words.

"Look," Dom said, leaning forward to keep the same distance between us, "I can't tell you how to work things out with Brian and Lugh. Your situation is different, after all." He grinned. "Adam's host isn't putting the moves on me, and if the two of them have anything romantic or sexual going on between them, I don't know about it and I don't want to. Adam's host has, for the most part, recused himself from his mortal life. Lugh is very much front and center, even though you're usually in control of your body. You and Lugh are more separate from each other than Adam and his host are."

"Yeah. I guess." Now I was depressed enough that even the delicious food wasn't enough to cheer me up. I pushed aside my half-eaten dinner and wondered if I wouldn't have been better off staying home. This conversation reminded me there was a *reason* I didn't usually share my troubles with anyone. I know some people find it helpful and comforting, but for the life of me I can't figure out why. It never seems to solve anything. At least, not for me.

Dom glanced at the plate I'd set aside, and I was

pretty sure he was about to either nag me to eat more or ask what was wrong with my dinner, but I was saved by a loud knock on the front door.

"Police! Open up!" Adam's voice announced.

Dominic groaned softly. "Oh, shit. I don't want to do this *now*."

I bit the inside of my cheek to keep myself from laughing. Dom looked comically chagrined, but he'd already said there was only so long he could keep his stepmother and Adam from meeting.

"At least I'm here to referee," I said cheerfully as Adam banged on the door again—drawing the attention of the entire staff.

Dominic gave me a baleful look as he stood up and trudged toward the front door.

"Go back to work," he instructed his staff, and most of them ducked back into the kitchen. Not his stepmother, though.

Adam looked like he had just come from work, though I bet he was the best-dressed cop in the entire Philly police department. He'd ditched his tie and unbuttoned the first couple buttons of his dress shirt, but his pinstriped trousers fit like they'd been customtailored, and the sport jacket he carried over one arm probably cost more than my entire wardrobe.

Damn, he looked good. But then, he always did. Demons tend to favor residing in attractive hosts, and when you paired that hunky host with a bad-boy demon, the result was basically sex on legs.

Adam invited himself in and draped his jacket over the hostess stand. Then, before Dominic could get a word in, Adam grabbed him, pulled him close, and planted a wet, showy kiss on his mouth. Dom tried to pull away, but if a demon has hold of you and doesn't want to let go, you aren't going anywhere. Dom's stepmother put a hand to her chest as if she were about to have a heart attack. There was a bit of a gleam in Adam's eyes as he gave her a visual once-over, and I realized that particularly exuberant display of affection had been for her benefit.

"Asshole," Dominic muttered when his mouth was no longer occupied, giving Adam a halfhearted shove on the shoulder.

Adam made a clucking sound with his tongue. "Watch your language, or I'm going to have to teach you a lesson later."

Dom's face went beet red, and the glare he shot his lover was obviously genuine—and heartfelt. "Don't," he said tightly. "Not here; not now."

It's not all that easy to make Dom angry, but there was no question he was pissed off right now. Obviously he'd mentioned to Adam that his stepmother might be a problem, and Adam had decided to stage a confrontation at his own convenience.

It never ceases to amaze me that Adam, whose name should be in the dictionary beside the word "hard-ass," will actually back down to Dom, but I'd seen it happen on more than one occasion. Adam held up his hands in a gesture of surrender, and though he didn't verbally apologize, the apology was in his body language and his facial expression.

The damage, however, was done. Dom's stepmother—who I knew from her first few words to me was perfectly capable of speaking English—said something angry and accusatory-sounding in Italian. She was fingering her crucifix again. Dominic answered in kind, complete with expansive hand gestures. He was Italian by heritage only, but from the way he was talking and gesticulating now, I could almost convince myself he'd just flown in from Italy yesterday.

Dom's stepmother whirled and slammed the kitchen doors open. Without a look at either Adam or me, Dominic ran to follow her. I couldn't tell if he was following to continue their argument, or whether he was hoping to appease her. All I knew was he wasn't happy.

"Nice work," I said to Adam with a grimace of distaste.

He took that as an invitation to come join me at the table. "Dom's been tap-dancing his way around this for two weeks," he said as he grabbed my leftover risotto and pulled it to his side of the table. "I didn't think putting it off was doing anyone any favors."

I crossed my arms over my chest. I considered Adam to be something that at least bore a mild resemblance to a friend, but no one could ever accuse me of *liking* him.

"You should have left that up to Dom," I said.

Adam shoved a fork full of cold risotto into his mouth and chewed vigorously before answering. "If I'd left it up to Dom, he'd have ended up being the bad guy in his wicked stepmother's book. This way, *I* get to be the bad guy. It won't make things go *smoothly* for him, but it might make the bumps in the road a little smaller."

One of the reasons Adam so often rubs me the wrong way is that he does these totally obnoxious things, then manages to explain them away so that I end up feeling he's right.

"Help yourself to my risotto," I said, because I refused to acknowledge that he might have a point.

"Don't mind if I do," he said around another mouthful. "I wasn't expecting to find you here," he continued. "Anything wrong?"

I almost laughed. I might feel comfortable confiding in Dominic, but Adam was a very different story.

"Nothing I plan on sharing with *you*."

"You cut me to the quick."

"Yeah, I'll bet." But as I sat across from Adam, resentfully watching him polish off the last of my dinner, it occurred to me that there *was* something I should discuss with him.

"Shae paid me a visit today," I said.

Adam's jaw visibly tightened, but that didn't stop him from scooping the last few grains of rice onto his fork and eating them. He and Shae had a history, and it wasn't a very nice one. Since he was the Director of Special Forces, he'd had to deal with Shae in her role as informant on a regular basis. Shae had always resented him for it, and whenever she had a chance, she lashed out at him. I was almost surprised she hadn't met with an unfortunate accident yet. But then Adam was one of the good guys, so he only murdered people if it was for a good cause, not just because they pissed him off.

Dom's stepmother burst out of the kitchen, her head held high while her eyes gleamed with tears. She sneered at Adam, ignored me, then stomped out the front door. Dom had followed her out of the kitchen, but he stayed inside the restaurant, his head bowed so that I couldn't see his face. I suddenly wanted to be anywhere but here. If Adam and Dom were about to have a lovers' quarrel, I didn't want a front-row seat.

"Well, I'd better get going," I said, pushing my chair back from the table. It didn't come off sounding like a smooth exit line, but I wasn't a good enough actress to hide my spike of discomfort.

"Oh, no, you don't," Adam said, grabbing me by my wrist. "First you need to tell me what Shae wanted with you."

"Um…" I responded intelligently, my eyes fixed on Dominic. Tension screamed in his shoulders, reminding me again that I wanted out. "I'll tell you all about it later." I tried to pull my arm from Adam's grip, but I wasn't going anywhere unless he allowed it.

Adam followed my gaze to Dom and shook his head. "You can yell at me later," he said to Dom. "We have all night for that."

Dom finally raised his head, and the expression on his face wasn't one of anger. I winced at the pain in his eyes. I knew what it was like to be scorned by my own family. Unfortunately, I didn't know any words that would take the pain away.

"Fuck," Adam muttered under his breath. He let go of my wrist, stood up, and gathered Dom into a hug. Dom didn't return it, his arms held stiffly to his sides, his fists clenched. But I knew how much he loved Adam, and I knew the two of them would work it out.

Swallowing a lump of unreasonable envy that had gathered in my throat, I slipped away from the table and out the door. Neither Dom nor Adam seemed to notice me leaving. So I ended up leaving Dom's restaurant feeling even worse than I had when I'd come in.

That's what I got for trying to open up and talk about my problems.

four

I T WAS ALMOST MIDNIGHT, AND I WAS IN MY PJS, WHEN the front desk called to let me know I had a visitor. Adam, of course. I should have known he'd come after me once he'd done his best to make Dom feel better. In the old days, I'd have told the desk not to let him up. But then Adam would pull his badge and pretend he was on official police business, so it did me no good.

"Send him up," I said with a sigh of resignation.

I didn't feel like changing into respectable clothing, so I merely covered my PJs with my disreputable robe and waited.

It took the better part of forever for Adam to make it to my twenty-seventh-floor apartment, seeing as our elevators are so slow it was arguably faster to walk. I opened the door before he had a chance to knock, having heard the ding that signaled the elevator's arrival. He raised an eyebrow at my outfit.

"Did I get you out of bed?"

I'd have loved to lay a guilt trip on him, but I doubted he'd feel guilty, so it wasn't worth the bother of trying. "Nah. I was still up." I opened the door wide enough to let him in, and Adam headed for my couch without any further invitation. He plopped down heavily and ran a hand through his short-cropped hair.

"How's Dom?" I asked as I sat cross-legged on the love seat.

Adam waggled his hand in the gesture for "so-so." "I tried to talk him out of reconnecting with his family once Saul was exorcized, but he didn't listen to me."

"It's his *family*," I protested. "You can't seriously expect him to just cut them off." A funny protest coming from someone who had as many family troubles as I did, but I knew how strong family bonds could be, even when you could barely stand one another.

"Why not? My host severed ties with his family even before he became a host."

Adam had told me about this before. His host had come out of the closet when he'd turned eighteen, and his family had been so appalled that they'd kicked him out. And, as far as I knew, they hadn't spoken to him since.

"Not everyone's that much of a homophobe," I said.

Adam shrugged. "You saw the expression on that harpy's face. And she's probably the most accepting of them. After all, she wanted to help out in the restaurant, as long as she could live in the land of denial and pretend Dom and I were 'just friends.' " He shook his head in disgust. "I simply can't understand why you humans are so hung up on this sexual orientation thing."

I remembered the crucifix Dom's stepmother had fingered. "I'm guessing they're old-school Catholics. According to Catholicism, homosexuality is a sin. If she thinks he's going to burn in Hell forever because of his lifestyle, then..."

"Don't get me started on religion," he said grimly. "I understand that even less."

Despite all the contact I had with demons, despite the fact that I should know better by now, I still sometimes found myself thinking about them as if they really were human. They are similar to humans in so many ways that it's easy to forget that they're *not*.

"Demons don't practice religion?" I asked, curious despite myself.

Adam shook his head. "No. My host has tried to explain it to me, but he was never religious himself, so his understanding isn't so great."

I held up my hands. "Don't look at me for an explanation. I was brought up in a Spirit Society household." The Spirit Society practically worships demons, but they've never gone so far as to declare demons deities. Perhaps it's a religion in its own right—actually, in my opinion it's more like a cult—but since it had failed to indoctrinate me, I can't say I have that great an understanding of it.

I was in danger of having a nonessential conversation with Adam—something I tried to avoid at all costs—but I was saved by Adam's sudden change of subject.

"It's late and I want to get back home. Tell me why Shae came to see you."

So I told him everything, watching his face carefully for a reaction, but I could read nothing in his expression. Despite his distaste for Shae, Adam was a member of The Seven Deadlies, and I knew he still visited there on occasion to satisfy some of his more dangerous urges with demons who could heal whatever damage he caused. Dom wasn't exactly happy with the arrangement, but he seemed to have accepted it as necessary, knowing that Adam was not having sex with his playmates at the club.

"Have you noticed an increase in illegal demons at the club?" I asked.

Adam shook his head. "I don't go there as a cop—unless I'm meeting Shae. I don't socialize there, either. I try to get in and out as fast as I can. But the next time I'm there, I'll pay attention. And I'll do some discreet inquiries at work, see if there's any rumbling on the street about people 'disappearing.' "

"What do you think it means, if Shae is right?"

His expression was troubled. "Nothing good."

"Yeah, that much I figured out on my own."

"I don't have enough information to be making guesses, but I'll make one anyway. Dougal's got to know that Lugh won't stay in hiding forever. Even if Dougal's abandoned his quest to kill Lugh, he can still take advantage of Lugh's absence."

I followed Adam's line of thought easily. "By sending more of his supporters to the Mortal Plain."

Adam nodded. "That's what I'm thinking. There are a limited number of willing hosts available, so maybe he's institutionalized a program to funnel demons into *un*willing hosts."

"Using people from the fringes of society so no one will kick up a fuss. Or possibly even notice." Adam nodded again, and I shivered in a phantom chill. The more I thought about this, the less I liked it. "And if that's really what's going on, what are the chances it's only happening in Philadelphia?"

Adam didn't have to answer that, because we both knew the answer was zilch.

"Just how many demons are there who want to come to the Mortal Plain?" I asked.

He met my eyes with a steady stare. "Enough that the waiting list is decades long."

"That's a lot," I muttered, wondering how many of these demons had managed to come to the Mortal Plain in the months that we on Lugh's council had been growing complacent. Sure, we knew that eventually we were going to have to take some kind of action against Dougal. His original plan had been to use Lugh's True Name to summon him into a host who would be immediately burned at the stake. Raphael had foiled the plan by summoning Lugh into *me*, but Lugh could not afford to return to the Demon Realm while Dougal and his followers had his True Name, or the original plan would go into effect again. Since I'm not immortal, Lugh will have to go back to the Demon Realm eventually, and if we haven't wiped out every trace of the coup by then, his goose is cooked. So to speak.

With Lugh in residence I was likely to live to a ripe old age, so there had been no great urgency to find a solution. But if Dougal really had created some kind of illegal pipeline onto the Mortal Plain—if it wasn't just some localized anomaly—then we needed to get our act together and soon.

As king of the Demon Realm, Lugh *should* know the True Name of every demon who had earned one. If theory were reality, we could simply use Dougal's own strategy against him. However, in a moment of naivete, when Lugh had ascended to the throne, he'd tried to reconcile with his brothers by not forcing them to reveal their True Names. Ah, the famed twenty-twenty hindsight!

"I guess we need to call a council meeting," I said.

"I'd suggest tomorrow," Adam responded, clearly feeling the same urgency that I did.

"I'll call everyone first thing in the morning," I agreed, suppressing a yawn. Adam gave me a look that said I shouldn't be yawning at a time like this, but it was after midnight and I couldn't help it.

"We can meet at noon," I said when I finished yawning. "That ought to give me enough time to catch everyone. Now go home to Dom and let me get some sleep."

"I should go to The Seven Deadlies," he responded, looking less than thrilled with the prospect. "Maybe I can spot one of these illegals Shae was talking about, and we can have a little chat."

"You can go tomorrow night. Dom needs you tonight."

Adam's lips compressed into a thin line. "Lugh's needs come before Dom's. Or mine."

Tell him to go home, Lugh said. *If he's going to go to The Seven Deadlies, he should wait until after the council has had a chance to discuss it.*

I relayed the message to Adam, who accepted it without question. Once upon a time, he would have questioned whether the message really came from Lugh, but he knew from experience that I was a shitty liar, so these days he usually took what I said at face value. Someday I'd have to learn to take advantage of that.

I wasn't surprised that Lugh didn't let me sleep peacefully until morning. Unlike me, he was a big fan of the therapeutic conversation—though his therapy methods were highly irregular.

I "woke up" in Lugh's living room, though in reality, my body was still sound asleep and the room was a figment of my imagination. An imagination over which Lugh had total control, I might add. I saw what he wanted me to see, and usually the setting gave me some hint about what kind of conversation we were about to have.

The living room was a relatively neutral setting as long as I wasn't lying on the couch and there was no fire in the fireplace. That meant he probably wasn't making an attempt to seduce me, as he would if he'd conjured his bedroom, nor was he going to try to cow me with his authority, as he would if he'd conjured his throne room.

Lugh was sitting on his favorite couch, which was upholstered in the softest leather I'd ever encountered. I'd been hosting him for several months now, and I'd seen him—at least, I'd seen the image of himself he created in my dreaming mind—more times than I could count. But that didn't stop me from feeling a tug of attraction every time I set eyes on him.

He's about six foot five, with long, raven-black hair, golden skin, and a body to die for. He was eye candy from head to toe, and he liked to dress in such a way as to show off his masculine beauty.

The black leather pants and the knee-high black boots were practically a uniform for him, but what he wore—or didn't wear—on top changed with his mood. Tonight, he wore a black tuxedo-style shirt, the tiny buttons undone to about the middle of his chest. He smiled at me—the smile that reminded me he knew *exactly* how I responded to him, no matter how much I wished that I didn't.

I folded my arms over my chest and declined to sit down. It got incredibly tiresome to talk to someone from whom you could hide absolutely nothing.

Lugh's smile broadened. "And it gets tiresome to always feel like you have something to hide."

I answered through gritted teeth. "You know the one way to guarantee that any conversation between us will go badly is to start it by responding to my *private* thoughts, so why do you do it?"

He didn't answer me, merely fixing me with a steady

stare. He'd told me before that he responded to my thoughts just to remind me that they weren't really private. It was a form of honesty I could do without, although he had a point when he said I'd resent it if he allowed me the illusion. The illusion wouldn't hold, and when it faded, I'd feel like he'd lied to me.

"I suppose that's your justification for butting in with Brian earlier," I grumbled. "That he'd feel deceived if the status quo continued."

Lugh's chin dipped in a barely perceptible nod. "It was time to acknowledge that you cannot have a relationship with each other without having a relationship with *me. You've* accepted me. Now it's time for Brian to do the same."

I plopped heavily into a cushy love seat across from Lugh. I'd spent two months living in the land of denial, and the universe seemed determined to tear the carpet out from under me. First with Shae's ominous news, then with Lugh's latest machinations.

"Is it a coincidence that you decided to butt in on the same day Shae came to talk to me?" I asked, already knowing the answer.

"I'd been meaning to do it for a while," he said, "but I'm afraid I was growing a little complacent, too. After Shae's visit, I realized I was procrastinating, so I decided to get it over with. I have never been anything but honest with you, and I owe Brian the same courtesy. When he makes love to you, he makes love to both of us. If he can't learn to deal with that, then it's best to find out sooner rather than later."

I pinched the bridge of my nose. I didn't have a headache, but after that little speech, I *should* have. Lugh had never lied to me—that I knew of—but that wasn't quite the same as being completely honest. It didn't take a rocket scientist to know there was more to this story than he was telling.

"If it was best that he find out sooner rather than later, then why did you wait until *now* to make your point?"

He flashed me a rueful smile. "With all the troubles you and Brian have had since I've been in residence, do you really think he'd have been in the proper state of mind to deal with that dose of reality?"

I wished I had a snappy comeback for that, but none leapt to mind. There had been a lot of bumps in the relationship road for Brian and me, and I doubted things would ever be easy. But we loved each other, and though I don't believe love truly conquers all, it conquers a hell of a lot. Could it conquer Lugh?

"I'm not the enemy," Lugh reminded me, and I scowled at him.

I tried to remember what it was like in the days before I had Lugh in my life, but they seemed impossibly distant.

I blinked, and suddenly I wasn't sitting on the love seat anymore. I was sitting on the couch beside Lugh. I hated it when he did that, but there was no point in protesting.

He laid a hand on my shoulder, the touch innocent and yet strangely intimate. "Brian will come around," he said. "He's fought too hard to keep you to give up because of me."

"You can read *my* mind. You can't read *his*."

Lugh's mouth quirked into a grin. "I can make an educated guess. And my guess is that he'll come around eventually. It's just going to take a little time and ... adjustment."

I regarded him suspiciously. "You think he'll 'come around' to the idea of you trying to seduce me, too?" In Lugh's mind, there was no competition between himself and Brian, because I never had to choose between the two of them. Lugh could only interact with me as something other than a phantom voice in my head when I was asleep. Brian could only interact with me while I was awake. Therefore, in Lugh's opinion, no conflict.

"That might be a little harder for him to accept," Lugh admitted, startling me. This was the first time he'd ever indicated that he thought there might be a problem with his cozy little plan.

Once again, he answered my unspoken thoughts. "After seeing his reaction when he thought you'd had an affair with Adam, I can hardly pretend that I don't know he's the jealous type."

I laughed halfheartedly. "You say that like it's unusual, like most men would have no objection to their girlfriends having sex with another guy. If that's what you think, then you don't understand humans anywhere near as well as you've pretended to."

To my surprise, Lugh leaned back on the couch, cocking his head and seeming to give my words serious consideration. "It's not that I don't think other men would be jealous. But there is a certain...territoriality to humans that is foreign to the demon experience. Still, perhaps my lack of a separate physical body would lessen the strain on most men. There is no one he can lay his hands on and fight, if that makes sense."

Perhaps to Lugh, but not to me. "So if demons aren't 'territorial,' as you call it, about their lovers, then that means Adam wouldn't mind if Dom screwed around on him." Not that Dom ever would, but I had no doubt that Adam would object vociferously. After all, he was already at least mildly jealous of Saul, who had resided in Dom's body when he and Adam first became lovers.

"Walking the Mortal Plain changes us. It's hard to live within our human hosts, knowing their deepest thoughts and feelings, without being influenced by them. That's part of the reason why my brothers were so eager to develop a less intelligent host. Raphael said it's because he doesn't like hearing his host's opinion of him, but I suspect he's more concerned with how his host's opinion might influence him."

"So Adam has become territorial because his host is territorial?"

"That would be my assumption."

"And yet you haven't absorbed any of that territoriality even though I'm not your first human host."

He shrugged. "Humans aren't all the same. Surely you don't think demons are."

"Whatever. Why are we having this conversation?

You already explained your position to me earlier, so why can't you just let me get a good night's sleep?"

Yes, I was technically still sleeping, but these dream interactions with Lugh took something out of me. The longer we spent talking, the more tired I'd be in the morning.

"Since you called a council meeting for tomorrow, and since Brian is a member of the council, I thought it would be best if you and I worked things out beforehand."

"This isn't something we can 'work out' just by talking."

"I know, but it's a start. I hope that you at least understand my position, and understand that I'm not arbitrarily trying to make things difficult for you."

I heaved a sigh. I already knew that. One of the things I could count on with Lugh was that he had good intentions. Too bad those good intentions didn't make everything better.

"Get some sleep," Lugh said, like it was somehow *my* fault I wasn't soundly asleep right now. "I have a feeling that by tomorrow, all of our personal lives will have to take a backseat once again."

And on that cheerful thought, I drifted off into la-la land.

five

THERE ARE ABOUT A MILLION AND ONE GOOD WAYS to spend a Saturday morning. Calling each member of Lugh's council and telling them to drop everything for an impromptu meeting is not one of them.

Lugh's council had grown to eight members, with the recent inclusion of Barbara Paget, a private investigator who'd found herself roped into our cozy little nightmare. We were *not* one big happy family. My brother, Andy, who'd been forced to host Raphael on more than one occasion, hated Raphael. Saul, Raphael's son, also hated Raphael—though in his case, for causing the death of his mother. Raphael despised Andy for reasons I didn't fully understand.

Come to think of it, if we could just get rid of Raphael, the rest of us wouldn't have it quite so hard. But Raphael was loyal, and—though I hated to admit it— useful. Not to mention that whole being-Lugh's-brother thing.

Andy was the first to arrive. Not because he was so all-fired eager to attend a council meeting, but because he wasn't doing anything more important than hanging around his apartment when I called. He just hadn't been the same since the last time Raphael had possessed him. He was quiet and withdrawn, almost listless. He'd improved a little after some tough love from Raphael—you've got to love the irony—and at least he wasn't losing weight anymore. But I was still both worried about him and exasperated by him.

Andy had become a host because he wanted to be a hero. It was incredibly shitty luck that he'd ended up stuck with Raphael. The last time he'd been possessed, he'd been so desperate to get rid of Raphael that he'd been willing to foist him off on a God's Wrath fanatic who would hate Raphael even more than he did. The guilt was still eating him alive. I understood how he felt—I wasn't exactly guilt-free myself, having allowed it all to happen—but the wallowing was getting on my nerves.

I busied myself preparing an oversized pot of coffee so the awkward silence between us wouldn't feel so... awkward.

Dominic and Adam arrived next, and their playful flirtation lightened up the mood. Next came Saul and Barbie, who were either dating or fuck-buddies; I hadn't figured out which yet, and I wasn't sure I wanted to know. Brian showed up right on their heels with two dozen doughnuts. The guys fell on them like a school of rabid piranhas, and Barbie and I laughed at them from behind our coffee cups.

When the front desk rang to let me know Raphael was on his way up, there were two doughnuts left in the box. Saul, who still had powdered sugar on the corners of his mouth from his last victim, picked up one, and Andy took the other. Yes, they were petty enough to eat the last of the doughnuts so Raphael wouldn't get any.

Raphael noticed the decimated boxes when he walked in, and raised an eyebrow. "What?" he asked in feigned shock. "You didn't save any for me?"

Saul opened his mouth, and I knew it wasn't his doughnut he was about to take a bite out of. I was getting used to being quick on the trigger to stop their bickering before it began.

"Serves you right for being late," I said as I handed Raphael a cup of coffee.

He glanced at his watch. "Hmm. Must be running slow."

I doubted it. Raphael was rarely, if ever, annoying by accident. He'd give Machiavelli a run for his money. I'd given up trying to figure out what he was up to every time he pulled one of his little mind games.

While waiting for everyone to get here, I'd pulled the dining room chairs into the living room and made a big circle of them with the couch and love seat. Now that all the council members were present, we took our seats, and I told everyone what Shae had told me. Then I opened the floor for comments and waited for the fireworks to commence.

"How reliable is Shae's information?" Barbie asked. "You've said she's a mercenary. Can you be sure she's not feeding you a bunch of crap in hopes that you'll give her something she can use?"

"Sure? *Hell,* no," I answered. "But my gut instinct says she's telling the truth. You should have seen the look in her eyes when she talked about being given a gag order. She was seriously pissed."

"Yeah, but you can't be sure exactly what she's pissed about," Barbie said.

"Shae wouldn't come to Morgan on a random fishing expedition," Raphael said. "Not when she knows there's a chance Morgan would sic me on her. Something's going on."

I nodded my agreement. "Yeah, but what? And is it just happening in Philadelphia?"

More discussion ensued, though no one seemed to have anything useful to say. For the time being, I just sat back and listened, ready to jump in if my services as referee were needed. But Raphael kept his mouth shut, which kept the bickering to a minimum...and aroused my suspicions. Raphael is not one to keep his opinions to himself.

I was sitting directly across the circle from him, and the expression on his face said he was thinking deeply about something. Something that didn't make him happy.

"What do you think is happening?" I asked him, and everyone else fell silent to stare at him.

"I told you that we couldn't sit around twiddling our thumbs forever," he said. Before I could protest his tactless description of our recent activities, he continued. "I think Dougal is taking advantage of the fact that Lugh isn't around to stop him and is funneling a higher number of demons onto the Mortal Plain. And the longer we stay out of his hair, the more demons he'll send through. And whose side do you think they'll be on if this conflict goes public?"

"Christ," Brian muttered. "It's the Invasion of the Body Snatchers."

"Something like that," Raphael agreed.

Adam had come up with the same theory earlier, but although it seemed like a logical—if terrifying—conclusion, I wasn't convinced we had enough evidence.

"Let's not panic yet," I said. "All we know for sure is that Shae says there have been more illegal demons in her club than usual lately. We don't know if it's happening all over the place or just here."

"Forgive my ignorance," Barbie said, "but if Dougal simply wanted to send more demons to the Mortal Plain, why wouldn't he just try to get the Spirit Society to lower their standards?"

Like I said, the Spirit Society practically worshipped demons—or "Higher Powers" as they called them. They felt it was beneath a demon's dignity to reside in an unattractive host.

"Maybe they have," I answered. "But even within the Spirit Society, there are a limited number of people who actually want to be hosts. The rest of the membership likes to kiss demon ass, but that isn't the same as being willing to give up your life for a demon."

Adam gave an exasperated grunt. "How many times do I have to tell you that our hosts don't 'give up their lives'? My host is alive and well and perfectly content in this body."

Yeah, we'd had this argument before. And on a rational, logical level, I knew he was right, at least about many demon/host relationships. But emotionally, it would always feel to me as if the hosts were dead, because they were so completely cut off from the outside world.

"We don't give up our lives when we agree to host," Dominic said. "We just give up *control* of our lives. There is a difference."

I held up my hands to signal my surrender. "Fine. I get it. But there still aren't all that many people who are willing to 'give up control of their lives' to host a demon. So if Dougal wants to get more of his minions onto the Mortal Plain, yeah, he can ask the Society to lower their standards, but that wouldn't…widen the pipeline as much as he might want." I raised an eyebrow at Raphael. "Right?"

He nodded. "Dougal is not a big fan of subtlety. If he wants more demons on the Mortal Plain, then he wants *lots* more demons on the Mortal Plain, not just a handful."

"Do we even want to speculate about why?" Dominic asked.

I shuddered to think of the possibilities.

We're getting ahead of ourselves again, Lugh told me. *First, we have to confirm that our guesses are correct.* Then *we worry about what it means.*

I conveyed his message to the council, and no one argued the point.

"So, how do we confirm our guesses?" I asked of no

one in particular, though I had a feeling I already knew the answer.

Raphael grinned at me. "Sounds like another visit to The Seven Deadlies is in order."

This was yet another one of those times when I really hated being right.

Considering how much I loathed The Seven Deadlies, it was amazing how many times I'd set foot in the place. Enough that the bouncer at the door recognized me and let me in, even though I wasn't a member. Adam *was* a member, and he claimed Barbie as his guest. Raphael wasn't technically a member himself, but Tommy Brewster, his host, had a membership card from back when he'd been possessed by a different demon.

I always thought of The Seven Deadlies as a sex club, and it is, in part. But when you first go in, it looks and sounds just like any other nightclub, complete with ear-splitting music, dim lighting, and a floor that vibrates with every bass note. There's also the standard bar and dance floor.

But once your eyes adjust to the light, you start to notice the differences. The first thing you notice is that bunches of people in the crowd are wearing cheesy halos or cheesy devil horns, which they picked up from a table near the entrance. Adam had explained to me that one wore a halo if one was shopping for a partner for some vanilla sex, and one wore the horns if shopping for something more...exotic.

There was a sign above the dance floor that labeled it "Purgatory," and I'd always thought that an apt description. There were rooms to rent on the second floor for the halo crowd. The balcony of the second floor looked down onto the dance floor, and was labeled "Heaven." And then there was The Door, as I'd come to think of it. The Door led into a section of the club called "Hell," and it was where the S&M crowd hung out . . . and played. I'd only been down there once before, but the things I'd seen remained burned on my retinas, and you couldn't pay me enough to go down there again.

I'd have been repulsed enough if what happened down there were human S&M, which Dominic assured me was about mutual pleasure, even if that pleasure was obtained in unconventional ways. But unlike humans, the demons loved the pain itself. They are incorporeal in the Demon Realm, and many of them find physical sensation—*all* physical sensation—fascinating. Add that to the fact that they can heal wounds that would kill a human being, and you have a scene from your worst nightmare and scariest horror movie all wrapped up into one.

"I'll go get a room," Adam shouted into my ear.

I didn't feel like screaming myself hoarse, so I merely nodded. Raphael, Barbie, and I hovered in an especially dark alcove near the entrance, trying not to attract attention. It wasn't that hard. People were mostly occupied with their prospective partners, or so drunk they didn't care what was going on around them.

Adam returned shortly with a magnetized key card. He and Raphael went upstairs to unlock the room, then

Adam came back down and handed the key card to Barbie, who tucked it in the back pocket of her jeans.

"Happy hunting!" Adam yelled with a lascivious lift of his brows. Barbie laughed, but I just scowled at him.

Barbie snagged one of the halos and put it on, looking positively ridiculous, in my opinion, then headed toward the bar with me in her wake. Raphael, the author of our nasty little plan, had been very specific on the criteria for our mark. It had to be a demon who wasn't into pain, for one thing. Even the demons who liked pain had their limits, but interrogating one of them would be...especially unpleasant. Which was why Barbie had donned the halo. It also had to be a demon who fit Shae's description of these new illegals, with the look of someone who wasn't far removed from a street person.

And that's where I came in. Because these demons wouldn't look like the stereotypical drop-dead gorgeous specimens, it would be hard for Barbie to tell the difference between a nouveau demon and a skanky human. I would have to discreetly slip into my exorcist's trance and check the aura of anyone she was considering taking upstairs for the glow of demon red.

I wasn't entirely sure I could get myself into the trance state under these circumstances. I don't need the whole dog-and-pony show many exorcists require to induce the trances, but I feared the music and crowd might be a tad distracting, even for me. Still, I'd managed to induce the trance in less-than-ideal circumstances before, so I hoped I could manage it here.

The reason I still insist on calling Barbara "Barbie," despite her repeated attempts to get me to stop, is that she looks so much like a Barbie doll. She's petite and blond, with a curvaceous figure and a china-doll face. Yes, I hate her, even though I actually like her against all my expectations.

Her delicate good looks made her the perfect bait, and we hadn't even swallowed the first sips of our drinks before we had a candidate sniffing at her skirts. I shouldn't have been surprised that said candidate was female. This was a demon club after all, and I've already mentioned their lack of gender preferences.

Barbie's admirer fit our profile perfectly. She was way too skinny to be wearing a spaghetti-strap camisole, which showed off her bony shoulders and jutting collarbone. Her cheekbones were dagger-sharp slashes across her face, and there were hollows under her eyes. Her hair was a brittle, frizzy bottle-blond, with a stripe of brown roots showing at the part. She might have looked pretty enough at a healthy weight and with a decent dye job, but as she was, she was an eyesore. Definitely not the kind of person the Spirit Society would approve as a legal demon host.

I didn't hear what Ms. Skin-and-Bones said to Barbie, but her smile was lascivious enough to get the meaning across. It also showed a chipped front tooth. I knew without even checking her aura that she was one of the nouveau demons. With Shae's sense of aesthetics, she'd never have granted membership to a human who was so patently unattractive.

I expected Barbie to start up a flirtation, but instead she slipped an arm around my waist possessively and shook her head, smiling gently. Ms. Skin-and-Bones pouted, and I stood stark still, trying like hell not to show my surprise. I'm a shitty actress, so it's a good thing our would-be mark only had eyes for Barbie.

Ms. Skin-and-Bones reached out and gave Barbie's shoulder a squeeze. "If you change your mind, I'll be at the bar," she said, then sauntered off, probably thinking the way she shook her ass was sexy, rather than pathetic.

Barbie dropped the arm she'd put around my waist and gave me back my personal space. I frowned down at her.

"She was a perfect candidate," I protested. "Why did you turn her down?" I doubted it was due to any homophobia, considering Barbie had pretended to be with me, but I couldn't understand it.

"I thought we'd be better off with a male," she answered, leaning close to me again so she wasn't broadcasting her words to the whole room. Not that anyone could hear her over the blasting music. "I didn't want Adam and Raphael to get squeamish."

I was glad I wasn't in the middle of sipping my drink, because I'd have spit it halfway across the room as I laughed my ass off. Barbie had been a member of our council for a couple of months now, but since nothing much had happened, she hadn't gotten to see Adam and Raphael in action. If there were ever two people less likely to get squeamish—about *anything*—I sure didn't want to meet them.

"Believe me," I said between bouts of laughter, "they won't let chivalry—" The laughter threatened to take over again, and I sucked in a couple of deep breaths to quell it. "They won't let chivalry get in the way," I finished when I could get the whole sentence out.

"All right," Barbie said, the flush in her cheeks the only sign that my laughter pissed her off. "Maybe *I'm* squeamish. I'd rather pick someone who doesn't look so pathetic."

"That might be tough, since 'pathetic' is kinda one of the traits we're looking for."

We both looked toward the bar, where Ms. Pathetic sat sipping some kind of fruity drink. No one was talking to her. Hell, no one even looked at her. She might be one of the only demons in this club who'd have trouble getting laid.

Barbie bit her lip. "Are you sure she's a demon?"

Yes, I was. But not sure in the way Barbie was asking, so I took a deep breath and closed my eyes.

"I'll let you know in a minute," I said, adding a mental "I hope," because I still didn't know if this was going to work. The music pounded through my body, distracting me even as I tried to tune it out. No pun intended. When I breathed deep, I smelled booze and sweating bodies and a miasma of conflicting colognes.

Without opening my eyes, I reached into my pocket and pulled out the tissue I had stashed there. Before coming to the club, I'd dotted the tissue with some vanilla-scented oil. I made a pretense of wiping my nose as I drew the scent of vanilla into my lungs.

By the third breath, the club began to fade around me, the music suddenly seeming to come from far away. I let the trance take me, then opened my otherworldly eyes.

The sight I saw was almost enough to shock me back out of the trance, though I should have been braced for it. This was a demon nightclub. I *knew* most of its patrons were demons. But that didn't stop the moment of existential terror when my otherworldly eyes took in the sea of red auras that surrounded me. There were humans here, too, of course, their blue auras dotting that red sea like buoys. But the ratio of demons to humans was higher even than I'd expected.

I forced myself to calm, then focused on the bar. This was harder than it sounds, because in my otherworldly sight, I can't see objects, only living beings. The bar, being an inanimate object, was invisible to me. My depth perception was also kind of screwy, and I couldn't figure out how far out I needed to look to find the bar.

For a moment, I thought I couldn't do it. Then I noticed a set of auras that formed an almost straight line, behind which only a single human aura appeared, and I realized that had to be the bar. Aside from the bartender, there was only one human present, and he or she was at the far end.

I shook off the trance and opened my real-world eyes. Ms. Pathetic still sat alone and ignored at the bar, and since she wasn't at the far end, that meant she wasn't the human I'd seen in my trance.

"She's a demon," I told Barbie.

Barbie sighed. "All right, then. I'll go tell her I changed my mind." She still didn't look happy about it, but I knew that was because of her limited exposure to demons. It was hard for her to look past the external package and see the powerful, nearly immortal being within.

I watched as Barbie pushed her way past the milling crowd and approached the bar. Ms. Pathetic's face lit up when Barbie sidled up to her, and even *I* felt a tug of guilt for getting her hopes up like this only to dash them. And worse.

I was sure Barbie felt the same guilt, only stronger, and I halfway expected her to walk away. But she had committed herself to this path, and she wasn't deviating from it. Her mark didn't stand a chance. Barbie could coax a preacher into robbing a bank with the crook of a finger.

After only a couple of minutes of conversation, Barbie slipped her hand into Ms. Pathetic's and started leading her toward the stairway to the second floor.

I pulled out my cell phone and texted Adam a one-word message: "Incoming." Then I followed in Barbie's wake, giving her a big enough head start that Ms. Pathetic wouldn't notice me coming toward them. Not that she was likely to notice anything other than Barbie right now.

The club was air-conditioned, but no air conditioner in the world could combat a night this hot and humid, not with a couple hundred people packed together, radiating body heat. Half the dancers looked like they'd just come out of the shower, their hair wet, their clothes plastered to their skin by sweat.

By the time I got across the room, I was sweating, too, and about ready to deck the next person who grabbed me and tried to pull me onto the dance floor. The alcohol was flowing freely tonight, the crowd more boisterous than I'd seen in my past forays here.

Barbie and our mark were just disappearing into a room at the end of the hall when I made it to the head of the stairs. I glanced down at the dance floor as I was shoving my way through the loiterers, and caught sight of Shae. She was strolling gracefully through the crowd, surveying her domain. I moved away from the balcony, hugging the wall and hurrying. I doubted Shae would object to what we had planned, but what she didn't know wouldn't hurt us.

Struggling through a sweating, inebriated crowd of mostly demons was hard work. I felt like I'd run a marathon by the time I finally made it to the door behind which Barbie and Ms. Pathetic had disappeared.

I knocked on the door—two series of three knocks, which was our agreed-upon signal—and moments later, the door cracked open just wide enough for me to slip inside.

It was Barbie who'd opened the door. Her already fair skin was even paler than usual, and there was a sheen of tears in her eyes. Her halo was crumpled in a corner, where presumably she had thrown it. She wasn't a wuss by any stretch of the imagination, but I doubted she'd been exposed to as much violence as the rest of us.

Ms. Pathetic lay on the floor, curled into a fetal position and whimpering. Raphael stood between her and the door, and Adam circled her like a shark.

"I was hoping you'd be more talkative, Mary," Adam said, in a purring voice that held more menace than the fiercest growl. Even with the door closed, the music from downstairs was uncomfortably loud, but Adam's voice carried over the ambient noise.

"Let me try asking you this again," he said pleasantly. "How long have you been on the Mortal Plain?"

"All they've been able to get her to say so far is her name," Barbie said to me in a deliberately low voice. I think she was trying to hide a quaver, and it occurred to me that it wasn't a good thing that this scene wasn't bothering me like it was her. A few months ago, it would have.

There was no crumpled furniture, no dents in the wall, no broken glass, so I had to presume Mary hadn't put up a fight when Adam and Raphael had jumped her. She wouldn't have been able to take them, but I was surprised she hadn't even tried. Demons weren't usually wimps, even the ones who didn't like pain.

"How long?" Adam roared, and Mary curled more tightly around herself.

"T-two d-days," she stuttered, her voice hard to understand because she had her chin ducked to her chest and her arms over her head. The fact that she was blubbering didn't help, either.

"Very good," Adam said in his most condescending manner. "Now, it seems clear to me that you are in an unwilling host. I'd like to know how you got to the Mortal Plain, and why you're in this particular body. Just keep talking, and I won't hit you anymore."

She didn't uncurl, but she relaxed just a little. Giving in to the inevitable, I suppose. "My host performed a summoning," she said, sounding defensive.

"There's a difference between being willing to do something and actually *wanting* to do it. Tell me, Mary dear, did your host perform that summoning ceremony of her own free will?"

Mary didn't answer, and Adam punished her with a brutal kick that made me wince and Barbie gasp. I had to remind myself once more that this was a demon, not the fragile mortal she appeared to be. And that she had taken this host when the host was unwilling—stealing her life, violating her every boundary. Mary did not deserve my pity. No matter how pitiful she seemed.

"Do I need to repeat the question?" Adam asked. "Or would you prefer to answer me?"

"No, my host isn't really willing," Mary sobbed desperately. "They hurt her, then threatened to kill her if she didn't perform the summoning."

"*They?*" Adam prodded. "Who are 'they'?"

"She doesn't know. They were strangers, and they wore masks."

"I didn't ask whether your host knew them. I asked who they were."

"Please," Mary said with another sob. "I don't know. I didn't care enough to ask. I just wanted to get out."

"Get out of where?" Adam asked, his brow furrowed.

"Prison," she hiccuped.

"Shit," Adam said. Raphael's response was even more colorful.

I didn't know exactly what this meant to them, but I wasn't about to ask in front of Mary.

"How many prisoners have been sent through?" Raphael asked, and it was just as well Mary still had her chin tucked protectively down and couldn't see the look on his face or she might have died of fright.

"I don't know."

Adam growled, and Mary raised her head for the first time since I'd entered the room. I thought she'd looked pathetic before. She looked positively hideous right now—mascara-stained tears leaving tracks across her battered face, a line of blood snaking down her chin from a split lip, and a look of terror and hopelessness in her eyes.

"Please," she begged. "Please! I don't know. I'm no-body. I'd been imprisoned for centuries. They pardoned me and let me out early, but as soon as I was out, I was ordered to come to the Mortal Plain."

Adam was still circling her, and Mary followed him with her eyes until he was out of her line of sight. She didn't turn her head to watch him, instead closing her eyes and tensing, every muscle in her body quivering.

Was this what happened to demons who were imprisoned? Or had she been this pathetic beforehand? I had a nasty suspicion it was the former. I couldn't imagine this terrified bundle of nerves having the gumption to break a law.

"Again I ask you, who are *they*?" Adam said. "Name some names for me."

But Mary shook her head. "I don't know who they were. I only know they were elite, and they told me if I was still in the Demon Realm when they came looking for me next, they would destroy me."

Barbie frowned, interested in spite of herself. "I thought there was a decades-long waiting list to come to the Mortal Plain. How did you get here so fast?"

Mary cringed. "I jumped," she said in a whisper, tensing even more, like she expected to be hit.

I cocked my head to one side. "What does that mean?"

Adam's jaw tightened. "It means she cut into the line. We can all feel the call of a general summoning, but it's against the law to answer when it's not your turn." He glanced down at Mary, a knowing look on his face. "What were you imprisoned for?"

She hesitated, but answered before Adam had to bully her. "Jumping."

He nodded. "Right. So no one would be particularly shocked that you'd jump again as soon as you were out."

"I wouldn't have done it if they hadn't made me!" she protested. "I don't want to go back to prison."

Adam ignored the protest. "And what were you told to do once you reached the Mortal Plain? Because I don't believe for a moment that 'they' sent you here with no strings attached."

"No," she said with a wet snuffle. "There are strings."

"Go on," he prodded when she didn't continue.

"There's a demon. I don't know his name. I'm to check in with him once a week, and he may have orders for me."

"This just gets better and better," Raphael muttered under his breath, shaking his head.

Adam ignored him. "So when are you supposed to check in with him next?"

She flinched. "Please. I'll go back to prison if I betray him!"

Adam reached out and grabbed her by the throat. The poor creature was too mousy even to fight against *that*.

Great. Now I was thinking of a demon who'd taken an unwilling host as a "poor creature." Talk about your bleeding hearts!

"There are worse things than going back to prison, Mary," Adam said, his voice once more that menacing croon. "When do you meet with him next?"

"Thursday."

Adam kept his hold on her throat, but he didn't seem to be squeezing. The threat was enough to keep her compliant. "And where will you meet?"

She swallowed hard. "I don't know. He's supposed to call me at two and tell me where to meet him." Her eyes widened with renewed terror, like she was sure Adam wouldn't believe her and was going to hurt her again.

Adam processed that a moment. "All right. Here's the plan: I'm going to give you my card," he said, letting go of her throat and reaching into his back pocket for his wallet. "As soon as you hear from the mystery man, you're going to call me and tell me where you're meeting him."

"Please—"

"Don't even *think* about running, or not calling, or lying to me. I can get to you wherever you go, and believe me, you wouldn't like that."

Her shoulders slumped and her head bowed. She didn't say anything, just nodded, her body language a picture of defeat and misery. I felt another pang of pity.

I think even Adam was starting to feel sorry for her, because his voice, when next he spoke, was surprisingly gentle.

"The bathroom's right there," he said, pointing. "Why don't you go wash your face? Then you can get going."

I think if Mary'd had a choice, she'd have bolted from the room immediately, bloody, mascara-smeared face or no. But she interpreted Adam's offer as a command and slunk into the bathroom. If she'd been a dog, her tail would have been tucked firmly between her legs.

The four of us waited in silence as Mary washed her face in the bathroom sink. No one was making eye contact. Was it possible that even *Raphael* felt pity for our soon-to-be informant?

Mary looked a lot better when she emerged from the bathroom. Not only had she washed off the mascara and the blood from her cut lip, but she'd washed her face clean of makeup entirely. The lack of eyeshadow made her eyes look less sunken. And the cut had already sealed itself, though there was still an angry red line where it had been.

She watched us with wary eyes, her back against the wall, her shoulders hunched.

"You can go now," Adam told her, and we all moved away a little bit, giving her room to get out without having to pass too close to any of us. "I assume it goes without saying that we never had this conversation?"

She nodded, then slowly backed her way toward the door, eyes darting this way and that, showing too much white. When she reached the door, she yanked it open then threw herself through it, slamming it behind her. Even over the din of the music, we could hear the crowd on the balcony protesting as she shoved her way through in her rush to get away from us.

six

"WHY DO I FEEL LIKE I NEED A SHOWER AFTER THAT?" Barbie asked, crossing her arms over her chest and shivering.

No one answered her. I wished I hadn't pushed her into picking Mary. Yes, anyone we'd picked would probably have looked pretty puny, but it was hard to imagine a more beaten, miserable creature than Mary.

"So," I said into the awkward silence, "we assume Dougal and/or his cronies are behind this, right?"

"It's the logical assumption," Adam agreed. "And if he's sent one prisoner through, he's doubtless sent others."

"Cannon fodder," Raphael muttered.

"Huh?" I said.

"They're cannon fodder," he said more loudly. "I don't know what he plans to use them for, but the fact that he's sending prisoners through—perhaps ahead of others who've been on the waiting list for decades—suggests he's going to use them on missions that require demons he considers expendable. Maybe missions his real supporters aren't willing to undertake."

The only thing that can kill a demon is fire. The thought that popped into my mind at that moment almost made me sick to my stomach.

"Suicide bombers," I whispered.

Barbie gasped and covered her mouth. Adam sat heavily on the bed. And Raphael stood there looking grim.

"Do you really think..." Barbie started to ask, but her voice died before she got the question out.

We all turned our gazes to Raphael, who knew Dougal best.

"I don't know about suicide bombers," Raphael said. "He wouldn't need demons for that, considering how fanatical his human followers are. But I can't help thinking that maybe he doesn't want to be king of just the Demon Realm. Maybe he wants to rule the Mortal Plain as well. I wouldn't put it past him."

"So he's just going to ignore Lugh completely?" I asked, wondering if the covert war had just passed us by.

"I doubt it," Raphael said.

"It's a challenge," Adam said. "He *meant* for Lugh to find out about this. He thinks it will bring Lugh out of hiding."

"Maybe," Raphael said, but he didn't sound convinced. He looked at me. "Has Lugh got anything to say?"

I waited a beat to see if Lugh would answer, but he didn't. I shook my head. "He appears to have declared radio silence."

"Don't even *think* about doing anything stupid, Lugh," Raphael said. "Even if Dougal *is* tweaking you, there's nothing you can do about it."

Still no response from Lugh. I found that as unsettling as Raphael did, and I wished I could see into Lugh's mind like he could see into mine.

"Before anyone goes off half-cocked," Adam said, "let's find out what's really going on. Maybe Dougal's emptying the prisons because he wants to use them as cannon fodder to help him take over the Mortal Plain. Or maybe he's trying to flush Lugh out of hiding. Or maybe he's planning something we haven't even thought of."

The possibilities are not mutually exclusive, Lugh said, breaking his silence.

Yeah, I don't know if mentioning that is a good idea, unless we want to have Raphael and Adam sitting on us for the rest of my life to make sure you don't "do something stupid."

"So what do you, in your infinite wisdom, suggest we do?" Raphael asked Adam with one of his trademark sneers.

Adam can be a hothead at times, but he kept his cool, despite Raphael's attempt to provoke him. "We wait until Thursday and have a talk with Mary's handler. He'll be a step higher on the totem pole, and will know more."

"Do you really think she'll call you?" Barbie asked.

"She'll call." Adam's tone said there was no doubt in his mind, and I tended to believe him.

"So once again, we sit around and wait," Raphael grumbled.

"Do you have a better idea?" I countered. "Because I don't think jumping up and down and screaming 'The sky is falling' is all that useful unless there's something you plan to do about it."

Raphael shot me a glare that would have frozen molten lava, and I was glad I wasn't within his easy reach. He'd slugged me before, and he looked like he wanted to do it again. But he obviously didn't have a better idea, because he kept his mouth shut.

"All right then," I said. "Let's all go home and fill in our significant others before they worry themselves to death."

The only way we'd been able to keep Brian, Dominic, Saul, and Andy from coming to the club with us as "backup" was by promising a full report as soon as it was all over.

Raphael laughed. "Our significant others, eh? Does

that mean I should give Andrew a call when I get home? He's the closest thing I have to a significant other."

"You leave Andy alone!" I snapped. "I'll call him as soon as I've talked to Brian."

Raphael shrugged nonchalantly. "Whatever you want. Let's get out of here. I've had quite enough of this place for one night."

I couldn't have agreed more.

It was after two A.M. when I got home. I'd kind of hoped that Brian would be waiting there for me, preferably in my bed, but he wasn't. Trying to deny the hurt that stabbed through me, I changed into my PJs then sat cross-legged on my bed as I dialed Brian's number.

He answered on the first ring, which suggested he'd been waiting by the phone. Even if he was suddenly struggling to deal with my dual personality, he still worried about me, I guess. That couldn't be a bad sign.

I filled him in on what had happened at the club, though I left out some of our more alarming speculation. He'd probably come up with the same ideas on his own, but until we had solid facts, I didn't want to worry him any more than necessary.

If Brian had any theories of his own, he kept them to himself. I thought about trying to talk a little more about our Lugh issue, but like I said, it was after two. I was exhausted, and I was sure Brian was as well. The likelihood that we'd have a productive conversation was low.

After an awkward and uncomfortable good-bye, I called Andy.

"I just got off the phone with Raphael," he told me as soon as he picked up.

You know how in cartoons, steam blows out of characters' ears when they're pissed? That's how I felt at that moment.

"I told that asshole to leave you alone," I said through gritted teeth. If I'd thought Raphael was serious about calling Andy, I'd have done it myself first thing and let Brian wait.

"It's okay," Andy said. "He was relatively civil. No harm, no foul."

Maybe, but Raphael had harmed Andy so much already...

"Morgan? You still there?"

"Yeah," I said, releasing a deep breath and trying to relax. "I just don't want you around him any more than absolutely necessary."

"Believe me, I don't want that, either. But all he did was call and tell me what happened at the club. No big deal. Honest."

"Okay," I answered, unconvinced. It was hard not to look at everything Raphael did upside down and sideways, searching for a self-serving motive.

Andy and I never did too well with chitchat, so we hung up shortly after that. Tired as I was, I didn't feel like sleeping yet. I'd have said I was afraid of having nightmares, but Lugh had put a stop to all nightmares, even all regular dreams. I plopped down on the couch and turned on the TV. The chance of finding anything interesting to watch at this hour was approximately zero, but channel surfing at least gave me something to do.

I practically dropped the remote when I came upon a commercial I'd never seen before. It looked like one of those glorified army commercials—the kind that made it look like joining the army automatically transforms you into Macho Hero He-Man, who can leap tall buildings in a single bound. Only I knew immediately this wasn't an ad for any of the armed forces.

It was a montage of scenes, strung together with rousing orchestral music in the background.

A fireman leapt out of a blazing building, carrying a small child in his arms.

An EMT bent the twisted frame of a wrecked car just enough so his team could extricate an unconscious woman from the driver's seat.

A policeman chased an armed thug, catching up to him and tackling him even though he'd taken two shots to the chest.

Another uniformed man—National Guard, I thought— helped shore up a levee in a blinding rainstorm, carrying so many sandbags his feet should have sunk into the ground from the weight.

There was no narrative, no voice-over. But the commercial ended with the words "Make a difference" in stark white letters on a black background. Below that was an 800 number and a Web address.

I stared at the TV in horror. We'd speculated that the

Spirit Society might be persuaded to lower their standards for demon hosts, but we hadn't thought about a national recruitment campaign.

Make a difference. It was what ninety-nine percent of all demon hosts wanted to do, and I could easily see it as a siren call to people with self-esteem problems.

I tried to tell myself that they wouldn't drum up much business running the ad at two in the morning, but of course I knew they were likely running it in prime time as well. A century ago, belonging to the Spirit Society had been a federal offense, punishable by life in prison; now they were recruiting on national TV.

I clicked off the TV and dropped the remote on the coffee table. Then I convinced myself I had a headache and downed a couple Tylenol PM before climbing into bed and pulling the covers over my head.

I woke in the morning to the sound of the phone ringing. I'm always groggy in the morning when I take something to help me sleep, so instead of answering, I snuggled deeper into the covers. A minute passed, and then the phone rang again. I groaned and jammed a pillow over my head to drown out the noise. Whoever it was could leave a message, damn it!

When the phone started ringing a third time, I dragged myself into a sitting position and glared at it. The clock told me it was only seven-thirty, which meant I'd had about five hours of sleep. So it wasn't just the Tylenol PM making me groggy.

The phone in my bedroom doesn't have caller ID, so

I had no idea who to expect when I picked it up and growled, "If you're selling something or looking for a donation, or doing a survey, I'm going to hunt you down and kill you."

"And good morning to you, too," Adam said.

I groaned again and fell backward onto my bed, the phone still pressed to my ear. Adam calling at this time of the morning was not a good thing. And whatever not-good thing it was, I didn't know how I could face it before I had my coffee.

"What is it?" I asked, closing my eyes and thinking wistfully of sleep.

"Mary's dead."

His words banished most of my grogginess, and I sat bolt upright. "What? How? And *when*?" It wasn't that many hours ago that we'd been having our guilt-inducing interview with her.

"Not very long ago, and slowly."

I swallowed hard. "What happened?"

"She was beaten to death. I haven't been to the crime scene—officially, she was a human murdered by another human, so therefore it's not in my jurisdiction—but I talked to one of the officers on the scene. Sounds like whoever beat her broke practically every bone in her body."

I winced, trying not to picture Mary's miserable, frightened face. Whoever killed her must have had a heart of stone. Of course, since she was a demon, the beating had really killed Mary's human host, not Mary herself, who would have returned to the Demon Realm when her host died. "What are the chances it's a coincidence that she was murdered shortly after we talked to her?"

"Pretty damn low," Adam said with an unhappy sigh.

"Did she still have your card on her when she was found?"

"Yeah. That's why the officer called me. I told him I met her at the club and gave her my card in case she witnessed anything hinky there. It's not the first time I've done that, but she's not the type I'd usually approach. I'm still going to have a bunch of explaining to do. The cops don't know she was possessed, and it's best if it stays that way."

"Why? If the cops know she was an illegal, then the crime will fall under your jurisdiction. Surely that would be better for you."

I could almost hear Adam squirming. "You know there have been...questions about my conduct lately." Thanks to me, though he was kind enough not to say it. "I'm not sure how safe it is to call attention to myself by admitting I failed to follow standard procedure."

I shrugged, though he couldn't see it. "Whatever. I'll trust your judgment on that. But where does that leave us?" I hadn't felt like we'd gotten as much as I'd hoped out of last night's interrogation, but without Mary to lead us to her contact, we had *nothing*.

"Back at square one," Adam confirmed. "I think another council meeting is in order."

Great. One problem with this concept of having a

council is that they expect to be kept in the loop, and even to take part in decision-making.

"Guess I'll be spending the rest of the morning on the phone again," I grumbled.

"Better than how *I'm* going to spend the morning," Adam quipped back, and I had to agree, no matter what he decided to tell his comrades.

seven

BECAUSE ADAM WAS TIED UP WITH POLICE BUSINESS, our second council meeting in two days didn't convene until after four. As I waited for the council to arrive, I watched a Phillies game on TV, hoping to keep myself from thinking too much. It even worked, for the first couple of innings. Then I saw another Spirit Society recruitment commercial, and I lost all interest in the game. I turned off the set and wondered if I'd ever enjoy watching TV again.

The council members straggled in by ones and twos, just like the day before. And just like the day before, Raphael was the last to arrive and was about ten minutes late. But no one said anything to him about it, so at least we didn't immediately start the hostilities.

Adam filled us in on the details of Mary's murder. Not surprisingly, Mary's host, Helen Williams, had a long rap sheet, even though she'd been only twenty-two years old. Arrests for drugs and prostitution riddled her record, and, as is unfortunately often the case with people like Helen who live high-risk lifestyles, the police weren't going to spend lots of manpower and taxpayer money to hunt down her murderer. So far, there'd been no sign of any friends and family beating on their doors demanding justice. The prevailing theory was that she'd run afoul of a drug dealer and been "punished."

If Helen Williams had been a different sort of person—the kind the police saw as valuable members of society—the authorities might have pressed Adam harder about why she'd had his card. His explanation, after all, was a bit thin. But there was only so much time and effort they were willing to put into the case, and Adam was a high-profile, upstanding citizen, so he was getting something of a free pass. Damn convenient for us, but I couldn't help feeling a surge of disgust at the police department's lack of interest in the death of a young woman. I understood all the reasons why it wouldn't be a priority, but I didn't have to like it. It gave me another reason to really hope we caught up with whoever had forced Helen Williams to summon a demon she didn't want. A little vigilante justice might hit the spot.

How many more people like Helen Williams were out there right now? I shuddered to think.

"I guess we need to go on another hunting expedition," Raphael said. His compassion for the dead woman was underwhelming, but then I hadn't expected anything more from him.

"No," Barbie said. She sat rigidly on her straight-backed chair. "We just got that poor woman killed. I'm not doing that again."

"Fine," Raphael said with a nonchalant wave of his hand. "We'll use someone else as bait."

"No, you won't," Barbie retorted. Anger flushed her cheeks, but her voice remained level and reasonable. "The only reason to do it would be to try to get to the next rung in the ladder, which isn't going to happen if whoever we question gets murdered within hours of us talking to them."

It was a very reasonable-sounding argument, though I felt certain Barbie's refusal to take part was out of something other than cold logic. She'd felt guilty last night, when Mary had only been roughed up a bit. I bet she felt really horrible right now, knowing that Mary . . . no, that Mary's *host* had been killed.

I glanced over at Andy, the guilt king. He might not have been present for the interrogation, but he'd raised no objections during the council meeting where we'd concocted the plan. Sure enough, he was staring at his feet, his lips pressed together in a thin, unhappy line.

"I don't feel good about getting Helen Williams killed, either," I said, still looking at Andy, "but it's not like we could have guessed it would happen."

Raphael followed my gaze to Andy, then rolled his eyes dramatically. I clenched my teeth and ordered myself not to tell Raphael what I thought of him. Never mind that Andy and his hangdog act were getting on my nerves, too.

"We'll just have to pick a better mark this time,"

Raphael said, quickly losing interest in his former host. "Mary had only been on the Mortal Plain a couple of days. She hadn't had a chance to meet with her contact yet. If we can question someone who's been here at least a couple of weeks, he or she might be able to give us a name, or at least a description."

Barbie sat forward in her chair. "So it doesn't bother you at all that a woman was beaten to death because of us?"

Saul, sitting beside Barbie, laughed bitterly. "Do you have any idea how many people have died because of the things my sire has done? Expecting him to feel remorse is like expecting him to grow a halo and wings."

I tensed, thinking this conflict was about to escalate, but Raphael surprised me with the mildness of his answer.

"Whether I feel remorse or not doesn't matter," he said. "I know what you all think of me, and, frankly, I don't give a damn. I'm giving you my opinion of what I think we should do next, but it will ultimately be Lugh's decision." He looked at me. "The council is here for discussion and advice, but we all know who's in charge."

"Care to comment, Lugh?" I asked.

I'm afraid remorse is not a luxury we can afford, he answered. *We need more information, and these newly arrived demons are the key to getting it.*

I didn't like his answer—even though I knew he was probably right—so I didn't share it. "Does anyone have a better idea?" I asked, hoping I didn't sound like I was pleading.

"Lugh agrees with me," Raphael said, reading Lugh's

answer in my face. "But perhaps there's a way to make our course of action more palatable."

"I'd love to hear it," I muttered.

"When we've finished questioning our next subject, Morgan can perform an exorcism. Without the demon in residence, there would be no reason for our enemies to kill the host."

Adam looked dubious. "Even if the demon was keeping the host shut out, the host might know something damaging enough that they'd kill him anyway."

Raphael shook his head. "After we've already questioned him and wrung every possible drop of information out of him? What would be the point? It would be an unnecessary risk."

"Of course, if the demon's had a couple of weeks to do a hatchet job on the host's psyche," I said, "the host might not survive the exorcism."

"But you believe that exorcism is the lesser of two evils when an unwilling host is involved," he countered. "Even if by some miracle the demon and host get along famously, they're going to be under the thumb of someone who regards humans as nothing more than cattle, to be used and discarded as necessary."

"You mean like you?" Saul muttered, but Raphael ignored him.

"It's a good plan," Raphael said. "We get the information we need, and the host gets rid of an unwanted visitor. Surely even *you* can't object to that, son."

Usually, Raphael shows a remarkable amount of restraint around Saul, considering how heavily Saul goads him. But every once in a while, he got his subtle verbal jabs in, almost like he couldn't help himself. We all knew how Saul objected to any reminder that Raphael was his father. Hell, Saul wouldn't even use the word "father," but insisted on calling Raphael his "sire," if he had to refer to him at all.

Saul bared his teeth. "Don't call me that!"

Barbie reached over and put her hand on Saul's leg. "Down, boy," she said. "You know better than to let him get to you."

Sometimes, when Saul works up a head of steam, as it looked like he was doing now, it was really hard to rein him back in. Apparently, Barbie was having a good influence on him, though, because as soon as she spoke, he relaxed back into his chair and shook his head.

"You're right," he said, crossing his arms over his chest. "He's not worth it."

I had to bite my tongue to keep from laughing at the sulky, sullen look on Saul's face. Neither Saul nor his host was a kid, but he looked like your stereotypical rebellious teen.

Raphael was examining his fingernails with sudden fascination, his lowered head keeping his face in shadows. Sorry to say, I knew him too well to be fooled by his apparent apathy. It hurt him every time Saul denied him.

So why the hell does he keep poking his pins in Saul, when he knows very well how Saul will react? I asked Lugh silently.

Because when Saul strikes back, Raphael can think "Oh, poor me" and throw himself a pity party, Lugh responded. *Sometimes, I think he's really changed. Then he pulls something like this, and I realize he's still the same old Raphael.*

I wasn't sure I agreed with Lugh on this point. Yeah, Raphael was a pro at feeling sorry for himself, but it seemed to me he had ... matured since I'd first met him. Specifically, I remembered a time when Lugh had taken over my body to confront Raphael. I'd thought he just meant to have a conversation, but it had quickly turned into a fight. But although Lugh and Raphael were about evenly matched in power, Raphael had refused to fight back, willing to let Lugh send him back to the Demon Realm and Dougal's tender mercies rather than risk a fight that could get Lugh killed.

Do you really think the old Raphael would have made the same decision? I asked Lugh, trying not to think about how ironic it was for me to be defending Raphael, whom I loathed.

Perhaps not, Lugh conceded, then fell silent.

"Another trip to The Seven Deadlies, then," Adam said, bringing us back on topic.

Barbie let out an unhappy sigh. "I guess so."

"You don't have to be the bait," I told her. "I'm sure someone else can do it." Not that anyone seemed in any rush to volunteer.

"No, it should be me," she said. "This is the kind of stuff I do for a living." She frowned. "Well, not really, but..." She huffed. "You know what I mean."

And I did. Barbie had once described the biggest part of her job as "convincing people to tell me things they're not supposed to tell me," with an obvious corollary of "convincing people to do things they're not supposed to do." She was the right person for the job, even though she didn't like it.

"I guess that means we're all settled," Adam said. "The club isn't open on Sundays, so let's head out there tomorrow night."

"Whatever you say, coach," I said, feeling tired now that we were winding down and I could let myself relax a bit. I don't function well on less-than-optimal sleep.

There was a little more chitchat after that, but nothing of great importance, and no one came to blows over anything. As the council members trickled out my front door, I noticed that Brian was hanging back. I couldn't decide whether that was a good thing or a bad thing. On the one hand, he and I really needed to talk. On the other hand, this wasn't the kind of talk we should have while I was tired and grumpy.

When Brian and I were finally alone in the apartment, he turned to me. I held up a hand to forestall whatever he'd been about to say.

"Can it wait until I've made a fresh pot of coffee?"

Dominic had brought me some fabulous, extra-strong Italian roast that I was dying to try. He'd probably meant me to make it for the meeting, but I wasn't about to share my treasure with seven other people.

Brian gave me one of his boyish grins. "It can wait. I know better than to get between you and your coffee."

"Smart-ass," I replied, but I meant it affectionately.

Brian followed me into the kitchen and watched in silence as I scooped out fragrant coffee and filled the pot with water. I set the pot to brew, then turned and leaned my butt against the counter, examining the man I loved, trying to get a feel for what he was thinking. But, unlike me, Brian was a pro at hiding his thoughts.

"Okay," I said as the coffeepot began to gurgle. "What's up?"

His eyebrows arched. "I need an excuse to want to talk to my girlfriend?"

"Of course not," I answered irritably. "But considering how we left things, I don't think you're here to make small talk."

Brian reached into the cabinet beside my head and got out a coffee mug. Without another word, he pulled the carafe from the coffee maker. A couple drops of coffee hissed against the hot plate, but I'd never abide a coffee maker that made you wait until the pot was done before you could get a cup, so there wasn't much of a mess. There was only enough coffee in the pot for about a third of a cup, but Brian poured it into a mug and handed the mug to me before putting the carafe back.

"For medicinal purposes," he said.

I rolled my eyes at him, but that didn't stop me from taking a cautious sip from my mug. I managed to burn my tongue despite my caution, but it was worth it for the rich, dark flavor. It was a shame to dilute that with cream and sugar, but I only drink coffee black if I have no choice. I closed my eyes and inhaled the scent, letting the comfortable familiarity of the coffee ritual calm me.

When I opened my eyes, I saw that Brian had gotten the half-and-half out of the fridge and put the sugar bowl in front of me. Ah, the joys of being predictable. But it was nice to be able to doctor my coffee so I could pretend not to notice how intently Brian was watching me.

"I had an idea during today's meeting," he said. "I want to run it by you, but I don't want you to answer right away. Just promise me you'll think about it."

Uh-oh. I didn't like the sound of this. I tore my attention away from the coffee and glanced at him cautiously. "Is this one of those ideas that requires me to put down breakable objects before you present it?" I asked, holding up the coffee mug for display.

A smile tugged at the corners of his mouth. "I'm not sure. Why don't you put it down just in case?"

I made a face at him, but put the coffee mug down. I had no clue what he was about to say, and that made me nervous.

"Okay," I said, bracing myself. "Lay it on me."

"Again, remember that I don't want you to answer me now. I just want you to keep it in the back of your mind."

I nodded and made a "keep talking" gesture.

"It occurred to me that we're probably past the point where it's necessary to keep Lugh hidden behind your human aura."

Because of my unique relationship with Lugh, no one examining my aura could tell I was possessed, as long as I was the one driving my body. When Lugh took control, I *did* show up on the radar as possessed, but that happened so rarely it hadn't been an issue. This had made my body the perfect hiding place for Lugh when Raphael first tricked me into calling him to the Mortal Plain.

It wasn't hard to see where Brian was going with this, and I immediately bristled. "You want me to pass

Lugh off to some other host?" I had so many objections to this idea I couldn't even figure out which one to lob out first.

Brian held up his hands. "Let me finish before you bite my head off."

I narrowed my eyes at him, my chest feeling tight and achy. I didn't have to hear him out to see the danger signs. Brian had thought about what life would be like continuing to date me with his new understanding of just how *present* Lugh really was, and he wasn't able to accept it.

I was so stunned and upset by the implications that I couldn't think of anything to say. Brian took that as a sign it was safe for him to keep talking.

"When you were first hosting Lugh, it was pretty much just the two of you against the world, and secrecy was your best weapon. But now...Now Lugh has the council and powerful demon allies. Plus, Dougal doesn't seem to be actively hunting him."

"And just who would you 'volunteer' to be Lugh's new host?" I asked through clenched teeth. "Not that I'm conceding your point, you understand. And if you say Andy, I'm going to..." I couldn't think of a creative enough threat. "Let's just say it won't be pretty."

Brian gave me an affronted look. "I'm not a complete moron. I'd never suggest you should give him to Andy, even if I thought Andy was willing to host him."

"Then who?"

"If all goes as planned, tomorrow night, you'll be kicking a demon out of an unwilling host. Who might not be in good shape when the demon's gone. And who we've already determined is unlikely to have friends and family who would be distressed—or even notice—if he or she disappears."

My jaw dropped, and I stared at Brian in utter shock. "You want me to transfer Lugh to an unwilling host who, I'll remind you, might recover even if he's catatonic after the exorcism?" I tried to keep my voice down, without success.

Never in my wildest dreams would I have guessed he'd propose something so patently immoral. In the past, I'd always seen him as a model citizen, law-abiding and ethical almost to a fault. True, I'd found out that I'd put him on a bit of a pedestal, but still…

Brian wouldn't meet my eyes. "You could always have Lugh transfer temporarily, and Lugh could tell you whether he thought there was any chance of recovery. Besides, for all we know, the host will be brain-dead, not just catatonic."

It was true that in about one percent of all cases, a host would be brain-dead after an exorcism, unable to function on even the basest level—like, say, breathing—without the demon in residence. I shook my head violently.

"So you'll be *hoping* the poor schmuck we exorcize tomorrow turns up brain-dead?" I wasn't making any attempt to keep my voice down anymore. I was so pissed I wished I hadn't put the coffee mug down. Brian had subtly nudged it out of my reach, and if I wanted to grab it and pitch it at the wall, I'd have to go through him to do it. Actually, that wasn't sounding like such a bad idea.

"I can't believe what I'm hearing," I said with a shake of my head. "You're supposed to be one of the good guys! The good guys don't condone possessing unwilling hosts just because it's convenient."

The look on his face hardened. "Oh, so it was okay to let Raphael take Tommy to save your brother the trouble of hosting him, but it's *not* okay for you to give Lugh to a host who's already damaged beyond repair?"

I couldn't help flinching. It was a low blow, but I probably deserved it. I was being a hypocrite. Yet even knowing that, I was still fighting to rein in my temper. "What's happened to you, Brian? I never thought I'd hear you argue that two wrongs make a right."

Now *he* was getting pretty angry, too. "Oh, I don't know. Maybe it has to do with being kidnapped and tortured." I flinched again. "Or helping Lugh commit murder. Or letting the council talk a mentally challenged host into summoning a demon. You can't expect me to do all this crap and not be changed by it."

I refrained from pointing out that this was one of the reasons I'd tried to break up with him when Lugh first came into my life. I didn't want to drag him into the mud with me. But it seemed to have happened anyway.

Brian visibly calmed himself, and when next he spoke, his voice was a lot softer. "Just think about it, okay?"

"I don't need to think about it. The answer is no, and the answer will stay no. I'm not palming Lugh off on some random stranger, even if the host is brain-dead after the exorcism. And if I *did* decide to do such a thing, it wouldn't be because you can't bear to be with me because I'm possessed."

Brian rolled his eyes. "I never said—"

"You don't have to say it. I'm getting the message loud and clear. And I think it's time for you to go."

"Morgan—"

I pushed past him and headed for the front door. He hurried after me and grabbed my arm. It didn't improve my disposition.

"Let go," I said, and though I wasn't shouting anymore, there was no doubt he heard the simmering fury in my voice. "We're done with this subject, and if you don't get out of here, I'm going to let Lugh take control so he can bodily remove you."

Brian let go of my arm and shook his head. "Fine, I'll go. I'm sorry I offended your delicate sensibilities."

I jerked open the front door and pointed to the hallway. "Out!"

His shoulders slumped in defeat. "Gee, *that* went well," he muttered under his breath as he stepped out into the hallway.

I slammed the door after him.

eight

I T DIDN'T OCCUR TO ME UNTIL ABOUT A HALF HOUR after Brian left, while I was still fuming, that Lugh hadn't uttered a peep during my little talk with Brian. True, Lugh didn't always intervene in our arguments, but it seemed to me that that particular discussion was one he had a stake in. It wasn't like him not to let his opinion be known.

I waited a couple beats after this surprising realization, expecting Lugh to chime in to answer my thoughts, but he didn't.

"What's with the silent treatment?" I asked him.

To my surprise, he didn't answer.

"Lugh?" I prodded. "Hello?"

Still nothing.

When I'd first begun hosting Lugh, he'd only been able to communicate with me through dreams. Then he'd progressed to being able to talk to me when I was under a lot of stress and my mental barriers were weakened. Eventually, it had gotten to the point where my mental barriers were down altogether, and he talked to me whenever he felt like it. I'd gotten so used to it that this sudden silence was strangely unsettling.

Had my barriers inexplicably gone back up? Did Lugh not feel like talking? Or was there something wrong? Alarm stabbed through me. I couldn't imagine what could be wrong, but since everything about our relationship was outside the norm for demons and their hosts, who knew *what* could happen.

"Come on, Lugh. You're freaking me out here."

No answer. It had to be my mental barriers, I decided. Somehow, my fight with Brian had raised them again. My subconscious is so powerful it's scary, and I'd never had much luck pushing it around.

I cursed my subconscious now. I wanted to talk to Lugh, find out what he thought of Brian's proposal. Did he think I was trying to sabotage my relationship with Brian—yet again—by being so completely obstinate about this? I didn't think that myself, but then I've never been the best judge. Loving Brian as much as I did was arguably scarier for me than being the demon king's human host. And there were times I'd been scared enough by the intensity of my love for him to do really stupid things.

But the truth was, I wasn't sure Brian and I would have lasted as long as we had if it hadn't been for Lugh's help. I'd shot myself in the foot about twenty times since Lugh had moved in, and I'm not sure I'd ever have noticed myself doing it if I didn't have my own internal psychoanalyst.

I had a long and strange evening. It's not like Lugh and I are in constant conversation with one another. We could easily go a couple of days without a word passing between us, and it never bothered me. But now, I hadn't heard from him in a handful of hours, and I was ready to tear my hair out.

By bedtime, I felt like a junkie who hadn't had her fix. As illogical as it was, I could hardly wait to fall asleep and talk to Lugh. Maybe he would understand why my subconscious walls had suddenly gone up again. And, of course, I could ask him if he thought I was being a stubborn, self-destructive bitch for reacting so violently to Brian's suggestion.

I wanted to fall asleep so badly that it was actually pretty hard to sleep. But eventually, I drifted off.

When I woke up at eight in the morning, having slept dreamlessly through the night, I was on the verge of tears. Lugh had been able to talk to me through dreams almost since the very beginning, and yet last night he hadn't talked to me. What the hell did it mean? I was having trouble believing my subconscious barriers had gotten so strong he couldn't even talk to me in my dreams. I pressed a hand to my chest.

"Lugh, where are you?" I asked the empty room. There was, of course, no answer.

I spent the day trying not to worry about what was going on with Lugh. Of course, you know how successful it is to order yourself not to worry.

And anticipation of another trip to The Seven Deadlies didn't make the day any better. But it turned out I needn't have worried about our planned visit.

At a little after five, the front desk called and let me know Adam was there. I wasn't expecting him, so right away I suspected that something bad had happened. I told them to send him up and spent the time it took him to get to my door worrying about what was going on. It sure would be nice if these demons would call me every once in a while instead of just showing up. But I guess talking on the phone is less than discreet.

The look on Adam's face when I opened the door confirmed my suspicion that bad news was coming my way yet again. He looked as grim as I'd ever seen him, and I had the cowardly urge to shove him out the door and cover my ears so I didn't have to know what had put that look on his face. Of course, we'd already established that shutting the door against a demon wasn't going to do a lick of good.

"How bad is it?" I asked as I led the way into the kitchen for the ritual pot of coffee.

"Pretty damn bad," Adam said as I started shoveling the last of Dom's Italian roast into the filter basket. "Shae's dead."

I dropped the coffee scoop, scattering grounds all over the counter and the floor. "What?" I asked, hardly believing what I thought I'd just heard him say.

"Neighbors heard a commotion this morning before dawn, Shae and some guy yelling at each other. It sounded like it started getting violent, so they called the police. By the time the police got there, smoke was pouring out the windows."

"Holy shit!" He didn't just mean Shae's *host* was dead—he meant Shae, the demon, was dead.

"The fire was relatively easy to contain, so at least there were no other casualties," Adam continued, his voice flat. "It was set in Shae's bedroom, and the killer made a tidy little bonfire there, complete with some kind of accelerant. It doesn't take a lot of expertise to tell that her body was ground zero."

I swallowed hard. There was something primally terrifying about the idea of burning to death, and as much as I'd disliked Shae, I wouldn't have wished it on her. "Are you sure it's her?"

"The body's burned beyond recognition and we'll have to wait for dental records to be legally sure. But *I'm* sure it's her."

I started sweeping grounds off the counter and into the sink, but I think I was spilling as much onto the floor as I was getting in the sink. I kept doing it anyway, because as long as my hands were moving it was harder to see how much they were shaking.

"Do you think it's because she gave me that information?" I asked, and my voice sounded thin and tight to my own ears.

"I don't believe in coincidence."

Yeah, neither did I.

I frowned as a confusing thought occurred to me. "The bad guys, whoever they are, beat Mary to death, but they didn't burn her, didn't kill the demon. Why did they burn Shae?"

"I don't know for sure, but I have a guess. You remember what Mary was like—about as weak and miserable a creature as there is. Shae was anything but weak. Maybe they thought they needed a more permanent solution than killing her host. I doubt she's the kind of person anyone would want as an enemy."

I could see his point. I dusted the coffee grounds off the palms of my hands, then glowered at the floor. I wondered if my vacuum cleaner would work on the linoleum. I didn't feel like doing the broom-and-dustpan thing.

"You're not actually feeling guilty about Shae, are you?" Adam asked.

I winced. "Of course not. Why should I feel guilty that I've gotten one woman beaten to death and another burned alive?"

I bent to open the cabinet under the sink. At least if I did the broom-and-dustpan thing, I could keep my hands occupied. I was pretty sure I had a whisk broom under here somewhere.

Adam bent over me and closed the cabinet door. I barely got my hands out in time. I was very aware of his body as he loomed there behind me.

"I wouldn't have wished that on anyone," he said. "But the truth is, Shae was bound to get into trouble eventually, considering who she consorted with."

I remained where I was, squatting on the floor with my forehead leaning against the cabinet doors. "So that makes it okay that someone burned her alive? She led a high-risk lifestyle, so she was bound to be tortured to death?" My voice was rising, but it wasn't just from anger. "That's like saying Helen What's-her-name was bound to be tortured into summoning Mary because she turned tricks and did drugs." I'm not given to fits of hysterics, but one might have hit the spot right then.

Adam grabbed my arm and hauled me to my feet.

"Go sit down for a bit," he ordered, giving me a little shove toward the living room. "I'll handle the cleanup, and I'll brew some coffee."

I could have argued with him, but I just didn't see the point. I trudged into the living room and sat on the couch, pulling my feet up and wrapping my arms around my legs. I ordered myself not to cry over Shae's death, no matter how horrifying it was, and no matter how responsible I felt.

Eventually, Adam brought a couple mugs of coffee into the living room. Since the good stuff was now down the drain or scattered on the kitchen floor, we were reduced to plain old Colombian, but at least it was fresh, and the mug was a soothing warmth in my hands.

"I don't know what's going to happen with The Seven Deadlies now that Shae's gone," Adam said as he sat beside me on the couch. "What I *do* know is that it won't be open tonight, or likely anytime in the near future."

I grimaced and inhaled the fragrant steam from my coffee. I wasn't heartbroken that I couldn't go to The Seven Deadlies tonight, but… "If we can't troll for illegal newbies in the club, that puts us back at square one. Again."

The corners of Adam's mouth tightened. "That about sums it up. I don't know about you, but I have a bad feeling about all this. Like we don't have all the time in the world to figure out what's going on before it's too late."

I had to agree with him. But without the club and without Shae, I didn't know how we could get our hands on one of these new illegals.

Then I thought of the new Spirit Society ad campaign, and was struck by an idea. "Did you know the Spirit Society's been running recruitment ads on TV?" I asked.

Adam nodded, his lip curled with distaste. "Yeah, and it's not just on TV. They've got recruitment posters all over the buses and subway stations."

My idea of public transportation is a taxi, so I hadn't been aware of the posters. But I imagined there were plenty of citizens of our fair city who were less than pleased to see these Satanist (in their worldview) advertisements leering at them wherever they went. I hoped they outnumbered the impressionable young people who saw those posters and thought, "Hey, I could be a hero!"

"What do you think the chances are that the Spirit Society is behind the illegal recruitment campaign as well as the legal one?" I asked.

Adam cocked his head to one side as he thought about it. "It's possible, I suppose," he said, though he sounded mildly skeptical.

"They had no moral qualms about helping Dougal and Raphael with their sick experiments," I pointed out. Although the Spirit Society supposedly worshipped all demons, there was no doubt that their leadership favored Dougal. Hard to believe they would sell out the entire human race to appease the "Higher Powers," but all the evidence suggested that was exactly what they were doing.

"Do you really think they wouldn't be happy to help Dougal and his allies take over humans that even the police sometimes think of as expendable?" I asked.

Adam scrubbed the top of his head—a gesture of frustration. "Damn it! Of course they'd be happy to help. I keep wanting to think the Spirit Society at least gives lip service to the law, but I know you're right. Maybe the rank-and-file members know nothing about this, but the upper echelon almost certainly does."

I nodded. "Well, then, at least we have a lead we can follow up on."

Adam raised an eyebrow. "Cooper again?"

Bradley Cooper was a regional director of the Spirit Society. Adam and I had questioned him once before about his involvement in Dougal and Raphael's experiments. Cooper had been less than cooperative, and Adam had ended up taking temporary possession of his body so he could rummage through his mind.

I nodded. "Might as well go straight to the top."

Adam grinned. "What do you think the chances are he'd open his door if you and I paid him a visit?"

I suppressed a shudder. I loathed Cooper, both because of what he stood for and because he was such a nasty little weasel of a man. But Adam's amusement at Cooper's expense still made me uneasy. It was true that possessing Cooper had been more...humane than some of the other ways we might have gotten information out of him, but I would never be comfortable with allowing anyone to be possessed against their will, even temporarily.

"Slim and none," I answered, fighting down my unease. "Which is why *we* won't be the people he sees on his doorstep."

nine

BARBIE IS ABOUT AS HARMLESS-LOOKING A PERSON AS I can imagine, which made her the perfect candidate to charm Cooper into opening his door when he shouldn't. We kept our raiding party small—just me, Adam, and Barbie—for the sake of simplicity.

Cooper was divorced and lived in the suburbs in a house that was meant to hold a family, not a single man. A *rich* family. Possibly with live-in help.

The lights were on inside when we drove up, and there were no other cars in the driveway. It looked like we would have Cooper all to ourselves, which was just the way we wanted it.

We parked by the curb across the street, not wanting to attract Cooper's attention by pulling into his driveway. If he caught a glimpse of me or of Adam, there was no way in hell he'd open the door without a scene, so we were going for maximum stealth. Instead of walking up the well-lit path to his door, we picked our way across the lawn in the shadow of the decorative privacy hedge that blocked the view from the neighbor's house. Then we ducked down under the window and crept up to the front porch.

Adam and I plastered ourselves against the wall beside the door. Cooper wouldn't be able to see us without sticking his head outside, and if he did that, we'd be inside before he knew it. Barbie raised an eyebrow at us, and we both nodded to indicate we were ready. Then she rang the bell.

Footsteps echoed in the foyer. Barbie stood up a little straighter and licked her lips, adding a faint wet sheen.

The footsteps stopped by the door. Cooper was probably checking out the view from the peephole. Like I said, it was hard to imagine anyone more harmless-looking than Barbie—though, of course, she wasn't as harmless as she looked. I expected Cooper to open the door right away. What middle-aged, heterosexual male *wouldn't* open the door when a twenty-something blond bombshell was standing there?

Apparently, Bradley Cooper.

"Who is it?" he asked through the closed door.

Barbie batted her eyelashes. It probably looked pretty sexy, but I knew it was a sign of surprise rather than a come-on. "My name is Barbara Paget," she said. There was no point in using an alias, since Cooper would recognize Adam and me anyway. "My car broke down, and I was wondering if I could use your phone. I'll only be a minute." She smiled up at the peephole hopefully.

Cooper hesitated a moment longer, but apparently even *he* wasn't immune to Barbie's charms. I heard his faint sigh, then the rattle of chains and locks being undone. Barbie stepped back a bit, and the moment the door started to open, Adam jumped in front of her and gave the door a hard shove.

Cooper, having been knocked back on his ass by Adam's shove, cried out in surprise as Barbie and I slipped in through the door that Adam held open.

"Get out of here!" Cooper commanded, but it was hard to sound too commanding when you were sprawled on the floor. Especially when your looks were a perfect match to your weaselly personality, complete with the buckteeth and beady eyes.

Cooper scrambled to his feet, glaring at the three of us. "Get out or I'll call the police!"

Adam laughed. "Are you forgetting that I *am* the police?"

Cooper sneered at him. "It doesn't mean you're above the law. Or do you have a warrant you'd like to show me?"

Adam took a step closer, smiling. It wasn't a nice smile, and a sheen of sweat broke out on Cooper's forehead. He took a corresponding step backward and held out his hands.

"Stay away from me!" Cooper shrieked.

Adam stopped his advance. "No need to get your panties in a twist," he said, still smiling. "We just want to have a little chat with you is all."

"I remember our last 'little chat,' " Cooper said, taking another step backward. "I think I'll pass."

I frowned. Cooper's eyes were darting about nervously, and he was backing away from Adam like he was a dangerous predator, but his words didn't match his actions. Ordinarily, Cooper wouldn't know dry sarcasm if it bit him in the ass.

"Don't take another step, Brad," I warned, wondering if he was trying to get within reach of a weapon. Maybe our last visit had made him a little more cautious. "And keep your hands where we can see them."

Cooper stopped retreating and put his hands out to his sides, fingers splayed. It was just what I'd expect Cooper to do, but something about him was...bothering me. Still keeping my eye on Cooper, I opened my purse and started rummaging for my Taser. I pretty much never went anywhere without my Taser anymore, but since I hadn't expected to use it tonight, it was buried somewhere in the depths of the black hole.

"I'd like to ask you a few questions about the Spirit Society's new recruitment campaign," Adam said.

Cooper blinked like he was surprised. "What kind of questions? There's nothing terribly mysterious about it. You can go to our website for the details."

"Not *that* recruitment campaign," Adam said. "The *other* one."

Cooper shook his head. "I have no idea what you're talking about. There's only one campaign, and the information is all very public. I think you should leave now."

Adam clucked his tongue. "Are we really going to have to have a repeat performance of my last visit? I was pretty gentle with you last time because I knew you had every reason to be afraid of Raphael, but I'm not feeling as charitable tonight."

Cooper blanched and swallowed hard. "I can't stop you from having a 'repeat performance,' as you call it, but it won't get you anywhere."

My questing fingers finally found my Taser as my paranoia spiked again. Cooper looked appropriately terrified, but his words...They were too calm, too measured. Something was wrong, I felt sure of it. Maybe Cooper wasn't alone in the house after all. Threatening him or illegally possessing him in front of witnesses would be really bad.

Adam didn't seem to feel the same qualms. He surged forward, slamming into Cooper and tackling him to the floor. I armed the Taser by feel as Adam grabbed both of Cooper's wrists and pinned them above his head.

That should have been all it took for Adam to slip out of his host's body and into Cooper's. The transfer via skin-to-skin contact takes about a millisecond to complete.

Adam's eyes widened at the same time I realized Cooper might be alone in his house, but not in his body.

"Shit!" Adam said.

Cooper smiled and drew his legs up, sharply, catching Adam in the gut with both knees. Adam grunted in pain and lost his grip on Cooper's wrists. Cooper then tossed him halfway across the room as if he weighed no more than a child.

I tried to fire my Taser, but nothing happened. Damn it! I'd let the charge run down. Cooper grinned at me, then advanced on Adam, who was still looking woozy.

Barbie leapt between Cooper and Adam. I hadn't known until this moment that she was carrying a gun. Unfortunately, guns aren't the best weapons to use against demons. If your first shot isn't lethal, you might not get in a second.

Barbie didn't even manage to get in that first shot. Cooper's demon-enhanced reflexes allowed him to knock the gun out of her hand before she squeezed the trigger. She yelped and collapsed to the floor, clutching the hand that had been holding the gun. When demons hit, they tend to break things.

"Get out of the way!" I screamed at Barbie. There was nothing she could do to help Adam—all she'd do was get herself killed. Not being the airhead some people assumed she was because of her looks, she scrambled out from between the two demons. At least she'd distracted Cooper enough to give Adam a little recovery time.

"Surprise," Cooper gloated as he grinned at Adam.

In retrospect, it should have occurred to us that if the Spirit Society was recruiting as heavily as it seemed they were, Cooper would finally get his wish and become a host himself.

"Geez, you must have been *really* desperate to come to the Mortal Plain if you were willing to take a host who looks like *that*," I said with an exaggerated curl of my lip. It was true, though, that Cooper was about as unattractive a specimen of manhood as existed.

The demon snarled at me. Somehow, he managed to make that rodentlike face look threatening.

"You two get out of here," Adam said to me and Barbie as he advanced on Cooper.

Adam *should* have had an advantage on Cooper, since his host outweighed Cooper by maybe seventy pounds. And though I didn't like the idea of leaving him to fight Cooper on his own, with my Taser not working, I wasn't much more use than Barbie.

"Oh, I don't think so," Cooper said, and instead of engaging with Adam, he launched himself at Barbie and me.

Lugh surfaced without warning or conscious thought on my part. One moment, I was just a puny human trying to brace against an attack that would probably break me in half; the next, my body was no longer my own.

Despite the imminent danger, I couldn't help one exasperated burst of thought: *Where have you been?*

Later, was his only answer. He pivoted to avoid Cooper's charge, moving just barely slow enough to be within the realm of human possibility. He then "accidentally" lost his footing and plowed into Barbie. She screamed in pain when her wounded hand hit the floor, but at least Lugh was now between her and Cooper.

Cooper skidded to a stop, and I was reminded of a bull circling round for another try after charging the matador's cape. Barbie, whimpering in pain, was trying to wriggle out from under us, but Lugh kept her firmly pinned. If Cooper came for us again, Lugh was going to have to use his supernatural strength and quickness to protect us, and that would make this whole encounter a hell of a lot more complicated.

But Adam hadn't just been standing there twiddling his thumbs while Cooper attacked. He was required to carry his sidearm at all times, and now that he and Cooper weren't grappling, he'd had a chance to draw his gun.

"Don't even think about it!" he shouted at Cooper, drawing his attention.

Guns might not be the weapons of choice against demons, but Adam had the reflexes to get a shot off in time, unlike Barbie. And he was close enough that he could make that one shot count.

Cooper froze, staring at the gun that pointed unwaveringly at his head.

Lugh decided his services were no longer needed and receded into the background. Predictably, the change of control made my stomach lurch and made my head ache like a son of a bitch. I rolled off Barbie, then regretted the motion as my stomach protested. I swallowed hard and managed not to puke. Score one for me!

Cooper stood with his hands open at his sides, looking awfully relaxed for a man who had a gun pointed at his head. Of course, the gun could only kill Bradley Cooper, not the demon, so I supposed the demon had no reason to sweat. Then he smiled, and a shiver trailed down my spine.

"I do wonder what you plan to do now, Director White," the demon said to Adam. "You've forced your way into my house without a warrant, and now you're threatening me at gunpoint. I'll have you know Mr.

Cooper is a legal, registered host, and your attack is completely unprovoked."

Adam grunted a laugh. "Tell that to Barbara," he said, indicating Barbie with a point of his chin. She was sitting with her back against the wall, clutching her wounded arm to her body, her face white with pain.

Cooper raised an eyebrow. "You mean the young woman who tried to shoot me? Strangely, I interpreted that as a provocation."

"The law says you can't hurt a human even in self-defense," Adam said, but he sounded less certain.

It was true that the laws in Pennsylvania were draconian where demons were concerned. Self-defense was generally not an acceptable excuse if a human was badly injured. But even if Barbie's hand was broken, it wasn't really that bad an injury considering she'd been meaning to shoot. Even a Pennsylvania judge might let Cooper slide on that.

"Of course you can always shoot me," Cooper continued. "I'm sure you'd have no trouble explaining to your comrades why you shot an unarmed man."

I probably should have kept my mouth shut, but that wasn't my style. "You're a demon. You don't need a weapon to be dangerous. And he's got two witnesses who can testify that you attacked us."

"And you'll have no trouble whatsoever explaining to the police why you all decided to pay me a visit and ended up shooting me," Cooper countered with a smug smile. "If that's the case, then go ahead and shoot, Director White. Don't worry—I won't hold it against you and come back for revenge against your little friends after the state has brought you to justice." He frowned theatrically. "Though on second thought, that might be fun."

Whose great idea had it been to come and question Cooper? Oh, right, it was mine. Shit.

"Grab me a pillow off the couch in there," Adam ordered me, jerking his head toward the living room.

"Planning to take a nap?" I asked under my breath, but I did as he asked. If I'd been Sherlock Holmes, I would have noticed as soon as we'd gotten here that the living room was way too neat—Cooper had the aesthetic sense of a typical single guy, and the last time I'd been here, the place had been a mess. Now it was spotless. Of course, even if I'd noticed, I'd have assumed he'd hired a maid, not been possessed by a demon.

I brought the pillow to Adam. I'd seen enough TV to guess he was going to use the pillow to muffle the sound of the shot. Did that mean he was planning to shoot? And if he didn't, what was our next move?

Shoot, or don't shoot? I didn't like either option. We'd have to revisit the question eventually, but I was always big on putting off till tomorrow what I didn't want to do today.

"Don't kill him unless you have to," I said to Adam. "We still have plenty of questions for him, don't we?"

Adam managed a feral grin as he buried the hand holding the gun in the pillow. His grin didn't have quite the edge it usually had, but I think only someone who knew him real well would have noticed. Cooper's argument had Adam spooked. Not a comforting thought.

Cooper crossed his arms over his chest. "I'd be curious to see how you're planning to convince me to answer your questions."

The look Adam gave me out of the corner of his eye said he was a bit curious himself.

"Where are the car keys?" I asked, and I could see by the look in his eye that Adam immediately understood. We'd driven out here in his unmarked, and I happened to know he kept a Taser in his trunk. He wasn't required to carry the Taser all the time, but he needed to have one readily available, seeing as he often found himself chasing down demons. I couldn't tell from the look on Cooper's face whether he got it, too.

"Right front pocket," Adam said.

I cursed under my breath. I really didn't want to be reaching into his pocket, especially not when he wore his jeans so damn tight. But he needed both hands—one for the gun, one for the pillow—and it didn't much matter what I wanted.

"Can you hang in there a while longer?" I asked Barbie. I was probably stalling, but I couldn't help it.

She nodded. "I'll be fine. The leg hurt much worse." She managed a pained smile. The last time we'd faced down a demon together, said demon had kicked her legs out from under her and broken one of them. Human against demon is never a fair fight.

With a little grimace, I approached Adam to get the keys. I was pretty sure the expression on his face could be called a smirk, but since he didn't take his eyes off Cooper for an instant, I didn't feel like I had legitimate grounds for complaint.

The fact is, Adam is drop-dead gorgeous, so it was impossible for me to reach into his pants pocket without being painfully aware of him as a man. The spicy aftershave he wore. The well-toned thigh muscle I had to brush over to get to the keys. And his ill-disguised, um, enthusiasm at my touch. Have I mentioned that Adam swung both ways? He was one hundred percent loyal to Dominic, but that didn't mean he didn't have impure thoughts now and then.

I'm pretty sure I blushed, but I tried to play it cool as my fingers closed around the keys and I withdrew my hand. Cooper snickered, but I refused to look at him or at Adam.

Cheeks still flaming, I hurried out to the car. I hoped Cooper would find it entertaining to stand there with Adam's gun pointed at his head while I dug out the Taser.

I moved as fast as I could, not sure how long the impasse in the house could possibly last. I ran across the street to the car, hoping I didn't look as conspicuous as I felt, then opened the trunk. Unlike mine, Adam's Taser was fully charged. I tried to close the trunk quietly, but it still made a solid thunk.

Firing the Taser might be as damning as letting Adam fire the gun, Lugh said.

I was glad to see we were back on speaking terms, but though I was anxious to question him about his mysterious silence, I had better things to do at the moment. He was right about the Taser. If I fired it, it would release a flurry of confettilike ID tags that could be traced to Adam. Not to mention that the Taser would store a record of exactly when it was fired.

Unless you've got a better suggestion, I thought at Lugh, *keep your comments to yourself.* Yeah, I was getting a bit testy, but I was beginning to think the odds of Cooper surviving this interview were very low. If he lived, he could make a lot of trouble for us—particularly for Adam. If he died...Well, if he died, and we did a good job of disposing of the body, then it was possible we could get away with it.

"I can't believe what I'm thinking," I muttered under my breath. Surely I drew the line at cold-blooded murder. Didn't I?

I let out a hiss of breath. Yeah, maybe *I* drew the line at murder, but I knew for a fact Adam didn't. He'd do whatever was necessary to protect Lugh, and even though Cooper didn't know I had Lugh, Adam would see him as an indirect threat.

Dithering over my moral qualms had caused me to slow down. I had my hand on the front doorknob when I heard a muffled bang from within, followed by a cry of pain.

Holding the Taser at the ready, I rushed through the door, not knowing what I was about to find. My heart hammered in my chest, and adrenaline surged through my system.

The sound I'd heard had to be a gunshot, and I assumed that meant Cooper had tried something. I also assumed it meant either Cooper was dead, or Adam was in deep trouble. Neither assumption turned out to be correct.

The first thing I saw when I burst through the door was Adam standing calmly in the foyer, his gun in his right hand, pointed at the floor, the pillow in his left. Then I saw Cooper.

He was crumpled on the floor halfway between where I'd last seen him and where Adam stood. He was rocking slightly, a soft moan escaping his throat, and his hands were clamped over a bleeding wound in his thigh. Based on the sounds Cooper was making, his demon wasn't a big fan of pain, but a nonfatal gunshot wound on a demon would heal completely in a matter of hours, and might only keep Cooper incapacitated for a few minutes.

"What happened?" I asked.

Adam looked grim. "He decided to call my bluff. I thought he might still be useful, so I went for the leg instead of the head shot."

Cooper's voice was gaining strength, and I was pretty sure the moan would soon turn into a scream. I didn't think the neighbors would have heard that gunshot—or realized what it was even if they heard it—but we'd be in even deeper shit than we were already in if Cooper started screaming. We'd made enough noise as it was. It felt a little less than sportsmanlike, but I pointed the Taser and pulled the trigger.

Electricity mucks with a demon's ability to control its host body. So much so that they can't even talk, much less move. Cooper might feel like screaming, but he wouldn't be able to control his voice enough to get the sound out.

"In for a penny..." I muttered. "Now what?" I asked out loud.

"Now we call in reinforcements," Adam said, and he tucked the gun back into its holster, dropped the pillow, and grabbed his cell phone.

ten

ADAM'S IDEA OF "REINFORCEMENTS" DIDN'T EXACTLY make my day, but we needed another demon to help us keep Cooper contained. We could have called Saul, but Barbie pointed out that her presence—more specifically, her injury—might distract Saul too much to make him useful. Which is how we ended up stuck with Raphael.

Raphael lived in Center City, so it took him more than twenty minutes to drive out to Cooper's house outside the Main Line. We'd had to juice Cooper a second time to keep him down, and the Taser's battery was starting to run low. If Raphael had gotten stuck in traffic, we would have been in trouble.

I guess Raphael didn't feel the same need for subtlety that the rest of us did, because he drove his car straight up the driveway, parking in front of the house in full view of anyone who drove by or who was watching from across the street. No, there was no reason for anyone to be suspicious of the car, but my paranoia instincts were on high alert, and I was tempted to tell Raphael to park elsewhere. I finally convinced myself that time was of the essence, and Raphael's car was fine where it was.

One of the side effects of the Taser was that Cooper hadn't been able to heal the bullet wound. I'd never thought of it before, but since the electricity ruined the demon's control over the host body, it ruined the supernatural healing ability as well.

The wound was still bleeding, though not as badly as before. The bright red puddle of blood on the floor and the coating of blood on Cooper's hands made my stomach turn, but ugly as the wound was, it wouldn't be fatal—not unless we kept Cooper incapacitated for a long, long time.

Raphael—whom we would all have to remember to call "Tommy," to keep his true identity secret—circled Cooper's limp body while Adam kept a watch on him, ready to pounce if Cooper made a sudden move. Not that he was making any moves, sudden or not, under the circumstances.

"You need to exorcize the demon," Raphael said to me after a moment's thought.

I shook my head in confusion. "What? Why?"

"So that Adam can do his special interrogation technique on Cooper. I can probably make the demon talk, but these aren't ideal circumstances for it. There's not enough privacy for me to get terribly creative, and, of course, information obtained under duress isn't always accurate."

As usual with Raphael, I looked for hidden ulterior motives behind his rather merciful-sounding suggestion. Raphael wasn't big on mercy. "Do you know this demon?" I asked him suspiciously.

Raphael shrugged. "You know we can't recognize one another on the Mortal Plain." He scowled at me. I guess he'd finally figured out why I'd asked him that question. "I don't know if I know this demon, and I don't give a shit. I'm making a practical recommendation, but if you'd like me to try to torture some information out of him, I'd be happy to oblige."

He grinned at me—a feral, angry expression. I could have apologized for my implications, but why should I? Raphael was a devious bastard, and he knew it. He shouldn't be surprised when people—especially me—suspected his motives.

"What do you think, Adam?" I asked, and Raphael's scowl darkened.

Adam looked grim. "I think he's right. If we keep Cooper Tasered, he won't be able to tell us anything, and if we don't, he's liable to kick up enough of a fuss to have the neighbors calling the police. We've got a sticky enough situation on our hands already."

It would have been nice if Raphael had mentioned his plan on the phone. I could have had Cooper exorcized by now. But Adam had given Raphael a very abbreviated account on the phone and had stressed the need to hurry. Maybe Raphael just hadn't fully appreciated the situation until he'd seen it himself. Giving Raphael the benefit of the doubt ran contrary to my nature, but I tried.

Cooper was starting to twitch, the first sign that his muscles were coming back under control. I wasn't sure how well I was going to do at getting into the trance state under the circumstances—I hadn't thought to bring anything vanilla-scented with me—but I sat cross-legged on the floor beside Cooper anyway, ready to begin the ritual.

"Not yet," Raphael said, grabbing me and unceremoniously pulling me to my feet.

"Get your hands off me!" I snapped, and he let go with gratifying speed.

I hadn't even noticed him taking the Taser away from me until he gave Cooper another jolt. He looked at me with a sneer. "You're supposed to be a pro. Don't you know better than to get that close to a demon who's not restrained? If he were more recovered than we thought, he could have grabbed you and transferred before you even blinked."

I had to bite my tongue hard to keep any number of snappy comebacks from leaping out of my mouth. I would have looked pretty stupid saying them, though, since Raphael was right. If I were a normal, nonpossessed human, I'd have been much more cautious around an unrestrained demon who might be starting to regain control of his body. In my arrogance, I hadn't thought of Cooper as a threat, since Raphael and Adam were here to jump on him if he made a hostile move. But if Cooper had tried to transfer to me and found me already occupied...I was getting careless.

So I swallowed my protests and took up my post again.

I was getting better at reaching the trance state under less-than-ideal conditions. Even with the lack of scented candles, the lingering resentment, and the gross-out factor of the still-growing pool of blood, I struggled only briefly to relax enough to open my otherworldly eyes.

The demon's red aura writhed around Cooper's body, smothering the human aura underneath. Performing an exorcism is an exercise in visualization. The specific visualization technique you used didn't matter, just so long as it worked. I always visualized a sudden gust of wind blowing the demon aura away. I gathered my energy around myself, then blasted it out at the demon, imagining a gust of wind blowing that aura to wisps.

Usually, that first blast was all it took to drive a demon out of its host body. But apparently, this demon was stronger than average and wouldn't be as easy to expel. Sudden fear tingled along my nerves. I was, as far as I knew, the strongest exorcist in the U.S., possibly one of the strongest in the world. But there still were some demons who were too powerful for me to exorcize—like Raphael, for example—and this would *not* be a good time to encounter one.

I took a deep breath to calm myself and bury my doubts. Then I concentrated once more on drawing energy into myself. This time, I didn't stop when I had "enough"; I just kept drawing more and more in—like taking a very deep breath, until your lungs feel like they're about to explode. When I could draw in no more, I let myself unleash that energy and thrust it at the demon.

To my intense relief, the demon aura shattered and disappeared, leaving a patch of human blue behind.

I opened my eyes to find Cooper gasping in pain as he pressed his hands to the wound in his thigh. He wasn't doing a great job of it—Tasers don't bother humans as much as they do demons, though they certainly have an effect—but I was glad to see someone was still home in his body. If the demon I'd just sent back to the Demon Realm had made mincemeat of Cooper's brain, this whole escapade would have been an exercise in futility. Not to say there was a guarantee it wasn't even now.

Cooper was moaning, his face shiny with sweat and tears. Weasel or not, I felt sorry for him.

"Let's get on with this," I said.

Adam seemed to have no objection. He dropped to his knees beside Cooper's curled-up form and touched his hand to the back of Cooper's neck. Instantly, Cooper stopped moaning. His hands fell away from the wound, and I saw that his movements had started the blood flowing faster again.

Adam's host—whose name was, confusingly, also Adam—rolled Cooper over onto his back. Losing his original demon hadn't cured Cooper's Taser problems, and Adam would be unable to control the body, at least for another few minutes. He could, however, still rummage through Cooper's brain while he waited.

"We need to get the bullet out of his thigh," Adam's

host said. "Once we get the bullet out, Adam will heal the wound enough to save Cooper a trip to the emergency room that might be difficult to explain."

"Hello to you, too," I said under my breath. It was decidedly weird to look at the person I've always known as Adam the demon and know that an entirely different person was looking out of his eyes.

"Can't Adam get the bullet out himself?" I asked out loud. "Demons don't generally go to hospitals, so I assumed they somehow..." I made a vague motion with my hands.

Adam's host smiled at me. "If Adam were going to stay in there for a few hours, he could make the body expel the bullet without help. However, for reasons I can't understand, he finds *my* body more appealing." He grinned at his little joke—no one in their right mind would *want* to look like Bradley Cooper, especially not with a stud muffin like Adam's host available.

Adam's host looked up at Raphael. "I need you to rip the pants leg for me so I can get to the wound."

Something sparked in Raphael's eyes. I didn't think he much liked being ordered around, but he didn't argue. Who needs scissors when you've got demon strength?

Adam's host had orders for me, too. "I need a sharp knife."

I blinked at him. "You think Cooper has a scalpel sitting around somewhere?"

"A kitchen knife will do."

My eyes widened. "Are you sure you know what you're doing?"

He made a shooing motion with his hand. "Yes. Now go on before he loses any more blood."

I found my way to the kitchen easily enough, but then realized I should have asked Adam's host what size knife he needed. I rummaged through Cooper's drawers and selected a paring knife, a steak knife, and a utility knife. Surely one of them would be what he was looking for. The thought of him cutting into Cooper's thigh with a steak knife brought back my urge to hurl, and for a moment, I didn't think I could keep my gorge down. The nausea I experienced when Lugh and I exchanged control was bad enough without the blood and gore.

When I returned to the foyer, Cooper's pants leg was ripped all the way up to his hip, giving me a glimpse of his tightie whities, which I could have done without, thank you very much. Adam's host was using a piece of material torn from the pants to wipe blood away from the entry wound.

I laid my selection of knives on the floor beside Adam's host. "Do you need me to find some alcohol to sterilize these with?" I asked.

He shook his head. "Adam will make sure there's no infection."

He picked up the paring knife, and my stomach lurched again. I turned my back, figuring there was no way I could keep from throwing up if I watched the proceedings.

Adam gave an incoherent grunt that I couldn't help but interpret as a sound of pain.

"Sorry," his host said. "It's going to get worse. Do you need something to bite on?"

Adam is one of those demons who has a fascination with pain, but he's more interested in *other* people's pain than his own. Having a bullet removed without anesthesia by an amateur with a paring knife was not going to be fun, even for him. Again I fought the nausea, trying not to imagine what it would feel like.

"You'd better be shielding Cooper from feeling this," I told Adam, still without turning to look.

He hadn't regained enough control of the body to do more than grunt his answer. I had no idea if that meant he was or he wasn't, but apparently his host could interpret his caveman grunts.

"He's shielding him. Unfortunately, he can't shield himself."

The wordless cry that followed needed no interpretation. I supposed Adam had been too macho to accept the offer of something to bite on—or maybe he didn't have enough control to bite—but he couldn't keep himself quiet. The sound wasn't particularly loud, his body still being too discombobulated to muster a whole lot of noise, but I flinched at it anyway.

With my back turned to the drama in the foyer, I had a clear view of Barbie, lying on the living room couch with a big bag of ice covering her hand. Our eyes met, and Barbie smiled grimly at me. No doubt she was in plenty of pain herself, but she wasn't enjoying the show any more than I was.

After that last cry, Adam had fallen eerily silent. I

fought the urge to turn around to see what was happening. I hoped he'd passed out, though I wasn't entirely sure if a demon could do that.

Finally, Adam's host said, "It's done," with an obvious tone of satisfaction.

I started to turn around. I'm not sure what I was thinking, because the scene was likely to be considerably messier than before, when it had almost made me toss my cookies. But I didn't get all the way around, because Raphael—who'd been so quiet I'd almost forgotten about him—grabbed me by the shoulders and gave me a little push toward the living room.

"We already have quite a mess to clean up," he said. "I don't want to deal with puke all over the floor."

That was Raphael, all right. Always full of compassion. Too bad I couldn't argue his point. Just listening to the impromptu surgery had my knees shaky and my face coated with sweat. Even if I managed not to vomit, I might pass out, which would be even more humiliating. So I didn't object to Raphael's callousness, and I didn't turn around. Instead, I made a beeline for an armchair tucked in the far corner of the living room, one that would have no view of the foyer.

eleven

THERE WAS A LOT OF ACTIVITY OUT IN THE FOYER FOR the next half hour or so. I participated in none of it, couldn't even see what was going on. But I could guess from the sounds.

Someone did his best to vacuum up the AFID tags the Taser had spewed all over the place. Someone else—or maybe the same someone—mopped the blood off the floor, sending the scent of bleach wafting into the living room. My stomach turned over yet again and I considered going to wait out in the car.

Eventually Adam, still in Cooper's body but wearing a clean pair of pants, limped his way into the living room, his host and Raphael bringing up the rear. If Adam was able to walk unassisted, then he must have gone a long way toward healing Cooper's wound already.

Adam drove Cooper's body to the love seat catty-corner to the couch Barbie still occupied, and sat down.

"Is Cooper still alive and kicking in there?" I asked Adam.

"Yeah. He's kicking pretty hard, in fact. And he's healed enough not to require any medical assistance.

Tommy, why don't you come over here and make sure Mr. Cooper stays seated when I'm gone. And Adam, please come rescue me!"

Adam's host smirked at him. "Not enjoying your stay?"

Adam made a growling sound that sounded all wrong—and not terribly threatening—coming from Cooper's throat. His host laughed. But he crossed the floor and reached out his hand for Adam to grab.

Adam clasped his host's hand, but waited for Raphael to come loom over Cooper before transferring.

Even before anyone spoke, it wasn't hard to tell when the transfer occurred. Adam's host, obviously, looked exactly the same whether Adam was in residence or not; however, there was a subtle shift in the body language, one I'm sure I wouldn't have noticed if I didn't know Adam as well as I did. And if I hadn't picked up that cue, the sudden hunching of Cooper's shoulders would have been a dead giveaway.

Adam came to sit on the edge of the couch, forcing Barbie to scooch over. "Let's see that hand," he said, lifting the ice bag without asking permission.

I couldn't tell how bad it was from where I was sitting, and I wasn't about to stand up to take a better look. Adam frowned down at her.

"Would you like me to heal it for you?" Adam asked. "It would take hours to get it fully mended, but I could get it far enough along so it doesn't hurt so much anymore."

Barbie regarded him with wide, wary eyes. She and I weren't terribly alike, but I had no trouble guessing what was passing through her mind right now. She was remembering Adam's performance at the club with poor Mary and wondering if she could stand the thought of allowing that creature into her body, even to heal her.

"I think I'll pass," she said. "No offense, but if someone's going to take over my body, I'd rather it be Saul."

Adam nodded, and I wondered if he'd seen what I'd seen in Barbie's eyes, or if her excuse fooled him. "Just make sure no one sees your hand while you're injured. Having an injury miraculously heal overnight tends to inspire questions."

Even in the most demon-friendly states, transferring a demon via skin-to-skin contact is illegal, even if both participants are willing. Those who hate and fear the demons—and that's about half the population of the U.S.—feel safer with that kind of legal protection and don't care how many lives could be saved and how much pain avoided if demons could be used as healers. Of course, I suspected Adam was far from the only demon to do this kind of illicit healing.

"I'll be careful," Barbie promised, and Adam put the ice bag back on her hand. Her eyes squinched at the corners, but she made no other sign that it hurt.

We all turned our attention to Cooper, who looked small and fragile with Raphael looming over him.

"Did you get anything useful out of him?" I asked Adam.

He nodded, but I got the impression that something about what he'd learned bothered him. "I have the name of the leader of the illegal recruitment drive:

Jonathan Foreman. Cooper didn't have an address for him, but I'm sure I can find it myself."

Raphael, standing behind the couch, bent and put his hands on Cooper's shoulders, right next to his neck.

"Oh, good," he said. "That means we don't need Cooper anymore."

Cooper let out a squeal of alarm as Raphael's hands slid to encircle his neck. He clawed at Raphael's wrists, leaving red marks on Raphael's skin, but his efforts probably wouldn't have dislodged Tommy, much less Raphael.

"Don't you dare kill him!" I said, glaring at Raphael.

Raphael raised his eyebrows, looking mildly curious as Cooper continued flailing at his hands. "Why on earth not? After everything that's happened tonight, he's a considerable liability."

Cooper's face was turning red, and he was making pathetic little gasping sounds. I loathed Cooper, had loathed him for all of my life. And I had good reasons to want him dead for some of the things he'd done to me in the past. But it turns out I haven't yet found it in me to just turn my head and let someone be murdered. And I hope I never do.

"Because we're the good guys," I said, "and good guys don't go around murdering people. Now let go of him!"

Raphael, of course, ignored me. I wished my Taser were charged, because there was nothing I could do against Raphael my own puny self without a weapon.

"Adam!" I snapped. "Do something!"

Adam gave me a look, at once impassive and full of

meaning. He probably approved of what Raphael was doing. Even if he didn't, Raphael outranked him. No, only Lugh could stop Raphael, and he didn't seem to be volunteering for the job.

I was trying to come up with a plan C, but Raphael suddenly dropped his hands from Cooper's neck. Cooper sucked in great, gasping swallows of air, his hands going protectively to his neck as if to stop Raphael from choking him again.

Raphael smiled pleasantly. "My advice would be to kill him and hide the body where it will never be found." He looked at Adam. "You've had intimate contact with him. Do you think if I reminded him that I could change my mind and come back for him at any time he would see the wisdom of keeping his mouth shut?" Raphael turned his unnerving attention to Cooper. "You'd have to make yourself disappear so you wouldn't have to tell your Spirit Society friends your demon is gone, but I know you have the means to do it."

Adam flashed Cooper a feral grin. "What do you think, Brad? Are you going to run around flapping your lips, or would you rather live?"

Cooper, still gasping and coughing, managed to sputter out a promise that he wouldn't say a word to anyone about what had happened here tonight. To be honest, I wasn't sure I believed him. But Adam seemed to think he'd keep his mouth shut, and Raphael, for the second time in one night, was showing something that resembled mercy. I wasn't going to be the one to start baying for Cooper's blood, not when I'd been about to make a heroic effort to save him.

We trooped out of the house together, leaving Cooper sobbing on his love seat. Adam carried a garbage bag that contained Cooper's bloody clothes, the bag from his vacuum cleaner, the pillow that had served as a makeshift silencer, and the rags they'd used to clean the floor—the hard evidence that we'd been here tonight and done Cooper harm. Adam was going to have to "lose" his Taser somehow. It wouldn't go over well with the brass— losses like that couldn't help but be suspicious—but he'd have a hard time explaining why the Taser had been fired not just once, but multiple times, when he was off duty.

As we closed Cooper's front door behind us, Raphael turned to me with a little grin and a spark of what looked suspiciously like mischief in his eye.

"You and I do a very nice good cop, bad cop act. We should do it again sometime."

"Fuck off," I said, with my usual tact and grace. "He could have died before you decided to listen to my good cop." And I *still* didn't understand why he had listened.

Raphael dismissed that with a wave. "Did you hear the little noises he was making?" he said with a chuckle.

I curled my lip in a sneer. "You think that's funny? Why, you despicable—"

Raphael didn't let me finish, cutting me off with a glare and a growl that made me take an involuntary step backward. He shook his head at me in what looked like disgust, then ducked into his car, pulling the door shut so hard I was surprised the metal didn't crumple. I caught a glimpse of his face as he slammed the car into reverse and practically flew out of the driveway. He was seriously pissed, and I hoped he wouldn't plow down any innocent passersby.

I shook my head. "Why is he mad at me?" I asked of no one in particular. "He had to know gloating like that would offend me."

"He wasn't gloating," Adam answered. "He was pointing out that Cooper was making noise, which meant he could breathe. No air, no noise."

Adam didn't glance at me after making me realize what an idiot I'd been, and Barbie didn't either. So much for my efforts to give Raphael the benefit of the doubt. By the time I'd recovered my poise enough to follow, Adam and Barbie were halfway across the street and I had to run to catch up.

The ride back into Center City was a quiet one. Barbie was in too much pain to make conversation, and neither Adam nor I was much into small talk. I still didn't get why Adam and Raphael had let Cooper live. It seemed so...unlike them.

Any ideas, Lugh? I asked, but apparently we were back to the silent treatment. I didn't understand what was going on with *that*, either.

My stomach still wasn't happy, and I felt the beginnings of a headache stirring behind my eyes, so I let my questions go, for now. I closed my eyes and leaned my head back against the headrest, willing the nausea to recede. At least Adam drove with reasonable care, not screaming around any corners or jackrabbiting when lights turned green. He probably just didn't want me puking in his car.

Our first stop was at Saul's apartment, where we dropped Barbie off. Saul lived in a small, intimate community. You had to buzz to get in, but there were no doormen, and there was no front desk. No one to see Barbie's obvious injury before Saul swept her behind closed doors to heal her.

I closed my eyes again as soon as Adam pulled away from the curb. I could hardly wait until Adam dropped me off so I could fall into bed in a dark room and, hopefully, sleep through the remainder of these aftereffects.

"It was really nice of you to offer to heal Barbie," I found myself saying without having intended to say a word.

I didn't open my eyes, but I could hear Adam's shrug. "It seemed like the thing to do at the time. She may have saved my life, after all. At least, my host's life. Cooper's demon was not rank and file."

I'd gathered that from the extra effort it had taken me to toss it out. It didn't seem like a good sign. If we had to have more demons than usual flooding the Mortal Plain, why couldn't they all be weaklings like Mary?

"Why did you and Raphael let Cooper live?" I asked, my mouth still running on autopilot. My conscious mind would have preferred I not ask, in case talking about it would make Adam change his mind. But being sick to my stomach lowered my inhibitions, and my mouth asked without permission from my brain.

Again, I could hear Adam's shrug. "I can't speak for Raphael. But personally, I didn't dare kill him. We cleaned up the evidence as best we could, but all it would have taken was one stray hair, or one witness who saw us enter, or who saw the car, to implicate me if we'd left a body behind. And if we *didn't* leave the body behind, we'd have to get it out of there somehow, which would have been too risky."

I cracked one eye open and glanced at Adam's profile. "So if you thought you could have gotten away with it, you'd have killed him?"

He stopped at a red light, but didn't turn to face me. "Yes. I'm sorry if that offends your moral code, but leaving Cooper alive is dangerous. He may be frightened enough of Raphael to keep his mouth shut. Then again, he might find his courage when we're not right there in his face."

The light turned green. I closed my eye again and didn't comment. Everything Adam said was true. I didn't have to like it, or even agree with him. At least I understood him. Raphael's mercy was much more mysterious, but then I probably never would understand him. His mind was the most complicated maze I'd ever seen, and I would lose my way in a heartbeat trying to solve it.

I suddenly remembered how unhappy Adam had looked when he left Cooper and returned to his host. He hadn't told us anything that justified the look on his face, though it wasn't surprising that he'd decided not to talk too much in front of Cooper.

"What else did you learn while you were getting to

know Cooper up close and personal?" I asked. "There was something bothering you."

Adam's heavy sigh said he was not happy. "We were right about the recruitment campaign not being restricted to Philly. And Cooper thinks about a hundred new demons—some legal, some not—have come to the Mortal Plain in the last six weeks. And that's just in Cooper's region."

That made me sit up straight and open my eyes. "Shit! That's a lot of demons." If we let this go on much longer, Dougal would have a freakin' army at his disposal.

"Yes, it is," Adam agreed, but apparently he had nothing more to add. Which was probably just as well.

Worry struck me out of the blue while I was riding the elevator to my apartment. If Cooper was a legal, registered demon host, that meant the Spirit Society had seriously lowered their standards. Unfortunately, Cooper wasn't the only person I knew who'd had hopes of hosting a demon.

I dove for the phone and called my mom as soon as the door to my apartment closed behind me. We had reached an uneasy truce after my father's death, but still we hardly ever spoke. I was pretty sure that even the lingering tension between us wouldn't keep her from calling to let me know if she finally got her wish to become a host, but "pretty sure" wasn't good enough.

To my surprisingly intense relief, she assured me that she had no plans to host. "That was a young woman's dream," she told me wistfully. "But I'm not a young woman anymore."

I managed to keep my opinion of that "dream" to myself, so it turned out to be one of our most civil conversations ever. Afterward, my head and stomach still feeling less than their best, I decided to make an early night of it. Everything would look rosier tomorrow, after a good night's sleep, I assured myself.

But I was dead wrong about that.

twelve

I DON'T KNOW HOW LONG I WAS *ASLEEP* ASLEEP, BUT IT felt like I had closed my eyes only moments before I opened them to find myself in Lugh's imaginary bedroom. Last night, I'd willed Lugh to appear to me in my sleep, and he hadn't done it. Tonight I wanted nothing more than oblivion, and here he was. Contrary bastard.

It wasn't that I didn't want to talk to him about his unusual reticence. It was just that the headache and queasiness that came with control changes had followed me into my dreams. Also, it was never a good sign when I found myself in Lugh's bed.

I was lying on my back, staring up at a cream-colored ceiling. My head lay on a fluffy down pillow, and the sheet that caressed my skin had the luxurious softness of pure silk. It was a fantastically comfortable bed, but I couldn't help noticing how much of my skin was in contact with that silk sheet. Which was practically every inch. Which meant I was naked beneath.

A shadow loomed in the candlelit darkness beside the bed, but I didn't turn toward it. I knew who it was, and the bedroom combined with the silk sheets and nudity told me just what was on Lugh's mind tonight.

The bed dipped beneath his weight. I knew he was about to lean over me, take away my option not to look at him, so I closed my eyes. I didn't want to see what he was wearing—or *wasn't* wearing, as the case might be.

"Let me go back to sleep," I said, my voice sounding unflatteringly petulant.

Lugh chuckled, the sound so full of warmth that I felt a flush rising on my face. "You *are* asleep," he reminded me.

I kept my eyes closed, but that didn't keep me from sensing his presence, his *closeness*. His breath caressed my face, smelling faintly of coffee and cinnamon. Of course, he didn't really breathe, and his breath didn't really have a scent. He just thought I'd find the scent of coffee and cinnamon enticing, and so he crafted it to please me.

I felt him shift on the bed beside me, then heard the silky slither of his hair as he loosed it from whatever confinement he'd had it under. The strands stroked across the skin of my chest, right above where the silk sheet came to a stop. My traitorous nipples hardened, and desire kindled low in my belly, despite my best efforts to squelch it.

Would I have better success fending him off if I

opened my eyes, or if I kept them closed? I felt sort of silly lying there with my eyes closed like he was some kind of monster under the bed and was about to go away. But if I opened my eyes...Lugh was an expert at pushing my buttons—he probably knew what they were better than I did—and adding visuals might tempt me to do something I'd regret later. So I kept them closed, though I still felt silly.

"Will you quit with the mind games already?" I snapped. I wanted to try to sit up, but I had a feeling I'd end up flinging myself into his arms if I did. Besides, silk sheets are kind of slippery, and it might be hard to keep this one over my naughty bits if I sat up.

He laughed again, the sound peppering my skin with goose bumps. "Is that what you think this is?" he asked, sounding terribly amused. The bed shifted under him again, and suddenly I felt the touch of bare skin against my hip.

Cool, sophisticated grown woman that I am, I let out a little yip of surprise and jerked away. My eyes popped open, and I tried to sit up while clutching the sheet to my chest.

Lugh was lying on his side beside me on the bed, under the crimson silk sheet. Well, *some* of him was under the sheet. If he so much as twitched—or if I pulled on the sheet any harder to keep my boobs covered—I'd be unveiling something I didn't want to see. Or at least, something I didn't *want* to want to see.

Lugh's head was propped on his hand, his hair draping his chest and shoulders like a shiny black cape, his sensual mouth lifted at the corners in a subtle smile. His skin was golden over his well-defined but not-too-bulky muscles.

I couldn't imagine a single thing he could have done to make himself look sexier. It just wasn't fair!

Lugh patted the bed beside him with his free hand. "No need to move on my account," he said, his voice a bass grumble that made my toes curl. I've always had a thing for men with really deep voices. But of course, Lugh knew that—had known that from the very beginning when he'd first spoken to me in my dreams.

"Knock it off!" I said, but my own voice sounded breathy. I wasn't convincing *myself,* much less Lugh.

Lugh sat up. The silk sheet probably slid down, but I didn't get to see, because before I could even begin to guess what he was up to, he had grabbed me and rolled me under him. The movement should have sent us off the side of the bed, but I guess that wasn't how Lugh wanted it to work, so it didn't.

I put both hands on his chest in a fruitless effort to shove him off me, but I doubt I'd have been able to do it in real life, much less in a dream that he controlled.

"What the fuck do you think you're doing?" I snarled at him. He'd been pushy with me before, but never anything like this. I punctuated my question by banging my fist on his chest, which had zero chance of hurting him.

To my shock, Lugh sat up a little—just enough to grab my wrists, gather them both together in one of his large hands, and pin them over my head. I was too surprised to struggle. My mouth gaped open, and my heart suddenly hammered from what felt like my throat.

Lugh's head lowered toward mine, and I realized he meant to kiss me. I quickly turned my head away.

"Haven't you ever heard that no means no?" I demanded. I couldn't figure out what I was feeling right at that moment. I should have felt helpless, and scared, and maybe even betrayed. He could control this dream, effortlessly destroy my every defense, do whatever he wanted to me. And even though it was a dream, anything he did to me, I would feel. I might lust after him in theory, and might have let him take certain, er, liberties in the past. But I didn't want to have sex with him, despite the temptation he offered.

So why couldn't I help noticing how good his body felt against mine, how warm, how strong? And why couldn't I help noticing his unique, spicy, musky scent? When his lips feathered over my cheek, it was all I could do to keep my face turned away.

What the hell was the matter with me?

Lugh's breath was a flush of warmth as his kisses trailed over my face down to my jawbone, then up to my ear, which he nipped very gently. "What's wrong with you is that you trust me," he whispered in my ear.

His words were startling enough that I turned my head toward him after all. He pulled back enough for our eyes to meet comfortably, though he didn't get off me or release my wrists.

I swallowed hard, part of me trying not to believe what he'd just said. Trusting was something I sucked at.

I didn't trust *anyone,* not deep down inside. I was always on the lookout, afraid of wounding words or actions, braced to defend myself. I'd known that about myself for a long time, and although I didn't like it, it was just the way I was. I'd made progress at trusting Brian. But I'd had no idea I'd made this much progress at trusting Lugh.

And yet, I did.

Whatever he was up to at the moment, I knew with unnerving certainty that he wasn't going to rape me, wasn't going to hurt me, despite the evidence of naked skin on naked skin, or his dominant position, or his hold on my wrists.

"You bastard," I said, but it came out in a whisper.

He smiled softly and stroked a finger down the cheek he had kissed. "Telling you things never seems to work. Showing works better."

"If you had real balls, I'd be putting my knee in them right now," I informed him. He had positioned himself in such a way as to give me a clear shot, but how do you hurt a dream?

He planted a chaste kiss on my forehead, then let go of my wrists and rolled off me. The sheet went with him, and I gave a little squeak of alarm as I grabbed for it. But suddenly, I was wearing a pair of silk pajamas in a midnight blue that looked almost black against the crimson sheets.

I sat up slowly, keeping a wary eye on Lugh. He'd put pajamas on me, but as far as I could tell, he was still naked himself, the sheet draping across his hips artfully. I tried not to imagine what lay beneath that sheet.

His head was propped on his hand again, and his smile was sin and temptation rolled together. "You don't have to imagine," he murmured. "All you have to do is give the sheet a little tug."

Lugh had been trying to seduce me from the moment we first "met," and he'd never been subtle about it. But as aggressive as he'd been at times, he'd never been like *this* before. The strangeness of it helped me fight off some of the temptation.

"What's gotten into you tonight?" I asked, keeping my eyes firmly focused on his face. "And what was with the silent treatment?" I couldn't have said exactly why, but I was sure now he'd been silent of his own accord, that it hadn't been my subconscious blocking him out after all.

"Brian wants you to get rid of me," he said. "I wanted to remind you what you'd be missing if you did—just in case the idea started to sound appealing to you."

Anger, hot and sweet, swelled in my chest, and my hands curled into white-knuckled fists. I was so furious, I couldn't even speak.

He'd put me through all that anxiety and discomfort just to prove a point. A point he could have made just fine by letting me know he was still there, even if he refused to talk to me.

"It wouldn't have been the same," he said. "If you'd known for sure I'd be back, the silence wouldn't have bothered you. But if I take a different host, then I won't be back."

My eyes prickled and burned with angry tears—tears I absolutely refused to shed. Lugh, who knew exactly what I was thinking and feeling, regarded me with an expression of mild regret.

"I'm sorry I distressed you," he said. "But, as I said before, *telling* you things rarely works. You needed to see that you would miss me if I were gone."

I knew it wouldn't hurt him, but I couldn't stop myself from hauling back and slapping him across his smug face. My palm stung and burned from the blow, but Lugh didn't even wince. Of course not. The cheek I had slapped wasn't real. The hand I'd slapped him with wasn't real either, but Lugh could make it feel real.

I cradled my hand against my chest. Something warm and wet trickled down my cheek, and I realized one of the tears I'd been desperately trying to suppress had escaped.

Lugh sat up, and even in the midst of my anger and hurt, I couldn't help glancing at his body. The sheet slid down and away, baring one leg all the way up to the hip, but a corner of the sheet still draped over his groin, kind of like a fig leaf on a statue.

My temptation to look made me even more furious, and I hurled myself to the other side of the bed, meaning to get out and run. Not that I'd be able to go anywhere, but it's the thought that counts, right?

Lugh didn't let me get that far. His hand fastened on my ankle, and he yanked me back onto the bed. I tried to grab for a bedpost, but even if I'd succeeded, Lugh was way too strong for me. Instead, I ended up sprawled facedown on the bed. When I tried to get up again, Lugh covered me with that big, strong body of his, pinning me in place. The hot, hard length of him nestled between my buttocks, and I realized I'd lost the pajamas again.

"Get off me!" I yelled, struggling helplessly.

He brought his mouth down to my ear, his tongue darting in for a taste before he spoke.

"You don't want to get rid of me," he whispered. "You like me. You *want* me, even if you won't let yourself act on that want." He wiggled his hips against my butt to emphasize his point, and my body betrayed me with a pleasurable shiver.

I could have argued with him, but really, what was the point? I could only *feel* my feelings; Lugh could *understand* them. My own personal, highly invasive therapist.

Tears continued to drip from my eyes, soaking into the silk pillowcase. But I stopped struggling.

"You didn't have to do this," I said, my voice a tear-strained whisper. "I told Brian no."

Lugh brushed his lips against the side of my neck. "I know. But not for the right reasons." His tongue trailed a path across my shoulders, and I had to bite my lip to keep from groaning.

I was in love with Brian. I shouldn't want Lugh so badly!

"I fulfill different needs than Brian does," Lugh whispered against my skin. His hair tickled my sides, but I didn't have the slightest urge to laugh. "You can want me and love Brian at the same time."

I couldn't talk—my throat was too tight—so I settled for shaking my head violently. The evidence that Lugh was right was overwhelming, and yet I refused to believe it. I was a firm believer in monogamy, and, damn it, I wasn't about to change my mind!

But Lugh wasn't finished talking. "Just as I can want Brian and love *you* at the same time."

His words took the last of the fight out of me, shocking me into immobility. I lay still and passive beneath him, painfully aware of every minute point of contact between us, of the heat of his body, of the dominance of his position, and of my utter lack of discomfort with that dominance. And I tried to convince myself he hadn't said what I thought he'd just said.

"You heard me," Lugh said, then started trailing kisses down my spine. The farther down those kisses trailed, the more freedom of movement I had. And yet, I didn't move.

Could it really be true? Could Lugh really love me? I'd always interpreted his interest as casual lust, but maybe that's what I'd wanted to see.

The kisses began to travel upward again, his skin stroking sensually against mine as he moved. God, he felt good!

His cock slid into the valley between my buttocks once more as his mouth returned to my ear, and against my will, I found myself arching into him. Desire clouded my mind, and I wondered if it would really be such a bad thing if I were to let Lugh make love to me. It was, after all, just a dream.

"No," Lugh whispered in my ear. "You're not ready to let me make love to you yet. You would regret it afterward, and that I cannot allow."

The truth of his words pierced the cloud of lust, and though my body was still all for a boisterous roll in the hay, my mind recognized it as the mistake it would be.

"So all of this has been one big tease," I managed to say. I guessed demons didn't suffer from blue balls—especially not when their host didn't actually *have* balls—but I was pretty sure I was about to experience the female equivalent.

Lugh's weight shifted above me. "Would I do that to you?" he asked, then turned me over onto my back.

He was smiling down at me, his amber eyes glowing faintly with a demon light, his hair forming a dark curtain around our faces. My breath came in shallow pants, and my mouth was dry with desire. Lugh had gotten me off before with some very naughty visual aids, and I wondered what he had in mind this time.

The fire in his eyes glowed more brightly. "No props this time," he said, his voice husky. "Just me."

He lowered his head slowly, giving me time to turn my face away again if I wished. But I didn't. I couldn't. I wanted his kiss too badly. Our relationship wasn't exactly what I would call chaste, but for all the sexual energy that surrounded us, we'd rarely kissed. I didn't have it in me to regret that that was about to change.

His lips touched mine, and it was like my body went up in flames. A decidedly unchaste moan escaped me, and I wrapped my arms around him, my hands buried in that gorgeous, silky hair. His lips were soft and warm, but there was nothing soft about his kiss. If he'd kissed me any harder, it would have hurt. His tongue thrust into my mouth, and I moaned again, loving the taste and feel of him.

I think I could have kissed him forever, forgetting the outside world existed, but he used his knee to nudge my legs apart, then settled in between them. My pajamas had reappeared, but Lugh was still nude, that thin layer of silk all that separated my flesh from his. He pressed himself hard against me, and my hips bucked against my will.

I desperately wanted to rip off the pajamas, to feel him inside me, but I kept my hands buried in his hair to resist the temptation as his hips began to move, his cock stroking me hard over the thin pajamas. It shouldn't have felt so amazing, not to a mature woman who was used to having sex with her boyfriend on a regular basis. But feeling him thrusting against me, his cock hitting my clit just right with each stroke, had me on the verge of orgasm in no time.

I arched up against him, wanting to take that next step into bliss, but he slowed his pace and lightened his strokes, tormenting me, playing with me, making me ache for release. I tried to hurry him along, but he would have none of it. And when I released his hair, meaning to hurry *myself* along since he wasn't cooperating, I soon found my hands pinned above my head again. I'd have complained, but it was hard to talk with his tongue halfway down my throat.

He kept me hanging there, right on the brink of orgasm, for what felt like forever and a day. The anticipation tightened every muscle in my body, and every once in a while I had to remind myself to breathe. But it also felt so good to be on that brink, knowing with total certainty that he would eventually push me over, and that it would be worth the wait when he did. I almost didn't want it to end, though that didn't stop me from straining my body up toward him.

Just when I was beginning to think I couldn't bear it for another moment, Lugh gave one last hard, perfect stroke, and the pleasure exploded through my body. I screamed something incoherent into his mouth as my back arched and my toes curled, and my heart threatened to hammer its way out of my chest.

He kept thrusting against me until he'd milked every last spasm of pleasure he could out of me and I lay there completely limp and panting for breath.

It was a while before coherent thought returned. When it did, I realized that as mind-numbingly good as it had been for me, Lugh hadn't come. He was still hard as a rock against me. I opened my eyes—not even having realized that I'd closed them—and saw a contented smile on his face, rather than the sexual hunger I'd been expecting.

He leaned down to kiss me again briefly. "Your body is my body," he reminded me. "When you come, so do I. I just chose not to include a physical manifestation of it in your dream."

Sometimes, these dreams were so damned realistic it was easy to forget they were dreams. The body that was still pressed up against mine wasn't real, and if he had an erection, it was because he chose to create that illusion for me.

"So basically," I said, still a little out of breath, "this is masturbation for you."

His eyes sparkled with something like mischief. "Another one of those human hang-ups that don't make a whole lot of sense to demons. Besides, since I feel your pleasure, it gives me additional incentive to do a good job."

The heat in my cheeks told me I was blushing—hard to believe I still had a prudish bone left in my body, considering what I'd been exposed to since Lugh came into my life, but there you have it.

He rolled off me, and I finally gave in to the temptation to take a good look at his naked body, scanning him from head to toe. And, I must admit, spending more time than I should have studying parts in between. Another wisp of arousal stirred in my center, but I was still limp and satiated and doubted I had the energy for another go just yet. Even as I thought that, my eyelids felt heavy and sleep tugged at me.

"Time to sleep now," Lugh told me.

"I *am* asleep, remember?" I murmured, but it was all I could do to suppress a yawn. How can I get sleepy when I'm already asleep? Beats me.

"We'll talk more about what to do about Brian later," he added as if I hadn't spoken.

Actually, it was a good thing I was suddenly so overwhelmingly tired; otherwise, I'd have been alarmed by those words. As it was, my eyes slid closed, and I drifted away.

thirteen

I WOKE UP THE NEXT MORNING GROGGY AS ALL HELL and mildly embarrassed about my encounter with Lugh last night. It was hardly the most embarrassing dream he'd ever given me, but it was much more... personal.

I zombie-walked to the kitchen to put on a pot of coffee, then stared at the pot as it brewed. It wasn't until I'd finished my second cup that my brain cells started to wake up, and I noticed the glaring omission from last night's conversation.

When I'd woken up in Lugh's bed, I'd gone into seduction alert, and that had pushed all thoughts of the real world and our much larger problem aside. Lugh flat-out didn't do things like that by accident. He'd put me in that bed and distracted me with sex either because he didn't want to talk to me, or because he'd been driving my body while I was asleep. Lugh usually had no problems with talking, so my money was on the latter, even though I didn't feel queasy at all—I never did if I wasn't conscious when Lugh took over.

I talked to Raphael while you were asleep, Lugh confirmed.

I wondered if maybe the silent treatment had been better after all. Time for more steam to come out of my ears. I really hated being used like that. "Couldn't you have just told me what you were doing?" I fumed. I felt silly having an argument with a voice in my head, but that didn't stop me from arguing. "Did you have to do the whole seduction thing and keep me in the dark?"

He didn't answer, but then, he didn't have to. I knew exactly why he hadn't told me he was driving my body around. Even though I could now let him take control when absolutely necessary, everything in my psyche recoiled at the idea. When I was awake for the process, I had to make a conscious effort not to kick Lugh out. When I was asleep, all it would take was a tiny knee-jerk reaction, and I would pop awake, thrusting Lugh into the background once again.

I folded my arms across my chest stubbornly. "The last time you wanted to talk to Raphael like that, you let me wake up." It had been hard as hell not to let my subconscious barriers go up when I awakened, but I'd managed it.

That was before you started getting so sick from the control changes. You were already feeling sickly. If you'd awakened while I was in control, you would have felt much worse.

I was running out of good reasons to complain about what he'd done, though I had to admit, the idea of Lugh and Raphael talking to one another while I couldn't listen in wasn't a comfortable one. I doubted they'd been reminiscing about old times.

"Care to comment?" I asked.

We were merely discussing our options, few though they are at this time.

"And what did you decide?"

We did not come to any firm conclusions. I heard an echo of laughter in my head. *Strangely enough, Raphael and I had difficulty agreeing on anything.*

I couldn't help a short burst of laughter myself. The two of them had gone a long way toward repairing their fraternal relationship, but I doubted they would ever see eye-to-eye. Still, at least it was better than the open hostility they'd started with.

For now, we must content ourselves with finding Jonathan Foreman, the demon Cooper revealed as the leader of the illegal recruitment campaign.

The mention of Cooper didn't make me happy. If he wasn't as much of a chickenshit as I thought, he could have spilled the beans already.

That won't be a problem, Lugh assured me, and something in his tone of voice set off all the alarms in my head.

"What did you do?" I asked in a near whisper.

What had to be done.

Heat rose in my cheeks—an angry flush, not a blush—and my hands curled into fists. "What did you do?" I repeated through gritted teeth.

I didn't do anything. But I did . . . approve Raphael's plan.

"Which was what?"

Lugh hesitated, and for a moment I thought he was going to chicken out and not tell me. But unlike me, Lugh doesn't run from conflict.

Cooper could not be allowed to live. But we couldn't afford

*to kill him when Adam might be a suspect. So Raphael went
back and made sure it looked like a God's Wrath attack.*

"Oh, God," I moaned. There was nowhere to sit in my
kitchen, so I leaned my back against the fridge and allowed my butt to slide down to the floor.

God's Wrath is the most militant of the anti-demon
hate groups. They specialize in "purifying" demon
hosts. By "purifying," they mean "burning alive." God's
Wrath didn't care that an innocent host was killed
when they burned these demons to death. According to
God's Wrath, only an impure person would allow a
demon to take over his or her body. They considered
that the case even with the most unwilling of hosts.
They probably think rape victims were "asking for it,"
too.

*Cooper was an obvious target for God's Wrath. Probably
was even before he was possessed.*

Certainly true. He was a high-ranking member of
the Spirit Society, after all, and the Spirit Society might
as well have been named the Satan's Little Helpers Society as far as God's Wrath was concerned.

*And since Raphael's host used to be a member of God's
Wrath, he knew how to stage an attack and make it look real.*

I made another moaning sound. I hadn't liked
Cooper, but even if I'd been willing to kill him, it
wouldn't have been a death like that!

*Raphael assured me that he would kill Cooper quickly be-
fore setting the fire. It was infinitely more humane.*

Who wants to take bets on whether Raphael gave a
shit about how humane Cooper's death was?

I care, Lugh said. *And Raphael promised to follow my orders, even though he didn't like them.*

"And you believed him?"

Yes, I believed him. Weren't you the one who was trying to convince me earlier that he had changed?

Yeah, I believed Raphael had changed some since I had first met him. But he hadn't changed *that* much. He would never be the soul of compassion, nor would he ever be the good little soldier and follow orders—unless he agreed with them.

We would never know for sure whether Raphael had followed this particular order, kept this particular promise. Even if he *did* kill Cooper quickly before the fire, he would have done it in a way that the police wouldn't be able to detect after the fact. If he'd broken Cooper's neck, or done something else that left an obvious physical injury, then the police would have to start looking at possibilities other than a God's Wrath attack, because God's Wrath needed the demon's host alive so the demon could die in the fire.

I shuddered and tried to make myself stop thinking about it. I had come close to being burned at the stake myself, and sometimes I just couldn't help putting myself in other people's shoes. I couldn't imagine what kind of pain Cooper must have been in when—

Raphael swore to me that he would give Cooper a quick death. I can't claim I trust Raphael in all things, but I believe his promise was sincere.

That made one of us. Then again, maybe killing Cooper first would have made Raphael's task easier, more foolproof. If Cooper had been alive when the fire was set, then there was always the chance he might escape. When I thought about it that way, it gave me a little more hope. The risks involved with Raphael killing Cooper first might have been less than those involved in letting him die in the flames.

I wouldn't believe Raphael had killed Cooper first because of compassion, or because of honor, or because he was following orders. I *would* believe he'd do it if he thought it expedient.

But the ugly truth was, there was nothing I could do about it now.

I was pretty damn pissed at Lugh, and I was glad he kept any further comments to himself. Regardless of how necessary Cooper's death had been, regardless of whether Raphael had shown mercy or not, Lugh had lied to me. Perhaps not in words—after all, I didn't think until this morning to ask what the hell he was doing with my body while he was busy seducing me—but a deception of that magnitude was as bad as a lie in my book.

I went into my office for a couple of hours in the early afternoon. I still had paperwork to file on my last exorcism, and I hoped dotting my *i*'s and crossing my *t*'s would get me out of my own head for a while.

The phone calls started coming in shortly after I stepped in the door. First was Barbie.

"Have you watched the news at all today?" she asked cautiously, without even bothering to say hello.

So much for coming to my office to escape. I should

have left my cell phone at home. Or at least not answered it.

"The news about Cooper, you mean?" I asked, and my voice sounded tired to my own ears.

Barbie hesitated a long time. "Where are you?" she asked. "I think we need to talk, and I'd rather not do it on a cell phone."

She had a point about the cell phone, but I didn't want to get together and talk about it in person, either. In fact, I didn't want to talk about it at all.

"We'll talk later," I told her. "I'm . . . not up to it right now, okay?"

Another long silence. "Just tell me one thing."

I should have known better than to hope Barbie would let it go. She was kind of like me that way. "Maybe," I said, drawing the word out a bit, not trying to hide my discomfort.

"Saul has a theory. Do you think he's right?"

The question almost made me smile. Barbie was really good at being cagey. Even if somehow signals got crossed and someone was overhearing our conversation, they would never in a million years guess what Barbie was asking me.

If Saul had a theory, it had to be that Raphael had something to do with Cooper's death. Saul was even quicker to think ill of Raphael than I was.

"Can you keep him from doing a Godzilla impersonation if I say he's right?"

"Damn," she said, and she sounded as tired as I felt. "That'll be tough to pull off. He's already pretty testy, if you know what I mean."

I grimaced. Yeah, I did. I doubted he was happy with any of us for letting Barbie get hurt, and for making her wait so long to take care of her injury. Not that we'd actually *made* her wait—she'd never have voluntarily left Cooper's house when there was still a lot of shit left to hit the fan—but Saul wouldn't see it that way.

"You're the one who decided you wanted to date Bad Tempers 'R' Us," I said, trying to sound funny. I think it came out more sour than funny. "Don't let him do anything stupid." What I expected petite little Barbie to do if the demon Saul decided he wanted to have a knock-down-drag-out with Daddy was beyond me. I just knew I didn't want any part of it.

She sighed. "I'll do my best."

A male voice—Saul, no doubt—spoke in the background. Barbie must have put her hand over the receiver, because I couldn't make out the words.

"I've got to go," she said when she came back on, her voice tight with tension.

My conscience twinged a bit at leaving her to deal with Saul's temper on her own, but since she'd volunteered for the job, I tried not to let it bother me.

"You gonna be all right?" I asked. So much for not letting it bother me.

She laughed a bit nervously. "I'll be fine. It's Saul's security deposit I'm worried about."

As if to punctuate that point, there was a loud crash in the background.

"I've got to go," she said again, and this time she hung up without waiting for an answer.

fourteen

AFTER BARBIE, THERE WAS BRIAN. THIS TIME, I CHOSE not to answer. I didn't want to talk to him about Cooper's murder. Once upon a time, I'd have expected moral outrage from him. Now I wasn't so sure. Would it bother me more if Brian was pissed at me for whatever role I may or may not have played in Cooper's death, or if he took the demons' side and agreed it was necessary? I didn't know, and I didn't want to find out until I absolutely had to.

After Brian was Andy. I almost answered that one. Andy had been so withdrawn that any attempt he made to reach out was a good thing. But in the end, I chickened out on that conversation, too. He wouldn't jump up and down and yell, but he'd be...disappointed in me. Even though I hadn't known what Raphael was going to do. Maybe he would start to wonder—as I was beginning to—whether I should have figured it out on my own and tried to do something about it. After all, I'd been so terribly puzzled over Raphael's mercy. Why had I not come to the natural conclusion that he had something else up his sleeve?

The more I thought about it, the more naive I felt. I

really should have known what Raphael was going to do. Yes, sometimes his mind works in ways that I don't understand, but this shouldn't have been hard to guess. But my subconscious sometimes does an amazing job of not letting me see what I don't want to see.

Great. Now I was getting as broody as Andy. Probably a good thing I'd chosen not to take his call, as I suspected he'd have made me feel even worse.

The phone rang yet again. This time it was Adam. Adam I could bear to talk to—especially since I had some choice words for him. I might have been naive enough not to guess what Raphael was up to, and Barbie might not have known him well enough, but there was no way I'd believe Adam's mind hadn't traveled the same road.

I answered the phone, trying not to feel disloyal for having blown Brian and Andy off.

"Did you know?" I asked, skipping the pleasant greeting. I wasn't feeling too pleasant, and Adam never bothered with pleasantries anyway.

Adam hesitated a beat before answering. "I didn't know. But I can't claim I was surprised. You can yell at me for not telling you later. I've found that address we were looking for."

I'd been so busy building my anger against Raphael that I'd almost forgotten we'd gotten some useful information out of Cooper last night. Before Raphael went back and killed him.

I shook my head to try to clear it. Cooper's was far from the first death I'd had a hand in since Lugh had come to town, and with the damn demons invading the Mortal Plain, I didn't have time to wallow in it.

"Great. So are we going to be paying our friend a visit?"

"Seems like the thing to do. I'll pick you up at your apartment around six."

"So I'm going to have to yell at you in the car? Because don't think I'm letting this drop." It would be easier to have a good fight if he came up to my apartment. I didn't want him crashing into anything while he was distracted.

"If that would make you happy, be my guest. But since I'll have Raphael with me, I suspect you'll have a more appealing target."

"No," I said, and it was almost a yell. "You are not bringing him with you. Period."

Adam gave a long-suffering sigh. "Of course I'm bringing him with me. You know all the reasons why, so don't make me repeat them on the phone."

There were a lot of things I wanted to say—and most of them weren't safe to say on the goddamn phone. "If you insist on bringing him with you, then you're both going to come up to my apartment and we're going to have a come-to-Jesus meeting before we set foot anywhere near our friend. Got it?" So far, we'd spoken to three people about the sudden influx of demons, and all three of them were dead. It was a streak I was anxious to put an end to ASAP.

Another of those long-suffering sighs. "I'll see what I can do. But if Raphael doesn't want to come up, I won't be able to make him. You know that."

"Tell him he's coming up, or I'm not coming down."

If I hadn't been pissed at Adam, too, I'd have felt bad for putting him in the middle. As it was, I hoped he was squirming. Not that I really thought I could make Adam uncomfortable.

"Fine. I'll tell him. We'll see you tonight."

Adam hung up without saying good-bye, as usual. The only person who hung up on me more often than Adam was Raphael. Which was why I didn't even bother trying to call him and let him know what I thought of him.

I doubted Adam would have much trouble getting Raphael to come up to the apartment. Sometimes, I thought Raphael rather enjoyed locking horns with me, though only if he was winning. He might think he'd win tonight, but I had a fully charged Taser that said the odds were against him.

I left the office after talking to Adam. I'd done as much paperwork as I could stomach, and I was distracted enough to screw up anything else I tried to work on. I wasn't anxious to get back to my apartment, where anyone who wanted me would find me, but I couldn't see myself strolling around the city on this hot, muggy day.

When I got home, I had about three hours to kill before Adam and Raphael were due to arrive and make my day more...interesting. I thought I'd spend that time taking a nap, making up for some of the rest I'd lost thanks to Lugh's visit. But once again, I'd forgotten

Brian had a key—though in my defense, I would have expected him to be at work on a weekday afternoon. Apparently, he felt like he had better things to do today than earn a living, because I opened my apartment door to see him making himself at home in my living room.

He was still wearing the conservative business suit he'd worn to work, but the jacket and tie lay draped over the love seat, and he'd rolled the sleeves of his shirt almost to his elbows. Suits and long-sleeved dress shirts just weren't made for ninety-plus-degree weather, but it was a rare law firm indeed that didn't make its employees wear them.

Brian had also taken off his shoes and socks, propping his bare feet on my coffee table. I don't actually eat on the coffee table, so I don't know why I object to people putting their feet on it. But I do, and Brian knew that. I frowned at him.

"You've been hanging out with Raphael and Adam too long," I said, though Brian didn't exactly "hang out" with them. "You used to have better manners."

Okay, so it was a rude way to greet my boyfriend, and the love of my life, but in the mood I was in, it was the best I could do.

Brian shook his head, but he sat up straight and put his feet on the floor, where they belonged. "Is *that* all you have to say to me?" he asked, and he sounded terribly disappointed in me.

This was so not what I needed right now. "I didn't give you a key to my apartment so you could barge in here and yell at me whenever you felt like it." I dropped my purse on the side table a little more forcefully than was necessary.

He gave me a look of pure innocence. "You consider this to be 'yelling' at you?" His voice, naturally, hadn't risen an iota.

I pried off my sandals, leaving them by the door, but instead of going to the living room with Brian, I headed for the kitchen. My apartment was small enough, and had an open enough floor plan, that it was still possible to have a conversation. Unfortunately.

"I'm assuming the yelling's going to come later," I said over my shoulder. It was too hot for coffee, but that didn't stop me from beginning the brewing ritual.

I heard Brian rise from the sofa and pad toward me, but I didn't turn to look at him, my full attention on trying to separate one filter from the stack. In my peripheral vision, I saw him lean against what would have been a doorjamb, if my kitchen actually had a door.

"Why do you always assume the worst of me?" he asked. "I don't know exactly what happened last night, but I know you too well to believe you were behind the murder. And even if I didn't, I'm in no position to throw stones."

The anger I'd been trying to build up seeped away, and my shoulders sagged. For all my life, I'd used anger as a shield against all of life's unpleasantness. Before I'd started dating Brian, it had never occurred to me to want to change that. Anger was—for me, at least—much easier to deal with than pain, or fear, or even confusion.

I rubbed my suddenly gritty-feeling eyes and shoved the brew basket back into place in the coffeemaker. My self-defense instincts wanted me to grab the carafe and fill it at the sink, which would allow me to continue not looking at Brian. I fought those instincts off, slowly turning toward him as I crossed my arms. I realized as soon as I'd done it that crossing my arms was another defensive gesture, but decided I was allowed.

There was a shadow behind Brian's eyes, one I couldn't remember being there before. I knew what he was thinking about.

There had been a demon, known as Der Jäger, who had had the unusual ability to recognize and hunt other demons on the Mortal Plain. Due to circumstances beyond my control, Der Jäger had learned that I was still hosting Lugh. Lugh and I had fought Der Jäger and won, but we couldn't afford to let him go back to the Demon Realm and tell Dougal who was hosting Lugh. It wouldn't have mattered who had been hosting Der Jäger; I still wouldn't have been happy with the idea of roasting a human being alive to kill the demon. But Der Jäger had taken my father—at least, the man who had raised me, even though he turned out not to be my biological father—as his host. I'd never gotten along with dear old Dad, but there was no way I was ruthless enough to kill him.

To make a long story short, Lugh had taken over, and Brian had helped him stage a fiery car accident for my father to die in. In Brian's words, he'd had to choose between my father and me, and he'd chosen me. But no human being could make a decision like that without something inside them breaking, and Brian, with his

Boy Scout ethics, was probably far more broken up about it than he'd ever let me see.

But he was letting me see it now. Letting me see the shadow of horror that haunted him. It made my chest and throat tight with pain.

Without thinking about it, I took the two steps I needed to close the distance between us and put my arms around him, pressing the side of my face against his chest. His arms wrapped around me, and he let out his breath in a long, shuddering sigh.

There were no words that could soothe his pain— none that I knew of, at least—and there was a part of me that still kind of hated him for what he'd done. Not a rational part of me, mind you, but then emotions are rarely rational.

"I didn't know Raphael was going to kill Cooper," I said into Brian's chest. I knew I was avoiding the true issue here, but avoidance is one of my favorite things. "In retrospect, I think I should have. But I didn't."

Brian's arms tightened around me. "Things are always clear in retrospect." His hands slid slowly up my back, then up my neck, until they were cupped around the sides of my head. He threaded his fingers through my hair. I used to wear it spiked with gel, but I'd been toning it down lately, for which I'm sure Brian was grateful.

I tilted my chin upward and found his mouth coming to meet me halfway. His lips were a familiar warmth against mine and I opened my mouth for him. His tongue dipped in for a taste, and I made an incoherent little sound of pleasure.

Lugh's voice hummed in the back of my mind, reminding me he was there, feeling everything I felt, lusting after Brian just as I did. Reminding me also that an issue far more dangerous than Cooper's death lay between us.

Reluctantly, I pulled away from Brian's kiss, though I kept my arms around his neck and my body pressed up against his. His eyes had darkened with desire. He licked the taste of me from his lips, and I had to suppress a groan. Brian could do amazing things with his tongue, and my hormones were screaming that now would be a good time for him to demonstrate. I tried to swallow the desire back down.

"What about Lugh?" I whispered.

The fire dimmed in Brian's eyes, and he lowered his forehead until it rested against mine. "Couldn't you just have gone with it?"

I shook my head without breaking contact. "He won't let me. Now that he's brought the issue up, he's not going to leave it alone until we both come to terms with it."

Brian let go of me, taking a step backward to put some space between us. That single step sent a stabbing pain through my chest. I'd worked so hard to hold on to Brian. If there were any justice in this world, my efforts would be rewarded for it. But justice is a rare and precious thing.

Brian wasn't making eye contact, but at least he wasn't retreating any further.

"Have you thought at all about what I suggested the other day?" he asked.

"You mean about finding Lugh a new host?"

He met my eyes now with a look of mild reproach. Of course that was what he meant—what else could he possibly be talking about? But for reasons I didn't fully understand, I wanted him to verbalize it, so I met his reproach with pure stubbornness. Brian lost the staring contest.

"Yes, about finding Lugh a new host," he said.

Images of last night's dream with Lugh flashed through my mind. Heat rose in my cheeks, and I tried to force the images away. The last thing I wanted was to reinforce Brian's jealousy, and he was too observant to miss the blush. And too smart not to understand what it meant. I did my best to divert him.

"After you suggested it, Lugh stopped talking to me for a while," I said, not sure telling this to Brian was the smartest move. "He made me realize how...comfortable I've gotten with having him inside me." A lump formed in my throat, and I couldn't for the life of me tell whether it was because I feared losing Lugh, or because I feared losing Brian. Maybe both.

"You of all people know how isolated I've been," I continued. "I used to like it that way, but now..." I shrugged, my shoulders tight with tension. "Now I'm not sure I can go back."

Brian reached out and grasped my shoulders, giving them a firm squeeze. "You don't have to go back to being isolated," he told me earnestly. "You're learning how to open up and let other people into your life."

I shook my head, picking my words carefully. "I don't think I can do it without him." Brian opened his mouth to protest, but I put my fingers to his lips to silence him. He had no idea how much influence Lugh had had on me, how much Lugh had helped me repair the damage I'd done to our relationship. "Think of Lugh as a pair of training wheels," I said. "With the training wheels on, I can ride like a big girl. But I'm not ready to go without them yet."

Brian took another step back from me and scowled. "You're using him as another excuse to keep me from getting too close."

It used to be that Brian never got angry. Well, not *never*, but *almost* never. It used to drive me crazy when I argued with him. My voice would rise to somewhere in the vicinity of a sonic boom, my emotions boiling over, and Brian would respond calmly and logically. He was like a black hole for my anger, sucking it in and letting none escape. Being with me had changed him, hardened him. I hated that.

"I'm not the one using Lugh as an excuse," I said quietly. "Nothing's changed for me since the last time we made love. You're the one who's looking at me differently."

The scowl deepened. "You really think nothing has changed? I asked you to consider finding a new host for Lugh, and now you're telling me you don't want to. Am I supposed to just take that in stride?"

Jealousy flared in Brian's eyes, and I didn't know what to say. I couldn't even tell him he had no reason to be jealous of Lugh, because that would be a lie.

Brian's Adam's apple bobbed as he swallowed hard,

and I had to look away from the pain on his face. I hated seeing Brian hurt, but my first instinct was always to lash out. I'd gotten better at controlling that instinct lately, but my control wasn't perfect.

"I seem to remember a time when you got mad at me for assuming you'd be jealous," I said, still not looking at him. "You said I didn't give you enough credit. It's beginning to look like I was right all along."

Brian made a sound of frustration. "That was when Lugh was coming on to you. I can't be mad at you for what Lugh does. But this...this is all you."

My head flew up suddenly, and it wasn't because I wanted to look at Brian again. In fact, what I really wanted to do was turn my back, just in case the tears that hovered behind my eyes decided to fall. But when I met Brian's gaze, it wasn't *me* looking out from my eyes, it was Lugh. And he was pissed.

"I'm sorry if this makes you sick later," he said, speaking to me, not Brian, "but I've heard enough."

"Huh?" Brian asked, frowning in puzzlement, because, of course, he didn't realize yet what had happened.

Lugh uncrossed my arms and took a decidedly aggressive step in Brian's direction.

What the fuck do you think you're doing? I screamed at him, but he ignored me.

"You selfish little bastard," Lugh said through my mouth, glaring at Brian. "All this time you've hounded Morgan to open up to you, to trust you not to hurt her. Then the moment she says something you don't like, you slam the emotional door in her face."

Some of the color left Brian's face. I guess he was finally figuring out it wasn't me who was speaking anymore. "Lugh?" he asked tentatively.

Lugh didn't bother to answer. "Have you given even a moment's thought as to what you're asking her to give up?" he asked, poking Brian in the breastbone hard enough to make Brian take a step back.

"With me in residence, she has all the advantages of being a demon host. She will never get sick—except for these unexplained illnesses that happen with control changes. She can heal any injury short of a mortal wound, and even some of them. If anyone ever attacks her, I can protect her. And I can help her cope with some of the horrors she's faced. Someone else who's been through everything she's been through might suffer from posttraumatic stress for the rest of her life, but because of me, Morgan won't. All this she gains, without having to give up control of her body and her life. And you think she should throw it all away just because I make you uncomfortable?"

Brian was rarely at a loss for words—something of a survival trait for lawyers—but he was struck speechless now. He stood there in the kitchen doorway, gaping at Lugh and absently rubbing the spot on his chest that Lugh had poked. I wondered if it would leave a bruise.

But Brian wasn't speechless for long. I could see him pulling the shreds of his composure back together. His shoulders straightened and his chin rose, the lines in his jaw showing how tightly his teeth were clenched. He leaned ever so slightly forward, into Lugh's personal space, and if it were anyone but Brian, I would have suspected he was seriously considering throwing a punch.

"You think you're the best thing that ever happened to her, huh?" Brian asked, and there was no missing the fury in his voice. "Because of you, she was almost burned at the stake. Because of you, I was kidnapped and tortured. Because of you, her father is dead. And none of this is going to stop until you're out of our lives once and for all. So don't give me all this self-righteous bullshit when we both know all you really want is to get into her pants."

Internally, I winced. I'd seen Brian angry before, but not like this. Not almost-out-of-control angry.

He's angry because he knows I'm right, and he doesn't like it, Lugh said, his mental voice sounding much calmer than he was making my own voice sound out loud.

"Don't forget, I'm just as happy to get into *your* pants as hers," Lugh said, twisting my lips into a nasty smile.

Brian's face, already red with anger, turned almost crimson, and both fists clenched at his sides. Lugh folded his arms across his chest...that is, folded *my* arms across *my* chest. "Go ahead and hit me if it will make you feel better," Lugh said. "I won't let Morgan feel it."

And, for reasons I didn't even begin to understand, Brian's shoulders suddenly sagged, and the anger drained from his face.

"Jesus Christ," Brian said, scrubbing at his hair with both hands—trying to find an outlet for all that rage, I suppose.

"I've told Morgan this many times," Lugh said, his

voice now much softer. "You and I are not in competition. She loves you, Brian. You have no idea how much power that gives you over her, or how terrified she is of that power. I've helped her manage that fear, you know I have. I'm not your competition, and I'm certainly not your enemy."

Brian looked defeated. "I know that, I guess. I just..." He shrugged.

I felt one corner of my mouth lift in a wry smile. "You just want some evidence that if she had to choose between you and me, she'd choose you."

Brian laughed, but it was a nervous sound. "It sounds so childish when you put it that way."

It is! I wanted to yell at him. Probably just as well Lugh was in control at the moment.

Lugh reached out with my hand and cupped Brian's cheek tenderly. Brian jumped at the touch, clearly not sure what to do. It was, after all, *my* hand. I just didn't happen to be the one controlling it.

"It's you that Morgan loves," Lugh said, his fingers—*my* fingers—tracing a line down the side of Brian's face. "Don't back her into a corner to make her prove it. Some things are meant to be taken on faith."

Brian shied away from Lugh's touch, but there didn't seem to be any real rancor or distaste in the gesture. "You've made your point. Now will you put Morgan back in control?"

Lugh sighed. "I will if you promise to drop the argument and nurse us back to health."

Brian almost smiled at that, but not quite.

I tried to brace myself as Lugh faded into the background and put me back in the driver's seat, but the headache still slammed into the back of my eyes like a semi truck. I groaned and let myself sag into Brian's waiting arms.

fifteen

I WAS NOT A HAPPY CAMPER. WHEN LUGH AND I change control too often, I invariably get sick to my stomach and am gifted with a raging headache. The closer together the control changes are, the worse my symptoms. Twice in two days was very definitely too much, and I felt like an industrious blacksmith had taken up residence in my skull.

I felt too lousy to continue my deep discussion with Brian, or even to complain about Lugh taking over like that. Brian didn't seem much inclined to continue the conversation, either. He sent me off to my bedroom to hide in the comforting semidarkness as I waited for the aftereffects to go away. If previous experience was any guide, I'd feel better in a few hours as long as Lugh didn't take control again. If he did, I was in for at least three days of misery.

Brian brought me some aspirin and a glass of water. I took them even though I knew they wouldn't help. My head throbbed steadily, and I hoped that, miraculously, this time the aspirin would work.

True to his word, Brian spent the rest of the afternoon with me. We didn't talk much—it was hard to be coherent when my head hurt so badly—but I did find his presence strangely comforting. I spent the entire time lying in my bed with my eyes closed, willing the pain to go away. Brian tried to distract me with a back rub that would have felt heavenly under other circumstances.

I guess I must have drifted off to sleep despite the pounding in my head, because time seemed to pass without all the hours of the day being accounted for. One moment, I was curled into a little ball of misery with my pillow over my head, as if that could somehow keep the pain from getting to me. The next, I was listening to a ringing phone and deciding to let my answering machine get it. I had no idea I'd fallen asleep until Brian came in and sat on the side of the bed.

"Adam and Raphael are on their way up," he said, keeping his voice low in respect for my headache. "They said you were expecting them."

I groaned and rolled over, lifting the pillow off my head and squinting at Brian as if there were a bright light shining in my eyes. "I'm not expecting them until six," I said, then made to hide under the pillow again.

"Morgan, it's ten after six."

I let out a little squeak of alarm, sitting up so fast it made my head throb even worse. I glanced at the bedside clock, even though I knew Brian wouldn't be playing games with me when I wasn't feeling well. Sure enough, it was after six.

"Shit," I said, with feeling.

Brian frowned at me. "Should I have told them to go away?"

I started to shake my head, then thought better of it. "No. Besides, they'd have come up anyway." Adam's badge worked like an all-access pass to my apartment when he wanted it to. It was probably illegal to use the badge under false pretenses, but Adam wasn't about to sweat legalities.

"Can you go let them in while I get dressed?" I'd taken off my top and bra so Brian could get his hands on bare skin while he massaged me.

"Sure," he said, but I caught the quick little glance he gave my bare breasts. It almost made me smile.

I took my time getting dressed. I wasn't thrilled with the idea of leaving Brian in Adam and Raphael's company for very long, but whenever I tried to move too fast, the pain in my head spiked.

Eventually, I made my way out into the living room. The guys had been arguing about something, but they all shut up the moment I stepped into the room. Brian was sitting on the couch, looking pissed off again. Adam was sitting on the arm of the couch, looking neutral. And Raphael was sprawled on the love seat, looking smugly amused.

I remembered belatedly that I was planning to chew Raphael a new one, but it was hard to build up a head of steam when I felt so lousy. It also occurred to me that I might not be in the best shape to join this interrogation squad, but there was no way in hell I was letting Adam and Raphael do it without supervision. Never mind that they would ignore my "supervision" whenever they found it convenient.

"You up to this?" Adam asked, right on cue. I didn't want to know what Brian had told them about why I was sick.

I held my head a little higher, squaring my shoulders. "No, but let's do it anyway." Adam and Raphael stood up, but I wasn't ready to get going yet. "Before we leave, I want to know what the plan is, both for this demon and for his host."

Adam and Raphael shared a glance, then turned nearly identically bland faces toward me.

"Our choices are somewhat limited," Adam said. I guess he'd appointed himself the spokesperson.

"Then let me make this abundantly clear to both of you," I said, mustering every scrap of authority I could find. "We are *not* killing anyone tonight. And you," I continued, pointing at Raphael, "are not going back later to kill anybody."

Raphael raised a single eyebrow. "I'm not?" I glared at him, but he met my gaze steadily and without flinching. "And how, exactly, are you planning to stop me?"

He had me stumped there. If I could count on Lugh to back me up, I'd have had at least some hope of making Raphael toe the line. But if Lugh had condoned Bradley Cooper's murder, there was no reason to assume he wouldn't condone the murder of Jonathan Foreman, the illegal recruitment czar, too. I put my fingers to my temples and tried to massage away the damned headache. I had enough deaths on my conscience! I didn't know if I could stand any more.

"If we can find a way around killing anyone," Adam said, "we will." I wasn't sure if he could legitimately speak for Raphael, but I was pretty sure he was telling the truth. I was also pretty sure he'd already determined there was no way around it.

"Remember, Dougal's the one with total disregard for human life," Brian said, putting his arm around my shoulders in solidarity. "We're supposed to be better than that."

Raphael gave Brian a contemptuous glance. "What would you have us do? Reveal ourselves as Lugh's supporters to a high-ranking demon under Dougal's control and then release him so he can destroy us?"

"You're going to exorcize the demon, aren't you?"

Raphael shrugged. "Probably."

"So he'll be back in the Demon Realm, where he can't hurt us. And his host is not our enemy."

Raphael looked even more contemptuous. "How the hell do we know that? There's every chance he volunteered for the job, just like Cooper. A human bearing tales is just as dangerous to us as a demon. Maybe even more so, since he can accuse us of various crimes. You know the human courts would take his side if at all possible."

Brian looked uncomfortable and frustrated. I knew how he felt. It was hard to feel like the angels were on your side when you were contemplating murder. But it was hard to argue Raphael's logic. As far as I could tell, there was no moral high ground to be found.

My head pounded steadily, and I pinched the bridge

of my nose. "Let it go, Brian," I said. "You're not going to win these guys over. They'll do whatever they think is necessary, and they don't give a rat's ass what we think about it." I looked back and forth between Adam and Raphael. "Does that about sum it up?"

Raphael flashed a sardonic grin. "Yeah, that sounds about right."

Adam didn't look as happy about it, but he still nodded.

"Enough talk," Raphael decided. "Adam and I are going to go question Mr. Foreman. Morgan, you can come with us or not; it's your choice. But don't fool yourself into thinking you can stop us from doing whatever needs to be done."

"I'm coming," I said with a resigned sigh. Brian opened his mouth—I think to say he was coming with us, even though we hadn't invited him. I silenced him with a quick kiss.

"Will you wait for me?" I asked, desperately wanting him to say he would. I had a feeling when this little field trip was over, I was going to need his loving arms around me.

"Do you want me to?"

I put my arms around him and hugged him fiercely. "Yes, I want you to."

His hug was more tentative than mine. "Then I suppose I'll wait. But be careful, okay?"

Head still pounding, stomach still giving the occasional lurch, I pulled away from Brian's arms and nodded.

Jonathan Foreman lived in South Philly in an over-whelmingly Italian neighborhood, which consisted of one cookie-cutter row house after another, differentiated only by the trim. Some had painted brick, some had plain brick; some had shutters, some didn't; and a couple actually had window boxes with flowers in them, though those were only on second- or third-story windows. Growing up, I've learned from my parents' experiences that if you planted anything within reach of the street, someone would eventually dig it up and take it as a souvenir. Ah, the joys of living in the big city!

Even postage-stamp-sized backyards are almost nonexistent in the city proper, so the only approach to Foreman's house was from his front door. Adam knocked on the door while Raphael and I stood on the stoop a couple of steps below him. It was a rare city dweller who would open the door for an unknown and unexpected visitor, but since Foreman was a legal, registered demon host, we figured he might not be as cautious as us mere humans tended to be. Of course, he might also recognize Adam's face—being the Director of Special Forces meant that Adam occasionally made the local news—and that could make him cautious anyway.

We waited breathlessly to see what Foreman would do—assuming he was even home. He could even now be out hunting the city streets for another "expendable" human being who could be coerced into hosting a demon.

I didn't hear any sound of movement from behind the door, but Adam must have heard something, because his posture stiffened ever so slightly. I expected someone to open the door, or tell us to go away, but nothing happened.

Raphael climbed the last step, I guess in case Adam needed help breaking down the door. Whatever the reason, it was a damn good thing he did, because the next thing I heard was a loud bang, like the sound of a car backfiring. Raphael apparently heard something before that, because he shoved Adam out of the way just in time to avoid the bullet that punched a hole in the door.

Raphael cried out in pain and doubled over, clutching his gut. Adam did an involuntary backflip over the railing that bordered the landing. He went down hard on the pavement below, but it was no doubt better than being shot.

Without needing anyone to tell me, I vaulted over the railing myself and pressed my back against the stoop, which gave me some semblance of cover. The door to the house burst open, and a fist smashed into Raphael's face, sending him tumbling to the bottom of the steps. He left a brilliant trail of blood in his wake.

Compared to demons, I move practically in slow motion. I was fumbling through my purse, trying to find my Taser, as someone—Foreman, I presumed—barreled down the steps, gun in hand, and took off running down the street. Adam, apparently not hurt by his fall, drew his gun and dashed off in pursuit. They were both out of range before my hand closed on the Taser.

People around us had noticed the commotion—and the guns—but no one seemed to be panicking. I could see the people driving down the street glancing out the window at the action, but they kept driving, and the pedestrians—most of them, anyway—just changed directions and walked hurriedly the other way. And they call Philadelphia the "City of Brotherly Love." Yeah, right.

A gum-cracking teenaged girl called 911 on her cell phone while she stared, wide-eyed, at the trail of blood Raphael had left on the steps. I was way too shaken up to walk, so I crawled over to where he lay on the sidewalk, his arms wrapped around his belly, his body curled around itself. He was making little moaning sounds as if he were in dire pain, but when I got close enough, he made eye contact and I could see he was fine.

You see, Tommy Brewster isn't just any old demon host. He was a product of Raphael and Dougal's genetic experiments, and he healed even more quickly than normal demons. In fact, I'd seen Dick—Saul's current host, who was from the same "batch" as Tommy—get shot in the head twice and barely pause long enough to blink. Of course, the general population doesn't know about the experiments, or the superhosts those experiments produced. And it's probably better that way.

The teenaged girl was the only pedestrian to make any move to help us in the heat of the moment, but now that it seemed like the shooting was over, we were beginning to draw a crowd. No one seemed to want to get

too close—like they were afraid getting shot was contagious—but it was far more attention than I was comfortable with. I don't know if the bullet Raphael had taken
would have killed a normal host, but it certainly would
have hurt one very badly.

The teenager closed her phone, though not before
surreptitiously snapping a photo. Camera phones have
to be the devil's own invention.

"An ambulance is coming," she said, leaning over
Raphael to get a better look. "Is he gonna die?"

I wanted to tell her to back off, but she *had* called an
ambulance, which made her into something like a
Good Samaritan. I try not to bite the heads off Good
Samaritans even when my head hurts like a son of a
bitch and I have problems up the wazoo.

"He'll be all right," I said. "He's a demon."

The girl's eyes widened. She made the sign of the
cross, then backed away hastily. I think she was regretting calling the ambulance. I guess when you're in a
heavily Italian neighborhood, you have to expect a lot of
Catholics, and the Catholic church would never accept
demons as the good guys.

Raphael started sitting up, and now it wasn't only
the girl taking a step back. I bit my lip, wondering
where Adam was. I couldn't figure out whether I hoped
he'd caught Foreman or not. At least I hadn't heard any
more gunshots.

"Should you be sitting up yet?" I asked Raphael. It
was just beginning to dawn on me that Raphael had
maybe saved Adam's life and had taken a bullet for his

efforts. I couldn't quite wrap my brain around the concept.

"I'm fine," he said, one arm still pressed tightly to his abdomen. "It's just a flesh wound." He managed something that passed for a sickly grin, but I suspect the wound had healed completely already.

I looked at the blood that soaked his shirt and that trailed down the steps. The evidence pointed to far more than a flesh wound. And in broad daylight, with witnesses surrounding us and an ambulance and police on the way, there was no way we could hide anything.

Sirens wailed in the distance, and I would have loved to flee. The police had seen far too much of me since Lugh had come into my life, and my being at the site of yet another violent crime was not going to help my less-than-squeaky-clean image. Where the hell was Adam? I wasn't doing *his* reputation much good, either, since he'd been forced to extricate me from a number of delicate situations, but I really hated the idea of talking to the police without him present.

My silent prayers went unanswered, and the emergency vehicles converged before Adam put in an appearance.

sixteen

I DIDN'T MAKE ANY NEW FRIENDS IN THE POLICE DE-
partment that night.

Despite his showy wound, Raphael managed to
avoid being shuffled off to the hospital. He wouldn't
even let the EMTs take a quick look—probably because
the wound was already gone, and even a demon should
still have some sign of injury left. I have no idea what
they would have made of the nonexistent wound, and I
was just as happy not to find out.

While Raphael was arguing with the EMTs, one of
the officers who'd arrived on the scene took me aside to
get my statement. That's when I started making a nui-
sance of myself.

Obviously, I couldn't explain to the police exactly
what I was doing here, nor could I offer any theories on
why Jonathan Foreman had shot at us. But I'm a lousy
liar in the best of times, and with that blacksmith still
hammering away at my skull, I just didn't have the...
creativity to come up with a plausible explanation. Just
as well, because Raphael's story and mine wouldn't gel,
seeing as we hadn't had a chance to consult with each
other. So I decided to tell the nice policeman the facts,

and only the facts. Adam knocked on the door. Raphael pushed him out of the way, getting shot in the process. And someone, presumably Foreman, had taken off with Adam in hot pursuit.

I refused to say what the three of us were doing on Foreman's doorstep. I can't imagine how many red flags my refusal set to waving, but I figured if I couldn't come up with a plausible story, I was better off saying nothing. I hoped Raphael was doing the same, even though he could probably come up with three plausible-sounding stories without breaking a sweat.

Things were getting pretty tense, and I was afraid they were about to arrest me—for what, I'm not sure— when Adam finally sauntered back onto the scene. Okay, he wasn't really *sauntering*, but he couldn't possibly move fast enough to satisfy me. I hadn't exactly been watching the time, but it felt like approximately forever since he'd run off after Jonathan Foreman, and I couldn't imagine what had taken so long. With their demon-enhanced endurance, the two of them could have run to New Jersey and back in the time Adam had been gone!

The cops turned their attention to Adam, who I suppose they felt was a more reliable witness than Raphael and me. We were told in no uncertain terms, however, that we were not to leave the scene. We sat together on the steps—careful to avoid the blood—and didn't speak to each other. I think we both noticed the cop who was "nonchalantly" hanging out within hearing distance, no doubt hoping he'd get to overhear the real story. He clearly wasn't cut out for undercover work, though he tried to keep up the illusion that he was busy.

I was overflowing with questions myself by now, but I knew I wasn't getting answers anytime soon.

What had happened to Jonathan Foreman? Why had he shot at us? He couldn't possibly know we were after him, could he? And what story was Adam telling his fellow officers that would explain this mess away?

Raphael and I sat in silence for the better part of an hour as twilight fell, then faded to full dark. He kept one arm pressed against his midsection, where the bullet wound should have been, the whole time. Me, I'd have forgotten about it and flashed the healed skin as soon as my concentration waned. Of course, if you're going to be any good at lying—and Raphael was a master—you've got to learn to stick to your cover story.

Finally, the police were done with Adam. They had some stern words for me and Raphael, but said we could go home. Hallelujah!

We'd driven to Foreman's place in Adam's unmarked, which was parked around the block. By unspoken agreement, none of us spoke until we were in the car and on our way. I doubt anyone could possibly have overheard us, but you can never be too careful. Raphael even kept up the injured act until he was safely sprawled in the backseat.

"What happened to Foreman?" I asked, as soon as my paranoia thought it was safe to speak.

"If all went well, he'll be at my place right about now," Adam said.

I swallowed a laugh. All had most definitely not

gone well! "How the hell did he get to your place? Assuming he did."

"I caught up with him a few blocks from here. I
Tasered him, then called Dom and Saul to come pick
him up. That's why it took me so long to get back to the
crime scene—I had to wait for them to show up."

Raphael stirred in the backseat. "You left him with
only Dominic and Saul as guards?" He didn't sound
happy.

Adam glanced at him in the rearview mirror. "I
didn't have a lot of options. But they've both got Tasers,
and they're not idiots. They'll keep him contained."

"If you get my son killed, I'll eat your liver," Raphael
said, his voice as calm as if he'd said "I think it's going
to rain tomorrow." Saul might despise Raphael, but
Raphael didn't seem to hold that against him.

I could see Adam's hands tighten briefly on the
steering wheel, and it occurred to me that with someone like Raphael, that threat might have been meant literally. I fought to suppress a shudder.

"What did you tell the police?" I asked Adam, figuring now was a good time to change the subject.

"I kept it pretty vague and mostly stuck to the truth.
I told them we'd stopped by to talk to Foreman on a personal matter, and that none of the three of us had ever
met him in person. Then I told them what happened—
though of course I told them Foreman got away after I
fired my Taser at him and missed."

"And they were satisfied with that?" I asked with a
raised eyebrow.

"No, of course not. I had no good explanation for why a complete stranger would shoot at us when we came to the door. And they didn't much like me not telling them why we were coming to see Foreman. But there's no law that says I have to tell them, so I didn't. My lack of cooperation isn't going to go down well with the brass, especially so soon after I 'lost' my Taser, but what else could I do, especially when I didn't know what the two of you might have said?"

Raphael made a disdainful noise in the backseat. "We were smart enough to keep our mouths shut even without having you there to advise us."

Adam gave him a dirty look in the rearview mirror, but didn't otherwise comment. I had a feeling "the brass" was going to be giving Adam more than just a hard time about this. He hadn't exactly been flying under the radar lately, and his involvement with me and all of my troubles had put him on the hot seat before. Still, that was his problem. I had enough problems of my own to worry about.

We were silent until we came to the next red light, at which point Adam looked at Raphael over his shoulder.

"Why did you push me out of the way?"

"I heard—"

"A gun being cocked. Yeah, I heard that, too, about half a second too late. I didn't ask how you knew Foreman was going to take a shot at us. I asked why you took the bullet for me."

The light turned green, and despite the weighty question, Adam turned to face front and kept driving. I

kept an eye on Raphael, who was looking out the side
window, his expression thoughtful.

"Because I could survive even a gunshot wound to
the head," he finally answered. "You couldn't." He
turned his head, meeting Adam's eyes in the rearview
mirror. "If I'd known it would be a gut shot, I'd have
been more than happy to let you take it."

Adam made a soft snorting sound. Then, after a
brief hesitation, he said, "Thank you." I don't think the
words came easily.

Raphael's only answer was a silent shrug.

We didn't speak for the remainder of the ride back
to Adam's house. Adam's posture eased somewhat
when we pulled into the tiny private lot across the
street. I guess he was happy to see Dom's car, though
just because the car was there didn't mean Saul and
Dom were safe.

Still giving each other the silent treatment, we
trooped into Adam's house, heading immediately for
the stairs to the second floor. We all knew where Saul
and Dominic would be keeping our prisoner. It would
be far from the first time that room had been used for
an interrogation.

The Dreaded Black Room loomed at the head of the
stairs and, as always, I felt a flutter of fear in my stomach when we approached it. It was in that room that
Adam had interrogated and then murdered the woman
I'd once believed to be my best friend. It was also in that
room that Adam had whipped me bloody for his own
amusement. Nothing good ever came of setting foot inside its confines, but here I was yet again.

I call it the Black Room because everything in it is black. The floor is gleaming black tile. The walls and ceiling are painted a light-absorbing matte black. A massive black iron bed, draped with black silk covers, dominates one end of the room. And one wall is dotted with black pegs, each of which holds a coiled whip, illuminated by the track lighting above.

Jonathan Foreman sat in the far corner of the room, his back against the wall, his knees gathered up to his chest. Foreman was better-looking than Cooper, but he still wasn't the pinnacle of perfection that used to be required for a Spirit Society member to host a demon. He was kind of pudgy and soft-looking, and his nose was too big for his face. I doubted he was more than twenty-five years old, but he had a severe case of male pattern baldness that made him look middle-aged at first glance.

He looked up when Adam and Raphael and I entered the room, but he made no aggressive moves. Possibly because both Saul and Dominic had Tasers trained on him and he knew it would be pointless. There was a little too much white showing around his eyes, and even at a distance, I could see his chest rising and falling too fast as he panted. He hugged his knees more tightly to his chest and pushed himself more firmly into the corner. Call me crazy, but he didn't seem much like a shoot first, ask questions later kind of guy.

Adam turned to Raphael. "You're going to let me handle this, right? Because if you're planning to Taser me the moment my back is turned, I'd just as soon leave."

Raphael grinned, apparently enjoying the memory of one of his more badass moments. We'd been interrogating a demon, and we all knew Adam was planning to torture him if he didn't talk of his own free will. But Raphael came up with his own plan, which was to Taser Adam so he wouldn't interfere, then douse the demon with gasoline and threaten to light him. The demon had started talking real, real fast.

"This one's all yours," Raphael said. "Unless it turns out you need help."

Adam gave him a long stare, then turned his attention to Foreman. Foreman cringed slightly, reminding me of the pathetic Mary. *This* was the ringleader for the illegal recruitment campaign? I'd have said Cooper was lying to us, but since Adam had plucked the information straight from his mind, that wasn't possible.

Adam stalked closer to Foreman, his eyes glowing slightly with demonic light, his body lithe and predatory. Foreman swallowed hard and looked like he might pass out. Adam stopped just out of reach, looming over what looked like one very frightened demon.

"Care to tell me why you tried to shoot me?" he asked. His voice wasn't particularly sharp or loud, but he still managed to make the question drip with menace.

Foreman swallowed hard again. "I thought you were coming to arrest me," he said. His voice was thin and whispery, but at least it didn't shake.

Adam cocked his head. "Why would you think that?"

"You're Adam White," Foreman said. "I recognize

you from TV. They said they'd report me as a rogue if I didn't cooperate. When I saw you at the door, I figured I hadn't cooperated enough."

Adam had only asked two questions, and already Foreman had raised about a million more with his answers. I had to bite my tongue to keep from butting in. Patience has never been my strong suit. But Adam did this kind of thing for a living, so I figured he'd do a better job than I would at picking the right questions to ask.

"Who are 'they'?" Adam asked.

Foreman hugged his knees tighter. "If I tell you, will you protect me from them?"

"You say 'if' as though you think you have a choice."

"They'll kill me," Foreman said, shaking his head. "I don't mean they'll just kill my host, they'll kill *me*."

"Would it be more to your liking if *we* killed you instead?" Raphael asked. We all should have known better than to expect him to keep quiet.

Dominic and Saul were still standing guard, though Dom had lowered his Taser to his side. I could hardly blame him—I couldn't imagine Foreman making a break for it.

Adam glanced at Saul. Some kind of silent communication must have passed between them, because Saul suddenly grinned and turned his Taser toward Raphael.

"You said you'd let Adam handle this," Saul said. "I suggest you keep your word. You have no idea how much I want to shoot you."

Raphael crossed his arms over his chest and leaned against the wall as if it didn't bother him in the least that his own son was threatening to Taser him. I knew it *did* bother him—I'd been around him too long not to know that—but he sure didn't let it show on his face. He feigned a bored look and kept his mouth shut.

Adam turned his attention back to Foreman. "I'm going to be brutally honest with you," he said. "I can't promise you protection. Not when I don't know who I'd be promising to protect you from. What I *can* promise you is that this will be a very long night for you if you don't start talking before I lose patience. So, tell me who you think is going to kill you."

There was a sheen of tears in Foreman's eyes, and if he'd been any more scared, he'd probably have wet his pants, but he started talking.

"The recruitment team I'm supposed to be running," Foreman said, looking at the floor instead of at Adam. "We've been picking up street people and, er, persuading them to summon demons."

This time *I* was the one who had trouble keeping my mouth shut, but I bit my tongue and resisted the urge to say something indignant.

"Now why would you be doing that?" Adam asked.

Foreman looked around as if hoping to find an ally in the room. He was out of luck. He seemed to shrink in on himself as flop sweat made dark circles under his arms.

"Answer the question!" Adam demanded.

Foreman squirmed. "Um..." He cleared his throat. "We're trying to shorten the waiting list for demons who want to walk the Mortal Plain. The Spirit Society has been recruiting hard, but they haven't been able to provide enough willing hosts. So we were trying to… make more hosts available."

"You do understand that that's against the law," Adam said in a suspiciously mild voice.

Foreman shuddered. "I know. But I didn't have much choice."

"Oh? I thought you said this was *your* recruitment team."

"No, I said it was *supposed* to be."

"Meaning what, exactly?"

"Meaning I'm not really running it. I'm just the stalking horse. Anyone who isn't one hundred percent trustworthy thinks I'm in charge. Only I'm not."

"So Bradley Cooper wasn't one hundred percent trustworthy?"

Foreman started at the mention of Cooper's name. "I wouldn't have expected him even to know *my* name. Humans, by definition, aren't trustworthy."

This time, I couldn't suppress my outrage. "Gee, could that be because you're pulling an Invasion of the Body Snatchers on us and trying to make us into your handy-dandy puppets?"

Adam made a growling sound from deep in his throat. "Shut up!" he snarled at me. "If one more person butts in, I'm going to kick you all out of the room."

Raphael snickered, and for once I got his humor. With three members of the royal family present, Adam wasn't kicking anyone out unless they wanted to go.

I shut up, but that didn't stop me from giving Foreman a death glare, which he ignored. I guess with Adam looming over him like that, the rest of us didn't seem all that threatening.

"So if you're not really in charge, who is?"

Foreman took a deep breath and let it out slowly before he answered. "His name is Julius. He's not a royal, but he's definitely of the elite. And his host was a football player in college. He's about three hundred pounds of pure muscle."

Adam shrugged. "It doesn't matter how big he is. A Taser will stop him like anyone else."

"You'd have to find him first. He didn't trust me anymore, so I'm sure he's been having me watched. Now that I've been captured, he'll assume I've told you everything I know and will take evasive action. That was the whole point of making me the leader in name only. Besides, even if you could track him down, stopping Julius won't do you any good."

Adam raised an eyebrow. "Why not? Generally, when you chop off the head, the monster dies."

I wouldn't have thought it possible, but suddenly Foreman looked even more scared. His thinning hair was plastered to his scalp by sweat, and his eyes were practically bugging out of his head. Call it a hunch, but I think he was regretting his last words.

Adam nodded in understanding, though Foreman hadn't answered him. "Julius isn't really the head, is he?"

Foreman closed his eyes and shook his head.

"Dougal's the one who's really in charge," Adam said. He hadn't made it a question, but Foreman nodded anyway.

"If you manage to track down Julius and take him out, Dougal will just send someone else. He's gotten so many people sucked into..." Foreman's voice died, and he stared at the floor.

"Sucked into his conspiracy to take the throne," Adam finished for him.

Foreman flinched, but again he nodded. "The only way to stop it," he said softly, "is to stop Dougal. And the only way to stop Dougal is to kill him."

Adam cast a quick glance back at the rest of us. "It's on our to-do list. But you're working with Dougal, so why do you sound like you think killing him would be a good thing?"

Foreman rubbed his eyes, wiping away some tears. "Because he lied to me. He lied to a lot of people. I supported him in the beginning, but I didn't know he actually planned to kill the king. I just thought he was taking advantage of Lugh's absence to arrange things more to his liking. He tricked me into throwing in with him until I was in too deep to back out."

Adam suddenly looked a lot more...intense. "He lied to you personally, you mean. You're not just some peon."

Foreman blew out a breath. "I am now. But yes, I know Dougal. At least, I thought I did. I used to consider him my friend. But his only true friend right now is his ambition, and he's making that more and more clear as the water gets hotter."

"What do you mean, 'as the water gets hotter'?"

Bitterness and anger did wonders to calm Foreman's fear. "Dougal never made any contingency plans for what he would do if the coup failed—or at least didn't succeed on his first attempt. He made a lot of promises to a lot of people, but without the power of the throne behind him, he can't keep them."

"What kind of promises are we talking about?"

Foreman grimaced. "He promised a lot of people that we would move them to the front of the waiting list to go to the Mortal Plain, for one thing. That's how he got Alexander to throw in with him."

Adam's face registered shock. "He has a *council member* in his pocket?"

"He did," Foreman agreed.

Lugh let out a quiet sigh. *Remember when I decided to form my council on the Mortal Plain? I told you I feared some of my official council members would side with Dougal. Apparently, I was right.*

"But Alexander got cold feet a few weeks back," Foreman continued. "He insisted Dougal let him leave for the Mortal Plain, or he'd take the conspiracy public. Dougal had no choice but to let him go, but without Alexander, he can't get the council to vote his way all the time anymore."

"And that's making the rest of his coconspirators nervous," Adam said.

"Yeah. It was bad enough when Raphael betrayed him, but Alexander's defection could turn out to be the last straw if Dougal isn't careful. That's why he sent some of us to the Mortal Plain to try to find more hosts so he can make the waiting list shorter. He hopes it'll appease some of his supporters for a little while. I don't know how well that's working for him."

Adam chewed that over for a minute, looking puzzled. "We talked to one of those newly arrived demons the other day."

"I know."

I think we all must have been wearing our thoughts on our faces, because Foreman paled and held up his hands as if to ward off a blow.

"I didn't have anything to do with what happened to her!" he said in a voice tight with fear. "That was Julius. He said he needed to discourage the others from talking too much."

Adam gave him a look of disgust, but soldiered on. "She said she was a prisoner. She was freed and then told to jump the line."

Foreman nodded. "That was another promise Dougal made, to free some prisoners who were friends and family of his supporters. But once Alexander left and the council started being difficult, Dougal couldn't show such blatant favoritism without being blocked. So he pardoned a bunch of jumpers who'd served at least half their sentences, using them as camouflage for the ones he'd promised to free."

Adam decided to stop looming and sat on the floor facing Foreman. I guess he was trying to develop some kind of rapport.

"What's your name?" Adam asked. "I mean *your* name, not your host's name."

Foreman stared at his hands. "William."

Both Raphael and Saul started, and I realized they knew him.

"William?" Adam repeated, sounding somewhere between surprised and appalled.

William nodded. "Yes, *that* William."

"Shit!" Adam said, with feeling, and I couldn't keep my mouth shut anymore. The curiosity was killing me.

"Who the hell is William? And why are you all so upset?" I asked.

William looked up at me and frowned. "How can you not know who I am?" he asked, and I realized he'd made the natural assumption that everyone here was a demon. Apparently, any demon should have recognized the name.

"Not everyone in this room is possessed," I answered.

William gaped at Adam. "You've brought *humans* into this?"

"The humans have the biggest stake of us all in what happens, so yes. And believe me, I don't require your approval."

"Is someone going to answer my question?" I asked. *Care to give me a hint, Lugh?* I added silently.

They'll tell you, and then Dominic can hear, too.

Adam was shaking his head. "He's one of the royal cousins." He turned his attention back to William. "That's why you tried to shoot me. You were afraid I'd arrest you and that no one would be able to exorcize you."

William nodded, his eyes going wide and his fists clenching in what I recognized as renewed terror.

"You said they threatened to report you. Why?"

William shuddered. "I raised too much of a fuss

when they killed that demon, Shae. I was a fool. Dougal had already shown me I had no way out anymore. I should have just kept my mouth shut."

Raphael pushed away from the wall and came to sit beside Adam, his legs crossed. Apparently Saul was too interested in what William had to say to remember he was supposed to Taser his father if he tried to interfere.

"There's always a way out," Raphael said, his voice soft and soothing. I blinked in surprise. Raphael flat-out didn't do soothing. "If you help me quell my brother's rebellion, I can promise you a royal pardon."

Everyone in the room gasped, and William's eyes went saucer-wide, this time with surprise, not fear.

"What are you doing?" Adam cried, looking at Raphael like he'd sprung a second head.

"Lugh?" William asked, and there was something very like reverence in his voice.

"In the flesh," Raphael answered with a gentle smile.

seventeen

WE WERE ALL SHOCKED SPEECHLESS. WHAT THE hell was Raphael up to *now*? I silently asked Lugh that question, and his response was *Your guess is as good as mine.*

It wasn't exactly the first time Raphael had veered

away from the official plan, but this was far more drastic than any of his previous deviations. I couldn't imagine where he was planning to go with it. I had a momentary temptation to argue with him, but I had little trouble squelching it. Whatever Raphael was up to, he'd committed us all to that course of action when he'd opened his mouth. I heartily wished we hadn't brought him along.

"Now that we've been reunited, cousin," Raphael said, "tell me what you're doing on the Mortal Plain acting as my brother's stalking horse."

William shook himself, and it seemed to effectively disperse whatever clouds were in his mind. "How do I know that you're really Lugh?" he asked. "For all I know, you could be one of Dougal's people trying to hammer the final nail in my coffin."

Raphael smiled, and there was just a hint of condescension in his voice when he spoke. "If I were one of Dougal's people, the lid would already be firmly nailed shut. But you can examine my aura if you don't believe me. And I can examine yours at the same time."

Neither Saul nor Adam looked surprised at Raphael's offer, but Dominic and I shared a puzzled glance.

Our auras are too indistinct on the Mortal Plain for us to recognize each other with absolute confidence, Lugh explained. *Der Jäger's ability to distinguish auras on the Mortal Plain was part of what made him so extraordinary. But we can sense each others' power to some degree. William will know from Raphael's aura that he is one of the royal brothers. Dougal would be able to tell the two of us apart even on the Mortal Plain, but William will not.*

And can Raphael tell whether that's really William? I asked.

No. He'll know if he's truly one of the royal cousins, but he won't know for sure which one. I don't suppose it matters much one way or another.

Raphael reached out his hand, and William clasped it. The two of them closed their eyes and sat motionless for maybe thirty seconds. Then they opened their eyes at the same time and let their hands fall back to their sides.

William was not looking quite so frightened anymore, the expression on his face showing a cunning that had been missing before. "How do I know you're not Raphael? Or Dougal, for that matter?"

Raphael's eyebrows arched. "Do you think this interview would be quite so... civilized if I were Raphael?"

William's face paled, and he shook his head. I wondered if there was anyone in the Demon Realm other than Dougal who wasn't terrified of Raphael.

"And surely you don't believe Dougal would show his face on the Mortal Plain?"

William thought that over for a moment. "He might," he decided. "If he thought coming here would lure you out of hiding. There's only so long he can keep his supporters in line with threats and unfulfilled promises. He sent me to the Mortal Plain and painted a big target on my back because he was afraid I'd break ranks and report him to the council. Once Alexander backed out..." He shrugged. "I'm sure I'm not the only one who's started thinking about damage control. Dougal still has plenty of advocates on the council, but if his supporters start talking, even his strongest advocates might agree that it's prudent to appoint a new regent pending word from you that the allegations are false and Dougal is your choice."

Raphael's lips curved in a satisfied smile that looked like no expression I could ever imagine on Lugh's face. "He would find that ... most awkward, I imagine."

William snorted softly. "That's one way of putting it."

"I'm glad to hear that Dougal's road is not as smooth as we'd thought. We'd feared that he had time on his side, but it sounds like it's more on ours. Most heartening."

"I don't understand why this is so heartening," I said. "So what if Dougal loses his position as regent? He still has Lugh's True Name." I belatedly realized I should have said "your" True Name, not "Lugh's," but luckily William assumed the question had been meant for him.

"He can't do anything with Lugh's True Name unless he has someone on the Mortal Plain who's willing to do a summoning. He's already losing supporters now; he'll lose a lot more if he has to step down as regent."

"But surely he won't lose them all," I protested. "And all it takes is one or two loonies and Lugh is toast. Literally."

William acknowledged my point with a nod. "I make no claim that Lugh's troubles are over. Merely that Dougal's foothold is not as strong as it once was. The throne will not be secure until Dougal is dead."

"Dougal and all his followers," I said.

It was Raphael who answered me. "No, only Dougal has to die. Unless they have Dougal to put on the throne in my place, they have nothing to gain by attacking me. If Dougal's dead and they kill me, then the throne would go to Raphael. And no one wants that."

I narrowed my eyes at him. "Are you *sure* no one wants that? What about Raphael? Maybe he thinks the throne looks comfy." Okay, so maybe this wasn't the best time to stick pins in Raphael. Still, he was making me very uncomfortable right now, and I didn't understand why he was pretending to be Lugh.

Raphael met my eyes steadily. But then, he's never had any trouble lying to someone to their face. "Raphael can hardly be bothered to care for a single human host. Do you really think he's interested in caring for all of demonkind? There's a lot of power that comes with the throne, but there's a lot of responsibility as well."

He has a point, Lugh said in my mind. *I honestly can't imagine Raphael wanting the throne.*

I held up my hands in surrender. "Just thought I'd ask."

"Was Dougal right to suspect you?" Raphael asked William. "Would you support me above him?"

"I would be a fool not to say yes, even if I didn't mean it. But yes, I will support you. I swear to you I didn't know what Dougal had planned when I started helping him." He held his head up high. "I can't expect you to trust me under the circumstances, but I'll do whatever I can to earn that trust."

Raphael nodded sagely. "You can start by telling me a little more about this team of yours. Mary said she was supposed to report to a handler once a week, and that he might have jobs for her."

"Dougal's trying to make the best of a bad situation," William replied. "He figured if he was getting pressured to send all these demons to the Mortal Plain, he might as well use them." He looked up at Adam. "When he first started sending them, he was thinking small. You know, coerce some undesirables to risk their lives to take out some of Lugh's known supporters, like you. If they got themselves killed along the way, it wouldn't matter a bit to him. Knowing him, he probably grew that small idea into a bigger plan, but since he doesn't trust me anymore, I can't say for sure."

Up until recently, this "war" had been so covert that Lugh was convinced only Dougal's inner circle even knew it was going on. But it was beginning to sound like the conflict was mushrooming. If it came down to open warfare, what would happen to the human race? Nothing good, that's for sure.

Raphael stood up in one fluid, lithe movement. Adam did the same, though William wisely remained where he was.

"I need to consult with my council on the Mortal Plain," Raphael said. "I'm going to ask you to stay right where you are. If you make any attempt to escape, I'm afraid I'm going to have to kill you. It isn't something I want to do, but now that you know who's hosting me, you are far too dangerous to be allowed to go free. You're either with me or you're dead. Understand?"

The fear was back in William's eyes, and he nodded. "I understand. And I'm with you, I swear it."

"Only time will tell."

I'm pretty sure Raphael was the only one even marginally comfortable leaving William alone in that room, but that didn't stop the rest of us from following him out.

We didn't go far. We gathered in the hallway outside the Black Room and conversed in low, urgent voices. Dominic, Adam, Saul, and I all asked some version of "What the hell are you doing?" at approximately the same time. We didn't consciously coordinate our movements, but we ended up forming a semicircle around Raphael, with his back pressed to the wall. Hostility rode the air like a static charge, and I hoped a fight wasn't about to break out.

Raphael held up his hands for silence, and to my surprise, we all obeyed, though the tension ratcheted up another notch.

"I made an executive decision based on the information at hand," Raphael said. "If Dougal's back is to the wall as William suggests, then he'll be actively hunting for Lugh again." He looked at me. "Dougal and his agents might not be able to tell that you're possessed right now, but they do know you were Lugh's original host, which puts a target on your back."

I had a few choice words I wanted to share about that, but Raphael turned his attention to Adam and continued talking before I could interrupt.

"You're one of Lugh's most high-profile supporters on the Mortal Plain, and it would take only the smallest amount of poking around to find out you've been spending time with Morgan. That's makes you—and, by association, Dominic—a target, too." He stood up a little straighter. "But if Dougal and company believe they already know who's hosting Lugh..."

A metaphorical lightbulb turned on over my head. "You're taking a page from William's book. Making yourself into Lugh's stalking horse." Suspicious, nasty person that I am, I immediately noticed the convenient coincidence that the only person outside of Lugh's council who knew Raphael's true identity—Shae—was dead. Could it have been Raphael who killed her, rather than William's team? But no, surely Raphael hadn't foreseen that he would be impersonating Lugh.

He nodded. "Exactly."

"That's not the kind of decision you should have made on your own," Saul growled, and he looked mad enough to put his fist through the wall. Or through Raphael's head, for that matter.

Raphael laughed, but it wasn't a happy sound. "If you expect me to be a good little soldier and do what I'm told, then you're obviously suffering from severe delusions. Lugh might have been too noble to let me put myself in the line of fire, so I took the decision out of his hands." Raphael always made "noble" sound like a bad thing. Perhaps to him, it was.

"It's not too late to turn back," Adam said. "If we do away with William, then no one will be the wiser." He said that with such a patent disregard for both human and demon life that I winced.

"That would be foolish," Raphael countered. "You heard what William said. Dougal's starting to lose control. That means he'll be getting desperate. That makes him even more dangerous than before. And it could also give us some leverage."

"What do you mean?" I asked.

"All his troubles go away if Lugh dies. Our king is completely above the law, so even if everyone in the Demon Realm knew Dougal had murdered Lugh, there would be nothing they could do."

"That's a monumentally stupid method of government," Dominic muttered.

Raphael shook his head. "You don't understand. It isn't how we *choose* to run things. It just *is*. There is nothing on the Mortal Plain analogous to the power of the demon throne. No one can stand against it. Not for long, anyway."

"At least, not in the Demon Realm," Adam amended. "We'd have had Lugh back on the throne in no time if he'd been able to wield his power here on the Mortal Plain."

I sensed more bickering was about to ensue, so I intervened before it could get started. "So how does your claiming to be Lugh give us any leverage?" I asked Raphael.

"It helps us because, with his back against the wall, Dougal would do just about anything to eliminate Lugh as fast as possible." His lips curled into what could only be described as an evil smile. "Maybe even come to the Mortal Plain in person."

eighteen

THIS DISCUSSION WAS TOO BIG—AND TOO IMPORTANT—
to have in a hallway. So I called the remaining members of Lugh's council—Andy, Brian, and Barbie—to come join us for yet another meeting. We'd met more often in the last week than we had all of last month.

Of course, having a council meeting while William was around posed some logistical difficulties. Unless we decided we trusted him—which wasn't going to happen anytime soon—we couldn't leave him unguarded. There wasn't a lock in the world that could hold a demon, and the only thing that made the Dreaded Black Room even marginally safe was the fact that it had no windows. I suspect that was a home improvement Adam had made personally, because I don't think the house would have met building code as it was.

Of course, if William was seriously trying to escape, he could break through the wall. But he'd make a lot of noise doing it, so we'd probably be able to stop him.

In the end, we decided to assign Barbie and Andy to guard duty when they arrived. They were the two least likely to kick up a fuss about being left out of the council meeting, and, although no one said it out loud, the least likely to make a useful contribution—Barbie because she was a relative newcomer, and Andy because he could rarely be bothered to care.

Barbie put up a token protest, but I think it was more out of curiosity than anything else. Andy just shrugged and said, "Whatever." I wanted to grab him by the shoulders and shake him to make him snap out of his persistent funk. God help me, I think I was beginning to understand why Raphael found my brother so annoying. I took a deep breath and reminded myself that Andy wouldn't be this way if it weren't for Raphael's mistreatment. But for the first time, I found myself not entirely convinced. Raphael had told me once that Andy wasn't as strong as I was. Maybe he'd been right.

We stationed Barbie at the far end of the hall. That would give her ample time to get off a Taser shot if William should venture out of the room. We then stationed Andy at the base of the stairs. He'd have a clear shot as soon as the door opened, too. Between the two of them, surely one of them would hit him.

Adam slipped into the Black Room alone to inform William that he had no chance of escaping and to describe what Adam would do to him if he was caught trying. I was just as glad not to have to hear that.

I can't say that any of us felt completely secure with our demon prisoner upstairs, but it was as secure as we were going to get. When we were all gathered in Adam and Dom's living room, I turned to Raphael and said, "Spill."

He never much liked taking orders from anyone, especially from me, but he managed to contain his natural knee-jerk reaction and settled for giving me a dirty look before addressing the rest of the council.

"We all know we can't secure the throne for Lugh as long as Dougal lives," he said. "Dougal will be in really bad shape if he loses most of his supporters, and he'll be in even worse shape if the council makes him step down as regent. He'll want to avoid that at all costs, and if it happens, it'll make it much more difficult for him to get to Lugh. But it won't make it impossible. Even if Dougal is ground into the dust, if he can eliminate Lugh, all his troubles will be over."

"We know all this," Saul interrupted. "Quit grandstanding and get to the point."

Raphael gave him a bland look, though I'm sure Saul had been hoping to piss him off. "The point will make more sense when presented in context. No one here completely trusts me, so I'm going to give you my entire train of thought." Usually, when Raphael made some comment about the rest of us not trusting him, he managed to sound sulky, as though it were somehow unfair of us to suspect him of shady dealings, no matter how many terrible things he had done, or how many times he had lied. But this once, he treated it like a matter of fact, rather than an insult. It made me think marginally better of him.

"So," Raphael continued, "no matter how badly things go for Dougal in the Demon Realm, we still have to kill him. We've known that from the beginning, but we had to get him to the Mortal Plain to do it, and we all know he's not stupid or arrogant enough to put himself in harm's way.

"But if what William is telling us is true, Dougal is seriously feeling the heat. We might not feel safe with him still at large, but his life could become very difficult if his supporters turn on him. Hell, if enough of them turn on him to convince the official royal council that he tried to kill Lugh, he could find himself imprisoned." Raphael shuddered, and I didn't think it was entirely for dramatic effect. "Believe me, that's a fate worse than death in the Demon Realm."

"A fate you, yourself, deserve," Saul muttered under his breath, but no one would believe he hadn't meant Raphael to hear it.

Raphael's fists clenched at his sides, and his eyes closed. It seemed Saul's barb had hit its target. Raphael had said long ago that Lugh was such a stickler for the law that he would put Raphael in prison for his crimes even if Raphael was instrumental in putting him back on the throne.

Would you really put Raphael in prison? I asked Lugh silently.

We'll talk about it later. Tell Saul from me that if he makes one more comment that is not constructive, I will send him to replace Barbara on guard duty. Lugh's mental voice was thick with irritation. *We don't have time for his pettiness.*

Reluctantly, I relayed Lugh's message. Saul didn't know me as well as the others and still didn't quite appreciate what a terrible liar I am. The rest of the council would believe the words really came from Lugh, but Saul might not. He shot me a lethal glare.

"We *should* be talking about how to catch and stop this Julius character, not wasting time trying to unravel the knots in my sire's thinking. We don't need the distraction."

Raphael rolled his eyes. "William's right; Julius will have pulled up stakes and relocated by now. And it doesn't matter how many of Dougal's supporters we take out if Dougal is still alive and kicking."

Saul's face said the reasoning didn't convince him, but he refrained from arguing any more.

"Go on," I urged Raphael. "I'm anxious to hear where you're going with this, even if Saul isn't."

Raphael gave me a faint smile. "Right. So, my point was that Dougal might find himself in deep shit if he doesn't eliminate Lugh fast. Possibly deep enough shit that he'd risk coming to the Mortal Plain in person if he thought that was his best shot at eliminating Lugh."

"What exactly are you proposing?" I asked.

"I'm proposing we send our friend William back to the Demon Realm and let him stir up some trouble."

The rest of us all started talking at once, our voices blending into such a babble that I couldn't tell who was saying what, and I bet the others couldn't, either. Raphael held up his hand for silence, and surprisingly everyone, even Saul, obeyed.

"It's a risk," Raphael said into the sudden, tense silence. "I don't believe William's an innocent victim in all this, no matter what he's said. I think he's just a weakling who will change sides in a heartbeat if he feels he's found a stronger position. But I can promise to

issue him a royal pardon if he contacts Lugh's supporters in the Demon Realm and tells them Lugh unequivo-
cally does not approve of Dougal being his regent."

Adam shook his head. "Lugh's supporters will believe it. But then they probably believe it already. It's not
like William could bring any proof with him."

"Maybe not," Raphael agreed. "But if the rumor gets
around, it will turn up the heat even more, and make
Dougal even more desperate to get to Lugh. And don't
forget about all the demons Dougal's been sending to
the Mortal Plain. If he's got some kind of mysterious
plan in the works, we need to disrupt it as much as possible, as fast as possible."

It was my turn to toss out an objection. "You know as
well as the rest of us that William's just as likely to go
blabbing to Dougal that you're Lugh. And Dougal will
sic his minions on you."

"Like I said, it's a risk. But it's only really a risk to
me, not to Lugh. Besides, since I'm playing the king,
Lugh can give me William's True Name, so I can summon him back to the Mortal Plain at a moment's notice.
Which means I will have more power over him than
Dougal. And greater means to make him suffer. He'll
have to choose whether he'd rather cross Dougal or me.
With the right incentive, I'm betting he'll cross Dougal."

"It's a ridiculous plan," Saul said, his face set in such
a scowl it looked almost painful. "And I don't see how it
helps us. So what if we make Dougal more desperate? It
doesn't follow that he'd show his face on the Mortal

Plain. He'll just whip his supporters into even more of a frenzy."

"The thing is," Raphael said, "at some point, it's going to occur to Dougal that the one thing he can do to flush Lugh out of hiding in time to keep himself out of prison is to come to the Mortal Plain and set himself up as bait. He knows we have to kill him, and he knows we can't get to him in the Demon Realm. But if he can come here and lure Lugh into a trap, he might finally be able to secure the throne."

Saul waved his hand dismissively. "That's not a plan. It's just wishful thinking."

"I disagree," Raphael said, still calm and reasonable. "I've been involved in many a plot with my dear brother, and I know how his mind works." He turned to me, but he was looking right through me, his gaze and his words meant for Lugh. "You and I will never fully understand one another. But *Dougal,* I understand."

"And he understands *you,*" I countered, not waiting for Lugh's reaction. "Won't he see your handiwork in all of this and know it's a trap?"

Raphael shook his head. "He *thinks* he understands me, but he doesn't. If he truly understood me, he'd never have let me in on the conspiracy to kill Lugh in the first place. He knows I've betrayed him, but I'd stake my life that he still doesn't understand why. I'm sure he thinks I did it because I felt it was in my best interests. The idea that I might actually be loyal to Lugh would never occur to him."

"Me either," Saul mumbled, though again it was clear he meant Raphael to hear him.

Raphael turned to glare at his son, and he had that weird glow in his eyes that demons seemed to get when they were well and truly pissed.

Uh-oh, Lugh's voice whispered in my head.

"I've heard just about enough out of you, *son,*" Raphael said, and the frost in his voice made me shiver.

Saul leapt to his feet so fast he knocked his chair over. He never took it well when Raphael called him "son," which was no doubt why Raphael did it on a regular basis.

Raphael stayed seated, but the glow in his eyes brightened. "Get over yourself!" he growled. "Is berating me really so important that you feel it appropriate to disrupt a council meeting for it? We're talking about killing Dougal, preserving Lugh's life, and putting him back on the throne, and all you care to contribute is the occasional insult in hopes that one will wound me?"

Saul stopped dead in his tracks, his face reddening with something other than anger. I was impressed with Raphael's strategy. There was nothing that Saul could say now that wouldn't make him look like a selfish hothead who'd be more useful guarding our prisoner upstairs than participating in our meeting. He swallowed hard, his cheek muscles twitching as he ground his teeth. But he managed to tamp down his rage.

Saul righted his chair and dropped into it without another word.

"Do you really think this plan will work?" I asked Raphael, trying to get our meeting back to order.

Raphael blinked a couple of times, like he'd forgotten where he was for a moment. Then his eyes focused on me.

"I think it *might* work. Nothing even close to a guarantee. But don't you think a plan that *might* work is better than no plan at all?"

I had to admit he had a point—if William was telling us anything that resembled the truth. "How confident are you that Dougal really is feeling the heat?" I asked. "If we're not sure we believe the rest of William's story, why should we believe that?"

"I'm pretty confident that he's telling the truth about Dougal's difficulties. People—both demon and human—are more apt to support a winner, and I'd say Dougal is looking less and less like a winner as time goes on."

"Since you were part of Dougal's inner circle once," Adam said, "you know a lot of the players involved, right?"

Raphael nodded. "Indeed. And I see where Alexander's defection would make them very uneasy. There are a handful who are as loyal to Dougal as we are to Lugh. But there are more than a handful of opportunists like William. And, apparently, Alexander. I would have pegged him as one of the loyal handful, but I guess I was mistaken." He turned toward me. "I believe William's story, and I believe Dougal's troubles give us a legitimate chance to lure him to the Mortal Plain. But it's up to Lugh to decide whether he thinks it's worth a shot."

"One question before we make a decision," I said.

"What are we going to do with William if we don't want to try Raphael's plan?"

The silence in the room was deafening, and suddenly no one wanted to meet my gaze. It didn't take a rocket scientist to figure out what that meant.

"We're going to kill him," I said, my voice barely a whisper. I'd been involved in a peripheral manner with the death by fire of several demons now, but each time it happened it was because someone—either Raphael, or Lugh, or, most recently, the state of Pennsylvania—had taken the decision out of my hands. I wasn't sure I had what it took to participate, or even look the other way, if I had a choice.

Raphael broke the silence. "If we don't have a use for him, then we can't afford to keep him alive. You know that."

I did, but that didn't mean I was happy about it. I turned to Brian, who'd been avoiding my gaze just like everyone else.

"What about you?" I asked. "Can you really just sit by while we commit premeditated murder?" He'd managed to stomach killing Der Jäger, but that had been in the heat of the moment, with a more tangible and immediate danger. This was an entirely different kettle of fish.

Brian shrugged. "I'm really hoping Lugh will go for Raphael's plan so I don't have to deal with it." He swept a glance over Lugh's assembled supporters and shook his head. "If these guys decide William has to die, there's no way you or I can stop them."

An uncomfortable truth, but truth nonetheless.

I decided I'd join Brian in hoping not to have to deal with it. "What do you think, Lugh?" I asked. "Do we go with Raphael's plan to send William back to the Demon Realm?" *Please say yes,* I added as a mental aside.

Yes. With some conditions.

I relayed his answer to the council while sighing in relief.

nineteen

LUGH'S CONDITIONS MADE A LOT OF SENSE. THAT didn't mean I had to like them. To guard against the possibility that William would continue to side with Dougal, we had to take extra precautions to ensure our safety, with Raphael being the most vulnerable of all. Therefore, Lugh decreed that none of us should be living alone right now, and every "household" should have at least one demon in it.

Even though the words came from Lugh himself, and were therefore tantamount to law, there was a lot of bickering about who would stay with whom. No one, of course, wanted Raphael, but Adam and Dom bit the bullet and invited him to stay with them. Brian could stay with me, and Barbie could stay with Saul—I think they were practically living together already anyway. That left only Andy. I wasn't real anxious to have him moping around my apartment, but neither Saul nor Barbie had a spare room in their apartments, and Andy and Raphael in the same house seemed like a recipe for disaster. That left only me.

With the living arrangements worked out, the council meeting broke up. Only Raphael, Adam, and I entered the Black Room to speak to our prisoner.

William was no longer huddling in the corner when we stepped in. He'd lain down on the enormous black bed, but with his arms crossed over his chest, and his legs crossed at the ankles, he looked anything but relaxed. He sat up hastily as we filed in, and he got that white-eyed frightened look on his face again. I guess he knew his life was in the balance.

Raphael, back in Lugh mode, stood slightly ahead of Adam and me. I guess we were kind of playing royal bodyguards, though I'm not good at "playing" anything. William slipped off the bed and rose to his feet, straightening his shoulders and making a reasonably successful attempt to look dignified as he waited for "Lugh" to pass sentence.

"Is your host intact?" Raphael asked, and William looked completely flummoxed by the question.

"What?"

"Is your host intact?" Raphael repeated. "Meaning, would he function without you in his body, or have you damaged his brain?"

William paled a little. I guess he knew Lugh didn't much approve of demons mistreating their hosts.

"He was already damaged when I took him," William said. "He was a longtime drug user."

"Just answer the question."

"I . . . I *think* he can function without me. But I don't know. I've been keeping him happy from the moment I first took him. I'm not sure how he'd take to returning to reality."

"Keeping him happy as in keeping him high?" Adam asked.

William nodded warily. Considering the truly awful ways some demons abused their hosts, I supposed keeping his drug-addict host in a permanent state of euphoria was fairly decent, but I would never feel comfortable with the idea.

Raphael pursed his lips, which was not an expression I'd seen on his face very often. He was usually so sure of himself. But then, he was pretending to be Lugh, and Lugh always thought things through before he acted. Eventually, he reached some kind of decision—or pretended he did.

"I'm going to exorcize you," he said, and there was no missing the relief on William's face. Relief that quickly faded when Raphael explained exactly what William was to do once he got back to the Demon Realm.

"I can't!" William wailed, almost hyperventilating. "If I start running my mouth, Dougal will throw me in prison!"

Raphael made a soothing gesture with his hands. "Calm down, William. Hear me out before you panic."

William's eyes showed too much white, and there was no missing the fact that he was still on the verge of panic, but he managed to rein it in. "Okay," he said in a choked whisper.

"The reason I was asking about your host's condition is that I plan to summon you back in three days' time. That ought to be enough time for you to stir up plenty of trouble. But even if Dougal imprisons you, I can summon you back. If your host isn't capable of performing the ceremony himself or isn't willing to, then I'll have one of my other human allies do the summoning and then transfer you back into your host."

I hoped that was just a soothing lie. No way did I want one of my friends to have to summon William the Wimpy.

William bit his lip, still looking worried, though the panic was gone. "If my host is capable, he'll be more than willing," he said, almost absently. "He's chased the ultimate high for his entire adult life, and now that he's found it, he'd do anything to keep it."

My face scrunched up with disgust, but I didn't say anything. Maybe someone as fucked-up as William's host—if he was indeed as fucked-up as William said— was just better off if he could completely check out of reality.

"Then it seems we have a plan," Raphael said with satisfaction. "But if you have any thought of betraying me, remember that you will be summoned back into our custody. I don't enjoy being cruel, but I will be if I find that you haven't obeyed me."

William swallowed hard and nodded. "I won't betray you. I swear it."

Raphael nodded in kingly approval. "Very well then. Give me your hand, and do not resist."

William's hand was shaking when he held it out for Raphael to clasp, but he did as he was told.

The exorcism took all of about forty seconds. I was impressed. I'd never timed myself performing an exorcism, but I knew it took me way more than forty seconds, and I was the most powerful exorcist I'd ever heard of. Of course, I'm not demon royalty, so I guess I was outclassed. Hmm. Outclassed by Raphael. Not a comfortable thought.

When William was gone, his host collapsed to the floor, but it wasn't because he was brain-damaged. Tears streamed down his face, and a piteous, wailing moan rose from his throat as his whole body began to shake. Sweat dewed his skin, and his eyes had an empty, glassy look to them.

"What's the matter with him?" I asked. I'd never seen a host act like this when his demon was exorcized before.

Adam shook his head in what looked like disgust. "At a guess, I'd say he's already having withdrawal symptoms." William's host raked one hand over his face, leaving five distinct, bloody scratches. Adam hastened to grab both his hands, at which point he started struggling and screaming. Who knows what he was actually seeing, but I was pretty sure it was nothing in this room.

"This is going to be a very, very long three days," Adam said, and I couldn't help agreeing with him.

Before we left Adam's house, I decided that the next three days were going to be unbearable if I didn't lay down some ground rules for Andy. Living with my older brother in a cramped apartment wasn't going to be much fun in the first place, but living with him *and* his own personal thundercloud of doom was going to get old so fast he might not survive three whole days.

I cornered him as soon as he set foot out the door, grabbing him by the arm and dragging him to a shadowed corner by the front stoop, where we could talk in relative privacy. His eyes widened at my manhandling, but he didn't protest. I might have preferred it if he did—that would at least be a sign of life. That he used to be even worse than this was a sobering thought.

I suppose, as his loving sister, I should have been warm and nurturing, full of sympathy and gentle words, but that was never my style. I didn't have it in me to be as brutal as Raphael, but I was sick and tired of the kid gloves.

"If you're going to come live with me for three days," I said, poking him in the chest, "then you're going to need an attitude adjustment. I can't have you sitting around my apartment crying, 'Oh, woe is me,' constantly, or I'll go insane."

His jaw set stubbornly. "When have I ever said 'Woe is me'?"

No, my brother is not an idiot. He knew perfectly well what I meant. "Just stop it, Andy! So you've done some things you're not proud of. So what? Who hasn't? Deal with it and move on."

He laughed, but the bitterness in that laugh was thick enough to make me wince. "That's your advice?" he asked, an angry glitter in his eyes. "Deal with it and move on?" He shook his head. "That's cold even for you."

I decided to try a low blow. *Anything* to knock some sense into him. "Did you learn all this mopey poor-me shit from Raphael? Because he's raised feeling sorry for himself to an art form, and you seem to be emulating him."

Andy's wince and gasp proved my low blow had hurt plenty. Unfortunately, it didn't seem to be a constructive sort of pain.

"If you can't bear to have me around, then I'll take my chances on my own," he said. "I don't care if Lugh likes it or not. I may be on his council, but that doesn't make me one of his subjects."

I'd been kidding myself to think that a few well-chosen words would fix whatever was wrong with him. "I think I liked you better when you were catatonic," I muttered under my breath. Yeah, it was another low blow, and I'm not proud of myself for saying it.

"You and Brian have a good time playing house," he said, then pushed past me.

I grabbed his arm before he could get too far. "You're coming to my place," I informed him. "I'm sick of your attitude, but that doesn't mean I want you in the line of fire."

He jerked his arm from my grip. "You're all heart." He started walking away.

"If you're not at my apartment by nine A.M., I'm coming to get you," I yelled at his back.

He held up his hand in a gesture that was either an agreement, a sign to shut the hell up, or the finger—I couldn't tell which in the darkness.

While I'd been witnessing William's exorcism, Brian had been at his apartment, packing a suitcase so he'd have everything he needed for an extended stay at my place. I arrived back at my apartment building to find him waiting for me in the lobby. He already had a key to my apartment, and he was already on my very short list of people who were allowed to come up without the front desk calling to ask my permission first. Now it was time for me to register him as a resident of my apartment, even if it was only on a temporary basis. His resident status would earn him a parking pass, and would mean he didn't have to sign in at the front desk every time he came in without me.

We rode the slow, cranky elevator up to my floor in silence, and it wasn't an entirely comfortable silence. The issue of Lugh still lay between us, and I, for one, didn't know what to say. I didn't know if Lugh's earlier intervention had made things better, or worse.

The silence followed us into my apartment, and I felt so awkward I was tempted to offer Brian the guest room, even though that room would be Andy's when he moved in tomorrow morning. Brian put down his suitcase, then pulled me into a hug. I wrapped my arms around his waist and gratefully leaned the side of my head onto his shoulder. Brian's amazingly good at knowing when I need a hug. I'm not what you'd call a touchy-feely type, so these moments were few and far between.

"Do you still love me?" I asked. I guess I was feeling needy at the moment.

Brian's arms tightened around me. "Of course I do. Even during our worst moments, I never stopped loving you."

I swallowed past the lump in my throat. "And what about Lugh?"

I felt him shrug, even though he didn't let go. "I'll learn to live with him." He pushed me away slightly, then cupped my face in his hands, tilting my head up toward his as his thumbs stroked over my cheeks. "After what he said to me earlier, I can't in good conscience ask you to get rid of him. Not when he can keep you from ever getting sick or hurt. When I asked you to pass him off to someone else, I didn't fully think about what I was asking."

The lump in my throat ached. Something told me living with Lugh wasn't going to be as easy as Brian was suggesting. Sure, he might logically admit that Lugh was good for me, and he might logically want me to have all the protections that came with being possessed. But emotions, damn them, aren't logical. Jealousy would rear its ugly head again; I knew it.

Brian bent and brushed his lips over mine. "Yes, I'm still jealous," he said against my mouth, but it was hard to get too upset by the declaration when he was teasing me with butterfly kisses. "But one way or another, I'll deal with it."

"I think it's time to stop talking now," I said, then pulled his head down to mine for a firmer, deeper kiss.

"How's your head?" he asked when we came up for air.

As soon as he mentioned it, I noticed the lingering traces of the headache that had started when Lugh took control. It wasn't bad anymore, just a minor discomfort.

I stuck my lower lip out in an exaggerated pout. "It was fine until you made me start thinking about it."

Brian smiled at me, his eyes dark with desire. He pressed his hips firmly against me, letting me know how happy he was to have me in his arms at the moment. "Do you think maybe I can find some way to distract you?"

I answered his lustful smile with one of my own. "There's only one way to find out."

And wouldn't you know it, I felt no pain for the rest of the night.

I went to sleep cuddled in Brian's arms, and woke up in Lugh's living room. I considered complaining about it, but there wasn't a whole lot of point to it, since my complaints never seemed to affect Lugh much.

"What's up?" I asked, feeling a bit wary, wondering if Lugh was distracting me with this dream so he could have a little private time with Brian.

He smiled at me. "No, I'm going to butt out of the Brian situation for the time being."

Color me shocked! Lugh didn't butt out often. As in *ever.*

The smile turned to a mischievous grin. "I said *for now,* not *forever.* I have an idea what our next step should be, but right now, the two of you are doing just fine." He gave a happy little sigh.

I blushed a bit, knowing he'd enjoyed this evening's romp with Brian as much as I had, but I think I was finally getting a bit desensitized, because I didn't feel like I wanted to melt through my seat in humiliation.

"If you're not planning to play Dr. Phil, then why *have* you brought me here?"

All signs of satisfaction faded from his face. "You asked me a question this evening—a question I told you I would answer later."

Enough had happened this evening that I almost forgot what the question was, but it came back to me fast. I'd asked Lugh if he'd really put Raphael in prison if he ended up back on the throne. Based on the look on his face, I didn't think I wanted to hear the answer.

"My brother has committed many, many crimes," Lugh said regretfully. "I highly doubt I even know about all of them. I would be honor-bound to punish him."

"Even though he's saved your life? Even if he's instrumental in putting you back on the throne?" There was a hint of outrage in my voice. In case you haven't noticed, I really despise Raphael. But there were moments—fleeting, but there nonetheless—where I saw shadows of myself in him. And that made it hard to hate him quite as much as I should.

"Even so," Lugh said. "I wouldn't *want* to. For all his

faults, I do love my brother. But I refuse to be the kind of king who alters the rules to suit his friends and family. Raphael has broken the law, and therefore he must be punished."

I could hear in his voice how much the idea hurt Lugh. When he said he didn't want to, he meant it. But in his own way, he was as much of a stickler as Brian.

"What exactly does it mean to be imprisoned in the Demon Realm? Raphael has described it as a fate worse than death, but I can't say I understand."

Lugh shook his head. "No, you can't. Imprisonment for us is to be shut away in what equates to a sensory deprivation chamber. Without bodies, we don't feel physical sensations, but that doesn't mean we don't have senses. We can 'see' each other, we can 'hear' each other. We can interact. But in prison, we can do none of these things. The isolation is...extreme." He met my eyes. "And we are nearly immortal beings. A life sentence..."

I gasped at the horror of the idea.

"I would not give Raphael a life sentence, although many would argue he deserves it. I can commute his sentence in light of the help he's given me, but I can't do away with it entirely without showing blatant favoritism. Even with a commuted sentence, he would...suffer."

Lugh's explanation shone a whole new light on just how much Raphael was giving up by trying to restore him to the throne. I had to admit a grudging admiration. No matter what his faults, Raphael was as loyal a creature as I could imagine.

"Do you think ill of me for my decision?" Lugh asked, although he had to know how I felt. It wasn't like there were any secrets between us, at least not when the secrets were mine. But sometimes he liked me to articulate things, even when he knew what I was going to say.

"I don't think less of you," I admitted. "You're trying to be fair, which is a good thing. But I have to admit, I think more of Raphael right now than I did before."

Lugh closed his eyes, as if in pain. "So do I," he said in a voice barely above a whisper. "So do I."

And the dream slipped away.

Wednesday was the dawn of William's first day stirring up trouble in the Demon Realm, but we didn't expect to feel any ripple effects yet. Which was a good thing, because Wednesday night was the private training dinner at Dom's restaurant. He'd invited all of Lugh's council, and he'd also invited his family, which seemed to include approximately one third of the population of South Philly.

Despite his conservative family's disapproval of Dominic's lifestyle, just about everyone showed up. Even his wicked stepmother, who looked like she couldn't wait to get out of there the moment she set foot inside. My guess was that Dom's father had bullied her into coming.

Dom had put place cards on the tables, so we all knew where we were supposed to sit. Of course, that did make the few empty seats with place cards in front of them very conspicuous, but it wasn't as bad as Dom had feared. He'd been afraid Wicked Stepmom would convince a bunch of the older women not to show.

The only no-show among Lugh's council was Raphael, but that was by plan. *Someone* had to stay at Adam's place and take care of William's host, who so far had been so busy frothing at the mouth—figuratively speaking, for the most part—that he could barely be considered a functional human being.

Lugh and I didn't much like the idea of leaving Raphael alone. Not because we didn't trust him—for once—but because he'd painted such a big target on his back. To my intense surprise, Andy had volunteered to stay behind with him. I guess his hero instincts were trying to come out of hiding. Maybe my stern talking-to had more effect than I thought, though perhaps I was flattering myself to think so. But Raphael had dismissed Andy's offer with a careless wave of his hand.

"I'll only be alone three hours, tops," Raphael had said. "I'll phone in an SOS at the slightest sign of trouble, and the restaurant's less than four blocks from here. Besides," he'd added with a feral grin, "I'm not that easy to kill."

Everyone had accepted that as adequate reassurance, but Lugh and I were both still worried. I understood why Lugh was worried—Raphael was his brother, after all—but I wouldn't have expected it from myself. I suppose my attitude toward Raphael had softened even more than I'd realized.

Even Lugh and I had to admit, though, that the evening was a lot more pleasant without Raphael present. For one thing, Saul acted far more civilized when his father wasn't around. For another, we didn't have to listen to the subtle, but nasty, digs that Raphael invariably managed to interject into any conversation.

To my surprise, the evening ended up being fun. It wasn't that I'd expected a dinner at Dom's restaurant to be a chore. It was just that it's hard to relax and really enjoy anything when you're a key player in a covert war and the fate of the human race rests on your shoulders. I was habitually on guard, and about the only time I allowed myself to let any of that guard down was in bed. Now don't get me wrong; letting down my guard in bed was fun. It just wasn't the same kind of fun.

Without Raphael around to jab pins in anyone, all the members of Lugh's council were more... relaxed. Even Andy seemed to shake out of his stupor for a while. He still didn't do a lot of talking, but I didn't get the sense he was tuning the rest of us out, either. And every once in a while, I caught him smiling at something. Like when Adam took advantage of a momentary lapse in Dominic's attention to pinch him on the ass. Dom jumped and gave a little yelp, but the restaurant was noisy enough to cover the sound, and his family members, at least, were engrossed in their food and their conversations. Dom turned to glare at Adam, who made innocent eyes at him.

"You promised you'd be on your best behavior," Dominic scolded, and Adam gave him a wicked grin.

"This *is* my best behavior."

Dominic rolled his eyes dramatically and heaved an exasperated sigh. Afterward, he was careful never to turn his back on Adam again.

The dinner went off without a hitch. But Dom and the rest of us had underestimated his family's ... staying power. The restaurant didn't have its liquor license yet—that took forever in Philly—but patrons were allowed to bring their own, and Dom's family had brought enough wine to inebriate half of Philadelphia. They were having a jolly old time trying to drink each other under the table, and I started to get antsy again about leaving Raphael unprotected for so long, no matter how hard he was to kill, and no matter how unlikely it was that anyone was gunning for him yet.

Adam and Dom tried engaging in a slightly more obvious public display of affection, hoping Dom's relatives would get uncomfortable and leave, but most of them were too drunk to care.

It was after eleven when Brian, Andy, and I excused ourselves from the festivities to go keep watch on Raphael. Dom was going to be stuck at the restaurant until the wee hours, and there was no way Adam was going to leave him there alone. It would be asking for trouble to send Saul and Barbie, which is why the three of us got the short straw.

My life had been so unpleasantly eventful lately that it was almost anticlimactic to arrive at Adam and Dom's house and find no enemies waiting to spring out at us. We explained to Raphael what we were doing there, and he kindly fixed us a pot of coffee to help us stay awake until we could go to our own apartment. I guess I was pretty tired, because I fell asleep on the sofa before the coffee was even ready.

twenty

INCONVENIENTLY, RAPHAEL HAD PROMISED TO SUM-
mon William back to his host on the Mortal Plain
three days after sending him to the Demon Realm.
Which meant we had to summon him back on the night
of the actual grand opening of Dominic's restaurant.
We'd debated whether to do the summoning before or
after the opening, then finally decided on after. Dom
was nervous enough without getting any worrisome
news from the Demon Realm—and it was hard to believe
the news wouldn't be worrisome.

Just as we'd done on Wednesday night, all the members of Lugh's council except for Raphael went out to
dinner at Dom's. It wasn't the joyous, rowdy occasion
that the practice dinner had been, but I was pleased to
see that he got a pretty good crowd. And that the crowd
seemed happy. Dom was a constant blur of motion, flit-
ting from table to table to check on his customers' satisfaction, then darting back into the kitchen to keep an
eye on the cooking. I had to suppress a smile when I noticed more than one female customer trying her best to
flirt with him. Although he was no longer a host, he
still had the typical demon-host good looks. He was also

modest enough not to realize it, which only added to his appeal.

We might have all stayed until closing time so we could walk back to the house together, but there seemed to be a crowd gathering at the door, and Dom needed the tables. We left Adam to escort Dominic home—with strict orders that Dom was to let his manager handle closing up instead of supervising it himself—then prepared for the ritual to summon William.

This was only the second time I'd been present for a summoning ceremony. They were usually the exclusive purview of the Spirit Society. But I was there when we'd summoned Saul, so I wasn't quite as nervous or intimidated this time.

Jonathan Foreman, William's ex-host, was still deep in withdrawal, but at least he had some grasp of reality. And William had been right: Jonathan was very, very anxious to have him back. To the point that I was tempted to tie him up and lock him in a closet somewhere just so we didn't have to listen to him anymore. The constant refrain of "Is it time yet?" got old fast.

Appropriately enough, Adam and Dom arrived in time for us to start the ritual right on the stroke of midnight. Dom had a happy glow in his eyes when he joined us in the basement, and I was sad to see that glow die down as he transformed from Dominic Castello, restaurateur, to Dominic Castello, member of Lugh's royal council.

I'd always imagined the summoning ritual to be something solemn, intricate, and complex. Probably when performed by the Spirit Society, it was. But the demons knew exactly how much ritual was needed to make the summoning work, and it wasn't much. There had to be a circle of people around the summoner, and those people had to be holding candles. Other than that, the only necessary ritual was the speaking of the incantation.

Jonathan, who was so strung out he could hardly hold still for more than about five seconds at a time, lay down on his back, with his hands crossed over his chest. Rather like a dead-body pose, come to think of it. The rest of us sat in a circle around him, each of us holding a lit candle.

The rest of the ritual was entirely up to Jonathan, and that was not a good thing. There was a Latin sentence he was supposed to repeat three times. Lugh informed me the sentence translated roughly into "I, of my own free will, invite thee to enter my world, to reside within my flesh, and to make of my body thine instrument." The sentence was to be followed by William's True Name, which Lugh had told Raphael so that Raphael could continue to play king.

The problem was it was all such a mouthful—especially the True Name, which sounded like a bunch of nonsense syllables strung together at random—that it was nearly impossible for the twitchy, still semidelusional, and easily distracted Jonathan to get it right three times in a row. I don't know how many times he tried, but it was at least twenty, maybe more, before he finally managed it.

And then William was back, and the twitching stopped. I think we all breathed a sigh of relief. I know I, for one, had begun to worry Jonathan wouldn't be able to manage the summoning at all.

William let out a deep, shuddering breath, then reached his hands up to cover his face. He wasn't twitching, but there was a tremor in his hands, and you couldn't miss the tension in his body. It looked like he hadn't had a fun time back in the Demon Realm.

Raphael broke the circle and went to kneel at William's side. The rest of us stayed put.

"Tell me what happened," Raphael said, and his voice sounded way gentler than usual. He laid a hand on William's shoulder in a comforting gesture. Being such a talented liar made him into a talented actor as well, and he was doing a pretty good Lugh imperson-ation.

Yes, he is, Lugh agreed in my head. *Rather... unnerving.*

William pulled himself together by bits and pieces. Eventually, he let his hands fall away from his face and allowed Raphael to help him sit up. He was still pale, but at least he was no longer on the verge of hysterics.

"What happened?" Raphael asked again, with no hint of anger or impatience in his voice.

William shuddered and looked at the floor. "I did as you ordered," he said. "I started telling people that I had spoken to you, and that Dougal was trying to take the throne." He swallowed hard. "Most people didn't believe me. But some did, and I know the rumor started to spread, because Dougal called me." His eyes closed and his fists clenched at his sides.

Raphael patted his back like he was comforting a

small child. "And what did Dougal have to say? Did he mean to put you on trial, or was this a private meeting?"

Again, a shudder rippled through William's body. "Private meeting," he said, his voice whispery. "He didn't believe I had talked to you. He thought I was spreading trouble in an attempt to blackmail him. I told him you would summon me back to the Mortal Plain and that would be proof that I was acting on your behalf. He still didn't believe me, but he did give me a message for you, on the off chance I was telling the truth."

Raphael arched his eyebrows. "And what message would that be?"

Once again, the whites of William's eyes showed. "You are not like Dougal, right? You won't kill the messenger?"

Raphael shook his head. "No, I'm not like Dougal. Tell me the message, and don't worry that I'll take it out on you if I don't like it."

William braced himself. "He called you an arrogant fool for coming out of hiding. He said it would be your undoing, and that he wished he could be here on the Mortal Plain to watch you burn."

Raphael blinked a couple of times. I think he had a little more trouble acting as the calm, impersonal monarch when his temper was roused, but he managed to answer with only the faintest hint of tightness in his voice.

"That doesn't sound like Dougal," he said, and gave William a narrow-eyed look. "His quarrel with me has never been personal. At least, not that I knew."

William had relaxed a bit when Raphael didn't immediately blow up at him, but he tensed again under the scrutiny. "It's personal now that things are starting to go so wrong."

Raphael cocked his head to one side. "And just how wrong are things going right now? How desperate is Dougal feeling?"

"Now that you've actually summoned me back and given my 'ravings' some credibility? Pretty desperate."

The rest of us had all been quiet, an audience to the conversation rather than participants, so I don't think I was the only one who jumped a bit when Saul spoke.

"Those who don't want to believe it will just say you gave your True Name to someone else so you could be summoned back. They don't have to believe it was Lugh who summoned you."

William shook his head. "No one who knows me would believe I'd do that. Give up my True Name in a quest for power of some sort?" He actually laughed, though there was a bitter edge to the laughter. "I don't have the . . . constitution for it."

"And even if some people believe it was someone other than Lugh who summoned him," Adam said, "there will be a hint of doubt in their minds. If Dougal's position was already tenuous . . ."

Time to take this conversation somewhere private, Lugh said, and I relayed his message to the council. Without saying the message came from Lugh, of course, since William thought Lugh was sitting right next to him. But either everyone got the hint, or it was just obvious that it was time to stop talking around William, because Dominic broke what was left of the circle to go turn on the basement lights, and the rest of us blew out our candles.

We made the same arrangements we'd made last time we'd had to have a council meeting while keeping William contained, Andy and Barbie taking up their posts while the rest of us gathered in the living room.

Once we were seated, all eyes turned to me. I guess the guys had figured out it was Lugh who wanted the private time. I waited for Lugh to tell me what was on his mind, but he was eerily silent.

"Well?" Raphael asked, obviously low on patience. "What does Lugh think we should do?"

"I'll let you know as soon as he tells me," I answered, my voice a bit sharp because I was finding Lugh's silence ominous.

The silence continued, but that didn't stop the rest of Lugh's council from staring holes in me, waiting breathlessly. If I were a better actress—or had a good idea—I'd have started making shit up just to cut through the discomfort.

As soon as that thought struck me, an idea came into my mind. I honestly don't know if it was purely my idea, or if somehow Lugh's thoughts had leaked into my brain, but I felt a shock of recognition that told me he and I were on the same wavelength. And I understood now why he was reluctant to speak.

I sat up straighter in my chair, hoping what I was about to suggest wasn't going to trigger a mutiny.

"So our plan was to make Dougal's situation more

desperate, in the hopes that he'd decide to come to the Mortal Plain to try to flush Lugh out of hiding himself, right?" I asked.

Everyone looked back and forth at each other, but it was Raphael who answered for the group. "That was the idea."

"But we'd rather get him here on our own terms than on his," I continued.

Adam snorted. "No kidding? Really?" I guess he knew I wasn't relaying Lugh's words, because I couldn't see him smarting off to Lugh.

I decided to ignore him, not even giving him the dirty look he deserved. Lugh wasn't jumping in to interrupt me, so I kept going.

"Dougal's shown an absolute fascination with the Mortal Plain. Aside from the experiments he did with you," I said, nodding toward Raphael, "he also decided to move on the throne as soon as Lugh suggested he was going to make it illegal for demons to possess unwilling hosts."

"Just get to the point," Raphael said.

I smiled sweetly at him. "I'm telling you all the reasoning that leads up to the point, so you'll understand what I'm thinking." I wished I could remember the exact phrasing he'd used when he'd made the same sort of comment to Saul, but even with the paraphrase, he recognized what I was saying. It shut him up.

"So Dougal—and his supporters—really, really want access to the Mortal Plain. And Dougal's gained his supporters by promising to give them unlimited access. If they're already starting to get out of hand now, just imagine what they would be like—and how desperate Dougal would be—if we threatened to cut off access altogether."

I looked carefully from face to face as I made this suggestion. Brian wore his lawyer face, hiding whatever he was thinking. Adam's face had frozen in a look of shock, his expression so raw that Dom felt the need to reach over and give his hand a firm squeeze. Saul looked mulish, as usual. And Raphael...Raphael looked grim, but not a bit surprised.

"This thought has occurred to you before," I accused.

Raphael examined his manicure while he spoke. "I thought of it as a last-ditch way to stop Dougal from getting what he wanted. I thought maybe if we made it impossible for him to get what he wanted, he might eventually decide it wasn't worth it to kill Lugh for the throne. But I never liked the idea enough to mention it. There are so many downsides..."

I laughed, but it wasn't a nice laugh. "You mean you'd lose your access to your own personal playground."

His eyes flashed, and he bared his teeth at me. "And so would every other demon, even the ones like Adam and Saul, who make your world a better place. Think what you want of *me,* but the reason the U.S. legalized demonic possession is because of how much we can contribute to your society."

In my usual tactful manner, I'd been about to remind Raphael that he wasn't the only demon who wouldn't recognize the concept of "conscience" even if it bit him in the ass, but Brian spoke before I did.

"What exactly do you mean when you talk about cutting off contact between the Demon Realm and the Mortal Plain?" he asked.

I gave him a grim smile. "Think about all we've learned about demons since we've gotten sucked into this mess. There's a reason demons keep all this shit secret, and it's not just because they like being mysterious."

Brian processed that thought for a moment. "You mean if we start telling the public about the secrets the demons have been keeping, the anti-demon lobby will get demonic possession outlawed once again?"

"Exactly. It's not like it would completely stop demons from getting to the Mortal Plain—it never has before—but it would make it a hell of a lot harder for them to get here."

"And a hell of a lot less fun," Adam contributed. "If we came to the Mortal Plain and then had to stay in hiding…" He shook his head. "I've gone that route before, as I suspect most of us have, since possession was illegal much longer than it's been legal. I enjoyed myself enough to want to come back, but now that I've seen what it's like to be out in the open, I don't know if I could go back to the way it was."

"But we're not actually going to *do* it, right?" Raphael asked, fixing me with a piercing look. Once again, I was pretty sure the look was directed at Lugh. "We're just going to *threaten* to do it if Dougal doesn't come to the Mortal Plain and fight like a man, as it were. Right?"

We'll try a threat first, Lugh said. *But I suspect Dougal will think we're bluffing. If we make the threat and aren't willing to back it up, we have gained ourselves nothing.*

I relayed Lugh's message. It might have been easier to just let him take control and do his own talking, but it hadn't been all that long since he'd last been in control, and I wasn't sure how my body would react to another control shift. I preferred not to find out.

Raphael looked very unhappy. He might not have wanted what Dougal wanted badly enough to kill Lugh, but he did still want it.

"We don't have to give away everything," Raphael said, and his voice sounded a lot calmer than his face looked. "We can reveal something humans won't like but that won't get us outlawed. That might convince Dougal we mean what we say." He looked at me, and this time he was really looking at *me,* not Lugh. "You've been a demon-hater all your life. Which of our secrets would piss you off but not make you want us all to be outlawed?"

They were all looking at me now, and I didn't much appreciate the scrutiny. Raphael made me sound like some kind of bigot when he called me a "demon-hater," and that was certainly not the way I'd ever seen myself. And yet ...

Before Lugh had come into my life, I had made no bones about my dislike of demons. If I knew someone was possessed, I disliked him or her on the spot, and no number of good deeds would make me let go of that dislike. It wasn't like I'd marched on the streets of Washington shouting "down with demons," but if you'd pressed me, I would have admitted I thought demonic possession should be outlawed again.

I didn't feel that way anymore, which was in a way kind of strange considering everything I'd learned and everything I'd been through. Demons had been the authors of all my worst troubles, and I'd dealt with the darkest, the most dangerous, the most evil of them. But I'd also dealt with Lugh, who could annoy the shit out of me at times, but who was so good and honorable that I couldn't really think ill of him even when I was pissed off at him. And I'd come to know Adam, who was far from one of the nicest people I'd ever met, but who was a hero in every sense of the word, and whose love for Dominic had shown me that demons really were capable of the same depth of emotion as humans.

Demons were *people* to me now, not inscrutable aliens. And I had no grounds to argue Raphael's assessment, even if I didn't hate them anymore. I knew what it was like to hate them and to want them gone.

"If we told people that demons don't die when they're exorcized," I said softly, "that would make a lot of people very unhappy."

There was a moment of shocked silence, but it didn't last long. Saul, Adam, and Raphael all started to protest at once, but Raphael's voice was loudest, and the other two reluctantly ceded the field to him.

"They wouldn't be just 'unhappy'!" he snarled. "That's the one secret that could very well fuel the effort to outlaw us again!"

"No," I said, very calmly, "the one secret that would

be sure to get you outlawed is the eugenics program you and Dougal ran for the last several centuries."

Raphael actually paled at my words, and all the starch went out of his spine as his fellow demons turned to glare at him. I almost felt sorry for him. But not quite.

"If the human population finds out that exorcism doesn't kill you," I continued, "then I can guarantee there will be some changes in the law. Maybe more states will go the execution route, but since it's killing the human host that made them balk before, they may well still balk even if they know the truth. Exorcism may not be the Old Testament eye-for-an-eye-type punishment that people think it is, but it gets the offending demon off the Mortal Plain and leaves the host alive, at least usually. Knowing the truth will give the anti-demon hate groups and the anti-demon lobby more power and fuel, but I doubt it would be enough to make you all illegal. Demons have made themselves too useful for us to get rid of you that easily. It would take something really heinous to destroy you all in the court of public opinion."

Raphael sank down lower in his chair. His head hung low, and he stared at his hands. "But we'd only tell people that as the absolute last resort, right? If Dougal doesn't take us seriously and come to the Mortal Plain?"

"Right," I agreed, trying not to think about what it would be like if we revealed to the general public that Dougal and Raphael had captured, bred, and destroyed human beings like experimental rats. I suspected outlawing them would be the least of their troubles. Those demons already on the Mortal Plain would be targeted by every hate group in the country, even though the vast majority of them had nothing to do with Dougal and Raphael's project. There would be murders, and riots, and general mayhem. I didn't want to see it happen any more than Raphael did.

But it looked like Dougal was vulnerable now, so now was the time to strike, before he found some way to solidify his power base. And before he funneled too many more of his supporters—disgruntled or otherwise—onto the Mortal Plain.

"Does Lugh support this plan?" Adam asked.

I heard Lugh's sigh in my head and sensed, rather than heard, his agreement. I nodded.

Adam squared his shoulders. "I would be the obvious spokesperson for us," he said. "Aside from the fact that Dougal already knows I'm in Lugh's camp, I also have access to the press through my job. I'll set up a press conference."

"But not right away," Raphael said. There was still a haunted look in his eyes, but even in the depths of turmoil, Raphael was still Raphael, full of cunning. "Wait until Monday. Then we can send William back to the Demon Realm with a message for Dougal that if he doesn't make an appearance before Monday, we'll have a press conference. I suggest we not say that Adam will be giving it, or Adam might not live until Monday."

"Dougal's going to call our bluff," Saul said, and for once, he wasn't sneering at his father, just stating a fact.

"The press conference will have to happen before he'll believe we really mean to do it."

Raphael examined his hands as he spoke. "I know. But we have to at least try."

And so, our path was set.

twenty-one

THERE WASN'T A WHOLE LOT OF CHATTER BETWEEN us as Brian, Andy, and I returned to my apartment. What was there to say, after all? William was once again back in the Demon Realm, delivering our ultimatum to Dougal, and we wouldn't know how that ultimatum was received until Monday morning, when once again we would summon him back to the Mortal Plain. I didn't envy Adam, Dom, and Raphael having to play nursemaid to Jonathan and his withdrawal again, but better them than me.

We were all exhausted by the time we got back to the apartment at about three in the morning. Andy made a beeline for the guest bedroom. I'm not sure he even bothered to get undressed or brush his teeth before he collapsed into the bed and started snoring loud enough that Brian and I could hear him in the next room.

We *did* bother to get undressed, and when I cuddled

up in Brian's arms, my back to his chest, I felt the evidence that he wasn't quite as tired as I'd thought. His hand trailed idly between my breasts and down my belly, making me shiver, though it wasn't cold. He touched his lips to that deliciously sensitive place where my neck meets my shoulder, and I decided that I wasn't as tired as I'd thought, either.

He kissed his way up toward my earlobe, which he sucked lightly, making my back arch in pleasure.

"I could get used to having you in my bed every night," Brian whispered in my ear as his hand moved up to cup my breast.

I thought about objecting to his not-so-subtle hint that he wanted to live together, but the truth was, I was beginning to think I could get used to it, too. Still, I was far from ready to admit it.

"Need I remind you that *you're* in *my* bed?" I teased.

He laughed against my skin, his breath warm and mint-scented from his toothpaste. I was guessing I didn't need to admit anything; Brian knew what my lack of protest meant. He pressed his erection into the crease between my buttocks, and I suppressed a moan at how hard and hot he felt against my skin. Andy's snores reassured me that he couldn't hear us, but Brian and I have been known to be rather loud, and I thought I might perish of embarrassment if we managed to wake Andy up.

Brian drew himself slowly downward, and I parted my legs to make room for him between them. I expected this to be more foreplay—Brian does love to tease unmercifully—but apparently tonight he was impatient for the main event to begin.

Usually, I don't like being taken from behind. There's something that feels too submissive about it. But I was beginning to think Brian could make me like just about anything—with the possible exception of Brussels sprouts. Instead of trying to turn over as I might have in the past, I simply relaxed into Brian's embrace and tried not to moan too loudly as he slowly slipped inside me.

Next door, Andy's snores stopped. That didn't necessarily mean he was awake, but still . . .

Brian's lips brushed my ear. "Be vewy, vewy quiet," he whispered, and I had to bite my tongue to keep from laughing. Then he thrust all the way in, and laughing was the last thing on my mind.

It was oddly exciting, trying to keep quiet during some fantastic sex. It was also surprisingly hard to manage. Even Brian, usually a master of control, struggled with it, little whimpers escaping his throat despite his best efforts. But by the time we both reached our climaxes, Andy was snoring again in the next room. Yay, us!

The exhaustion I'd been feeling when we first went to bed hit me like a brick wall when the adrenaline rush faded, and, with Brian's arms still cuddling me to his chest, I drifted off to sleep.

Sunday was hell. I'm a woman of action, and I hate waiting around. Unfortunately, there was a lot of it to be done. We couldn't make a move until we'd heard back from William, so as much as I wanted to leap into action, that just wasn't possible.

Because we were still on high alert in case William betrayed us, we were all still on the buddy system. Which meant that not only was Brian constantly at my side, but Andy was, too. We'd been pretty close as children—at least until the Spirit Society got its hooks into him—but things were almost unbearably awkward between us now. I kept thinking I should apologize for my harsh words of the other night, but I had the suspicion my attempted apology would lead to more harsh words, so I kept my mouth shut.

We were all up at the crack of dawn on Monday. Both Brian and Adam were due at their jobs today. Brian had missed enough time lately to make his boss grumpy, and since he did still care about his career, even in the midst of this crisis, he refused to stay home. Adam, as a public servant, had even less flexibility. So to accommodate their schedules, we'd decided to hold the summoning early in the morning.

Early in the morning is never my best time, even with Dom's extra-strong Italian roast coffee doing its best to jump-start my brain. I was glad to see I wasn't the only one yawning when we all sat in the basement of Adam and Dom's house with only the dim light of the candles illuminating the dark.

Jonathan was a total mess, his cheeks hollow, his eyes bloodshot and shadowed with dark circles. His hands shook, and sometimes we had to repeat ourselves to get him to even hear us. And even though he'd just learned the incantation to summon William a couple of days ago, it was as if he'd never heard it before. If it had taken him twenty tries to get it right at the first summoning, it must have taken him at least thirty this time. I hoped he'd have a few brain cells left to rub together if we ended up having to use William as our messenger to the Demon Realm again.

I'd expected the situation to improve when William was back with us. It didn't.

As soon as Jonathan's mind slid into the background and William took over, he started to scream. His arms and legs flailed, his back arched, and the screams rose from his throat one right after another, to the point where I wondered how he had enough air in his lungs to keep it up.

Raphael and Adam put down their candles to try to restrain the frantic demon, but he was fighting so hard Saul had to jump in and help them. Raphael, practically kneeling on William's chest like a rodeo star on a bucking bronco, kept repeating his name over and over, but there was no sign that William heard him.

Finally, Raphael slapped William across the face. The first slap was light, and William seemed not to feel it. The next slap was hard enough to make me wince, and I hoped he hadn't just broken William's jaw. But, to my immense relief, William stopped screaming.

He was conscious. You could tell that by how hard he was breathing and by how desperately he squinched his eyes shut. But it was hard to tell if he was in his right mind or not. Adam continued sitting on his legs, and

Saul kept hold of his wrists, although William didn't seem to be fighting anymore.

Keeping a careful watch on him, Raphael slid off William's chest and rested a soothing hand on his sweaty forehead. He then traced his fingers gently over William's cheek, where a bruise was forming.

"I'm sorry I hurt you," Raphael said softly as he once again transformed himself into Lugh. "I could find no other way to calm you."

William dragged in a painful-sounding breath. Both Adam and Saul tensed, anticipating another fight, but William merely opened his eyes. He looked up into Raphael's face.

"Lugh?" he asked, his voice scratchy from all the screaming.

Raphael nodded, and William proceeded to burst into tears.

"You can let go now," Raphael said to Adam and Saul. Adam let go immediately, but of course, Saul didn't. Not, I suspect, because he thought William might pitch another fit, but because he didn't want to do what his father told him to do.

When Saul finally let him go, William turned over on his side and curled into a fetal position, sobbing. Raphael murmured soothing sounds and stroked his hair, comforting him as you would a small child.

"What the hell happened to him?" I found myself whispering, though I hadn't meant to say it out loud.

Raphael shook his head in what looked like disgust. "I have a feeling Dougal did, indeed, try to kill the messenger."

William drew in a loud, shuddering breath. "He tried," he managed to gasp between sobs. "I'd have let him win if I could, just to make it stop." He started to push himself up into a sitting position, but his whole body was shaking. I think he would have collapsed back into a heap if Raphael hadn't reached out and supported him.

William closed his eyes again, fists clenched at his sides. "He wouldn't let up. Even when he knew he couldn't kill me, he kept trying."

Lugh had explained to me once that it was impossible for demons to kill one another in the Demon Realm unless there was a significant disparity in power between them. I guess William, being a royal cousin, was too strong for Dougal to destroy. But it sounded like the attempt had been something akin to torture.

"I suppose that means we're getting to him," Raphael said. If he'd been speaking like himself, he probably would have sounded dryly amused—like I've said before, he's not the soul of compassion—but in Lugh mode, he sounded grave and almost sorrowful.

William laughed—an awful, dry, not entirely sane laugh that I feared might turn into another crying jag. "Oh, you're getting to him all right. I've never seen him so enraged before."

"And does he plan to come to the Mortal Plain to stop me from announcing the truth about exorcism?"

I don't think any of us were surprised when William shook his head. "He says you're bluffing. He says you'd never endanger the lives of all the demons now on the

Mortal Plain by admitting something that would encourage humans to execute them rather than exorcize them."

Raphael heaved a sigh and looked grim. "Apparently, he doesn't know me as well as he thinks he does." He looked over at Adam. "Call the press conference for this afternoon."

"This ought to be interesting," I heard Saul mutter under his breath.

Adam merely nodded to acknowledge his orders. I had a feeling there were many words that could be used to describe the upcoming press conference. "Interesting" didn't even begin to cover it.

twenty-two

THE PRESS CONFERENCE STARTED AT A LITTLE AFTER three that afternoon. I doubt that Adam gave the reporters much of a preview, but they obviously knew he was going to say something very important, because they interrupted the local programming to televise it. For all I knew, they interrupted national programming as well. After all, it was quite a bombshell he was about to drop.

Andy and I watched in my living room. The tension was getting to both of us, and we hadn't spoken a word to each other in about three hours. Probably just as well. Tension makes some people act like asses, and I'm one of them. If we both kept our mouths shut, I would have much less chance of sticking my foot in mine.

Adam looks great on TV. I'd seen him give a press conference before, but this time I was struck again by his masculine good looks and by his aura of quiet confidence. He was dressed in a dark suit with a conservative striped tie, his bad-boy qualities completely buried beneath a layer of respectability. It was a side of Adam I rarely saw, and it made it easier to see how he'd risen to such an exalted rank within the Philly PD.

Cameras flashed as he stepped up to a podium that sprouted microphones like runaway weeds. The voices that had been murmuring in the background before he stepped up faded to nothing, as if the crowd were holding its breath to see what he would say. He laid a sheet of paper—his prepared statement—on the podium, then took a quick look around the room. I guess he was waiting to see if anyone was going to try to stop him at the last moment, but no one did.

"Good afternoon," he said, sweeping the assembled press before him with one last searching glance before he lowered his eyes to the paper on his podium.

"As many of you know, I am a demon. I am Philadelphia's Director of Special Forces, and am an official citizen of the United States. However, as a demon, I remain a citizen of the Demon Realm as well.

"Just as the United States is governed by individuals with differing opinions, so is the Demon Realm. And just as the laws and attitudes of the United States change when there is a change in government, so do they change in the Demon Realm.

"The Demon Realm has recently had a change in leadership."

The crowd wasn't quite so silent anymore, a low, urgent murmur starting up. I realized I'd clasped my hands together in my lap tight enough that my fingers were turning white, and I forced myself to relax.

"Because of this change in leadership," Adam continued, as if unaffected by the rumblings of the crowd, "I have been tasked with explaining to you a misapprehension that the United States—and other countries—has about demons. A misapprehension that our former leadership fostered and encouraged in an attempt to protect the demons who walk the Mortal Plain."

The rumbling in the crowd was louder now. If they hadn't guessed before that a bombshell was about to be dropped, they did now.

Adam looked up from his prepared speech, facing the crowd head-on as the flashes of photos being taken intensified. He swept the crowd with his gaze, then focused on the camera, like he was looking straight through it into the living rooms of all of us who were watching on TV.

"For the protection of our own people, we have allowed you to believe that exorcism kills us."

At this point, Adam had to raise his voice to be heard over the crowd. I saw the tightness in the corners of his eyes and mouth. This press conference couldn't be easy for him, and I wondered how much danger he was putting himself in by doing it. Dougal's supporters might already be gunning for him, but as the conveyor of this devastating news, he was probably going to attract the attention of every fanatic—both pro-demon and anti-demon—out there.

"The truth is," he continued, still looking straight at the camera, "that when we are exorcized, we are returned to the Demon Realm. Unharmed."

The place erupted, everyone shouting questions at once. Adam held up his hands for silence, but it was a long time before he got anything that even vaguely resembled it. The background noise was still pretty loud when he began to speak again.

"I realize that this information comes as a shock. I also understand that many of you will be troubled by the idea that demons are not punished for their crimes in the way that you have always thought. But rest assured that there is a system of justice within the Demon Realm, and just because we are not killed by your exorcisms does not mean we are not punished."

I had a feeling Raphael had advised Adam to add that last part. There certainly was no punishment now for demons who'd committed crimes on the Mortal Plain, but I supposed if Lugh ever got back on the throne, that would change.

The crowd noise rose in volume again, with more questions being shouted. Adam simply raised his voice to be heard over them.

"I ask you also to keep in mind that the vast majority of demons who are currently exorcized are exorcized for crimes that would fall far, far short of the death penalty if the perpetrators were human."

The questions now were coming so fast and loud that Adam would have had to shout to be heard over them. He said something else into the microphone, but I couldn't make out the words over the crowd noise. Then, with a handful of police discreetly guarding his exit route, he left the podium and slipped through a door off to the side.

twenty-three

THERE WERE REPORTERS CAMPED OUT IN FRONT OF Adam's house when Brian, Andy, and I arrived later that evening. They weren't blocking the way to the front door, but it wasn't like we could go in unnoticed, either. The press would have photos of all the members of Lugh's council before the night was out, and you can bet they'd dig up all the information they could about each and every one of us. Still, we'd all agreed it was a risk we had to take. We'd opened the can of worms, and now we'd have to deal with the aftermath.

After the press conference, the "special report" on the news had continued for most of the afternoon, with rampant press speculation. They speculated on why Adam was chosen as a spokesman; on whether he was acting on his own, or following orders; on whether he was some kind of activist, trying to foment unrest.

Some even thought it might be a publicity stunt, though publicity for what, I don't know.

The press had descended on any demon who would hold still long enough to be interviewed, trying everything they could to get more details. Most of the demons wisely stuck to "no comment," but there were a few who did their best to paint Adam as a member of the demon lunatic fringe and dismiss his claims.

I don't know what the general public believed—it's not like the news reports were unbiased when such a sensational story was in the air. But I knew that lawmakers throughout the country were getting together to reconsider the usefulness of exorcism and the status of demons in our society. Change was a-comin', and I doubted any of those changes would be to the demons' advantage.

Eventually, all the members of Lugh's council had fought their way past the gauntlet of press and arrived at Adam's house. We were beginning to be more confident of William's loyalties, such as they were, since acting as our messenger had obviously soured his relationship with Dougal. That didn't mean we were willing to include him in our council meeting, but we didn't set up a guard this time. Of course, we didn't tell William that, so as far as he knew, Andy and Barbie were at their posts, ready to shoot him full of electricity if he tried anything.

We gathered in the living room, all of us somber and thoughtful. If Dougal called our bluff, every demon who walked the Mortal Plain would be in the worst sort of danger. Because it wasn't a bluff. If Dougal didn't come, we were prepared—as prepared as we could ever be—to tell the world everything. It was a terrifying prospect.

"So what happens now?" Saul asked when we were all seated and a full minute had passed without anyone else speaking.

"We need to exorcize William again," Raphael said. "I'm sure word of what we've done will reach Dougal regardless, but we need to set up a meeting with Dougal when he reaches the Mortal Plain."

"You really think he'll come?" Adam asked.

Raphael nodded. "If we manage to get possession outlawed again, everything he's worked for will be in vain. If his supporters are already starting to turn on him now, he'll have a full-scale rebellion then, and he could very likely find himself imprisoned. I can't imagine him risking it."

"Is sending William again really the best idea?" Dominic asked. "You saw what Dougal did to him last time. I'm beginning to think it's akin to cruel and unusual punishment to make him go back."

"Who else would you send?" Adam asked. "We could send me or Saul, but the power differential between us and Dougal is too great. If he decided to kill the messenger, we'd die. That leaves only Raphael," he said, and we all turned to look at Raphael. "And the only one in this room who might be able to exorcize him is Lugh." Everyone then turned to look at me.

May I take control? Lugh asked. *It's been long enough since the last time that I doubt you'll suffer any ill effects, and I think it's important that I speak.*

I let out what I hoped was a silent sigh. I don't think I'll ever get comfortable with letting someone else drive my body, but if Lugh had lots to say, then it would get old acting as his interpreter. Besides, the rest of the council was more likely to listen to me if it was Lugh talking.

Lugh didn't wait for my answer, because he could sense my answer without my having to articulate it. I did a little mental shiver at the feeling of being shoved into the background of my own body, but I think I was starting to get a little used to it, because I didn't feel an immediate reflexive need to kick him out.

Lugh sat up a little straighter in the chair, and I think just by the change in body language he demonstrated to everyone in the room that I wasn't myself anymore.

"I could exorcize Raphael if he didn't fight me," Lugh said, "but I'd prefer to keep him out of this."

Raphael raised his eyebrows. "Oh? Why is that?"

"Well, for one thing, if you're in the Demon Realm, you can't be here pretending to be me. For another, I'm not sure your host would survive without you in residence."

"He wouldn't," Raphael admitted, bracing himself as if ready for attack. "Tommy shut down several weeks ago." He hunched his shoulders, and if I didn't know better, I'd swear he actually felt guilty. I know *I* did, since I'd sacrificed Tommy to Raphael to free my brother. And let's not even talk about how *Andy* felt.

"I tried to be kind to him," Raphael continued, "and

I tried not to break him. His sanity was already severely compromised when I took him…"

It looked like Saul was going to take this opportunity to get in one of his verbal potshots, but Lugh silenced him with a glare before he said a word. I was glad, figuring anything Saul said would hurt Andy more than Raphael.

"It's all right, Raphael," Lugh said. "We all knew the chances of Tommy remaining intact were negligible, no matter who took him. It was a group decision to let you take him, not yours alone." Actually, it had been more like *my* decision, but no one had really disagreed with it. "But the point is, we can't use you as our messenger. It has to be William."

Raphael met his brother's gaze. "He's not going to be happy about the prospect."

Lugh grimaced. "I know. But it can't be helped."

"And what shall I have him tell our dear brother?"

Lugh thought about it a moment. I really wished I could hear his thoughts like he could hear mine. "Tell him he has till midnight on Wednesday to come to the Mortal Plain and begin negotiations."

Raphael snorted. "He's not going to *negotiate* about anything!"

"Yes, he will. I'm going to propose we fight a duel and put an end to this conflict once and for all. We will need to negotiate the rules of engagement."

No one spoke a word for what felt like about ten minutes. They all stared at Lugh with varying degrees of shock. Finally, Raphael broke the silence.

"You can't seriously mean to do it," he said, his voice guarded.

Lugh raised his eyebrows. "How else do you suggest I get close enough to him to kill him? Besides, he needs to think coming to the Mortal Plain will end his troubles *and* keep us from going even more public with the truth."

Now that the silence was broken, everyone began speaking at once, voices getting louder and louder as each tried to shout over the others. Myself, I didn't know what to think. Challenging Dougal to a duel sounded like a terrible risk, but it might be less risky than doing nothing.

Lugh let the others vent for a couple of minutes, then held up his hands for silence. "We'll debate on whether I should actually meet Dougal for a duel later. First, we have to get the message to him, and he has to agree. Then we have to meet to discuss terms."

He turned to Raphael. "Tell William that when Dougal reaches the Mortal Plain, he should contact Adam. Adam will meet him in person to confirm that it really is Dougal, and we will plan our future from there."

Dominic squirmed in his chair. "But you said yourself Dougal could *kill* Adam."

Lugh nodded. "He could. But not on the Mortal Plain. Besides, if he shows up, it will be because he's chosen to confront me. If that's the case, he'll have no reason to kill Adam."

Dominic clearly didn't like it, but Adam reached over and squeezed his shoulder, murmuring some kind of reassurance so quietly the rest of us couldn't hear. I don't think it helped a whole lot.

"Does anyone else have an objection?" Lugh asked. "Because if not, I'd like to put Morgan back in control."

I liked the sound of that. The other members of Lugh's council looked from one to the other, waiting for someone to object, but it didn't happen. And between one breath and the next, Lugh slipped into the background of my mind and put my body back under my control. I breathed a quiet sigh of relief, then tensed for the headache and nausea. I felt mildly queasy, and my head hurt a bit, but it wasn't too bad. The nerves over what Lugh intended to do were far worse, but I did my best to shove my worries to the side for now.

William had been less than happy to discover we were sending him back to the Demon Realm once more—"less than happy" being the understatement of the century. The poor guy had begged and pleaded, but "Lugh" had been gently firm about it. In the end, William had caved and agreed to do Lugh's bidding—not that he actually had a choice. I think we all felt at least a little guilty about putting him through this. Well, all but Raphael, who didn't do guilt.

Knowing that Dougal might once again try to kill the messenger, and knowing that the attempt would be sheer agony for William even though it wouldn't succeed, we promised William we'd summon him back first thing in the morning. That would give him enough time to get the message to Dougal, but wouldn't leave him in Dougal's clutches for too terribly long. Of course, more than twelve hours of torture might seem kinda long to William.

I tried to assuage my guilty conscience by reminding myself that William had been the de facto leader of the illegal recruitment campaign. That he'd been put in that position despite his protests was a mitigating factor, but the fact remained that he'd sat idly by as his demon accomplices tortured human beings into inviting demons into their bodies. No matter how pitiable William was, he was a long way from being an innocent victim.

The reporters outside Adam's house had not magically disappeared, more's the pity. I was almost tempted to ask Adam to let me stay over, just to avoid the vultures. "Almost" being the operative word.

Those of us who weren't spending the night—Brian, Andy, and me, along with Saul and Barbie—all left together, hoping to stave off the press by sheer numbers. We studiously ignored them as we fought our way through the gauntlet, but that didn't seem to discourage them.

Most of them stayed camped out in front of Adam's, but a splinter group started following us. Then the splinter group splintered again when Saul and Barbie veered off. We had about five of them on our tail when we reached my apartment building. They'd been quiet for most of the walk, but when the doorman opened the door for us and we were about to enter private property—where the vultures couldn't follow—the questions started up again.

If they thought they were going to wear any of us down, they were sorely mistaken. Wear us *out*, maybe, but there was no chance in hell we were going to talk to them.

Once we were safely inside my apartment, Andy announced his plan to sleep for the next week and a half and disappeared into the guest room. I was tired, but not sleepy, if you know what I mean. I guess Brian felt the same way, because instead of heading for the bedroom, he said, "Have you got anything to drink around here?"

I blinked at him. "You've been living here almost a week. You know what's in the fridge as well as I do."

He rolled his head back and forth, his neck making little popping noises in protest. "I was hoping for something stronger than what was in the fridge. Don't you have an emergency supply of booze somewhere?"

I'm not much of a drinker. Not for any philosophical reasons, but just because I hate the taste of alcohol. But every once in a while, I can be persuaded to force it down for the greater good of humanity. (When I feel bad enough to want a drink, it isn't safe to be near me.)

Today had been enough of a strain that I had to agree with Brian that a drink was just what the doctor ordered. In the back of the cabinet over the refrigerator—the one that I could barely reach into despite my greater-than-average height—was a single, lonely bottle of rum, about three-quarters full. I pulled it down and set it on the kitchen counter. My fingers left an outline in the dust that coated the bottle. Guess it had been a while since I'd dragged it down.

I got a Coke out of the fridge, because I'd have to be desperate indeed to drink straight rum. Brian merely threw some ice cubes in a glass and poured himself a healthy shot. He took a tentative sip, then made a face.

"I'm not a connoisseur of rum," he said, his nose wrinkled, "but I'm guessing this isn't exactly the good stuff."

I shrugged. "I bought the cheapest I could find. The good stuff and the bad stuff both taste like shit to me, so why waste the money? Besides, unless I missed my guess, you're drinking it for medicinal purposes, not for pleasure, so who cares how it tastes?"

I took a sip of my own drink and made a face I suspected was very similar to Brian's. But I'd have made the same face if it had been the most expensive rum on the face of the earth. Brian gave a resigned sigh, then tossed back the rest of the contents of his glass, the ice cubes audibly clinking against his teeth. He shuddered, then put the glass down.

"Vile stuff," he said, and I had to agree with him. The look on his face suggested he was thinking of pouring another shot, but he resisted the urge.

I took another swallow of my own drink. The first taste had numbed my tongue a bit, so the second wasn't quite as repulsive.

"Lugh really means to fight a duel with Dougal, no matter what anyone else thinks, doesn't he?" Brian asked.

I waited a beat to see if Lugh would answer the question in my head, but he didn't. I sighed. "Like he said, let's take this one problem at a time. We have to get Dougal to the Mortal Plain first."

He gave me an annoyed look. "Don't brush me off. You know where I'm going with this."

Yeah, I had a pretty good idea. The rest of the council was worried about whether Lugh would survive a duel. Brian was wondering about *me.* Truth to tell, so was I. Demons are extremely strong, and their hosts can withstand a great deal of abuse. And the more powerful the demon, the more damage the host could take. But with Lugh and Dougal equally matched, the size and strength of their hosts might be the crucial difference between them. I'm strong, but there were plenty of stronger, bigger people out there in the world, and you can bet Dougal's host would be one of them.

"What do you expect me to say, Brian?" I asked. "If Lugh really does decide to fight a duel, I'm sure we'll spend hours in a council meeting listening to everyone trying to talk him out of it. But in the end, he's the king, and it'll be his decision."

A flush rose to Brian's cheeks, either from the booze or from anger. "But it's *your* body."

Tell Brian that if it does come down to a duel, I won't fight it in your body.

"Lugh says he won't necessarily be in my body if he fights a duel," I repeated, though I'm sure Lugh noticed my equivocation. It was true that using my body for a fight might put him at a disadvantage, but I would have a hard time pushing someone else into the line of fire in my place.

"That's very comforting," Brian said sourly. I was beginning to get the feeling he didn't much like Lugh. I guess I couldn't blame him.

"Let's not borrow trouble. Or put the cart before the horse. Or whatever cliché you like best. I'm too tired and generally wrung-out to think about this now. I say some heavy-duty procrastination is in order."

I'd have liked to procrastinate by taking Brian to bed and burying our powers of higher reasoning beneath physical pleasure, but the look on his face wasn't what you'd call promising. He dumped the ice out of his glass and poured another shot of crappy rum.

"Come to bed, Brian," I said, reaching out to cover the glass before he could raise it to his lips. "You still have to go to work in the morning. You don't want to go in with a hangover, do you?" I bet that wouldn't go over too well in the offices of Stuffy, Stodgy, and Serious, which was my nickname for Brian's firm.

Brian made a face, but put the glass down. "It's hard to care a whole lot about the day job with what I know about the war."

"Yeah, but we have to hope that someday this will all be behind us, and we'll get to go on with our lives. Before you got sucked into all this with me, you actually loved your job." A fact that was completely incomprehensible to me, but different strokes and all that. "You need to make sure that job is still waiting for you when this is all over."

Brian put his hands around my waist and pulled me closer to him, but it wasn't a prelude to anything romantic, just the need for a reassuring touch.

"I somehow doubt our lives are going to go back to normal when it's all over, even if Lugh does end up being the undisputed king. After all, it's not like anyone is powerful enough to exorcize him and send him back to the Demon Realm. He'll be with us for the rest of our lives."

I had to suppress a shiver. No, there was no one strong enough to cast Lugh out; however, it occurred to me that that wasn't the only way he could get back to the Demon Realm. My death would do the trick quite nicely.

I would never do such a thing! came Lugh's shocked protest in my mind. *Nor would I allow anyone else to do it,* he continued, before I could say something about how Raphael wouldn't have the same scruples. I believed him—after all, he had said he loved me. The fact remained that Brian was right, and my life would never return to what it had been like before Lugh came into it.

I leaned into Brian's body, putting my arms around him and holding him close. "Let's go to bed, okay?" I asked.

I knew Brian was far from appeased. But he let me lead him into the bedroom anyway.

twenty-four

I EXPECTED TUESDAY TO BE ANOTHER ONE OF THOSE tense, miserable days of waiting. Brian headed out to work first thing in the morning, looking none the worse for his late night. Andy and I were, once again, stuck with each other. It was beginning to feel a bit like house arrest for both of us. It did seem that Andy had lightened up a bit on the doom-and-gloom crap, but he still wasn't exactly fun to be around. Frankly, I didn't know how much longer this whole buddy-system thing was going to work. If I was tired of hanging out with my big brother, I couldn't imagine how Adam and Dominic were dealing with Raphael and William the Wimpy— whom they had summoned back as promised, only to find him even more hysterical than last time. Surprise, surprise, Dougal hadn't taken the message well.

The news stations were still buzzing about Adam's press conference, so watching TV was out, even if the Spirit Society had suspended their recruitment campaign, which I suspected they had. I was glad I didn't get the paper, because I knew damn well what the lead story would be. Whether this gamble paid off in the end or not, there was still plenty of fallout yet to come.

I was reading a book—well, more like staring at the pages of a book until the type all blurred together—and Andy was doing who-knows-what on the Internet when my phone rang. I expected it to be press, but the number that popped up on caller ID was Adam and Dom's, so I picked up.

"Hello?" Since Adam was at work today, I assumed the caller was Raphael or Dom. Alarm spiked through me when it was Adam's voice that answered.

"We've got a situation," he said.

Why was it that Adam never had *good* news to deliver? "What now?" I asked. "And what are you doing home? I thought you were working today."

"I was," he responded, and I could hear the grimace in his voice. "It's been suggested that now might be a good time to use some of those vacation days I've accrued. It wasn't quite an order, but I think it would have turned into one if I made an issue of it."

I sighed. "Is this because of the press conference, or because you didn't cooperate as much as they wanted when they questioned you about the shooting?"

"Both, I suspect. I get the feeling that I'm lucky I haven't been fired. Yet. But that doesn't matter. Like I said, we have a situation. I had a visitor at the station before I left for home. You won't believe this: It was Dougal."

"What?" I cried, my voice coming out an embarrassing squeak. Andy shut down whatever he was doing on the Internet and turned to me in alarm.

"He just strolled into the station and told them he

wanted to speak to me. I assumed it wasn't really Dougal himself, despite what he'd claimed, but when he came up to the office, he let me check his aura. And unless Lugh or Raphael has changed hosts and is playing an elaborate practical joke, it was Dougal."

"Holy shit." It was all I could think of to say.

"What?" Andy demanded, still looking worried.

"Adam's talked to Dougal," I said, because if I didn't answer Andy, he'd never shut up. "Let me talk, and I'll tell you all about it after I get off the phone." I waited a second to see if Andy would mutiny, but he didn't.

"So what did he have to say?" I asked Adam.

"He said he was coming in to see me to let me know he'd accepted our invitation, as he called it. He suggested he and Lugh get together at six tonight in the food court at the Gallery to discuss terms. He figures that ought to be public enough that both he and Lugh would feel safe from an untimely attack."

Crap! We'd all been expecting Dougal to drag his feet about this, not try to rush us. "What is he up to?" I murmured, not really meaning for Adam to hear.

"At a guess, I'd say he's trying to make sure we're unbalanced. We've kind of got him by the balls, and he's going to look for any advantage he can find."

Tell Adam to get Raphael and Dominic and meet us here.

"What about the rest of the council?" I asked.

"Huh?" Adam said.

"Talking to Lugh," I responded absently.

We don't have time to gather them all and have a huge debate, not if we want to keep open the option of making the rendezvous.

I didn't like the idea of keeping Saul, Barbie, and Brian in the dark. Especiálly Brian, who'd be pissed off at me later for not telling him immediately what was going on. Besides, it kind of made me wonder if Lugh was planning something he'd rather not have one or more of them hear.

Just tell Adam to get them here, Lugh said, his mental voice impatient.

I fought down my natural urge to dig in my heels when someone tried to order me around. It was already two in the afternoon, and four hours wasn't a whole lot of time to plan this meeting, if we actually decided to go. And Brian would be at work until after five, so if I really wanted him to keep up his semblance of a normal life, I should do what Lugh asked. That is, ordered.

"Lugh wants you to bring Raphael and Dominic here to talk things over," I said to Adam.

Adam hesitated for a beat. I'm not sure why. Maybe he was worried about leaving William alone—although he'd been so badly beaten down by now it was hard to see him as much of a threat. Or maybe because he didn't like the idea of Dom being included in whatever scheme Lugh was going to devise. But the alternative would be leaving Dom unprotected in the house, so bringing him was the lesser of two evils.

"I'll be there in about a half hour," Adam said.

I frowned. "Can't you make it sooner? We don't have a lot of time."

"I can make it sooner if you don't mind having the press on our tails for the rest of the evening."

"Oh. Take your time, then."

He snorted softly, then hung up. As usual, no polite good-bye.

I'm going to have to take control when everyone gets here, Lugh informed me once I got off the phone.

I always felt like a bit of a loony talking to myself, so I retired to the bedroom, where Andy couldn't see me doing it. Lugh, understanding my way of thinking as usual, waited until the door had closed behind me to talk to me again.

I'd like you to promise to hear me out, he said, and every brain cell in my head went on red alert.

"Whatever it is you have to say, I already don't like it."

Lugh hesitated for a moment, then soldiered on. *We need to have this meeting with Dougal. He's as vulnerable as he's ever been, but if we stand him up, he might get cold feet and go back to the Demon Realm.*

"How would he do that? No one's strong enough to exorcize him except maybe you or Raphael."

Lugh was silent, and I shook my head as I recognized the faulty assumption behind my words: the assumption that Dougal had any scruples I'd understand. All he had to do to get himself back home was kill his host, and that wasn't something he was likely to lose sleep over. Assuming demons actually sleep.

"Okay," I said, "I get that we have to rendezvous with Dougal. Now tell me whatever it is you think I'm going to get upset about. Other than the fact that you want to have control for the second time in two days, which is going to give me a killer headache."

To most demons—even royals like William—Dougal, Raphael, and I all look about the same on the Mortal Plain. But Dougal would be able to tell Raphael and me apart. Kind of like how human parents can see the difference between their identical twin children when others can't.

My heart sank a bit. Letting the bad guys know that Lugh was inside me did not put me in my happy place.

You misunderstand, Lugh said. Raphael has already claimed to be me, in Tommy Brewster's body. Even if William couldn't give Dougal a very clear picture of what Tommy looks like, he'd at least know that I was supposed to be in a male body.

"So what?" I asked, though the hairs on the back of my neck were starting to stand up. My subconscious often understands things before my conscious mind does. I guess because denial doesn't work on my subconscious.

So if I show up with you as my host, Dougal's going to start wondering who William was really talking to.

I gave a little snort. "He won't wonder. He'll know it had to be Raphael." I frowned. "Or that you've switched hosts since then."

He'll know it was Raphael. If I switched hosts, my new host would be a man, not a woman. Our natural inclination is to possess hosts of our own gender, and if Dougal thought I picked a female host, he would get very, very curious about why.

"I still don't get it. He's going to be suspicious no matter what. He knows we want to kill him. And what does it matter if he thinks it was Raphael who talked to William?"

It matters because it's better for Dougal not to know that Raphael is working with us.

I frowned. "Newsflash: He already knows that."

No. He knows Raphael didn't want to let him kill me. There's a big difference between interfering with Dougal's plans to kill me and actually, say, being part of my royal council. And as you may have noticed, Raphael is a great deal more . . . devious than I am. Dougal thinks that makes me weak. I'd like to keep him thinking I'm weak, so I'd rather he not know I've got Raphael advising me.

My subconscious mind bitch-slapped my conscious mind until I let go of my denial. "You want to go to this meeting in Tommy Brewster's body." I sat on my bed and lowered my head into my hands. "But to do that, you'd have to get Raphael out. That's why you want Dominic here. You want him to host Raphael."

Only temporarily, Lugh hastened to assure me. *It would be for a couple of hours, at the maximum. I don't think they particularly like each other, but they don't dislike each other, either.*

A dull ache started behind my eyes, but I was pretty sure it was all in my mind. Lugh could stop me from having physical ailments—except for the ones that hit me after control changes. As Lugh had obviously known, I really hated the idea of letting Raphael into anyone else's body. Especially someone as nice as Dominic. But our other human allies were Brian, Barbie, and Andy. I didn't want to see how Saul would react to the thought of Raphael taking possession of Barbie's body—and I suspect Lugh didn't, either. Brian was at work, and I'd already decided he needed to stay there. And it would be cruel and unusual punishment to ask Andy to host Raphael for a third time when he hated Raphael as vehemently as he did.

How difficult do you plan to be about this? Lugh asked, and his mental voice sounded vaguely amused.

"Would being difficult about it change anything?"

No. It would just make things more difficult.

"I'm glad you're finding this amusing," I said in my most surly voice. But I knew he was right.

Lugh had to be in the driver's seat to move from my body to that of another host. He could fight his way into control, given enough time, but that would be spectacularly unpleasant for me. And even if he couldn't fight his way into control, as soon as Raphael arrived, he'd know what Lugh and I were doing. All he'd have to do would be to knock me out, and all my mental walls would come crumbling down.

"I won't be difficult," I finally conceded.

Thank you.

I wasn't sure he had much of anything to thank me for. Fighting over control would be unpleasant for *me*, not for him. But though I was tempted to pick a fight, I realized I didn't have the energy for it. There was too much going on for me to waste my mental resources on pointless sparring.

———

Lugh let me stay in control until Adam, Dom, and Raphael arrived. As soon as I closed the door behind them, Lugh tapped politely on the barriers of my mind, and with a resigned sigh, I let him in.

"Will we be making the rendezvous with Dougal?" Raphael asked before Lugh even managed to turn around.

"Yes," Lugh said shortly. "Let's all take a seat, shall we?"

It was kind of scary that with only one full sentence and some body language, everyone knew it wasn't *me* in the driver's seat anymore. But it was obvious from the way they looked at me that they knew.

Adam, Dom, and Andy sat on the couch. Adam put his arm around Dom and pulled him closer, giving Andy a little extra breathing room. Apparently guys—straight ones, at least—get antsy when forced to sit too close together on a sofa. Raphael, in his usual lone-wolf style, sprawled on the love seat. Lugh remained standing.

There was a pregnant pause, and then Lugh launched into the same spiel he'd given me. He was a lot less apologetic-sounding when he explained to the guys. I guess apologizing wasn't very kingly.

No one interrupted him, though it was easy to see from the expressions on their faces that they figured out where Lugh was going long before he got there.

"And so I need to meet with Dougal in Tommy's body," Lugh finally concluded, putting it into words, although I was sure he could see the comprehension in

their eyes just as well as I could. "Which means someone else is going to have to host Raphael for a few
hours."

Dom's face paled, and Adam's arm tightened
around his shoulders. Andy folded his arms across his
chest and lowered his chin, refusing eye contact.

Raphael laughed, a brittle, bitter laugh. "Ah, what a
joy it is to be welcomed with open arms."

"Try not to make things worse, brother," Lugh muttered, giving Raphael a scathing glance. His attention
didn't stay on Raphael for long. Andy wouldn't meet his
gaze, but Lugh spoke to him anyway. "I know how
poorly you and my brother get along," he said. "I would
not ask you to host him again."

Andy's eyes closed, and his shoulders slumped as a
long breath of relief hissed out of him. However, something akin to mutiny flashed in Adam's eyes.

"You can't ask Dom to do it!" he said. I suspect his
hold on Dom was getting hard enough to hurt, but Dom
seemed disinclined to complain. His breath was coming
short, and his hands were clenching and unclenching
in his lap.

"Yes, I can," Lugh said with gentle insistence. "He is
a member of my council."

"He's—" Adam started.

"He's an adult," Dom snapped, "and doesn't need
you to talk for him." I'd never heard him speak to Adam
so sharply before. It showed just how upset the idea of
hosting Raphael made him.

Adam was rarely speechless, but he was now. He

looked at Dom as if he'd never met him before. "You expect me to just sit here and not say anything?" he asked incredulously, and while he kept his arm around Dom's shoulders, his hold visibly loosened.

"Don't you two fight about it," Raphael said. He'd lost the look of bitter amusement, his expression serious and devoid of malice as he stared at my brother. "It should be you, Andrew. Like it or not, you've dealt with me for a decade. You can handle a couple of hours more."

Anger surged through me, and if I'd been in control of my body, I'd have had a few choice words for Raphael.

Andy shook his head in refusal, his attention fixed on the coffee table as if it were fascinating. "I can't," he whispered.

Raphael's lips curled into a contemptuous sneer. "You can barely forgive yourself for letting me take Tommy, a total stranger and fucking lunatic. How are you going to live with yourself if you let me mind-rape Dominic?"

Dom cringed and pressed himself into Adam's embrace. Andy gasped, finally looking up with horror in his eyes. And I started trying to fight my way to the surface, though what I thought I'd do to stop Raphael was anyone's guess. Lugh remained firmly in control.

Do something! I thought at him frantically, but he shook his head slightly and didn't move.

Andy's eyes shimmered with tears as he met Raphael's challenging stare. "You bastard," Andy choked out.

Raphael shrugged. "I am what I am. And you are

what you are." He held out his hand, leaning across Adam and Dom to do so. "Now take my hand and let's get this over with."

"Damn you," Andy said. And then, to my surprise, he reached out and clasped Raphael's hand.

twenty-five

EVEN THOUGH THERE WASN'T ANY WAY TO FORCE Raphael out of my brother, I couldn't help trying to fight my way to the surface, so angry I expected a red haze to cloud my vision. I felt Lugh wince as my efforts made his head hurt.

But then Lugh turned us toward Tommy Brewster, and I stopped fighting for control.

Tommy was slumped forward in his chair, his arm lying limply over Adam's and Dom's laps.

"He's not breathing," Adam said.

Lugh took a couple of strides forward. *Don't get into any trouble while I'm gone,* he told me, and I think he was only half joking. Then he touched the back of Tommy's neck, and suddenly, for the first time in months, I was alone in my body.

It was so disorienting that my knees gave out, and I pitched forward, almost landing in Adam's lap. Adam caught one of my arms, and Lugh, in Tommy's body, caught the other, and they held me until I steadied. My head throbbed, and my stomach churned, but I tried to ignore them as I got my feet back under me.

As soon as I'd disentangled myself from Lugh and Adam, I stood up straight and glared at Raphael. If I hadn't been afraid he'd let Andy feel it, I'd have slugged him. He blinked at me calmly, unaffected by my glare. He even smiled at me.

"Believe it or not, I'm doing Andrew a favor. I told you he likes to beat himself half to death with guilt. He'd have had a field day if—"

"You're the one who laid the guilt trip on him, asshole!"

"Yes, I laid a guilt trip on him while he could still do something about it. If I hadn't said anything, he would have allowed Lugh to 'volunteer' Dominic and would have drowned in guilt afterward. He needed a swift kick in the ass, and I gave it to him."

Lugh made a grunting sound that could have been amusement or annoyance. "Even when you're doing what is arguably the right thing," Lugh said, "you manage to be cruel about it."

Okay, that sounded more like annoyance.

Raphael shrugged. "If I'd tried to be nice about it, it wouldn't have worked. I may not like Andrew, but I understand him." He turned to me. "Honestly, Morgan. Hosting me for another couple of hours will do him no harm." One corner of his mouth tipped up. "And since he took me voluntarily, it might remind him that, even if his shining armor is dented and rusty, he still has it."

What could I possibly say to that? I couldn't deny that Raphael knew Andy better than any of the rest of us did. I'd tried my own version of "tough love," and it had been an abysmal failure. Raphael had been even more brutal, but he'd prompted Andy into doing something I would never in a million years have expected. Maybe he really did know what he was doing. Even so, I just didn't have it in me to trust Raphael.

"Let's talk about the meeting with Dougal, shall we?" Lugh asked.

It felt weirder than I can explain to hear Lugh's words coming out of Tommy's body. Even when I was hearing his voice in my head, I always pictured Lugh as the gorgeous stud muffin he made himself into in my dreams. To hear him talking out of what had only minutes ago been Raphael's body was ... uncomfortable.

I sat on the arm of the couch, feeling a little too weak and shaky to stand. I was still fighting the headache and nausea, but there was another pain, too, a hollow cold ache in the center of my chest. I found myself rubbing my breastbone absently, but it didn't ease the ache.

"Raphael," Lugh said. "I want you to stay here with Morgan and Dominic."

Raphael sat up straight and gaped at his brother. "You must be joking! You're not going to meet Dougal with only Adam at your side."

Lugh arched an eyebrow. "I'm not going to bring a couple of helpless humans into Dougal's range, and we've already established that I don't want him to know about you."

I was sitting close enough to Lugh to give him a sharp kick in the shin.

"Ow!" he protested, giving me an affronted look.

"There are no 'helpless humans' in this room," I informed him. "And we're not expecting a melee in the food court. That was Dougal's whole point in choosing to meet there, right?"

"And if you show up with only Adam in your entourage," Raphael said, "you're going to make yourself look weak, like you have no supporters."

"I *want* Dougal to think I'm weak. I want him to underestimate me so he'll make a fatal mistake."

Raphael shook his head. "Tell me you're not really planning to go through with this whole duel thing."

"Why not? I might have more supporters than I was planning to let Dougal know about, but we all know he's got many more supporters on the Mortal Plain than I do. If you're thinking we can somehow hunt him down and get to him without putting me at risk, you're delusional."

Raphael was agitated enough to stand up and start pacing. "But Lugh, there's no way to know who would win if the two of you fought. And Dougal's too smart to set up the duel in any way that would let you get an advantage."

"Someday, somehow, it's going to come down to a fight between the two of us," Lugh said, his voice low and soothing. "You know that, even if you don't want to admit it." He turned to me. "And in case you or anyone else is worried, if we do succeed in setting up a duel, I'll fight it in Tommy's body, not yours. We have to assume that Dougal will have taken a superhost of some sort, and I would be at a severe disadvantage if my host were a normal human."

I'd have worried about what that meant for Andy, since no doubt he'd be Raphael's temporary host once more if Lugh marched off to battle in Tommy's body. But if Lugh fought with Dougal and lost, I had a feeling Andy's emotional well-being was going to be the least of our troubles.

Raphael still didn't look convinced. "We'll argue about whether you're going to duel Dougal or not later," he said. "Let's finish arguing about who's going with you today, first."

Lugh smiled wryly. "Adam and I are going alone. There's nothing to argue about."

Raphael stopped pacing, and the look in his eyes made the hair at the back of my neck prickle. I could almost smell the testosterone in the air as Lugh unfolded from his chair and met Raphael's glare with one of his own. I wasn't sure if this was about to get ugly, but just in case, I started backing away toward my dining room table, on which my purse currently sat. I had a Taser in there, and I was beginning to suspect having it out and armed would be a good idea. No one paid any attention to me, not with Lugh and Raphael facing off as they were.

"You're not going without me," Raphael said with quiet menace.

"Raphael, I am your king, and I am giving you an order. Stay. Here." Lugh was getting that eerie, pissed-off glow in his eyes.

Raphael shook his head. "To you, you're my king first, my brother second, and that's the way it should be. But to me, you will always be my brother first. So you can give me as many orders as you like, but don't expect me to crumble in the face of your royal authority."

I'd gotten to my purse by this time, and I fished out my Taser.

"I really hate to say this," I said as I armed and pointed the Taser, "but in this rare instance, I agree with Raphael."

All eyes turned to me. Lugh's jaw dropped open in shock to see me standing there pointing my Taser at him.

"There are too many things that can go wrong," I informed him. "You can't go with no backup other than Adam." I kept my eyes on Lugh as I spoke to Adam. "You're damn good backup," I told him, "but you're only one person. You can bet Dougal's going to have more than one minion with him, and we need to have more than one person there to defend Lugh if push comes to shove. You know I'm right."

Lugh had told me once that even the most loyal of his council members would defy him if they thought it was for his own safety. I was gambling that he was right and that Adam would see things the same way Raphael and I did. If I was wrong, this was a lost cause. Yeah, I could Taser Lugh, and Raphael would be able to keep Adam and Dom from interfering. But superhosts were able to shed the effects of a Taser jolt faster than mere human hosts, so it wasn't like I could keep Lugh down long enough to miss the rendezvous.

Lugh turned his fearsome glare to Adam, who looked very unhappy to be in the hot seat. He thought for a long, agonizing minute, then sighed.

"I'm afraid they're right, Lugh," he said, his head bowed with regret. "All Dougal has to do is kill your host, and victory will be in his reach. If you look too vulnerable, he might be willing to risk trying it even in the middle of a crowded mall."

Lugh's glare would have had more effect if Adam had actually been looking at him.

"I know I'm only a 'helpless human,'" Dominic chimed in, "and you probably don't much care about my opinion, but I have to agree. I understand you want to minimize the risks to the rest of us, but meeting Dougal with only Adam to guard you would be just plain reckless."

Lugh winced, as if Dom's words had hurt him. Maybe they had. Lugh slowly lowered himself back into his chair, and I lowered my Taser. I didn't put it away, though. I knew how fast demons could move.

"If I didn't care about your opinion, Dominic," Lugh said, "you would not be on my council." He looked around at the rest of us, and a wry smile played on his lips. "I had hoped that without the full council here to back you, I might be able to browbeat you all into seeing things my way. It appears I was mistaken."

Raphael laughed, a genuine, hearty laugh that broke some of the tension in the room. I disarmed the Taser and shoved it back into my purse.

"You thought you could browbeat *me*?" Raphael asked Lugh, still laughing. "Being housed in human flesh has addled your mind, big brother. In what alternate universe would that actually work?"

Lugh's lips twitched. I think he was suppressing a smile, though he gave Raphael a halfhearted snarl.

"Just so we're clear," I said. "We're all going. Right?" Everyone nodded. "Okay then, what's the plan?"

And it was a good thing Lugh had kept the rest of the council members out of this, even if things hadn't turned out as he'd hoped, because even with only four of us there to argue with him, it took every minute we had left to agree on how to make the approach to Dougal.

twenty-six

THE GALLERY IS A GINORMOUS, SPRAWLING URBAN mall that, under normal circumstances, I'd avoid like the plague. Crowds are not my best thing, but the Gallery and crowds go together like chocolate and peanut butter. At least we weren't within spitting distance of a holiday, or the place would have been unbearable.

We entered the mall at the street level. The babble of too many voices made the throbbing in my head worse, and I still felt that weird . . . hollow feeling in my chest. I remembered how Dom had rubbed his breastbone after I'd exorcized Saul, and now I understood why.

The food court was on the top floor, but we didn't want Dougal and company spotting us until we were good and ready. Adam went up first, to make sure Dougal was there in the flesh, so to speak, and to make sure our meeting place was as secure as possible. Dom watched anxiously as Adam rode the escalator up. As a police officer and demon hunter, Adam put himself in danger on a regular basis, and Dom had to know that. But I guess knowing it in an abstract way was easier than watching it unfold.

After a very long few minutes, Adam called Raphael's cell phone and let him know that he and Dougal were ready for us. There wasn't anything on the face of the planet that could force Adam to give us the all clear if he saw something hinky, but that didn't stop me from feeling a nervous flutter in my stomach. Dougal had been the bogeyman for so long now that I couldn't help being scared shitless at the idea of meeting him face to face.

There wasn't a whole lot of breathing room on the escalator, and I was glad I wasn't claustrophobic. The four of us stayed close together, doing our best to keep the shoppers—and the teenaged mall rats—from getting between us.

The food court, naturally, was mobbed. I looked at some of the lines in front of the restaurants and wondered why anyone would want to wait in line that long to get fast food. If I'd been in one of those lines, I'd be expecting nothing short of a filet mignon by the time I got to the counter. Though considering the lingering nausea from the control change, even a filet would have made me hurl.

Despite the mob, we had no trouble spotting Adam waving at us. Raphael and I led the way, one final layer of protection between Lugh and Dougal.

There were three people already seated at the long table, though I was pretty sure that the four people at the neighboring table belonged to Dougal's entourage, too. They weren't watching us, and they had food in front of them, but they all had the stereotypical demon good looks, and they were more playing with their food than eating it.

The three at the long table were all also demon-beautiful. There was a tall, slim Asian woman with shiny blue-black hair that trailed halfway down her back. There was a solidly built man who dressed like an MIB wannabe and whose face held the most neutral expression I'd ever seen.

And then there was contestant number three, a striking blond guy with piercing blue eyes and sensual lips. He slouched casually in his chair, while his two companions sat rigidly straight, their eyes busily scanning the area. Gee, I wondered which one was Dougal.

Apparently, Lugh blended in better than Dougal, because I could tell from the way Dougal looked from one of us to the other—mostly skipping me—that he was trying to figure out which one of us was Lugh. A long, silent staring match ensued, during which I noticed the foursome at the next table had stopped playing with their food, though they still weren't overtly watching us.

"Everyone keep your hands where I can see them," Adam said. "If I see anyone reaching for anything, I'll shoot you." His hand rested firmly on the gun holstered at his side. It was a good thing his superiors had merely pressured him into taking a vacation, rather than taking away his badge and gun. "I am a cop, so I can get away with it even if you're just pulling out a hanky."

My eyes darted around at the people sitting at nearby tables, but the noise level in the food court was so high it would be hard to hear anything unless you were listening closely.

"So paranoid," Dougal said with a mocking smile. "I'm here under a flag of truce, remember?" But he laid his hands on the table, and gestured for his two companions to do the same.

"Them, too," Adam said, jerking his chin toward the four at the other table.

Dougal rolled his eyes as if all these precautions were ridiculous. But he glanced over his shoulder and nodded at the demons at the other table, and they all kept their hands in plain sight. Dougal then turned back to the rest of us.

"Now, which one of you is Lugh? We have much to talk about, so let's not waste time posturing."

Lugh pushed past Raphael and me and stood towering over his brother. The rest of us kept up our careful scans of the people around us. We were each armed with a Taser, but this being a public place, we didn't dare have them out. That didn't mean we weren't ready to draw them at a moment's notice.

Lugh didn't say anything, just held out his hand. To the human beings around us, it looked like a handshake that went on for an abnormally long time, but I knew they were checking each other's auras, confirming their identities, although Adam had been tasked with confirming Dougal's presence before calling us to come up.

"Sit down, all of you," Dougal said when he let go of Lugh's hand. "We can't have a civilized conversation with you all looming over me like that."

Lugh raised an eyebrow, but took the seat directly opposite Dougal. The rest of us took that as a cue and sat as well, except for Adam, who was keeping an eye on Dougal's minions.

"There's only so civilized this conversation can be, considering you've been trying to have me killed," Lugh said. Even in Tommy Brewster's body, even with the effort he made to hide it, I knew Lugh well enough to hear the edge of pain in his voice. He refused to admit it—I'm not the only one who's good at denial—but his brother's betrayal had wounded him.

Apparently, Dougal knew him well enough to hear it, too. He lost his mask of polite disinterest and leaned forward, regret clear in his eyes. I was betting Dougal was as good an actor as Raphael, but there's always a chance it might have been genuine.

"It was never anything personal, Lugh," Dougal said. "I want what I want, and you're in my way. If there had been a way to take the throne without harming you, I would have done it."

Lugh snorted. "How very thoughtful of you. That makes it all better."

"If you'd be willing to abdicate the throne in my favor, we could end this without any further bloodshed."

Lugh actually laughed at that. "Come now, brother. Surely you don't believe I'm that stupid. I'd have to return to the Demon Realm to formally abdicate, and I don't for a moment believe that you wouldn't have your friends summon me back to the Mortal Plain for a bonfire. Even assuming I'd be willing to entertain the idea in the first place, which I wouldn't."

Dougal smiled and held his hands out to his sides in a "Well, it was worth a shot" gesture. "I had to at least ask," he said. The smile leaked away. "But I suppose there is no hope that both of us can survive this little squabble. It's a pity. I would be happy to kill Raphael with my own two hands. But I'd prefer not to kill you if I could think of a way to avoid it."

It took some serious effort for me not to glance at Raphael and see how he took that news, but I managed it. Which was a good thing, no doubt, because Dougal's lieutenants were obviously searching all our faces, trying to figure out if one of us was Raphael. I'm pretty sure Raphael's poker face held, since no one seemed to be staring at him in particular.

Lugh cocked his head to one side. "Is that so? I seem to remember William saying something about how you wished you could be here in person to watch me burn."

Dougal waved that off. "I was angry when I said

that." He gave Lugh a wry look. "You've made this all rather more difficult than I was planning."

"So sorry to be a bother."

"Yeah, I'll bet you are." Dougal swept the rest of us with a glance. "So where is our baby brother anyway?" he asked, and he made no attempt to hide the hatred in his eyes. Apparently, Lugh wasn't supposed to take it personally when Dougal betrayed him, but it was okay for Dougal to take it personally when Raphael did it to him.

Lugh made a face, and his voice dripped with contempt. "I have no idea where he is, and I don't *want* to know."

Dougal's eyebrows shot up. "Is that so? Had a falling out, have you?"

Lugh was still scowling. "He tried his best to cover it up, but I found out what the two of you were doing in your labs."

"Ah," Dougal said, and I had a feeling Lugh had just made a very convincing argument. "You do love riding on that moral high horse of yours, don't you?"

"If I couldn't convince Raphael that what he did was wrong, I certainly don't expect to convince *you*. But what the two of you were doing was unconscionable."

Dougal pinched the bridge of his nose, like the conversation was giving him a headache. "You see, that's the thing about you, Lugh. You see the world in black and white, and you have no concept of compromise."

"Oh, and compromise is your middle name? I think your worldview is just as black and white as mine."

Dougal shrugged. "Maybe. But you're wrong about

one thing—I *would* have been willing to consider a middle ground, had I any reason to hope you could be reasonable."

"*I'm* being unreasonable? I'm not the one who's killing and torturing his own people in fits of pique!"

Dougal sneered. "Ah, yes. You're the saintly brother who has never lost his temper. One would think to listen to you that you are the pinnacle of perfection—the ideal to which all of us lesser beings must aspire."

I think Dougal scored a point with that potshot, though Lugh tried not to let it show on his face. He crossed his arms over his chest and leaned back in his chair. "If we're going to catalog one another's faults, we'll be here till closing time. Let's talk about terms for a duel."

Dougal stared at him intently. "You really mean to do this? To risk everything on the chance that you can defeat me in a fair fight?"

"Yes, I do. I'm sure I don't know half of what you've been up to in the Demon Realm since I've been gone, but I know enough to see that you must be stopped."

"And why would you expect me to risk fighting you? I'm confident that you'll slip up eventually and my people will get to you and eliminate my problems for me. Since you've made William into your toadie, you must know my resources on the Mortal Plain are not inconsiderable these days. Why should I not just sit back and wait until they succeed?"

One corner of Lugh's mouth tipped up. "If you thought you had that luxury, you wouldn't be here right now. I hear tell you've made a lot of promises and you've had trouble keeping them. Your future in the Demon Realm is looking less than bright. And all I have to do to turn all of humanity against us is to tell them about the experiments you and Raphael conducted with your human subjects, which would mean you couldn't escape your troubles in the Demon Realm by coming here."

A muscle ticked in Dougal's jaw, but otherwise his poker face remained steady. "You would really risk every demon on the Mortal Plain just to spite me?"

"To spite you? No. But to stop you? Absolutely. I've already put them at considerable risk by allowing Adam to announce the truth about exorcism. I believe humans have a right to decide whether to host demons or not. I will not sit idly by and watch you take that choice away from them."

Dougal shook his head in amazement. "You would side with humans over your own people?" The lines of his face hardened, and his eyes glowed with his anger. "This is the greatest proof ever that you are not fit for the demon throne. Your loyalties should be to your own kind, not to *them*." Grimacing as if disgusted, Dougal made a sweeping hand gesture to encompass the crowd that milled around the food court.

"You've made your point of view on the subject quite clear," Lugh said, and his voice sounded calm and unruffled. Score one for the good guys! "Now, are we going to discuss terms or not?"

Dougal visibly tamped down his temper. "Fine. Have it your way. We'll discuss terms. Where shall the grand event take place?"

Lugh shrugged. "I don't have a location picked out yet. I'm sure we can find someplace sufficiently secluded for what we need, given a little time. I can have Adam find a suitable location and then contact you—or your lieutenant—to let you know where it is."

Dougal laughed. "So that you can booby-trap it?"

Lugh rolled his eyes. "Let's establish from the start that neither one of us is stupid. I won't suggest anything that will insult your intelligence, and I hope you'll do me the same courtesy."

"But—"

"Obviously I would have to allow your people to examine the location once it's been selected so that you need not fear a booby trap."

From the look of him, Dougal was thinking furiously, trying to find the flaw in Lugh's logic. He must have decided it was sound, for he nodded. "All right. I will not formally agree to a location until my people have had a chance to examine it, but I will... provisionally agree, as it were. What weapons shall we use?"

Lugh sat back and thought about it a minute. "It seems to me weapons won't be of much use, since the point of this endeavor is for one of us to kill the other, not for one of us to kill the other's host." His eyes narrowed in a shrewd frown. "You wouldn't be entertaining thoughts of trying to kill my host, now, would you?"

It would be a lot easier to kill Lugh's host than to kill Lugh himself. And, of course, if Dougal killed Lugh's host and Lugh was sent back to the Demon Realm, Dougal's minions would summon him back into a host who was already subdued and ready for roasting.

"I'd be lying if I said it wasn't a tempting possibility," Dougal said. "But I presume you mean to give me some motivation not to?"

Lugh nodded. "You are fighting this duel to stop my supporters from revealing your special projects to the human public. The only way you can do that is by killing me in a fair and honest fight. If you cheat by killing my host, or if your followers interfere in any way, the agreement will be null and void."

Dougal frowned. "And what would prevent them from doing so if you lost fair and square?"

"You can't believe I or any of my supporters actually *want* to do this, can you?" Dougal shook his head, but still looked suspicious. "I told you I would not endanger our people like that out of spite, and I meant it."

Dougal gave a little grunt that might have been a laugh. "And yet you would have your supporters tell all if I do not fight a fair fight. That sounds like spite to me."

Lugh shrugged. "Call it what you will. As far as I'm concerned, it's a deterrent, and a deterrent has no power unless I am willing to see it through. Make no mistake, Dougal: If you cheat, the truth *will* come out."

Dougal thought about that a while, then nodded. "I believe you. Now tell me what's to prevent *you* from cheating."

"Firstly, it's not as easy for me to cheat. Killing your host would do me no good, unless you're planning to tell me your True Name so I can do to you what you plan to do to me."

"Granted. But you can still let your supporters interfere with the fight."

"Since I feel confident you won't risk having our secrets exposed by cheating, I would feel comfortable limiting the number of my supporters who are present for the duel. You can bring as many as you like, and they can ensure that my own supporters do not interfere."

Dougal smiled ruefully. "Nice move, brother. You make it sound like it's a concession, when actually you need to have most of your supporters safely away from the duel so they can carry out your revenge if I cheat."

"What does it matter, as long as I've set the conditions so I can't cheat?"

I could almost picture the wheels in Dougal's head turning as he tried to find a hole in Lugh's proposal. I was beginning to think Lugh had already put a lot of thought into his plans for the duel—without ever discussing it with me or with his council.

Dougal sat up straighter, and I could tell he'd thought of something.

"Your supporters are loyal in the extreme," Dougal said. "What's to stop someone from coming to the duel in your place and then sacrificing himself with some kind of suicide bomb?"

Lugh thought about it for a moment before speaking. Apparently this was one contingency he had not previously considered. "You needn't face me until one of your people has had a chance to confirm my identity."

"Confirm that the demon who shows up is either you or Raphael, you mean."

Lugh grinned. "Even if Raphael and I were on speaking terms at the moment, do you really imagine he would show up in my place? Since the plan is for your people to outnumber mine, it would be suicide for him. If you believe he would take a risk like that for *anyone*, then you clearly don't know him as well as you think."

Dougal conceded the point with a gracious nod. "It's true I can't imagine the little bastard sticking his neck out unless he felt sure no one was going to chop his head off. All right, so one of my people will confirm your identity before we begin, and when he has done so, I will enter the battlefield, as it were." He raised an eyebrow. "And we will fight each other with bare hands?" There was just the faintest hint of eagerness in his voice.

Lugh sighed. "No, I don't suppose bare hands will work, since I'm sure your host is so...durable that disabling him enough for you to burn would be well-nigh impossible."

Dougal didn't try to hide his disappointment. "You *have* learned a lot about the experiments, haven't you?"

Lugh ignored the comment. "We will have to use Tasers."

"And whoever gets the first shot in is the winner."

Lugh nodded. "We will need to have a pyre ready, since we both know Tasers don't work as long on your lab-bred hosts as on human hosts."

For a moment, Dougal looked irritated. Lugh obviously knew more about the superhosts than Dougal had hoped. He'd probably have a cow if he knew that Lugh's host was a superhost himself. Then Dougal's shoulders slumped slightly, and his gaze dropped to the table in front of him.

"We really mean to do this, then?" he asked quietly. "Really mean to condemn each other to death by fire?" He didn't sound scared. He just sounded...sad.

Lugh's jaw tightened. "Don't pretend the thought distresses you! You've already tried to have me burned at the stake."

"Yes, I have," Dougal replied. "But I find thinking about doing it with my own two hands is a bit more... troubling than merely ordering it done." He met Lugh's eyes. "Are you sure you can do it, brother? Sure you could take my body, put it on a pyre, and let me burn?"

Lugh's expression didn't change. "Yes, I'm sure."

Dougal's face hardened, the melancholy fading as if it had never existed, which it probably hadn't. "Very well then. We have only to set a place and time."

"Give me a contact number," Lugh said, "and I will have Adam get in touch with you about the place. Once the place is set, we can choose the time."

There was a little shuffling among Dougal's minions until one of them came up with a piece of paper and a pen for Dougal to write his number down. Adam was very, very watchful, making sure no one reached for a weapon. I suppose he wasn't as confident in the power of Lugh's threat as Lugh was.

Once he had the contact number, Lugh rose without another word. The rest of us—who had not spoken at all during the war council—took that as a cue and rose with him. Adam stayed behind, guarding our backs, making sure we weren't followed. And then we all went back to my apartment, where I was pretty damn sure Lugh's council would have a lot to say.

twenty-seven

RAPHAEL STARTED THE FESTIVITIES AS SOON AS WE had my apartment door closed behind us. He grabbed Lugh's arm, yanked him around, and got right up in his face.

"You are not dueling with Dougal!" he said, and though moments before he'd seemed cool and self-contained, his eyes now glowed and it looked for all the world like he was considering throwing a punch.

Lugh's eyes glittered strangely as he glared at Raphael. Andy was taller than Tommy, so Lugh had to look up to meet his brother's eyes, but that didn't reduce his air of authority.

"Let go of my arm, Raphael," he said. He hadn't raised his voice even a little bit, but it was a command, not a request.

"And if I don't?"

Lugh rolled his eyes. "Don't be childish. This isn't helping the situation."

Raphael gave Lugh a little shove when he let go of his arm, but Lugh didn't retaliate. "Do you understand how many people will suffer if you ride out on your white horse and get yourself killed?"

"Of course I do," Lugh answered mildly. "That's why I don't plan to get myself killed. Now why don't you all sit down? I'll tell you what I have in mind, and then we can shuffle hosts again so that Andrew doesn't have to put up with you any longer than necessary."

"Shouldn't we call in the rest of the council now?" Adam asked.

"I promised Andrew his sentence would be as brief as I could make it," Lugh said, drawing a scowl from Raphael. "You can call the rest of the council members later and fill them in."

"All right," I said, "let's hear this plan of yours that's going to let you duel with Dougal without getting yourself killed."

Lugh pulled over a dining room chair and sat on it. Maybe he thought the straight-backed chair was more dignified—or more like a throne—than the sofa or love seat.

"When the time comes for the duel, we will switch hosts once more so that I am in Tommy's body. I believe Dougal won't dare cheat, so my chances against him should be fairly even." Raphael opened his mouth as if he was about to interject something scathing, but one look from Lugh shut him up. "If I win, then our problems are solved."

I was pretty sure that was an overstatement. Dougal had sent an awful lot of his supporters through to the Mortal Plain already, including who knew how many criminals and at least one demon who was powerful enough to be part of the official royal council. A change in leadership in the Demon Realm would have no effect on the demons who were already here. But killing Dougal would be a nice first step.

"But I have a contingency plan for what to do if I lose," Lugh continued, and I'd almost describe that little smile of his as smug. He looked at Adam. "When you go looking for a location, make sure there are woods nearby. On the day of the duel, you'll go to those woods early and find yourself a secure hiding place up in the branches. If Dougal Tasers me, you shoot my host."

We all started talking at once, but Lugh held up his hands for silence.

"Let me finish," he said, and we all subsided. "Morgan, you'll be stationed here, at your apartment. If I should fall, Adam will send you a signal on the phone, and you'll immediately begin the summoning ceremony. I will give you my True Name. You'll be able to get me back to the Mortal Plain before any of Dougal's people can manage it. We'll be set up to move faster, because we'll be expecting it.

"The situation will, obviously, not be optimal. Whoever is with me for the duel may well be killed by Dougal and his people when they figure out what has happened." He looked at Raphael. "And we would not have Tommy Brewster to move Raphael back into, so he would have to remain with Andrew, at least until another alternative appears. But I will not be dead, and Dougal will not have the power of the throne."

There was a long, painful silence as everyone chewed

that over. I had to admit, it sounded like a pretty good cheat. The worst-case scenario still sucked, but it was not the utter disaster that Lugh's death would be. And it was unlikely we were going to find a better way to kill Dougal.

"Do you have any idea how many things can go wrong with this clever plan of yours?" Raphael asked. "What if Dougal's people spot Adam? What if he can't get a good shot? What if he *does* get a good shot, but it doesn't kill Tommy? Remember, a superhost can take a bullet to the brain without dying. I'm not sure I know exactly *what* it would take to kill one."

"With the right kind of rifle and ammo," Adam said, "I can blow half his head away. I don't think even Tommy can survive that."

"Maybe not, but what if phone service hiccups? Or—"

"Calm down, Raphael," Lugh said. "I'll be the first one to admit we can't make this foolproof. But if you think we'll ever come up with a truly foolproof way to kill Dougal, you're wrong. When the full council is here, we can discuss plans for each of the contingencies we can think of. But the basic plan is solid. You have to see that."

Raphael scrubbed his hands over his face. "Jesus, Lugh," he muttered from behind his hands. Then he huffed out a deep breath and let his hands fall away from his face. "I know the plan is a good one," he said, every word spoken with great care and deliberation. "That doesn't mean I have to like it."

"No one has to like it," Lugh responded. "But unless

you have a better suggestion, this is the way it's going to be. Understood?"

Raphael pursed his lips, but he nodded.

"Good. Now I shall return to Morgan, and you can call in the rest of the council to work out all the details." He looked over at me and held out his hand.

I stared at that hand for a long moment. I'd have thought I'd feel reluctant to take Lugh back, that I'd have enjoyed my time alone inside my head. Instead, I felt a surge of eagerness. It scared me a little, made me wonder if I was a little bit like Jonathan, growing "addicted" to my demon.

But I took Lugh's hand nonetheless. The moment our hands touched, the weird ache in my chest went away, and Tommy collapsed in a heap.

The next several hours were probably the longest argument I'd ever had the pleasure to participate in. As soon as Lugh was back in me, and Raphael was back in Tommy, I called Saul and Barbie and told them to come over for a council meeting. Then I called Brian. I probably should have explained over the phone what had happened this afternoon—it wasn't like he wasn't going to find out anyway when he got here—but I chickened out and just told him Lugh had called a meeting.

The guys had gotten started with the arguing while I was still on the phone, and the tension level rose another notch when Saul arrived. I managed to stay out of it for the most part, at least until Brian made his appearance.

The others were still too busy debating details—none too politely, I might add—so it was left to me to explain to Brian that I'd gone to face Dougal without telling him. We managed not to have a screaming fight about it in the middle of the council meeting, but only barely. I understood where he was coming from—I had a long, shameful history of withholding information from him, and I'd promised I wouldn't do it anymore. But it wasn't as if I'd had a choice, not with three demons siding against me.

We went to bed well after midnight, the council meeting having raged on into the wee hours. The good news was that we'd managed to come up with a number of backup plans to make sure I'd get the message if Lugh went down. The bad news was that the council had decided that rather than Adam being the one in ambush, it would be Saul.

Lugh felt it important that he not show up for the duel with only human supporters at his side, but he didn't want anyone on the opposite side knowing the identities of Saul or Raphael, and anyone who was at the duel was sure to be examined and recognized. Cynical me, I wasn't sure that Lugh wasn't just making sure his family members were out of reach if things should go wrong and Dougal's supporters should turn on the bystanders.

Saul had never fired a rifle, but Adam assured us that he could teach him how with minimal effort. There is no physical activity that demons aren't better at than humans, and Adam guaranteed that even with his inexperience, Saul would hit anything he aimed at. But I still would have felt a hell of a lot more comfortable if Adam were the shooter.

After that, all we had to do was work out the time and place. Adam would begin searching for the perfect location tomorrow. Which meant that once again, all the rest of us could do was wait.

Brian and I were both too worn out to continue our earlier argument—thank God—but there was a chilly silence between us as we got ready for bed, and there was no affectionate cuddling. He was brooding, and I was just too damn tired to deal with it.

twenty-eight

FOR THE FIRST FEW MOMENTS AFTER I WOKE UP THE next morning, I lay in my bed in blissful ignorance. The fuzz of sleep kept my mind free of any inconvenient thoughts, and I just snuggled into the covers and considered allowing myself to drift back to sleep.

But when I tried to relax, I remembered the upcoming duel between Lugh and Dougal—the duel on which the fate of two worlds depended. The memory forced back the last vestiges of sleep, and I pushed myself into a sitting position. Brian's side of the bed was empty. I rubbed at my gritty eyes and looked at the bedside clock. It was nearly eleven. He must have gone in to work this morning, as usual. I'm not sure I could have managed it under the circumstances, but then I'd never been as career-driven as Brian. I hoped the fact that he didn't wake me before he left didn't mean he was still mad at me.

I'd woken up less than five minutes ago, and already I was in major grouch mode. Probably just as well that Brian wasn't around, or I might have picked a fight with him just to work off my frustrations. My nerves were buzzing with anxiety and good old-fashioned fear.

Perhaps coffee wasn't the best idea when I was so on edge I could barely sit still, but I feared I might spontaneously combust without it. I drank way more than was good for me and found myself pacing my living room as if it were a cage.

I was absurdly grateful when Andy emerged from his room. Yeah, we'd been getting on each other's nerves, but I needed a distraction from my worries.

"Did Raphael behave himself last night?" I asked my brother as I poured him a cup of coffee. He hadn't seemed any worse for wear when Raphael moved back into Tommy, but I'd decided then that I'd rather wait for a private moment to make sure he was all right.

Andy gratefully took the coffee I offered him and took a sip before speaking. "He was Raphael," he said, but he didn't sound particularly bitter when he said it. "But he was right. I'm kinda used to him, and we managed to tiptoe around each other without throwing off too many sparks."

I felt my brows lift at that. "Raphael doesn't seem to tiptoe much." I remembered him laying on the brutal guilt trip last night, and tried not to imagine what it must have been like for Andy to have had that in his head for ten years.

Andy smiled a bit. "No, not his strong suit. Mostly we just both kept our metaphorical mouths shut so we didn't have anything to fight about."

"That was a brave thing you did," I said, looking into my coffee instead of at Andy's face. "Allowing Raphael back into you to protect Dom." I raised my head, and it was Andy's turn to stare at his coffee. Guess neither one of us was real comfortable with this touchy-feely stuff.

Andy licked his lips, and I couldn't tell if it was a nervous gesture or if he was just thinking. "It's so easy for me to think the worst of him. Whenever he suggests something, my instant reaction is to not want to do it. And when he tells me something, I assume it's a lie or that he's wrong or that he's somehow trying to manipulate me." He grimaced. "Don't you dare tell him I said this, but every once in a while, he gets one right. If I'd let him take Dominic to spare myself..." He shook his head. "That's not the kind of man I want to be."

He took another sip of coffee. Not knowing what else to say, I did, too.

"I became a host because I wanted to do some good in this world," Andy said. "When I let Raphael take Tommy..." He shook his head and swallowed hard. "I couldn't help wanting Raphael out of my head, and logically, I know it was only human. But I felt like I could never...consider myself one of the good guys again."

"Well, shit, Andy. You've *always* been one of the good guys."

He smiled at me, and I thought there was a little more light in his eyes than there had been in the last few months. "Little sisters are required to think their big brothers are heroes, so your opinion doesn't count for much."

I gave him a mock scowl. "Well, big brothers are required to be assholes, so you're doing your fraternal duty."

He tried to cuff me on the side of my head, but I managed to evade him. And I didn't even spill my coffee. Go me!

Then the moment of levity faded, and the smile disappeared from Andy's face. But even without the smile, I thought he looked like a weight had been lifted from his shoulders. Maybe—just maybe—he was considering the possibility of respecting himself again. I couldn't exactly thank Raphael for that—since it was Raphael who'd almost broken Andy's spirit in the first place—but I was glad for it, nonetheless.

Late that afternoon, Adam called to let me know he'd found a location he thought would work well for the duel. He came to pick me up around six, with Saul and Raphael in tow. I wasn't excited to share a car with the terrible twosome, but we needed Saul to check the location out and make sure he had a place he'd be comfortable watching from. And we needed Raphael's devious mind to make sure we didn't overlook any potential pitfalls. I doubt I would have been invited to go myself, except Lugh was adamant that he needed to see the place to give it his personal stamp of approval. Since he was the one who'd be risking his life—at least, risking his life the most—I supposed it was a fair request.

It wasn't the most relaxed of car rides. Saul rode shotgun, and I got to share the backseat with Raphael. They were relatively civilized, and they only stuck verbal pins in each other four or five times during the long drive to the location Adam had selected. But at least they didn't get into a brawl in the car.

There was nowhere within the city limits we could have the isolation we needed to hold this duel. But as it turned out, Adam had found a place already guaranteed to be an effective demon-killing field. It was an industrial-sized farm out in the Brandywine Valley. The farm had once been owned by Jeremy Wyatt, who had at the time been the leader of God's Wrath. He'd also been possessed by one of Dougal's demons.

The last time I'd been there, it had been a working farm, and Lugh and I had been destined to be burned at the stake—which in this instance was a basketball hoop set into a concrete court behind a large barn. But the night had ended with Wyatt and all his fanatical followers dead, and it looked like the farm had died with them. Locked gates featuring a "for sale" sign blocked the driveway, but the fields and buildings beyond screamed of neglect. It didn't look like anyone had been in a hurry to buy the place out.

There isn't much that can stop a demon from going where he wants to. Saul got out and broke the lock on the gates, then Adam drove through. We left the gates closed behind us. Unless someone were to get out and examine the gate, no one would be able to tell we'd come through it. Not that it seemed likely anyone would be looking

I tried my hardest not to flash back to my last trip out here, tried not to remember the horror of the fate that had awaited me at the end of the drive. But it's damn hard to forget about the threat of being burned alive. I cast a sidelong glance at Raphael, wondering what his memories were like. He must have been pretty distressed during that drive himself, since it was looking at the time as if all his plans to keep Lugh safe were going to fail. But he hadn't let a bit of what he was really feeling show back then, and he wasn't showing it now.

The concrete basketball court was still there, behind the barn, though the net was gone. The barn loomed between the court and the road, so no one would be able to see us. A big plus. Another plus—and the primary reason Adam had selected this place—was the stand of trees about fifty yards from the court. The rest of the farmland was, well, farmland—flat, and severely lacking in hiding places. Because the farm wasn't in use, the fields were overgrown with weeds, but they were low and sparse enough that they would make an ambush impossible.

Raphael shook his head. "Dougal's people are going to search those trees," he said. "There's almost nowhere else within sight that someone could hide, other than in the barn. And that makes the trees damn obvious."

"Maybe," Adam said. "But they're going to be worried about bombs and incendiary devices, not snipers.

Remember, it does us no good to kill Dougal's host without killing Dougal himself, and they know that. Besides, even if they search, I bet they'd have a hard time finding him." He turned to Saul. "Why don't you go see if you can find a good spot to hide while the rest of us check out the barn? When we're done, we'll come looking for you and see if we can spot you."

Saul nodded and trotted off toward the trees. Checking out the barn was a formality at best, but since the point of the exercise was simply to give Saul time to pick a spot without us watching, we dutifully trooped in and looked around. Nothing quite so exciting as examining an empty, smelly barn.

We gave Saul a good ten minutes to get himself concealed, then we all went out into the stand of trees and started looking. I knew practically from the first moment I passed under those branches that it would be nearly impossible to spot anyone. The trees were tall and leafy, the canopy dense enough to make it dark and murky between them. When I peered upward, all I could see were leaves, leaves, and more leaves. I doubted anyone else was having any better luck, but I crisscrossed the entire patch of woods anyway and couldn't spot Saul.

No one found him, but Raphael insisted we walk all the way around the perimeter of the woods as well.

"No chance anyone's going to see him," Adam declared when we finally got all the way around. "Come on down, Saul," he yelled.

There were some rustling noises up in the canopy, even though there was no breeze. We all looked up and watched Saul magically appear from the cover of the branches, climbing nimbly down the tree as only a demon—or maybe a monkey—could manage.

Wiping the sap from his hands onto his jeans, Saul sauntered toward us, looking mighty proud of himself.

"Satisfied?" he asked his father with a smug smile. Obviously, putting one over on Raphael just made his day.

The look on Raphael's face said he was anything but satisfied, but he nodded anyway. "This is probably the best place we're going to find. But we'll have to see if Dougal will go for it."

"No reason he shouldn't," Adam said.

Raphael looked at me. "Is Lugh all right with it?"

Tell him it's perfect. And tell him to stop worrying so much or he'll be the first demon in history to have a heart attack.

I relayed the message, and everyone had a good laugh at Raphael's expense—even Raphael. It was a laugh I think everyone needed, because the drive back into the city wasn't nearly as tense as the ride out.

The place had now been chosen. All that was left was to determine the date and time. Adam would call Dougal as soon as he got back home. It was getting late for Dougal to come out and look at the place tonight, but maybe as soon as tomorrow he would put his stamp of approval on it. After that, it would probably take no time at all to agree on a date and time. Which meant the duel wasn't far in the future.

For someone who hates waiting as much as I do, I was beginning to think there wouldn't be anywhere near enough of it before the day of reckoning.

twenty-nine

THE CLICHÉ FOR DUELS IS THAT THEY'RE HELD AT dawn, or thereabouts. The duel between Lugh and Dougal, however, was to be held at nine o'clock on Saturday night. There were several reasons for the late start, none of them being my reluctance to get up at oh-dark-thirty. The first was that Dougal's minions needed time to do a thorough check of the location to make sure Lugh didn't have an army of accomplices tucked away somewhere ready to charge the moment Dougal appeared. The second was that it would take some time to build the pyre on which the loser of the duel would be burned. The most important reason, though, was that we wanted to minimize the risk that a prospective buyer might want to view the property and stumble upon the duel. From the looks of the place, buyers weren't exactly beating down the door to snatch it up, but it was safer not to trust to luck.

Which meant getting up at oh-dark-thirty anyway, because Saul needed to be in hiding before there was a chance of a buyer or real estate agent stopping by, and Raphael insisted we accompany Saul so we could confirm he was well hidden. The sun was just rising when we arrived at the farm. We drove past it and parked about a mile away, then came at it on foot from an oblique angle. It was still dark enough that we could cross open fields without being spotted, and we got to the woods without seeing—or, hopefully, being seen by— anyone. We sent Saul into the treetops once more, this time with a high-powered rifle slung over his shoulder, a canteen on his belt, and pockets full of granola bars and trail mix. He had dressed in army-surplus chic, and his face looked pretty damn awful beneath a thick layer of camouflage makeup.

We spent a good half hour trying to find Saul after he had hidden, but none of us spotted him. Lucky that we were putting on this little shindig in the summer, with all those leaves for cover.

By the time we left, there were people moving around in the vicinity of the barn. They had a couple of dogs and a metal detector, and we figured they were Dougal's people, checking for booby traps. They gave no sign of having seen us, their attentions much more focused on the search for potential bombs.

After getting Saul situated, the rest of us drove back to the city. We had already determined that Adam and Dominic would accompany Lugh to the duel, leaving William locked up in their guest room. Obviously, the lock wouldn't hold him if he really wanted to get out, but Adam and Dom were going to neglect to mention that they were leaving the house, and William was too much of a coward to attempt an escape when he might get caught. Raphael, residing in Andy's body, would remain at my place with Barbie and Brian and me. The three of them would form the "circle" around me as I awaited the signal that Lugh was in trouble and I needed to summon him. The demons all assured me that three people were enough to form the circle needed for the ritual—though it looked more like a triangle to my untrained eyes—and I had no choice but to believe them.

Adam and Dom went back to their place—I suspected so they could have a final frolic, just in case one or both of them didn't come back—but they would be back to pick up Lugh in plenty of time to reach the dueling ground. Raphael, too, went home for a while, which was probably a good thing, since the tension level in my apartment was high enough as it was.

I spent about an hour in the late afternoon practicing the incantation. I had no trouble with the Latin—though I wasn't sure how well I'd do under stress—but I was really worried about Lugh's True Name. To say it was a mouthful was an understatement. I counted twenty-six syllables that sounded like one nonsense sound after another. Lugh said it translated roughly into "he who shines in the darkness," which seemed too simple for twenty-six frickin' syllables.

"What language *is* this?" I complained to Lugh as I stumbled over it for the umpteenth time. "Please tell me it's dead; otherwise I'll have to go kill it."

I heard his soft chuckle inside my head. If he was at all concerned that he might find himself burning at the stake in a few hours' time, it didn't show.

It's how we express our own native language with human

mouths, so I'm afraid the language is not dead. Luckily, you only have to learn this one phrase.

Even when I learned it, I was terrified that I would muff it under pressure. I remembered the painful efforts Jonathan had made to summon William, and how very long they had taken.

You're not Jonathan, Lugh assured me. *You'll do fine. But let us hope you don't have to do any summoning after all.*

Yeah, I sure as hell hoped that!

Adam and Dom were due to pick Lugh up at seven-thirty. Raphael—for once showing up on time—arrived promptly at seven. At seven-fifteen, I let Lugh take control so he could move into Tommy Brewster. Raphael hadn't transferred into Andy yet, although Andy was holding out his hand, his face as set and hard as a soldier going into battle.

"Well, what are you waiting for?" Lugh asked. He sounded impatient to get going.

Raphael heaved a sigh, which didn't seem to lessen the tension in his face or posture any. But instead of reaching for Andy's hand, he drew the Taser that was meant to be Lugh's weapon for the duel.

None of us had a chance to react in time. Not even Lugh.

The Taser made its trademark pop, and the probes hit Lugh firmly in the chest and belly. He collapsed to the floor, though even in his surprise, he acted quickly enough to block me from feeling more than a fraction of a second of the pain.

Brian and Barbie both gasped. Brian took a step toward me, and Barbie drew a gun from a holster I hadn't realized she was wearing. Unfortunately, Raphael had a gun in addition to the Taser. I didn't want to know where he'd gotten it. Holding the Taser—its probes still attached to my body—in his left hand, he menaced the others with the gun.

"I don't want to shoot anyone," Raphael said, his jaw set grimly, "but I will if I have to." A faint sheen of sweat glowed on his brow.

Brian gave him a murderous look, but the only person in the room at the moment who could offer Raphael any threat was Barbie. And even her threat was minuscule, considering how little a bullet would harm him.

"Put the gun down, Barbara," he said. "Lugh would have been the only one here who could stop me, and he'll be out of commission for a while."

"Stop you from *what*?" Brian asked, outraged.

"From going to the duel in Lugh's place."

Lugh couldn't move a single muscle in my body, but I heard his howl of protest in my head. Raphael came to loom over the two of us. His face was paler than usual. He still held the gun out, though he wasn't pointing it at anyone in particular. He ejected the cartridge from the Taser and stuck the Taser into the waistband of his pants.

"You said once before that there was no foolproof plan to defeat Dougal," Raphael said. "But there is." He reached up with one hand and unbuttoned the first few buttons of his shirt, just enough to show us that he had something—a large flask-shaped bottle—stuck to his chest with adhesive tape.

"This bottle is full of napalm," he said, and once again I heard Lugh's wail of protest in my head as we both guessed what Raphael was planning to do. I sensed Lugh trying to transfer me back into control, since I would be less debilitated by the effects of the Taser than he was, but it didn't seem to be working. Perhaps the electricity was mucking with that ability as well as all his others.

"Dougal's minions will examine my aura and think I'm you. Dougal will know the difference when we check each other's auras, but by the time he realizes who I am, it will be too late." He pulled a miniature lighter out of his pocket, then palmed it so it looked like his hand was empty. "I'll break the glass and light it, then I'll grab Dougal. His followers may try to put the fire out, but fires fueled by napalm are really hard to kill." His eyes glimmered with a hint of tears, and I noticed a slight tremor in the hand that held the gun. Raphael was scared shitless, and I couldn't come close to blaming him.

"You're going to kill yourself," Andy said, the first reaction he'd shown to Raphael's turnabout.

Raphael swallowed hard. "Dougal can't be allowed to survive this duel," he said. "We can't take the chance that Lugh might lose, even if Morgan did manage to summon him back here. We'll never have a better shot at Dougal than we will today. We *have* to succeed."

"You don't like pain," Andy said. His voice was flat and uninflected. "Do you really believe you'll be able to hold on to Dougal while you're burning?"

Raphael visibly shuddered. "I can do it. At least long enough to get the napalm on him. I'll try to get us into the pyre while I'm still capable of rational thought." He pulled two pairs of handcuffs from his pants pocket, throwing one to Brian and one to Barbie.

"Put those on," he ordered. Barbie and Brian looked at each other, then back at Raphael, who managed to muster a pretty scary sneer despite his obvious terror. "Put them on, or someone's going to get shot. Not fatally, but it'll still hurt like hell."

We all knew Raphael well enough to know he wasn't bluffing. I could see how much Barbie hated the idea of putting her gun away, but I guess she hated the idea of being shot even more, so she stuck it back in its holster and put on the handcuffs. Brian hesitated a fraction of a second longer, but when Raphael glared at him, he complied.

"I don't get any handcuffs?" Andy asked, his voice still that flat, almost uninterested tone.

Raphael put his gun away. "No." He walked over to the end table by the door, where I kept my purse, then rooted around until he found my Taser. Andy watched him, but didn't say anything, and made no effort to stop him. Raphael armed the Taser and then handed it to Andy.

"Your job is to keep Lugh from coming after me. We all know my plan is better than his plan, but family members rarely act rationally."

Andy stared at the Taser. I willed him to take it and give Raphael a jolt. I supposed in theory his plan might be better. I had to admit, there was a better chance of killing Dougal this way. But Lugh's plan was to accomplish the same thing without getting anyone else killed. I'd never liked Raphael. There were plenty of times when I'm pretty sure I actually hated him. But not enough to let him kill himself.

Andy reached for the Taser, but he didn't turn it on Raphael. I hadn't really expected him to. After everything Raphael had put him through, Andy probably found the suicide plan rather appealing.

Lugh struggled to get my throat and tongue under control. I don't know what he was trying to say, but all that came out were incoherent grunting noises.

Save your energy, I thought at him. *You're not going to talk Raphael out of it even if you could make yourself understood. It's Andy we've got to try to reach, and I'll have a better chance to do it than you will. Put me back in control.*

He did, and my stomach lurched in protest. I tried to lie perfectly still, not to draw Raphael's attention. I wasn't going to be able to talk Andy into *anything* until Raphael was gone, though I hated to give him a head start.

While Andy held the Taser loosely at his side, Raphael reached into his shirt pocket and pulled out a folded piece of paper, which he laid on the coffee table.

"This is a list of all the lab facilities Dougal and I set up," he said. "I've also put down what each lab was trying to accomplish, and as much as I know about how successful they were. I wasn't lying when I told you I didn't know much about the day-to-day operations of the labs other than The Healing Circle. I wish I could give you more, but at least you'll have enough information to get you started if you want to try to clean up the mess Dougal and I made."

Raphael checked his watch. "Adam and Dom will be here any minute," he said. "I'll meet them downstairs. In case anyone gets past Andrew and tries to get tricky, let me assure you that calling Adam and Dom would be a very, very bad idea. I can overpower them easily if I have to, but they wouldn't enjoy the process. For once in my life, I'm trying not to let anyone else get hurt. I hope you will honor the effort."

He took a deep breath. It sounded shaky when he let it out, so he did it again. After the third one, he had visibly managed to shove his fear into the background. Color came back to his face, his hands steadied, and the sweat began to dry on his brow.

Amazingly, he managed to muster one of his sarcastic grins, and if I hadn't known any better, I'd have thought his plans for death by fire didn't bother him at all.

"Off I go to save the world," he said. "Who woulda thunk it, eh?" He nodded at Andy—I guess it was his version of a good-bye. Then he knelt beside me and gave me another jolt from the Taser. I choked on a scream and wished I'd left Lugh in control until Raphael left. "I'm sorry for everything," he said, and I didn't know whether he meant the words for me or for Lugh. Possibly both.

No one said a word as he rose to his feet and walked out the door.

thirty

AFTER RAPHAEL LEFT, ANDY PULLED ONE OF MY DINing room chairs in front of the door and sat. He wasn't pointing the Taser at anyone—not yet at least—but he'd obviously set himself up as our jailor.

"So what happens next?" Brian asked. He was sitting on the floor beside me, not touching, but lending moral support all the same.

Andy tilted his chair until its back hit the door. "We wait. You and Barbara can make yourselves comfortable, but keep your distance from me. I don't expect you can do much with the handcuffs on, but I'd rather not find out I'm wrong."

Barbie took him up on the suggestion, settling into the love seat with her feet curled up beside her. Brian stayed where he was. I kind of doubted either of them was in a great hurry to rush to Raphael's rescue. Raphael had, after all, had Brian tortured, and Barbie was dating Saul, whose hatred of Raphael was probably contagious.

They consider Raphael expendable, Lugh's voice said bitterly in my head. *He didn't need to put handcuffs on them. They're happy to just let him die.*

I'd never heard Lugh sound that bitter before. I couldn't feel his feelings like he could mine, but I could hear his pain in that bitterness.

Don't give up, Lugh, I told him. *I'll do everything I can to save him.*

Even if saving Raphael could cost Lugh his life? I asked myself. If we somehow managed to get to the farm before the duel was under way, we could force Raphael to give up Tommy Brewster, and the duel could then be between Lugh and Dougal as originally planned. But we wouldn't have our summoning circle ready and waiting, so if Lugh lost, there would be no saving him.

Lugh must have sensed my hesitation, because there was a hint of what sounded like desperation in his voice. *Please help me save him,* he begged. *It is my duty as king to protect my people, and if I have to do it by risking myself, so be it.*

You can't protect your people if you're dead.

And I would not be the king they deserved if I allowed Raphael to kill himself to protect me.

I thought about that a little while—it wasn't like I had anything else to do while we waited for the Taser shot to wear off. Demons as a general rule believe that the ends justify the means. I wouldn't say I was *surprised* that Lugh would risk everything for his brother, but it didn't seem to fit real well with what I knew of demons.

If I didn't have a fair chance of beating Dougal myself, Lugh said, *then I might have to let Raphael do this, no matter how much I hated it. But I do have a fair shot, and I mean to take it.*

Is a "fair shot" really good enough? Maybe when I was waiting here to summon you, but...

If I fight Dougal, I will win. There was no hesitation, no uncertainty in his voice.

You said the two of you are evenly matched. You can't guarantee you'll win.

We may be evenly matched in strength, but I believe my will is stronger than his. That will give me an advantage. He sighed. *But no, I can't guarantee it.*

I couldn't say his argument was particularly convincing. Especially not when I knew how desperate he was to save Raphael. He had never outright lied to me that I knew of, but that didn't mean he couldn't, didn't mean that wasn't exactly what he was doing now.

His voice in my head was a snarl of frustration. *When Raphael captured Brian, you were willing to do anything, risk anything, to save him. I could have stopped you. I could have protected myself at his expense. But I didn't do it. Please, Morgan. Please help me save my brother.*

And with that argument, all my defenses crumbled. As Lugh, the manipulative son of a bitch, had known they would. I remembered how awful I had felt when I found out Brian was coming to harm because of me, and Lugh was right. There was nothing I wouldn't have done to save him. Hell, I let Adam whip my back to shreds for his amusement just so I could get him to help me rescue Brian. I knew the anguish Lugh was feeling right now. And I knew there was no way I could stand by and do nothing while he suffered.

Of course, that meant I'd have to find a way to get

through Andy. Andy, who might feel that Raphael was getting exactly what he deserved.

I tried to sit up. Unfortunately, while I wasn't completely incapacitated by a Taser, as a demon would be, I wasn't in great shape, either. A miserable moan escaped my throat as I collapsed before I got halfway up.

The legs of Andy's chair thumped to the floor, and he pointed the Taser at me. I didn't try to move again. I probably would have fallen flat on my face anyway.

"Andy," I said, my voice slurred like I was drunk. "It's me. Morgan. Lugh's put me back into control."

The Taser remained pointed steadily at me. "I don't think that changes anything."

I sucked in a deep breath, wishing the room would stop spinning and pitching around me. I closed my eyes, but that didn't help much.

How could I get through to Andy? How could I get past his anger and hatred? No easy answers leapt to mind.

"Raphael's a bastard," I said, my words slightly clearer now as my tongue decided to cooperate with my brain, "but he doesn't deserve to die."

Andy snorted. "You've got to be kidding me! Do you have any idea how many people he's killed? And let's not even *talk* about the people he's hurt."

Hmm. Maybe that hadn't been the best tack to take. "Yeah, he's done some terrible things in the past. But he's changed." Suddenly, I felt like I was onto something, and I found myself talking faster, more earnestly. "Think of all the good things he's done over the last few months. He risked everything for Lugh's sake, even knowing Lugh would imprison him for his crimes if he ever went back to the Demon Realm. He set up that trust fund for Blair Paget's care."

Blair was Barbie's twin sister, who had been horribly injured in a car wreck when they were teenagers. Barbie had been practically bleeding herself dry trying to keep her sister in the best long-term care facility possible. Then a mysterious benefactor had appeared out of nowhere and set up a trust that covered all of Blair's medical expenses.

"He *what*?" Barbie asked.

She was sitting behind me, but I didn't want to take my eyes off Andy. Plus, I was afraid he'd Taser me if I moved.

"He's the one who set up your sister's trust. He refused to admit it because he knew if he did, everyone would assume he had some kind of ulterior motive."

"Then how do you know it was him?" she asked.

"Because I bullied and badgered him until he finally admitted it to me." It had been an oblique admission—he hadn't actually come out and said he was responsible—but it was an admission just the same.

"He didn't have to do that," I said. "He had nothing to gain." Except, perhaps, Lugh's approval, but I kept talking fast before anyone could mention that. "And think about what he's trying to do today! He's going to kill himself in what has to be the most painful way possible just to stop Lugh from taking a risk. He's changed. You *know* that."

Andy wasn't so quick to argue this time, but argue he did. "Even if he really has changed, I'm not sure that makes such a big difference. We're much more likely to take out Dougal if Raphael has his way."

I tried once again to sit up, because there was only so long I could glare at Andy while lying on the floor without feeling ridiculous. This time, I succeeded. He tensed, but refrained from shooting me as soon as I moved. I didn't try to get to my feet, and I moved slowly as I turned to face him squarely.

"Lugh is the demon king," I said. "It was his decision to fight the duel, and Raphael has no right to take that decision away from him." I glanced over my shoulder at Brian. "You were the one who taught me that." There had been many times when I'd made bad decisions in an attempt to protect Brian, when in fact he was perfectly capable of deciding himself which risks were worth taking.

Brian nodded to acknowledge my point. "But if Lugh loses, Dougal will give the demons free rein to do what they want on the Mortal Plain. There's just too much at stake."

Tell them that if I lose, they should reveal everything to the public. I told Dougal I wouldn't do it just out of spite, but I would do it to protect your people from our people.

I relayed Lugh's message, then gave everyone a moment to absorb it.

"Lugh is willing to risk his life for this. And he's got a backup plan to keep Dougal from really winning, even if he wins the duel." I let a hint of pleading sneak into my voice.

Andy looked indecisive, which was a step in the right direction. He glanced at his watch. "I'm not sure if we can really do anything at this point," he hedged. "Raphael's got a pretty big head start already."

"And every minute we spend debating is another minute he has to get ahead of us. Please, Andy. You can think about it some more on the way, and if you change your mind, you can Taser me. But if we don't get moving soon, it really will be a moot point."

It felt like it took about an hour for Andy to make a decision and stand up. He moved the chair away from the door, then tossed the Taser back in my handbag.

"We'll need a car," he said, and I almost wept in relief.

thirty-one

WE TOOK BARBIE'S CAR. IT WAS JUST ANDY AND ME riding off to the rescue. We had no way to get the handcuffs off Brian or Barbie, and they wouldn't be much help—and could easily get themselves killed—if they came with us. Plus, we needed them to spill the secrets of the demons' labs if we didn't come back. I suppressed a shiver at that thought.

I would have preferred to drive, but Andy insisted that he be the driver. I guess so he could Taser me without me wrecking the car if he changed his mind about trying to save Raphael. His knuckles were white where he gripped the steering wheel, and I could see the muscles of his jaw working as he ground his teeth. I wanted to say something to help persuade him that he was doing the right thing, but I got the impression that talking wasn't a good idea. For the moment, he was doing what I wanted; I needed to keep it that way.

Raphael had more than a twenty-minute head start on us, but we were driving faster—though not as fast as I would have liked. I found my right foot pressing down on an imaginary accelerator and tried to stop myself. There was only so fast we could go without risking getting stopped for speeding—a delay we could not afford.

The other factor in our favor was that the duel would not begin the moment Raphael arrived. Dougal's people would have to confirm his identity to the best of their ability first, then they'd have to let Dougal know it was safe to come out from wherever he was. There was sure to be some posturing and speech-making before the combatants actually had at it, and there would be yet another delay as Raphael and Dougal examined each other's auras. I couldn't imagine that Dougal would send an imposter, not when he was utterly convinced of what Lugh would do if he didn't show up, but Raphael would still insist on checking.

None of these reasonable arguments kept my heart from beating double-time, or my palms from sweating. I took a deep breath to try to calm myself, amazed that I felt this . . . depth of anxiety for Raphael's sake. Just because I didn't think he deserved to burn to death didn't mean I should feel this desperate need to save him.

I thought for a moment that somehow Lugh's anguish was leaking over into my brain. And that was when I realized where my sense of desperation came from. It wasn't for Raphael's sake. It was for *Lugh's*. Despite everything Raphael had done, I don't think Lugh had ever stopped loving him. I suspected that was true of Dougal, too, though I doubted Lugh would admit it. To kill with his own hands the brother who'd betrayed him would hurt Lugh badly enough. To lose *both* his brothers...

A burning sensation in my eyes told me I was on the verge of tears. Lugh and I had had our differences, but he was kind, and compassionate, and thoughtful, and wise. He didn't deserve the kind of pain he would suffer if Raphael killed himself.

I swallowed the tears as best I could. "Can you drive a little faster?" I asked Andy, my voice scratchy from fighting the tears.

Out of the corner of my eye, I saw him glance at me and raise his eyebrows, but I didn't turn to face him. I didn't know what expression my face was wearing, but I suspected it was too raw, too open to be one I wanted him to see. I was more grateful than I could say when the needle on the speedometer inched up just a bit.

The miles sped away, but warp speed wouldn't have felt fast enough to me just then. My fingernails bit into my palms, and I kept flooring my imaginary accelerator whenever I wasn't concentrating on keeping still.

"Never in a million years would I have guessed Raphael was capable of this," Andy whispered when we were about halfway there. "I can't reconcile the Raphael

I know with the Raphael who would sacrifice his life to save *anyone*."

I swallowed a lump that formed in my throat. "That's because he really has changed," I said, just as quietly.

Maybe this is the Raphael that would have been, if I hadn't been so overbearing and judgmental all his life, Lugh said.

It's not your fault, I assured him. *Raphael was a bastard because he chose to be. You can't seriously hold yourself responsible for that any more than you can hold yourself responsible for him choosing to be a martyr.*

"Maybe being inside your head for all those years was a good influence on him," I said out loud. "You never got along, but he keeps saying how he understands you, even if he doesn't like you. Maybe some of your better qualities rubbed off on him."

Andy gave me a sidelong glance that spoke of skepticism, but Lugh *had* said that demons were influenced by their hosts, so I didn't think it was that much of a stretch. Then again, this might have been the first time in Raphael's life he'd ever had to *fight* for something. He was used to keeping himself aloof and uninvolved. I think even the eugenics stuff was just a pet project for him, not something he really *cared* about. Maybe he found that once you start caring, it's hard to stop.

Was I really so different myself? Before Lugh had come into my life, I'd been a bastion of self-loathing. My parents had thought my unwillingness to become a demon host was a sign that I lacked the courage and decency to want to make the world a better place. They'd hammered into me the idea that I was the lesser of their children, because Andy had been willing to host, and I wasn't. They'd called me selfish, and though I'd fought them tooth and claw, secretly I'd believed them.

All the things I'd done in the last several months to try to aid Lugh's cause . . . If you'd told me before I was possessed that I would one day be ready to risk my life to save someone I didn't even like, I'd have laughed at you. I'd have felt like a shit for it, but I'd still have laughed.

So maybe people—and demons—were capable of change after all, when they had a good enough reason.

The moment I was able to make out the farm in the distance, I started staring at the sky, praying not to see the glow of a bonfire. No glow, no fire, no dead demons, right? I leaned forward in my seat and didn't care that I was pressing my foot onto the floorboard like I thought that would make the car go faster. My heart pounded, and though he was quiet, I could swear I felt Lugh's anxiety as much as my own.

If I'd been driving, I might have floored the accelerator and burst through the gate over the driveway. It would have been a stupid thing to do, guaranteed to attract unwanted attention, but I don't know that I'd have been able to help myself. I guess that made it a good thing that Andy was driving.

I had my seat belt off before he even started slowing down, and I was out of the car while it was still rolling. My hands shook as I pulled loose the unlocked chain and gave the gates a shove. I had no intention of closing them behind me, and if that meant a passing motorist noticed and called the cops—well, tough.

I felt like Andy was moving in slow motion as he drove the car through, but he barely slowed down enough to let me jump in before he barreled down the dirt driveway at a pace that probably wasn't safe. I guess he'd either caught my sense of urgency or he'd decided that now that he was committed to the rescue attempt, he was in it all the way.

There were fewer cars in the gravel parking lot than I'd expected, only three in addition to Adam's. I didn't know what that meant, and I didn't care. Without having to talk about it, I let Lugh surface once more. I would run faster with him in control.

Once again, I leapt out the door before the car had come to a stop. Andy yelled something, but both Lugh and I ignored it. If I'd been in control, I probably would have fallen, considering the car was still going pretty fast when we jumped out, but Lugh was able to keep his balance. Andy yelled again, but Lugh was already running all out.

We rounded the corner of the barn, and that was when we could see the dueling grounds. I didn't see anyone there I didn't recognize from the meeting at the food court. The Asian woman had hold of Dom, and the MIB wannabe had Adam, keeping them from interfering, as we'd agreed. The other four of Dougal's supporters who'd been at the original meeting were fanned out in a defensive position.

A few people turned to look as Lugh came into view, but most of them were staring at Raphael and Dougal, who stood in the center of the basketball court. They were gripping each other's hands in what looked like a handshake, but of course, that wasn't what they were doing.

Raphael turned and saw me coming. And everything seemed to slow down, my eyes, with Lugh's will behind them, taking in every excruciating detail while my legs seemed to drag through knee-deep mud.

Dougal, who'd been looking grim, but not particularly afraid, suddenly gasped. His eyes widened, and I knew that was the moment when he realized he was facing the wrong brother. But if the rest of us couldn't guess that Raphael would sacrifice himself, then certainly Dougal couldn't. He hesitated in what had to be shock.

"No!" Lugh screamed with my voice, and inside my head, I screamed with him.

Raphael looked at us, any fear he might have been feeling deeply buried beneath his mask. He smiled at us, faintly. Then, with the hand that wasn't grasping Dougal's, he hit himself, hard, in the chest.

Lugh screamed again, and both his supporters and Dougal's looked startled, confused. I could hear the sound of glass shattering.

Raphael pulled Dougal into what looked almost like a hug, his left arm trapped between their bodies. For a moment, nothing happened. Maybe it was just that time-delay sensation of everything happening too fast to take it in. Lugh was still running for all he was worth. But it was too late.

The fire seemed to come out of nowhere, great licks

of flame suddenly shooting out from between Raphael and Dougal's bodies. Lugh's screams echoed those of his brothers as their clothes caught fire. Raphael used that first second or so of confusion, when no one but him understood what was happening, to propel both of them toward the pyre that was set up around the basketball goal. They were both screaming—agonized shrieks that would echo in my memories forever. Dougal started struggling to push Raphael away, but he was blinded by flames and too far off balance. The momentum of Raphael's first push carried them all the way to the pyre, which went up the moment the first flame hit it. It wasn't quite an explosion, but almost. Lugh was about fifty yards away, and we still felt the enormous blast of heat.

It was hard to see anything through the sudden pillar of fire, but for a moment I thought I caught sight of two shadows, both trying to escape the conflagration. No matter how willing Raphael had been to make this sacrifice, even the iron will of a demon wasn't enough to counter the primal drive to survive.

Lugh fell to his knees on the concrete, his head bowed as he sobbed. I heard the hiss of fire extinguishers as the observers tried to put the fire out, but they had to know it was hopeless. The flames continued to soar into the air, the fuel making snapping and popping noises, sometimes sounding almost like gunfire.

Lugh retreated into the background of my mind, but I cried as hard as he had, sobbing hoarsely, breathing in deep gulps of scorching air tinged with smoke. I was vaguely conscious of Andy kneeling by my side, taking me into his arms and hugging me. I buried my face against his chest and let my misery and Lugh's pain pour out.

thirty-two

CHAOS REIGNED SUPREME FOR I DON'T KNOW HOW long. Everyone was shouting, confused, scared. The only thing anyone seemed to know for sure was that Dougal was dead. The fire raged on; no one was even trying to put it out anymore. I tried to drag myself out of the grief, fearing that Dougal's minions would retaliate, but when I raised my head, no one seemed to be fighting. Adam and Dom, no longer restrained, came over to Andy and me. I was still crying too hard to talk, so Andy explained what had happened.

By the time he'd finished explaining, Saul, still in his camouflage gear and with his rifle slung over his back, had made his way out of the woods to join us where we huddled together. He knelt on the asphalt in front of me and reached out to grab my shoulder, giving it a firm squeeze.

"Everything happened so fast, I couldn't figure out what the hell was going on down here," he said. "I don't know if I figured it out fast enough. He had already fallen by the time I fired, but perhaps he wasn't yet dead."

My head jerked up, and I felt a swell of hope in my chest. "You mean he might have survived?" I asked in something that sounded like a hoarse squeak. I heard a groan of mingled hope and pain in my head.

Saul nodded slowly. "If it was my bullets that killed his host, and not the fire, then he will be back in the Demon Realm."

Suddenly, out of nowhere, Andy started laughing. We all turned to stare at him like he was crazy.

"He knew," Andy managed to gasp out. "He knew all along."

We all looked at each other. So far, Andy was the only one in on the joke.

"What do you mean, Andy?" I asked.

Andy sucked in a deep breath. "Raphael knew there was a chance he'd survive. He was counting on Saul to shoot him."

I felt a surge of something dark and ugly rising from my chest. If Andy was going to suggest that burning himself alive was all part of one of Raphael's Machiavellian schemes, I was going to beat the shit out of him.

But he must have caught the sentiment, because he held up a hand. "Let me finish. The last time he possessed me, Raphael gave me his True Name."

We all gasped at that. Raphael's True Name was his most closely guarded secret, one he hadn't revealed even to Lugh. But he had told Andy, with whom he did not exactly have a warm and fuzzy relationship.

"I couldn't get him to tell me *why* he was suddenly giving me his True Name," Andy continued. "It made no sense whatsoever." He shook his head. "But now I get it. This was his plan all along, even before we met with Dougal the first time. He knew he was going to burn with Dougal, but he must have hoped he'd get a last-minute stay of execution, as it were."

Saul shook his head. "He couldn't have known we'd have a sniper at the ready. That wasn't even his idea. It was Lugh's."

"Just because he didn't mention it doesn't mean he didn't think of it," Andy argued. "He wouldn't be so dangerous if he weren't smart."

"You're speaking of him in the present tense. Remember, I may have been too late."

"When did you realize that it was your father?" I asked Saul, and I didn't even try to hide the accusation in my voice.

Saul met my accusatory gaze head-on. "As soon as I figured out what was going on, I knew it was him. There was no one else it *could* have been. But that didn't make me hesitate. I didn't do it for *Raphael's* sake." His lip curled a bit like it always did when he mentioned his father's name. "I did it because I knew it was what Lugh would want."

Dougal's supporters were still milling about, looking lost and aimless. I lowered my voice to a near whisper.

"Are those guys going to attack us anytime soon?" We weren't exactly on the alert right this moment.

Adam shook his head. "They don't have Dougal to protect them anymore. They've already established themselves as enemies of the state by coming here today and openly standing by Dougal, and they're probably hoping they can find some way to climb out of the hole they've dug." He lowered his voice even more. "Of course, they have no idea who's who right now. If they knew that Lugh and Saul, who's Lugh's heir—if Raphael is really dead—were here, they might decide killing us is a step in the right direction."

"Perhaps we should get out of here before they start speculating too much, then," Saul said. Casually, he slung the rifle off his back until it was in his hands. He wasn't pointing it at anyone yet, but it was good to know he had it. "They aren't going to want to risk being shot and sent back to the Demon Realm when they don't know where Lugh and Raphael and I are. Everyone head for the cars. I'll keep an eye on them as we go."

Adam drew his gun and came to stand beside Saul as they herded the rest of us toward the parking lot. Dougal's minions looked briefly like they might want to stop us, but one look at the guns convinced them they were better off letting us go.

thirty-three

W E HAD ONLY GONE A MILE OR SO WHEN WE HEARD the wail of approaching sirens. I looked over my shoulder and saw the orange glow that lit the night sky. Someone else must have seen it and called 911. As far as I knew, Dougal's demons were still hanging around the bonfire. I was sure they'd have tons of fun explaining themselves to the police.

I closed my eyes and rested my cheek against the window of the car. Now that the immediate crisis was over, I was aware of the characteristic headache and nausea that came with too-frequent control changes. I swallowed, and hoped I wouldn't need Andy to pull over before we got home.

I managed to make it all the way there without puking, which was a nice plus. I still felt wretched—sick, and sad, and utterly exhausted. I tried to hold on to the kernel of hope that Raphael might be alive and well in the Demon Realm, but I've never been what you'd call an optimist. From Lugh's heavy silence, I guessed he wasn't much of one, either.

Adam, Dom, and Saul had followed directly behind Andy and me, and we all rode the elevator up to my apartment in oppressive silence. When we got there, Adam unlocked the cuffs on Brian and Barbie—turns out most handcuffs use the same kind of key—and explained what had happened out at the farm in as dispassionate a voice as he could muster. I don't think Raphael's possible death bothered him all that much in itself. But like me, and like Saul, he genuinely cared for Lugh and hated to know Lugh was in pain.

I let instinct take over and brewed a pot of coffee, trying my hardest not to think. Everyone took a cup. Then we gathered in the living room, bringing in chairs from the dining room as usual so we could all sit. I noticed Adam pulled in one more chair than we needed. I didn't think it was by mistake. Once we were seated, we all stared at that empty chair.

It was Andy who broke the silence. "I'm willing to summon him."

Everyone's attention turned from the empty chair to Andy. I opened my mouth, but I had no idea what to say, so I shut it again.

"I would ask that you find someone else to host him once he's here, but I'll bring him over and host him while you find another volunteer."

"Andy—" I started, but he cut me off.

"None of us is going to rest easy not knowing if he's alive or dead. I can handle hosting him a while." He managed a rather feeble grin. "It's not like I haven't done it before."

All eyes turned to me. I wasn't sure if they were waiting for permission, or just waiting to hear my argu-

ment, or waiting to hear from Lugh. The attention actually made me squirm.

Lugh didn't speak to me, but then he didn't have to.
I knew how badly he wanted to accept Andy's offer. And
in all honesty, I couldn't blame him. If I had been in his
shoes, not knowing if my brother was alive or dead, I'd
probably be willing to do just about anything to learn
the truth.

"Are you sure, Andy?" I asked, my voice choked with
emotion.

"I'm sure," he said, nodding. "You'll be able to find
someone else willing to host him, even if it takes a little
while. And if you're worried that he might mistreat his
host, tell him we'll transfer him into me every once in a
while, just to keep him honest. I'll be all right. But let's
go ahead and do it and end the suspense."

I didn't have enough candles for everyone in Lugh's
council to join the circle, so two people had to sit out. I
wasn't at all surprised that Saul volunteered to be one
of them, taking Barbie with him. Although he hadn't
put up any argument, his face clearly said how much he
hated the idea of bringing Raphael back to the Mortal
Plain. He'd always been such a hothead that I half expected him to make a fuss, even knowing how much the
uncertainty hurt Lugh. But I guess he wasn't as selfish
as I'd thought.

We cleared a large space on the living room rug, and
Andy lay down on his back. Saul and Barbie watched
from outside the circle as I lit the first candle, then used

that flame to light Brian's. One by one, the candles were lit, until the circle was ready. Tension filled the air, and I think we were all having trouble remembering to breathe.

If the summoning works, I told Lugh, *I want you to take control again.*

I could almost feel his surprise. *That would be three times in one day. It'll make you sick.*

He was right. I'd be in for about three days of pure misery. But if Raphael was indeed alive, how could I deny Lugh the chance to speak to the brother he'd almost lost?

I can handle it if you can, I told Lugh. Since he got to experience all the physical symptoms right along with me, he knew exactly what we'd be going through. But I wasn't surprised that he was willing to endure it.

Thank you, he said, just as Andy began the incantation.

Andy spoke slowly and clearly, his concentration narrowed and focused on the words he was saying. He would not put us through the agony of having to listen to him fumble and flub and have to start over ten million times like Jonathan had.

By the time he finished the third repetition, I was gripping my candle so tightly it was a minor miracle I hadn't broken it in half and ruined the circle.

The last syllables of Raphael's True Name left Andy's mouth, and I held my breath. For a long, agonizing moment, Andy lay there blinking and not speaking, giving us no clue as to whose mind was controlling his body.

Then a smile broke over his face. "Holy fucking shit!"

he said, pushing himself into a sitting position. "It worked!" He gave a quick look around the circle—counting heads, I think, to make sure everyone had survived—then locked eyes with me.

Actually, with Lugh, who had taken control without a hint of hesitation. Lugh stood up, his hands curled into fists, his jaw so tight I was afraid he would break my teeth. I'd have bet my last dollar his eyes were glowing.

Raphael scrambled to his feet and held up both his hands in a gesture that was either supposed to be placating, or that was just supposed to hold Lugh off. "I know you probably want to beat the shit out of me right now, but believe me, the fire hurt bad enough. I don't need any more punishment."

Brian cleared his throat loudly. "I think I have something I have to do at home," he said, blowing out his candle and standing up. He swept his gaze over the remaining council members, just in case they didn't get the hint.

One by one, they blew out their candles and stood. Someone turned on the lamp beside the sofa, but I didn't see who. Lugh remained exactly where he was, his posture no less stiff. I couldn't literally feel what he was feeling, but I more than understood it.

Raphael kept a wary eye on his brother as the rest of Lugh's council members filed out. Brian stopped briefly in the doorway.

"If Morgan needs help when she's back in control, call me," he said, but didn't wait for Lugh to acknowledge his words.

Then it was just Lugh and Raphael and me. I wished I could do as the others had and slip away, giving the brothers their privacy, but that was not among my options.

You can never have privacy from me, Lugh said. *It seems only fair that I should not have it from you.*

"I don't know whether to hug you or strangle you," he said out loud.

Raphael's chin lifted a fraction of an inch. "I might have hoped you'd have a second or two of gratitude before you blew your top."

If I'd been in control of my mouth, I would have laughed. It was strangely good to know that some things about Raphael had not changed. Lugh was not similarly amused.

"I watched you die," he said, his voice scratchy. I felt the tears that burned in his eyes. "Do you have any idea...?" His voice broke completely on that, and he closed his eyes. When he opened them again, the look on Raphael's face had gentled.

"I'm sorry I put you through that, brother," he said, and I was pretty sure he actually meant it. "But maybe I'm the ultimate coward. Maybe I couldn't have borne to be the one watching *you* burn." His gaze dropped to the floor, and I had the feeling I was seeing the *real* Raphael for the first time, stripped of all his masks and defenses. "You're everything I've always wished I could be. I couldn't let you risk your life. Not when I could risk mine instead."

Lugh crossed the distance between them, grabbed Raphael's shoulders, and gave him a teeth-rattling shake. "You weren't just *risking* your life!" he shouted, getting up in Raphael's face. How he managed that when he was in my body and Raphael's borrowed body was at least three inches taller, I don't know. "You were committing goddamn suicide! I don't care what Andrew said, you *couldn't* have known you would survive."

"No, I couldn't know," Raphael countered. "But I could hope." He tried a cautious grin. "And honestly, how could I expect Saul to resist when he actually had the chance to shoot me?"

With an inarticulate cry of rage, Lugh shook Raphael's shoulders again, practically knocking him to the floor. Then he pulled Raphael to him and hugged him fiercely.

"Don't ever do that to me again!" Lugh growled in his ear.

Raphael returned the hug a bit awkwardly, like he wasn't used to such gestures of affection. "I don't plan to," he said with a shudder. "Believe me, once was more than enough."

The hug went on far longer than most human men would have allowed, but eventually they broke apart. Lugh glanced at the coffee table, where the paper Raphael had brought still lay unopened, practically forgotten.

"Did you leave that with me just because you thought you were going to die, or did you actually want me to know?"

Raphael stuck his hands in his pockets, looking uncomfortable. "A little of both, I guess." He grimaced. "I tried really hard not to think about facing you after you read it."

"I haven't looked at it yet. If you want to take it back, you can."

Raphael sighed and stared at the piece of paper. "Very tempting." The look in his eyes turned to one of cunning, an expression he'd worn often while residing in Andy's body before. "Perhaps we can come to an arrangement. I'll give you the paper and I'll help you clean up the mess. In return, you'll grant me a royal pardon."

Lugh let out a little groan, then pinched the bridge of his nose. He was acting all exasperated, but I'd bet anything what he was feeling deep down was relief that Raphael had given him a solid excuse for granting the pardon.

Raphael shrugged and reached for the paper. "Well, if you don't want my help..."

"Leave it," Lugh said with a sigh. "You have your pardon."

Raphael let the paper fall back onto the coffee table. "Try to remember you've already pardoned me when you read this."

Lugh shook his head, but resisted the urge to comment. "I'm going to put Morgan back in control," he said, and I could hear the reluctance in his voice. "This will be the third control shift of the day. We're going to be very, very sick."

Raphael nodded. "I'll call Brian and ask him to come take care of you. And I'll hang around till he gets here, in case you need anything."

Lugh nodded his thanks and squeezed his brother's shoulder. Then he considerately steered my body into the bathroom and raised the toilet seat before he put me back in control.

epilogue

I SPENT THREE MISERABLE DAYS ALTERNATING BE-tween kneeling in front of the toilet and lying flat on my back with a pillow over my face praying for death. I seriously considered shoving Raphael into the oven when I got better, figuring it was all his fault I was sick as a dog. Have I mentioned I get grumpy when I'm sick?

Brian did his best to take care of me, but even *he* knew better than to press his luck. I knew he was still sleeping over—even though we no longer needed the buddy system—but he slept in the guest bedroom instead of in my bed. For his own safety, no doubt.

By Tuesday, I was starting to feel a bit better and was cautiously optimistic that it was safe for innocent by-standers to be near me. Lugh and I had both been too miserable to put too much thought into the future, but when I woke up on Tuesday and was able to think about something other than my aching head and roiling stomach, I couldn't put off wondering how things were going to change now that Dougal was dead any longer.

Sure, Lugh was the undisputed king of the Demon Realm now, but he wasn't *in* the Demon Realm, and couldn't get there unless I died. (Yes, we could have found a different host to put him in and kill, but to my intense relief, Lugh was as adamantly against this plan as I.)

Raphael had resided in Andy's body for all of about twelve hours before the council—without consulting Lugh or me—decided we had the perfect alternative host available: Jonathan Foreman. William was not thrilled to be sent back to the Demon Realm, but since Dougal wasn't waiting there to make his life miserable, no one felt too bad about letting Raphael exorcize him. Including me, even though I thought they should have asked first.

The moment Raphael learned that Lugh was not planning to return to the Demon Realm in the immediate future, he had a few choice words for us.

"So he's just going to take a seventy-year vacation on the Mortal Plain while our kingdom is in turmoil?" he asked incredulously.

I snorted. "Hardly a vacation! It's not like you and Dougal between you haven't left enough crap to clean up on the Mortal Plain to keep him busy for my lifetime and more."

Raphael backed down, at least temporarily, but I was sure we hadn't heard the last of it. And frankly, I wasn't sure Lugh was being completely honest about his reasoning, either. Admittedly, I couldn't argue that there was plenty left to do here on the Mortal Plain, like finding a way to shut down all the remaining labs Dougal and Raphael had set up. And getting as many of Dougal's people as possible back to the Demon Realm—and in prison. And figuring out what Dougal had been planning to do with them all, and whether that plan was still extant now that he was dead. We may have secured Lugh's throne, but our troubles were far from over.

What I wasn't so sure of was that Lugh had to supervise those efforts personally.

If I could get back to the Demon Realm without anyone having to die, I might consider it, he told me. *But even if that were the case, I'm not sure I would go back just yet. For all the turmoil Dougal caused, there was only so much effect he could have in the Demon Realm without the power of the throne behind him. He could do a hell of a lot more damage here, so I suspect here may be where I'm needed most.*

All very logical, but I couldn't help wondering if a lingering attachment to me—and to Brian—had any influence on his decision.

Of course, it was all well and good to have Lugh stay on the Mortal Plain for the span of my lifetime—after all, to a demon, the lifespan of a human being was barely a drop in the bucket—but *someone* had to rule in the Demon Realm while Lugh was here, and it wouldn't be whoever Dougal had left in charge when he'd come to the Mortal Plain for the duel.

There was really only one logical choice. Raphael just wasn't regent material, even if we could have cast him out—no sure thing—and even if we didn't need him on the Mortal Plain to help clean up his mess. The only other member of the royal family whom Lugh could trust was Saul.

Neither Saul nor Barbie was what you'd call happy about the idea. They hadn't been together all that long, but it seemed like their attachment had grown pretty deep in that short time. Nonetheless, Saul had little choice but to do as his king commanded. Lugh did make a concession, however, promising to summon Saul back to the Mortal Plain once a month so that Saul could update him on what was happening on the home front. Saul and Barbie would get to spend a little time together, and then we would exorcize him and send him back to the Demon Realm once more. Talk about your long-distance relationships...

Even more fun for Barbie was that she'd have to take care of Dick, Saul's host, while Saul was away. We had once thought Dick was mentally challenged, but according to Saul, he was of perfectly average intelligence. He'd just been so badly abused as part of Dougal and Raphael's breeding program that he would never be quite self-sufficient. His condition had improved since he'd teamed up with Saul, but he would probably never be able to take care of himself without help.

And then there was Brian.

The whole buddy system is a thing of the past, but it seems like every day, Brian manages to get himself more firmly entrenched in my apartment. His underwear is in my dresser drawer, his clothes hang in my closet, and his toiletries sit on my bathroom counter.

If I didn't know any better, I'd say we were living together.

Someday, I might even find the courage to admit it to myself. And then we could both move into his condo, which is a hell of a lot nicer than my apartment. But I'm not ready for that yet, and I'm not sure Brian is, either. He understands now why I didn't want to give up Lugh, and he no longer brings up the possibility, but I know he still struggles with jealousy. I don't suppose I'd have felt any different in his shoes. Complicating the issue was the fact that we both knew Lugh's seduction attempts were going to continue. Even so, our relationship was on firmer ground than it had ever been—which was actually a rather scary commentary on its own, but there you go.

When I'd first found out I was possessed, I'd spent a lot of time wishing my life could go back to the way it was before I'd even known Lugh existed. But looking back now, it's hard to remember why I'd found the idea so appealing. Back then, I'd just been going through the motions of living my life. I'd kept everyone, even Brian, at arm's length, and I'd carried around so much anger and resentment it was amazing I didn't collapse under the weight.

Don't get me wrong: I'm not the poster child for sweetness and light now, either. But I have a man I love, and who loves me back. I have a demon I care about and respect—and, yes, still lust after, though I hate to admit it. I have friends—the real kind, who I can be myself with and actually trust. And because of Lugh, there's purpose in my life. Working with him and with his council, I can do good, both for my people and for his.

It's more than I ever dreamed of having.

Are people really capable of changing? My answer used to be a resounding "no." Now, I think the answer might be a tentative "yes." But it remains to be seen whether all those changes are for the good.